Alistair McNaught was born in Lennoxtown, Scotland and grew up in Bearsden, a burgh on the outskirts of Glasgow. After graduating in history and philosophy at Glasgow University, he moved to Oxford, where he worked as a bookseller for sixteen years, before becoming a sales representative for a London-based book distribution company. *The Tragicall History of Campbell McCluskie* is his first novel to be published. He now lives in Wantage with his wife, Sarah, their two daughters, Iona and Heather, and a melancholic white rescue cat named Alba.

The Tragicall History
of
Campbell McCluskie

ALISTAIR McNAUGHT

AWEN
Stroud

First published in 2018 by Awen Publications
12 Belle Vue Close, Stroud GL5 1ND, England
www.awenpublications.co.uk

Front cover design copyright © Andy Kinnear 2018

Back cover design: Kirsty Hartsiotis
Editing: Anthony Nanson

ISBN 978-1-906900-55-7

To Sarah

Kind solace in a dying hour!
Such, father, is not (now) my theme –
I will not madly deem that power
Of Earth may shrive me of the sin
Unearthly pride hath revelled in –
I have no time to dote or dream:
You call it hope – that fire of fire!
It is but agony of desire.

Edgar Allan Poe

It's all down tae patterns and figures.
If you can decipher them, the fucking
Devil will dance tae your tune.

Campbell McCluskie

Prologue

It was on my fourteenth birthday that I first saw one of Campbell McCluskie's plays. I was staying with my cousin while recuperating from a bout of dysentery. As I recall, it was a sunny morning and I was in a state of euphoria, arising no doubt from my excited anticipation of presents. I was eating my breakfast, when my uncle entered the kitchen wearing my aunt's faded green bathrobe. A man of considerable charm and intellect, who bore a resemblance to the singer Engelbert Humperdink, he handed me a yellow ticket upon which was printed:

> 'The Irresistible Rise of Tam McLean'
> A Play in Five Acts
> by
> Campbell McCluskie
> 16th June, 1968
> Admit One, Evening Perf. 7.30 p.m.
> Citizens' Theatre

I stared at it in silent perplexity as I swallowed the remains of a sausage sandwich spiced with Worcester sauce.

'It's a ticket to the theatre,' my uncle volunteered. 'I'm taking you and Jamie to see a play.'

Later that evening, we took the train to Glasgow and then travelled to the theatre on the upper deck of a Corporation bus. A drunk man dozed fitfully two seats behind us. He was leaning against the window with a grey fedora lowered over his eyes, his head nodding in concert with the jolts of the moving bus. I was convinced that his awakening would result in our violent deaths.

I did not understand much of the play, being too young to appreciate the grandeur of McCluskie's language. However, I was enthralled by the violence that accompanied McLean's rise to power in the gangster community. The scene that I remember most clearly is that in which Rowena, stricken by grief at the sight of her husband's dead body, rips open her blouse and thrusts a dagger into her bare breast.

This display of nudity caused a scandal when the play was first performed in 1947, in a small theatre club in Glasgow, and the scene was judiciously cut before its first performance in London. The critic Swinbourne, in his double-edged tribute to McCluskie on the occasion of the playwright's death, described it as 'melodrama at its worst' and 'an unforgivable flaw in a work of such clarity'.

I was merely dismayed that my view of the woman's breasts was blocked by a lamp post that formed part of the stage set. I squirmed in my seat, fearful that any attempt to peer round the post would unveil my sordid lust for all to see. McCluskie would have had no such qualms. I never gained a satisfactory view of the actress's breasts; just a hint of pale flesh and the scene was over. The only other memory I have of this performance is of Tam McLean, dressed in a grey zoot suit, chest thrown out, declaiming his ambition to an unheeding universe, and in the process launching several drops of spittle into my lap.

On the train home, Jamie and I sat facing my uncle. Duplicated in the window, his head bent forward, he perused the programme, while beyond the glass the Clyde valley swept past in a succession of orange street lamps, dark outlines and moonlight glimmers. At a certain moment, he looked at me with a surprised expression and said, 'Do you know it is the fourteenth anniversary of Campbell McCluskie's death?'

My uncle did not realise the full significance of what he had said. For him, the coincidence of my birth with the death of the playwright had no metaphysical implications. He regarded the world as an intricate and colourful painting hanging in a dark room. For my part, I like to think that when he uttered these words my face took on that dreamy look that is normally associated with a religious experience, but which I have also induced by twisting a cotton bud into my ear. In all probability, however, I was too preoccupied with my earlier disappointment to appreciate what he had said.

Six years were to pass before I had any further contact with McCluskie's work. Consequently, I was surprised to feel a strange shiver of recognition, one cold November morning during my third year at university, when I read Tam McLean's opening words: 'Aw stop yer stupit jabberin', woman. Ye're be'er aff wi' me than wi' yon eejit.'

His plays were seldom performed then and the public indifference was echoed in academic circles. Most commentators agreed with Swinbourne, who, in one of his metaphorical flights, described McCluskie as 'an idiosyncratic backwater in the turbulent stream of modernist literature'. So it was by chance that I discovered *The Irresistible Rise of Tam McLean* in the library. I subsequently wrote an essay showing the extent of Shakespeare's influence on the play.

That was not a happy period in my life. I was distracted from my studies by a hopeless infatuation with a second-year history student named Marion McDonald. With only a week to go before the deadline for my essay, I borrowed from the main library a book entitled *Campbell McCluskie: The Quest for Love*, by Anthony Shaw, and took it to the History Faculty Library with the small cloth-bound edition of McCluskie's plays which I still possess.

Two oak tables, pitted by use, were squeezed into the space left between the bookshelves. I was sitting at one and Marion McDonald was sitting at the other. I had placed two histories of Elizabethan England on the table to justify my unusual presence in that library, but I was certain that the librarian doubted my motives for being there. She eyed me suspiciously from her desk as I flicked absent-mindedly through one of the books, and only let down her guard when I scribbled in my notebook some nonsense I had gleaned from the text: 'After the masque, Essex informed the Queen about the dead man in Deptford.'

I cast a sly glance at Marion's bare forearm, which bore a small birthmark shaped like the Isle of Wight. In a veritable agony of excitement, I slipped the biography out of my bag and flattened it on the table to keep its title hidden from the librarian. Only then did I read, 'At half-past ten on the evening of Wednesday, 16th June, 1954, the playwright Campbell McCluskie died alone and drunk in a stinking side alley in Glasgow.'

McCluskie did not die alone. Shaw, a sometime pornographer, had cobbled the biography together to cash in on the playwright's murder. However, I did later manage to verify the time of death. To the best of my knowledge, that is one of the few correct facts in the book, but it was enough to alter the entire course of my life. For that, according to my birth certificate, was the very moment I was born.

The time of my birth had for several years been a private obsession of mine, as a result of a grotesque incident in my childhood. I was ten at the time, with one of those corpulent faces that seem to haunt the back row of every school photograph. My shyness made me the victim of much cruelty, and so when Paul Clegg discovered what day I was born I knew the consequences would not be pleasant. Clegg was dark-haired, foul-mouthed and diminutive. I shall never forget his ugly face chanting, 'Wednesday's child is full of woe,' while he delivered repeated blows to my kidneys; nor shall I forget those others who gathered round to jeer with him. I don't suppose that any of them realised that my mother had died of heart failure while giving birth to me, but I subsequently bore the stigma of my birthday through the many hours of tortured self-reflection which led me to the unpalatable conclusion that she might have lived had I been born only an hour and a half later.

All those years of hidden anguish seemed to dissolve in that instant of realisation in the library. It was as if someone had unveiled the intricate workings of the universe for me and me alone. I felt for the first time in my life that everything made sense: the fair down clinging to Marion's nape; the movement of her right arm as she scratched her shoulder; the blob of mascara at the end of one drooping lash; the sudden death of my mother; Anthony Shaw's bogus biography.

This revelation was interrupted by Marion's irate departure from the library. She strode past me muttering something I couldn't quite hear but the gist of which was conveyed to me later by a gloating classmate. Namely, that I had been playing with myself under the table while gawping at her with an expression of unrestrained lust. It was impossible for me to explain that my ecstasy was of a purely spiritual nature and that a hand will often fall unnoticed on to a plump lap. But I was not unduly worried about her misapprehension, for the discovery had given my life a new purpose.

I can remember nothing of that first essay on McCluskie. However, my mind still smarts at the unjust blow levelled at me shortly after by Marion's boyfriend, Duncan McFadden. It was a crisp, sunny morning. I was strolling through the park near the university, too absorbed in my thoughts to appreciate my surroundings: the glistening hoar frost; the two young men huddled in conversation beside the statue of Lord Kelvin; the shadows of the leafless trees trembling at my approach. Such is how I now picture the scene. At the time, I was too busy thinking about Campbell McCluskie to notice anything.

During the previous fortnight, I had devoured in quick succession the two available biographies of the playwright, together with the three slim volumes of criticism which his work had generated. It was a frenzied task which left me exhausted and disappointed. McCluskie remained scrupulously hidden behind the lamentable prose of his biographers and the conceited delusions of his critics. And I? I was completely unprepared for the savage kick directed at my genitals by McFadden, which left me squirming on the gravel in agony. With scarcely a backward glance, he rejoined his friend by the statue and together they walked away in the direction of the university.

As I lay on the ground sobbing and clutching my groin, two young girls approached from the road that was just visible through the trees. On catching sight of me, they began to giggle and whisper behind their hands, until they were shooed away by a stout, middle-aged woman. She helped me to my feet and brushed the gravel from my back with her powerful hands. Then, leaving me with some harsh words for my attackers, she continued on her way. My humiliation was complete.

During the days following this incident, I fell into despair so profound that even my father noticed it. One evening in late December, he was sitting by the fire watching the television with his hands resting on his belly. At that time, I tended to spend my evenings in the sitting room, because his company, such as it was, was preferable to the loneliness of my room. I was sitting at the dining table at the other end of the room, my book of McCluskie's plays lying open in front of me. I was attempting to read some notes I had scrawled on a sheet of A4 paper (narrow feint, no margin) but I could not stop thinking about Duncan and Marion. For days, I had thought of nothing else, and my imagination had reached such a pitch that I could clearly visualize them: Marion lying on her back smiling avidly while Duncan pressed himself against her and whispered the details of my humiliation in her ear.

I began to tear the notepaper quite methodically into strips, and then to tear those strips into fragments. Tears started to run down my cheeks. My father looked up, frowned momentarily, as if he had just become aware of my presence, and said, 'What's wrong, son?'

At that moment, a scrap of paper fluttered on to my right forearm. With a start, I realised that I had unconsciously torn it into the same shape as Marion's birthmark. The crisis was over. Once again, I glimpsed the secret meaning of things. The joy I felt reduced all else to insignificance. There and then I resolved to make Campbell McCluskie the subject of my honours dissertation.

Meanwhile, my father, drawn from his habitual indolence by my grief, was squeezing himself between the table and the wall. I believe to this day that he intended to comfort me with a hug, but his foot caught on the table leg and he collapsed on to me with all his weight. My chair fell backwards. My glasses flew off and landed on the floor behind me. My legs kicked against the underside of the table, launching McCluskie's plays towards the Christmas tree. Scraps of paper drifted around us like confetti, and the fragment shaped like Marion's birthmark was lost for ever.

I subsequently arranged a meeting with the Head of the English Department, Professor Archiebald Williams, to discuss my dissertation, but it did not follow the course I had expected. As soon as I mentioned McCluskie, he responded angrily, 'Why exactly do you want to make this change?' I was surprised by the vehemence of his reply and began to feel rather foolish sitting there with my head lowered and the edge of the chair digging into my plump calves. He continued in a shrill voice: 'You know, I rarely have students of your ability, and I'm not happy about this at all. Why don't you reconsider? I was delighted by your original suggestion, delighted, and, to be perfectly frank, I cannot see how a subject like the "Role of Artifice in Elizabethan Drama" can be matched by the mediocre works of one forgotten Scottish dramatist, who was a drunkard to boot. It's early days yet. I mean, you don't have to make a final decision until the summer term.' He stared at me in evident perplexity with his elbows on the desk and a fountain pen bridging the gap between his pale hands.

'I don't think I will change my mind,' I said in a tremulous voice.

'But the man was a scallywag. His writing was derivative. His plays were poorly structured. He was a dilettante and a liar.' Professor Williams pointed his pen at me and continued in a similar vein for some minutes, pausing only to flatten down some strands of hair that had come unstuck from his balding pate. 'Look, why don't we discuss the matter over a wee dram?' He unlocked the glass-fronted bookcase behind his desk and produced a bottle of malt from behind a copy of Goethe's *Faust*. Placing a glass of whisky in front of me, he indicated with a flutter of his fingers the jug of water that stood among his cluttered papers.

He told me that he had known Campbell during his undergraduate days and that he considered the playwright to be nothing more than a cheap hack who had used his talents to seduce gullible women.

'Surely you understand', he continued, 'that to produce a dissertation on such a person could seriously harm your career prospects.'

I replied that I had strong personal reasons for making the decision. Whereupon he slammed his glass on the desk and shouted,

'Have you ever been to the McCluskie Museum? Have you ever seen that ludicrous monument to his legacy?' I shook my head. 'Well, go there. That will convince you more than any arguments of mine. Nobody knows about the museum. Nobody gives two hoots about McCluskie; all that civic crap about a grateful city honouring its dead. It makes me sick.'

I quietly excused myself. Professor Williams was clearly losing all sense of decorum.

At the time I write this the McCluskie Museum no longer exists. Its caretaker, Alan Cairns, died in 1981, and the Corporation sold the premises. After my abortive meeting with Professor Williams, he refused to discuss the matter further. He had given up trying to talk me out of the venture and was determined instead to put every obstacle in my way. Consequently, it took me almost a month to find the museum. It was not listed in any tourist guide, and the staff of the other museums in the city denied all knowledge of it.

I was on the point of giving up my search when by chance I met Alan Cairns one evening in the Curlers Bar. As I was squeezing my way through a boisterous hen party, a young woman with an L plate affixed to her chest dunted my book into the lap of an elderly man with a thick moustache. He picked it up. I could have sworn that tears formed in his eyes when he read the title. He grabbed my sleeve and said, 'You're reading Campbell's plays.'

Within an hour, he was leading me through frosty streets to the museum. His appearance was elegant in a quiet way: grey moustache neatly trimmed; brown coat with epaulettes; Paisley pattern scarf. It was obvious that the scarf meant a lot to him. He told me, later in his room, that it had belonged to the actor who portrayed the hero of Campbell's earliest play, *Shona of Lismore*, when it first opened in London.

He showed me his collection of tickets for Campbell's plays, and there among them was a yellow one (just like mine but torn into a ragged rhombus by an impatient usherette) for the 1968 production of *The Irresistible Rise of Tam McLean*. We pored over his album of McCluskie ephemera, and he almost broke down when we came to the newspaper cuttings recounting the playwright's murder.

In reverential tones he told me that McCluskie had slept in the room below on the night before his death. I was gazing out of the window when he said this. The neo-Gothic university building stood on the hill opposite, and the Art Galleries were across the river on the left. I turned to survey Mr Cairn's cramped living room. This was the house where the playwright had lived for the last year of his life. I had touched the kitsch objects that had so obsessed Campbell. I had peered into cabinets at his manuscripts with his feverish corrections. I had seen the bed where he had tossed in hopeless frenzy with Helen Miriam on the day of his death.

There is a general consensus among those who knew McCluskie that Helen was the only woman he had ever truly loved. Renowned for her beauty and intelligence, she had been notorious during the austere years of the early fifties for her avant-garde clothes and succession of lovers. Campbell met her at the premier of his last play, *The Life and Death of Doctor Frost*, which was regarded as his crowning achievement. It was his agent, the improbably named Christopher Malquist, who introduced them. Helen proved to be more than a match for the loquacious Scotsman. They became lovers within a very short time, but their happiness was blighted by the despair that haunted McCluskie during his final months.

In January of this year, I managed to track Helen down to a crumbling house in Hillhead. She was a broken lady with a wandering mind, who looked older than her sixty-four years. When I mentioned McCluskie, she eagerly beckoned me into her damp bed-sit. A mangy cat kept pressing itself against my leg while we sat drinking tea. A photograph of Helen and Campbell stood upon a sideboard riddled with woodworm. Everything seemed squalid and sad. I found it hard to identify the beautiful woman in the photograph with the elderly lady who sat opposite me.

She spoke of many things, but they were all jumbled up: her childhood in Egypt; her life before McCluskie; her love of the playwright. She would start describing an incident with her mother when she was five, and by the end of the anecdote her mother had transformed into the playwright and the setting had changed. I despaired of learning anything from her, and prepared to leave. Just as I stood up, she said, 'Wait, I have something for you. Please don't go just yet.' Then she wandered around the room, lifting up plates, opening drawers, pushing aside magazines, until she discovered a small, battered notebook.

'Here it is,' she said, pressing it into my hand. 'Please take it. I can't read it anymore. It's all gone now. Gone.' Tears welled up in her eyes. I didn't know what to say. Fool that I was, I tried to give it back, thinking that it held some special meaning for her, but she refused it. So I put it in my briefcase and headed home.

It was only when I read the notebook later that evening that I discovered the extent of my good fortune. During the weeks following McCluskie's death, Helen had set herself the task of describing everything that had occurred between them on that last morning, in an effort, I supposed, to recapture the past or to make sense of it. She never completed this.

I think her principal difficulty lay in the fact that the events of the final morning were so tied to those of the previous weeks that she couldn't disentangle them. She had found Campbell's moods and behaviour to be growing more erratic. She assumed that it was writer's block, but he never discussed what was troubling him. He never had. Instead, he had taken to drinking heavily. On the night before he died, he was so drunk that Helen had to watch over him while he threw up into the toilet for over an hour.

The morning of Wednesday 16 June 1954 was hot and sticky. McCluskie woke at six thirty, after tossing and turning for about a quarter of an hour. Helen was half asleep. Responding to his anxiety in the usual manner, he went through to the bathroom, had a copious bowel movement and returned to bed with a book; a novel entitled *Bend Sinister*. It was a book that seemed to hold a special fascination for him during the days preceding his death. Through half-closed eyes Helen watched him climb into bed and turn away from her. His eyes were red rimmed. There was a scar on the right side of his chest, which was echoed by a slightly smaller scar below his right shoulder blade. She cuddled up against his back while he lay on his side, reading.

Her notebook makes clear that for some time Campbell had shown little inclination for sex. On this occasion, however, she decided to take matters into her own hands. She went on to describe their lovemaking in embarrassing detail: her difficulties in coaxing McCluskie's erection; his foul breath; the mixture of desire and amusement she felt at the sight of his penis. She mentioned the ticklish sensation in her stomach, which reminded her, as always, of the trickling sand on the dune where she had lost her virginity. Despite her caresses, McCluskie remained with his back to her, and so she swung her leg over him and straddled his hip. As she bent to kiss him her knee slipped over the edge of the bed. Campbell was caught off balance and they both tumbled to the floor in a laughing heap. It was the first time that he had laughed in quite a while.

Cradling her head in his hands, he kissed her desperately. Then, as he lifted her back on to the bed, he began to kiss her breasts and nipples. His stubble scratched her and left red marks on her body as

9

he drew his tongue down her stomach. She pulled herself further on to the bed and closed her eyes. He pressed his face between her thighs. Then he firmly parted her legs and raised himself over her.

Helen felt the swollen head of McCluskie's penis pausing in the opening to her vagina. She recalled that in happier days he had referred to it as his 'pleasure dome', and she smiled in anticipation. But her expectations were not fulfilled. The long-awaited visitor merely curled up at the entrance without seeking admission. Helen, choking a sob of frustration, opened her eyes. McCluskie's face bore an expression of indefinable horror. He suddenly yelled, 'Malquist, you horny bastard, why can't you leave me alone?' disentangled himself from her limbs and strode out of the room.

She felt hurt, angry and confused. He returned shortly after holding a half-empty bottle of whisky and dressed without looking at her. Neither of them spoke. She heard him moving about his study and cursing for a good ten minutes before the front door slammed shut.

And then silence; the next time she saw him he was laid out in the morgue with a knife wound over his right eye. 'Yes, that's Campbell,' she whispered and promptly fainted.

A police constable witnessed the following when he walked down a narrow street leading off from Park Road at ten forty-five on the evening of 16 June: Colin Milverton, a portly middle-aged man, was sitting on the ground, cradling McCluskie's head in his arms and weeping. The playwright had died fifteen minutes earlier of an air embolism caused by the knife wound. A silver-handled steak knife, engraved with the name of Laing's Restaurant and tipped with Campbell's blood, was lying near the two men.

The detailed inventory taken by the police of everything found on McCluskie's body is a fascinating document, which for legal reasons was denied to earlier biographers. I possess a photostat of the original, which was typed by Detective Cairncross on Thursday 17 June 1954, on the explicit instructions of Chief Inspector Alan Greig.

Before Greig was called into the case, the general consensus in the station was that Campbell had provoked an argument in a nearby pub and that he had been killed during the fight that followed. On two prior occasions, the police had been called out to the Doublet to deal with fights started by McCluskie when he was drunk.

However, Greig saw things differently and ordered the detailed inventory following a brief interview with Colin Milverton. The inventory was annotated by the inspector with some of his initial observations and then signed by both the inspector and Detective

Cairncross. A copy without the annotations was sent to McCluskie's family.

Inventory of belongings found on the body of Campbell McCluskie, on the night of Wednesday, 16th of June, 1954.

1. *A pair of white, cotton underpants.* A urine stain suggests that the victim urinated clumsily shortly before his death.
2. *A pair of Argyle socks: light green with contrasting diamonds of dark green.* A hole uncovered the big toe on the right foot.
3. *A white linen shirt, worn without collar or cufflinks.*
4. *A pair of black brogues.* A scuff on the toe of the right shoe indicates that the foot was scraped forcibly and awkwardly along the ground during the struggle.
5. *Dark green, tweed, two-piece suit, made by Donald McKellar & Son, Stirling.* There is a tear on the left sleeve and a blood stain on the right lapel. The trousers are badly stained on the right knee and the seat with reddish dust. Small pieces of debris and dust are fouling the back of the jacket. The fly was unbuttoned.
6. *A novel entitled 'Bend Sinister' by Vladimir Nabokov.*
7. *Two keys.* One was identified as the victim's house key. The other has not been identified.
8. *A brown, leather wallet.*
9. *£6, 6s & 6d.*
10. *The business card of one Christopher Malquist, Literary Agent, 28 Gallowgate, Glasgow.*
11. *A photograph of Helen Miriam.*
12. *Two sheets of paper with a letter to Campbell McCluskie on one side, and some notes on the reverse written by the victim.* The handwriting of the letter is bold and florid, and the notes appear to have been written in a hurry.

(A)

26th of September, 1952

Dearest Campbell,

Why haven't you written to arrange another date? I went to so much bother persuading Colin to take the children to his sister's without me. You could have told me you couldn't come. Mr Malquist is a terrible slave driver, I know, but you could at least have told me.

I simply cannot wait to see you again. Colin was such a dear. The children were so sad to leave. And all my little sacrifices came to nothing. You are a beast for not coming. I was alone in this big house, wearing my fancy frills just for you.

Colly suspects nothing. He's so unobservant. I swear I could walk naked through the house and he wouldn't even lift his eyes from his paper.

I keep thinking of our short time together: that reeking close; your large, confident hands. I was so full of you. I knew it was cruel to deceive Colin, but he suffocates me. There I go again. You must think me an awful [illegible word]. I could never imagine Colin doing anything like that.

Life is very flat here without you. When will you finish with that rotten play and come back to Glasgow? I simply can't stop thinking about you. However, I shall expect a good explanation for last weekend, or I know someone who won't get to nibble his moist little peach.

If you meet me next Saturday, I might find it in my heart to forgive you. I shall be waiting in the lounge bar of the Grosvenor at 8 o'clock sharp. Don't forget your little riding hoods this time. I don't want to get pregnant. I think even Colly would notice that.

Your disappointed
Madelaine
XXXX

(B)

Moonlight reflecting on water. A man is rowing to an island, where his married lover is waiting for him. They plan to go away together. He remembers various things from his past – a pattern of seaweed on a beach – his first view of his lover – the anticipation he felt before they had sex – a childhood fear. A dark image intrudes upon his thoughts: a shape; a ruined castle; a place with evil associations for him? As the story progresses, it transpires that the man has drowned and his mind has created all the images during his dying moments.

'Heather and Liam'
Moonlight reflecting on water; the creak and splash of oars; Liam looks over his shoulder at the dark outline of the island.

Above, the sky is deep blue, but black clouds are gathering in the north. [Passage heavily scored out.] A string of lights, twinkling on the distant shoreline, marks the straggling village where Heather is waiting.

He imagines her sitting by the door, wearing her green coat and clutching her case. She would worry. She always did; that he wouldn't come; that Fergus would return unexpectedly. Liam remembers the first time he saw her. He was crouching by a rock pool: a small hollow circle of quicksilver, forgotten by the retreating tide, with a garland wreath of seaweed around its pitted dimpled rim. Heather, in a shapeless grey dress, was hanging out some washing in her garden near the beach.

Somewhere beyond, or behind (for who can tell with memories?), he discerns the ominous outline of something else, but then a cloud veils covers the moon and he is left in the darkness with only his bobbing lantern and the distant village lights to guide his way.

This meticulous attention to detail more than anything else betrays the presence of Alan Greig. He has even noted the words that Campbell scored out; those first thoughts and rejected ideas that are so important to literary critics. What the inspector hoped to learn from them is not clear. It was merely his method to assemble every detail pertaining to the crime, in the hope of picking out from Fate's web the individual strands of human motive and malice.

It is a sad comment on Campbell's life that his last piece of writing should only be preserved in a police file. Helen Miriam burned the original in a fit of jealous despair after reading Madelaine's letter. But, as ever, this tantalising fragment throws up more questions than it answers. We shall never know the significance of those descriptive details – the 'green coat', the 'shapeless, grey dress', the 'dimpled rim' of the rock pool. All have been rendered senseless by his murder. We shall never see, as we did with *The Life and Death of Doctor Frost*, the subtle patterns McCluskie might weave from these details, and in this lay the real tragedy of his early death.

The pathology report has a morbid precision of its own:

The steak knife, found near the body, had slipped over the upper side of the right eyeball and entered the skull through the superior orbital fissure. Here the nerves from the eye and its muscles pass through to the brain accompanied by a large blood vessel, the cavernous sinus, which drains into the jugular vein and hence to the heart. A puncture from the knife point enabled air to enter this vessel, which spread rapidly through the system resulting in unconsciousness within a minute or so. Campbell McCluskie died of an air embolism.

Colin Milverton was very drunk when he was discovered with the body, and consequently spent the night in a police cell. He was in a sorry state when Inspector Greig met him. A dusting of fair stubble encircled his chin. His eyes were bloodshot and swollen.

He was quite certain that McCluskie had been unconscious when he found him. The inspector observed that it was a curious circumstance to be discovered weeping over the body of a stranger. Milverton pointed out that he had been very much the worse for wear. The inspector then confirmed his personal details: that he owned a brick manufacturer's; that he was married with two children. Greig was about to conclude the interview, when Colin's wife burst into the office, closely followed by Detective Cairncross and a handsome young man.

'O Colly, what have they done to you?' said Mrs Milverton, pressing her husband's head to her bosom.

'I'm sorry, sir,' said the detective. 'I couldn't stop her

'Not at all,' replied the inspector with the smug look of someone who has just solved a rather intricate puzzle. 'Mrs Milverton is just concerned for her husband.'

'Am I to take it that my client is free to go?' said the handsome man from the doorway.

'And who might you be?' said the inspector, rising from his chair.

'I am Mr Milverton's solicitor, Donald Usher.'

'Well, Mr Usher. I think we have finished with your client for the time being.'

From this brief exchange, Inspector Greig was to elaborate a tangled plot, which would have its own tragic consequences. But his motives were similar to mine. I, too, am trying to find meaning in Campbell's death. However, to find meaning in a person's death, surely you must first learn all you can about that person's life.

I.A.M
Glasgow
10 November 1990

BOOK ONE

THE LIFE OF
CAMPBELL MCCLUSKIE

PART ONE

Chapter One

It was always Campbell McCluskie's contention that he had been conceived in Bembridge on the Isle of Wight. He had the habit of mentioning this strange circumstance when things were going badly for him, as if it was the root of all his troubles; as if no greater misfortune could befall a man than to be conceived on the Isle of Wight. Unlike much of what he said or wrote, it was a contention that was almost certainly true.

His mother's maiden name was Katherine McArthur. She was a young woman of exceptional beauty. Her black eyebrows, tapering in horizontal lines over her brown eyes, and her dark complexion gave her a Spanish appearance that belied the small coal-mining town of her birth. Her father, Duncan, a cooper by trade, had moved the family to Clydebank when Katherine was six years old. Consequently, she retained only vague memories of the terraced cottage, shadowed by slag heaps, where she had been born one squally night in March 1902.

Duncan was an aggressive, short-tempered man whom Katherine despised, but it was from him that she acquired her strength of will and her love of literature. Her complexion and beauty she owed to her mother. Indeed, according to family legend, that quiet and nervous woman was descended from a Spanish sailor of the Armada, who had been washed up on the Irish coast.

The few remaining photographs of Duncan portray a handsome man of medium height, well built, with a neatly trimmed black moustache. Only his eyes betray his kinship to Campbell McCluskie. By all accounts, Duncan was a fanatically religious but petty-minded tyrant. He imposed a strict discipline on both himself and his family. Trivial misdemeanours would be punished with such severity that none of his five daughters felt any love for him. It was his wife, Anne, however, who bore the brunt of his temper. She could never live up to his standards, and he often accused her of 'raising a family of brazen harlots'.

His strict Presbyterian faith forbade dancing and encouraged a guilt-ridden response to all physical pleasures. The only weakness he permitted himself was in reading and re-reading the works of Charles Dickens. However, he started drinking heavily during his wife's final illness, when he had other reasons to be guilty. The diaries of his eldest daughter, Agnes, provide tragic evidence of his belief that woman are by nature evil.

From the surviving family papers, it would appear that Katherine was a moody child. As she grew older, her childhood memories resolved themselves into several vivid episodes, which she recounted to Campbell and which he recorded in his adolescent journals. Even at that early age, Campbell displayed a talent for writing which now breathes life into that sepia-toned woman.

There was the episode with her paternal grandmother, Jean, who had come to stay with the family when Katherine was twelve. Jean was somewhat senile. A poorly healed hip fracture had seriously impaired her mobility and often conspired with a weakening bladder to humiliate her. On one occasion, Katherine was interrupted while scrubbing the kitchen floor by the reedy-voiced old woman calling, 'Katherine, where are you, girl? Come quick! I'm needful!'

It was all described in Campbell's notebook. The old woman shaking as she tried to raise herself from her chair. Her hands, dappled with liver spots, gripped the curved wooden arms, knuckles swollen, veins gnarled. Katherine half carried, half led her to the commode, which had a rhomboid moulding set in the apex of its back support. After helping Jean out of her combinations, Katherine noted sadly the way her skin puckered in places with age. But she found it difficult to love that severe old woman, who spent her last years in that grey room, muttering darkly about the evil days she had lived to see and screaming abuse at Katherine for her youth and beauty.

Also described was the summer evening Katherine spent queuing for the local dance. As with the other episode, I have the suspicion that Campbell was inventing some of the details. Did Katherine really remember the silhouettes of those distant cranes; the road mounting the hill and disappearing into the distance; that exotic orange peel curling into the gutter?

She certainly experienced the humiliation of being dragged out of the queue by her father and led down a narrow side street. I imagine some quiet soul observing her punishment through a ground-floor window: the muscular, grey-haired man striking her cheek while he recited some piece of holy scripture. In a letter to her errant sister Dorothy, written shortly after the incident, Katherine described the insane gleam in their father's eyes and the greasy stain shaped like an island on his jacket lapel.

The childhood and youth of Campbell's father, John, are if anything even more elusive. He was born in the flat above the family's shoe repair shop in Clydebank in 1897. One photograph, taken when he was eight, shows him as a ghostly blur chasing a metal hoop that multiplies itself along a cobbled street. The next record we have of him was of his conscription in October 1915, after which he served as an infantryman on the Western Front until the Armistice.

In Campbell's journals there is only one reference to his father's past: an incident that occurred during the Battle of the Somme and which John recounted to Campbell's mother. He was at the front line with his friend, Hugh Brendan, on the eve of a major offensive. Katherine pictured a muddy landscape with torn trees and the silhouettes of four Tommies going over the top. The image was black and white. She always pictured the war in black and white. Hugh, standing on a wooden platform halfway up the front of the trench, was opening a packet of cigarettes sent to him by his fiancée.

'Here, look at this,' he said, handing John a small card. On it was portrayed a Glasgow Celtic football player with his arms crossed and his right foot resting on a ball. 'Remember that game ...' His sentence was cut short by a German sniper's bullet. It struck Hugh squarely in the back of the head. Part of his skull was blown off and landed with a squish at John's feet. Campbell wrote,

My father, in deep shock, gazed at the fragment of bone for several minutes. He was reminded of an incident in his childhood when my grandfather had smashed a porcelain vase in a drunken fury. On that occasion, a piece of the vase had landed at my father's feet. He told my mother that the two events had aroused the same sense of futility in him, but that Hugh's death had changed him irrevocably.

There follows a fairly convincing portrayal of how a charming, practical and intelligent man was inwardly twisted by tragedy. In Campbell's words: 'Hugh's death induced a profound pessimism in my father, which remained with him all his life and which led not only to his violent outbursts of temper but also to his savage sense of humour. It was as if he used irony and black humour to distance himself from the pain of the world.' Such a glib summing up would never have occurred in Campbell's mature writings.

One can sense in his description the antagonism Campbell felt towards his father, but it was Hugh Brendan who interested me when I first read the passage. I felt that he was the key to John's character, and I was eager to find out more about him. Unfortunately, the only clue I had to his identity was a photograph taken during the war. John is pictured in front of a ruined farmhouse with four of his comrades. Three of them are sitting on a felled tree, while another sits cross-legged in front with his hands on his knees. John, taken by surprise by the photographer, is standing with one foot on a clay-covered root while he supports his elbow with his raised thigh. His cap is set at a rakish angle and he is using both hands to shield a match while he lights a cigarette. On the reverse side of the photograph are five names (written in faded pencil) which are laid out thus:

Matthew, Keith, Joshua, John
& Hugh
March 1916
Farmhouse de Nooley

How I gazed at that man sitting in the foreground. His thin, white neck was shaded on one side. He had a prominent Adam's apple and protruding ears, and his hands were too large for his slight frame. Campbell's account of Hugh's death had prepared me for a much more robust man; one of those hearty fellows with a full moustache and twinkling eyes; someone like John McCluskie. It was a preconception I was loath to relinquish, and I found it hard to imagine what John could have seen in such an unprepossessing man. During the weeks preceding my meeting with Joshua Hamilton in a Faifley council tenement, I tried to picture what Hugh's personality and life had been like, but all my conjectures came to nothing.

Of the five men in the photograph, Joshua was the only one still alive. When I met him, he was staying with his granddaughter, Ellen, and her family. The old man, sitting huddled in an armchair with a car rug draped across his legs, held the photograph with shaking hands. His great-grandson knelt on the floor between us, bent over a world atlas. Ellen busied herself in the kitchen, making a pot of tea and singing 'I'm Nobody's Child' in a harsh soprano.

'That man's no called Brendan,' croaked Joshua, almost inaudibly. The boy, frowning with concentration, was resolutely obliterating the south coast of England with a red wax crayon. 'He was called Copeland, Hugh Copeland.'

During the remainder of my visit, Joshua told me that he had once witnessed a fist fight between John McCluskie and another soldier whose name he could not remember. He then fell into a reverie. I spent my remaining time in that house eating a snowball and sipping tea, but Joshua ignored all my subsequent enquiries about John. Ellen, now sitting in the other armchair, gazed apprehensively at the white flakes I shed with each mouthful. She made me feel so uncomfortable that I wolfed down my cake and left.

The sun was shining, but there was a cool westerly breeze. As I crossed an area of moorland on my way to the bus stop, I experienced a sudden panic. Everything appeared dreamlike and insubstantial – the rocky outcrop beside which I stood, panting; the glittering tower blocks, tenements and cranes of Clydebank laid out before me; the grand sweep of the Clyde valley stretching towards the west.

When I returned to my bed-sit, I re-read Campbell's description of Hugh Brendan. Hugh emerged from Campbell's bold handwriting smiling and winking on his wooden platform; the first of those grinning phantoms with which Campbell would later people the stage. However, I was no closer to finding the key to John McCluskie's character.

He met Campbell's mother when she was nineteen. She was stretching up to take a sheet from the line. John, aged twenty-four, leaned over the garden wall to speak to her on his way home from his father's shop. Katherine was taciturn. She was wary of young men, but she found something attractive in the way the evening sun made him screw up his eyes and lower the peak of his cloth cap, or so Campbell would have it.

Katherine's father opposed the relationship from the outset. When John came to the house a week later to ask permission to take Katherine to the theatre, Duncan completely lost his temper. He strode up and down the kitchen shouting, 'The theatre is the Devil's own whorehouse!' He accused Katherine of betraying his trust. He then threw John out.

Subsequently, Katherine saw John in secret until in April of the following year she wrote to him, 'I'm sorry that you feel that way, but it must be obvious why I cannot see you again. We are not brutes and should not act as such ...'

In the meantime, her mother had fallen ill with lung cancer. During the summer of 1922, it fell to Katherine to nurse her through the terminal stages of the illness, because by then Katherine's elder sister, Margaret, had married a locksmith named Fergus and had left home.

That Margaret was worried about Katherine is obvious from her letters to their sister, Bessy. However, it is difficult to ascertain precisely what it was that Margaret feared. Her words skirt about the issue in an alarming manner, as if it was a truth too horrifying to countenance. Only one or two oblique statements indicate that Duncan was the source of the threat.

At the beginning of August, Katherine took the initiative in restarting the relationship with John. From disclosures that John later made to one of his daughters, it is clear that Katherine seduced him beside the canal one night towards the end of that month. His gratitude soon turned to suspicion that Katherine had had other lovers. He was in a ferment of doubt when she told him six weeks later that she was pregnant.

They got married in October in a Roman Catholic Church. Katherine's father did not attend. A daughter, Mary, was born in May of the following year. The extreme frailty of the child prevented tongues from wagging over the seven-month lapse between marriage and cradle. Duncan died six months later, following a solitary drinking bout, when he choked on his bile. He left the house and all its contents to Katherine; a legacy that none of the relatives disputed.

Katherine suffered what would now be termed acute post-natal depression after Mary was born, which contributed its own cycle of reprobation and guilt. At first, the three of them had to share a room in John's parents' house. John's mother never forgave Katherine for forcing her son into marriage, and she would provide her with a daily inventory of her failings in child rearing.

After Duncan's death, their move to Janetta Street improved the family's material situation, but it led to further complications in Katherine's emotional life. By the summer of 1924, despite (or perhaps because of) her strong will, Katherine was on the verge of a breakdown. Perceiving her approaching crisis, and fearful for Mary's safety, Katherine's sister Margaret offered to look after the child for two weeks in July. Coincidently, John was offered the use of his Uncle Sam's cottage in Bembridge on the Isle of Wight while Sam was visiting Europe.

The cottage, set away from the road outside the village and shaded by the branches of a sycamore, proved to be the perfect haven for Katherine and John. During their holiday, it seems they began making the private adjustments necessary for a long life together.

I imagine my own parents twenty-nine years later, preparing for their life together in a cottage overlooking Kyleakin on the Isle of Skye. As a child, I would often lie awake at night listening to the sounds through the wall, of my father racked with sobs on his creaking bed. I would squeeze my eyes shut and try to conjure the image of my mother lying in a sun-filled bedroom in Kyleakin; imagining that in doing so I might bring her back to life. But sleep would inevitably cloud my thoughts. I would be prey to nightmares of fearsome machines grinding endlessly in darkness, or of elaborate instruments of torture. Only once did I dream of my mother slowly turning away from me while I tugged and tugged at her empty sleeve.

I vividly recall poring over a map of Skye, which even now reminds me of a lion rampant, as if my mother was still living on that paw-like projection. However, I came to realise the futility of such delusions, because all that was being prepared in that Highland cottage was my mother's death and my own sorry life.

The Isle of Wight is more like a rhombus in shape, but I wonder if events there did not in some manner also contain the seeds of Campbell's death. Late one afternoon, while the sky darkened and a symbolic wind agitated the branches of the sycamore, Katherine briefly overcame her hidden anxieties. To the rhythmic creak of the bed springs, she cried, 'Yes!' three times. On the final loud creak, a china washing bowl toppled from its bedside stand and broke into four pieces on the floor.

Nine months later, on 6 March 1925, at half past six in the morning, Katherine gave birth to a healthy, seven-pound baby boy, who was christened Campbell, after her maternal grandfather, James Campbell Scott.

Chapter Two

Shortly before Campbell was born, John McCluskie fell heir to the family shoe repair business. His ambitions could not be contained by that modest shop with its dirty, shoe-filled window and the cast iron boot suspended over its entrance. Within a matter of months, he had sold the business, obtained a loan to supplement the money and set himself up as a shoe manufacturer.

The decision infuriated his mother. When John next took his family over to pay her a visit, she curtly informed him that they were no longer welcome. It was a humiliating experience which long stayed in Katherine's memory. She had been trying to manoeuvre Campbell's pram up the step, while his sister, Mary, waited on the garden path. John, as usual, angered Katherine by thoughtlessly striding up to the house ahead of them, whistling. His mother opened the door. Standing in the entrance with her arms folded, she said her piece and tightened her lips in a characteristic manner that made her mouth resemble a drawstring bag.

John's first act was to buy two long sheds of ochre-painted brick, on a piece of wasteland close to Sighthill goods station, which, when renovated and made secure, provided him with a workshop and a warehouse. I can only conjecture about the queasy mix of anxiety and excitement he must have experienced during the months that followed.

Campbell's mother certainly had a very hard time of it. Mary had fallen ill with tuberculosis. The extraordinary demands this placed on Katherine prevented her from giving Campbell all the attention he required. There never seemed to be enough money to cover the medical bills and the housekeeping. Then there was the housework. As Katherine confided to her sister Margaret, it seemed as if she had spent her entire life cleaning those four cramped rooms in Janetta Street.

Reading was her sole pleasure. She never tired of re-reading Jane Austen and George Eliot. However, it was difficult for her even to indulge this pleasure. There would be the heart-rending distraction of Mary, sitting on her favourite rug in the corner by the piano, bravely chattering to her rag doll as she fought a losing battle against her cough. Or Campbell would start to cry for his feed in a manner impossible to ignore.

Come the evening, there would be the meal with John. An exalted expression would appear on his face as he told her of the order he had obtained, or conjured an army of stenographers who would click their way home in his shoes, but it would change to an expression of hurt when he realised she wasn't listening.

Afterwards, the golden sunset, lengthening the shadows on the playing fields across the street, would fill her with vague longings that – as she wrote to her sister Dorothy – she could never quite grasp. And John would never sit at peace for long. He would fidget about with newspaper or pipe. Invariably, the sound of coughing from Mary's room would elicit from him a guilty look in that direction (which I imagine was similar to the one directed at me by my father when I caught him looking at the photograph of my mother and her dog). Then he would clear his throat, search his pockets for his tobacco and, without looking at Katherine, announce that he was going to the pub.

Their lives continued in this manner until the spring of the following year, when John returned, changed, from a business trip to London. Katherine noticed that he was more relaxed than he had been since setting up his new business. He ate his meal and then read Mary a bedtime story before unpacking. When he finally settled down in the sitting room, his good-humoured evasiveness reminded Katherine of their courting days.

A week later, he informed her that his recent successes meant that he could double her housekeeping and that he had employed a home help by the name of Jessie Connolly. Turning round from the window, at which he had been standing with his hands clasped behind his back, he told her they could finally afford a specialist for Mary.

A specialist was found. I picture a tall man with a serene, reassuringly lined face in a dimly lit office. He put the child through an experimental (and rather painful) course of treatment and suggested that a holiday by the sea might help her convalescence.

And so the family once again went to Uncle Sam's cottage in Bembridge. The two weeks there did little to restore Mary's health, but they did provide me with my most cherished image of the playwright.

On the second day, John drove them to the seaside in Sam's car. As soon as they arrived, he laid out the car rug on an unoccupied stretch of sand and erected a striped windbreak around it. Mary lay down and began to suck her thumb. Katherine undressed Campbell and helped him into the bathing trunks he had inherited from his sister. When Mary had outgrown her first swimsuit, Katherine had cut it down to make trunks for Campbell. The frills, which she hadn't bothered to remove, made him look like a little girl as he squatted nearby pulling at the ear of his teddy bear.

John had to go back to the car to fetch something he had forgotten, while Katherine began the delicate business of getting into her bathing costume without exposing herself to a group of men who were playing football further along the beach.

Suddenly, Campbell began to run towards the sea, trailing his teddy bear behind him by its leg. Katherine, helplessly wrapped in her towel with her bathing costume half on, shouted to him to come back, but it was John who raced across the beach and plucked him into the air with a laugh just before he reached the water.

Afterwards, this incident turned into an oft-repeated family story, in which Katherine would claim to see evidence of Campbell's nascent personality. She would show rare animation when recounting it. Her face would take on a beatific expression as she described the one-year-old Campbell being held aloft by his father, 'pointing at a yacht and babbling fit to burst'. However, the anecdote filled Campbell with a sense of foreboding which he could not adequately explain.

When I think of Campbell making that childish bid for freedom, I am reminded of the summer holidays I used to spend with my uncle, my aunt and my cousin, Jamie. They lived near Loch Lomond and we often went to a sandy beach known as the Aber shore. My uncle would boil water for tea on a fire of piled driftwood, and on one memorable occasion he constructed a train out of damp sand. I never knew how my father spent his holidays in those days. It was only recently that I learned of his yearly pilgrimage to the cottage where he and my mother had spent their honeymoon.

I cannot now recall when I first heard about my mother's death. For my first six months, I was cared for by her brother, Rab, and his wife, Wilma. When my cousin Jamie was born, I was returned to the small house in Crow Road which my father had bought with my mother's life insurance money. The remainder of the money went towards paying a nanny to look after me while he worked.

My father's name was Alexander McDuffy. He worked as an accountant in a flour manufacturer's situated to the south of Byres Road. It is still there. Its huge machines, visible through the windows, still operate in an unsettling manner that makes you think that the whole building is moving up and down. When he returned from work, he would cook our meal and often he would spend the evening immersed in his history books. The nanny remained with us until I was seven or eight. One night, I chanced to see her coming out of the bathroom naked, but otherwise I remember her as a cold and distant woman given to unpredictable outbursts of temper.

I suspect that I only gradually became aware of my mother's death, through snippets of overheard conversations, sudden inexplicable silences and ominous hints. By the time my nanny left, I knew that my mother had died of heart failure. I also knew that Rottenrow was linked to her death in some mysterious manner. I did not know where it was, but for nearly a year it filled my nightmares. I pictured it as being like the derelict places I glimpsed from the train when my father took me to town.

It was my Uncle Rab who let slip that my mother had died in childbirth. I was spending the school holidays in their wooden bungalow in Alexandria, near Loch Lomond. It was a sunny day. My cousin had run off with his friends, abandoning me to a fat, wheezing and red-faced solitude. Kicking at stones on the garden path, I made my way to the kitchen door. Just before I pushed it open, I heard raised voices from inside. Aunt Wilma was saying, 'But it's been over eight years now. What can you possibly gain?'

'Look, if it hadn't been for that midwife, Dot would have been alive today,' replied my uncle.

'Just think what you're doing to yourself. Even Alex has given up on the negligence charge.'

'But Wilma, to die in childbirth ...'

I pushed open the door. My uncle was sitting at the kitchen table, crying. My aunt was standing behind him with her hands on his shoulders. They looked at me for a moment, and then she swept me out of the room with a kind of desperate gaity, responding with kindly prevarications when I asked her why they had been talking about my father and mother.

I often wish that my father had shared more with me. He did not tell me why the nanny fled our house in tears one night, a shiny triangle of material flapping loose from her suitcase. Nor did I ever find out why he spent so much time reading history books. Indeed, it was only the trembling excitement he displayed when one richly illustrated volume on medieval history arrived in the post that revealed to me the extent of his pleasure. I firmly believe that he loved me but that part of him blamed me for my mother's death and that his guilt at this emotion made him feel awkward in my presence.

How I envy Campbell that moment when his father held him aloft on that beach near Bembridge. I picture the clear blue sky; the foamy residue of a retreating wave; the diamonds of light flashing on the choppy surface of the sea; Campbell's mother wrapping her towel around her brown shoulders and laughing.

On their way back to Scotland they spent two nights in London so that John could meet some important clients. While there, Katherine and he attended a play, *Edgar Caym*, in which Katherine's sister Dorothy had a leading role. It is unnerving somehow to imagine Campbell sleeping in the hotel room under paid supervision, his small fingers curled into a fist by his head, dreaming unknown dreams, while the threads of his destiny come together on that nearby stage.

Back in Clydebank, Katherine discovered that she was pregnant again. She complained to John that the house was too cramped. She deplored her momentary weakness in Bembridge, and in her letters she bewailed the wiles and appetites of men. However, another two years were to pass before John felt secure enough to invest in a larger house.

Instead, he opened a shop in Sauchiehall Street at the end of February 1927, shortly before Katherine gave birth to a daughter they named Moira. A second shop, opened in Edinburgh at the end of that year, provided Campbell with his first recorded memory: 'maddening glimpses of the castle through steam and sun-drenched foliage as the train pulled into Waverley Station'.

Perhaps the most curious twist of John's career took place towards the end of the summer of 1928. He published a shoe catalogue containing some startlingly original designs that were attributed to an Italian named Giovanni Villanova. In actuality, Villanova was nothing more than a figment of John's imagination. John had correctly assessed that the wealthy clients he sought would have little truck with the son of a Clydebank cobbler, and so Villanova existed in a series of catalogues, the success of which would ultimately cushion John's business from the worst effects of the Great Depression.

Just as John began to feel more secure about the family's future, tragedy struck. At the beginning of 1929, Mary started complaining of headaches. Three weeks later, she was dead from tuberculous meningitis. As Katherine stood weeping beside her emaciated body, the doctor, rubbing his hands in embarrassment, explained that it was unusual for a child so young to be afflicted in the first instance with pulmonary tuberculosis.

Campbell would never refer to Mary in any of his writings, and in several interviews he casually mentioned that it was his conception that had led to his parents' marriage. Many have seen this as a blatant example of his egotism. However, in this instance, I find myself in agreement with his sole female biographer, Mary Ryder. She interpreted Campbell's silence as an inability to cope with the loss of his sister.

Coincidently with Mary's final illness, John had entered into negotiations to purchase a house in Albert Road. Understanding nothing of his father's business success, Campbell linked the move with Mary's death. On one occasion, he asked his mother if Mary had stayed on alone in their old house because her screaming had become too loud for anyone else to live there.

The move was a traumatic experience for Campbell. He remembered the removal van in some detail years later, belching smoke and rattling to a halt on the street outside. Under Katherine's watchful eye, two men, in worn leather aprons and dirty striped shirts, carried out a mirror. Campbell was perplexed to see drifting clouds and sky reflected in it, instead of the familiar objects it used to contain. Perhaps Katherine's anxiety communicated itself to him, for he was convinced that he would never see his belongings again.

For the first time, Campbell had a room of his own. From his window, he could see the back lawn stretching down to a sycamore tree encircled by a wooden bench. Mounted on one wall was a framed engraving of a cobbler, lifted from a nineteenth-century fairy-tale anthology, which had once hung in his grandfather's shop. Campbell was fascinated by the tiny elfin creatures that scurried around the elderly cobbler. Also in the room was a desk on which stood a row of toy soldiers; there was a leather football; there were bookshelves; there was a wardrobe; there was Mary's orphaned bed.

At night, the room took on a more sinister aspect. A light source, which Campbell never located, projected on to the flimsy curtains the shadows of the sycamore branches, which the wind would imbue with a mysterious and terrifying purpose. Consequently, he developed a profound fear of going to bed. As he wrote in a short autobiographical piece:

The grandfather clock would tick with ominous regularity. Light from a street lamp, shining through the glass in the front door, would gleam maliciously on the varnished floorboards at the edge of the hallway. The fifth step would creak when I stepped on to it, and squeak like a tortured mouse when I stepped off. My mother would press her hand firmly against my back, to encourage me to take those last reluctant steps into my room.

Bedtime stories were to remain a nightly ritual until Campbell was nine. When his mother finished reading for the evening, he would employ a number of desperate stratagems to keep her from going downstairs, which later became a source of embarrassment to him. In a letter to an actor friend, he was to describe this period in disparaging terms:

> I was in many respects a contemptible child. At about the age of four, I became unaccountably afraid of the dark, and I used to dread being left alone in my room at night. When I started school, I felt that there was something shameful in this fear, and I was terrified that my friends would find me out and despise me for my weakness. I still feel proud of the way I overcame it. I would make a point of going to bed ahead of my mother, or I would force myself to walk around my bedroom in the dark after she had gone, even going so far as to open the curtains in defiance of the creatures of my fancy.

Campbell started school in August 1930. Initially, he was persecuted by his classmates because of his father's relative wealth. All that ceased when, outside the school gates at the end of the third week of term, he knocked the class bully to the ground with a single punch. It was noted that Campbell had never cried as a result of the bullying. He subsequently secured his position as class leader by a not unusual combination of violence and charm. His teacher was quick to notice his ability to manipulate people and situations and mentioned it in a report to his parents.

Despite Campbell's success at school, he did not forget the bullying he endured there, and it may be that his antipathy to his father's work dated from that time. Certainly, it was with a sense of shame that he would recall a trip to his father's workshop during the previous summer. John had introduced him with mock gravity to his

31

workers. Then he had led him to a workbench on which were spread various lengths of leather. Here, 'like a merchant displaying his wares, he offered [Campbell] a piece of dyed hide, saying, "It's pure alchemy, Campbell; pure alchemy. I can turn this leather into gold."'

On returning home later that day, Campbell discovered the purple face of yet another sister, Joan, gazing up at him from the wool-covered bundle in his mother's arms.

In his second year of school, he had a young and attractive teacher on whom he developed a crush. He once had a dream in which he rescued her from nameless tormentors who had stripped her and bound her to a wooden frame. At the sight of her naked body, he experienced a sexual thrill that he was too young to comprehend. During the following year, he gradually lost interest in her, and she was finally ousted from his affections by the arrival of his Aunt Dorothy.

Dorothy was two years older than Katherine, and like Katherine she took after their mother. She had Katherine's brown eyes and dark complexion, which set them apart from their pale and lumpish sisters. Her relationship with their father did not develop the incestuous aspect of Katherine's, but it was nevertheless an unhappy one. Dorothy tried to avoid confrontations with him and was generally quiet and obedient around the house. Duncan was wrestling with demons of his own. Despite her efforts, she often aroused his anger and he beat her frequently. Katherine believed that Dorothy's passive nature irked Duncan more than her own defiance did.

It came as a shock to the family when, at the age of seventeen, Dorothy ran off with James Knox. James was better known as the music hall comedian Jocky Widjin. During his short stage career, his act and set were invariable. Against the painted backdrop of a row of tenements with a lamp post on the left-hand side, his sidekick, Wully Peg Leg (sporting a Prussian uniform, monocle, walking stick and baggy, checked trousers) would propel himself about the stage, nervously asking Jocky's whereabouts of the audience. Jocky would suddenly appear in a window behind him, grinning enormously, and shout, '*Here*'s Jocky,' drawing out the opening syllable to thunderous applause. Jocky would then kick the stick out from under Wully. Whereupon, in a hurly-burly of patriotic songs, Wully would be subjected to a series of painful humiliations, which would culminate in him being carried offstage on a stretcher in the direction of a signposted Berlin, closely followed by Jocky Widjin in characteristic bandy-legged jaunt.

James Knox was a tall, effete-looking man with slim, tapering hands. He was popular on account of his ribald humour and his deceptively attentive manner. His passionate attachment to Dorothy lasted for just over a year, characterised by disappointing love-play and ostentatious socialising. After they moved to London to take Jocky to a wider audience, he became moody and distant.

They shared a house in Chelsea with Paul McGuire, the long-suffering Wully, who provided Dorothy with welcome companionship. She was attracted by his shyness and doleful appearance, which contrasted with the extravagant behaviour of James, whose apparent charms were giving way to something altogether more sinister.

Early in 1919, Jocky began to lose his appeal. Audiences dwindled. Bookings were cancelled. James, struggling to create a new act, blamed Dorothy for his repeated failures. A sadistic element entered their sexual relations, aroused by James's (quite correct) hypothesis that she was sleeping with Paul. She later confided to Katherine, but not to her journal, that she initially enjoyed the sadism. But alcohol and inadequacy do not in themselves explain the cruelty of James's inclinations, which passed by degrees beyond the point of innocent fantasy.

One night, he interrupted their perverse lovemaking in order to drag Paul into the bedroom, whereupon the reluctant ménage à trois degenerated into a terrible travesty of the Jocky Widjin stage act. Dorothy, intimately and emotionally bruised, left the house the following morning with a suitcase of clothes, two diamond cufflinks and twenty pounds, while James slept on unaware of the theft.

After her departure, the erratic correspondence Dorothy had maintained with Katherine through a mutual friend ceased abruptly. It did not resume until Dorothy met the impresario Charles Kemp at a Soho nightclub at the end of 1920. Dorothy never told anyone what occurred during those months. The only record we have of her existence during that time comes from the trial of James Knox in February 1920.

The sensational aspects of the case earned James some belated publicity in the gutter press. It emerged that he had assaulted a French prostitute outside the Penny Dreadful in Scribner's Lane, Whitechapel because he believed that she was having a homosexual affair with Dorothy. Under oath, he claimed he had overheard the prostitute describing to a client what she had done with Dorothy on the previous evening.

When Dorothy was called to the witness stand, she gave her

address as 23 Chesterton Way, Saffron Park, and her occupation as chorus girl in the Ragged Urchin jazz club. She admitted to meeting the prostitute during a party celebrating Jocky Widjin's first performance in London. However, she denied any subsequent meeting. There was no evidence to link Dorothy and the prostitute. It was clear that the entire incident was a product of James's growing mental instability.

On 6 December 1920, a famous raconteur and observer of London theatre society wrote in his weekly gossip column that he had encountered Charles Kemp walking with a young woman in Hyde Park. He described the scene in detail: the morning mist enveloping the trees; the clicking heels of a passing lady; Charles emerging on to the path in front of him 'like a stately spectre with a vamp leaning on his arm'. He went on to describe Dorothy as 'a young slattern wearing a moth-eaten fur collar and worn shoes'. The columnist took particular offence at the fact that 'her coat was missing its third button from the top', and concluded (metaphorically wagging a finger at Charles) that she must have been a 'cheap trollop'; an impression of Dorothy that was shared by many of Charles's rich friends.

Judging by photographs, Charles was a physically unattractive man. He had podgy cheeks, very full lips and a receding chin. In startling contrast to his appearance was his deep and powerful voice, which unsettled many people when they first met him. Dorothy confessed to Katherine that she had initially found him repellent. However, after she had gone out with him regularly for several weeks, he began to exert a fascination on her which she was unable to explain.

I now want you to picture a neo-Gothic apartment building in St John's Wood. In the extensive lounge of one of the third-floor apartments, you will find a three-piece suite upholstered in cream, floral-patterned silk. A walnut cabinet near the couch houses a gramophone on which a popular jazz tune is playing. Dorothy is sitting cross-legged on the couch. Her hair is bobbed. She is wearing a black, dropped-waist dress with thin shoulder straps and a square-cut neckline. A silver, rhomboid-shaped pendant hangs just below her clavicles. Charles is at the far end of the room, pouring drinks. He is wearing a well-tailored dinner suit that lends elegance to his bulk. His complexion is pasty. For five years, he has been dividing his time between this flat, which he leased for Dorothy in April 1921, and the house in Hampstead which he shares with his wife and a pampered lapdog.

On this particular evening, Dorothy and he are going to dine with

the playwright Martin Colehurst, whose play *Edgar Caym* Charles has
agreed to stage. The play tells the story of an unhappily married
woman, Janice Elliot, who falls under the influence of an evil inter-
loper, the eponymous Edgar Caym, and is led into 'a twilight world
of deception, despair and ultimately murder'. It is precisely the kind
of melodrama that Charles liked to put on, to leaven his usual fare of
bedroom farces.

Charles had arranged the meal in order to discuss the possibility
of Dorothy taking the role of Janice Elliot. At first, Colehurst raised
objections about her accent and expressed doubts about her acting
ability, but by the end of the evening he was completely won over by
the idea. Scandalmongers later ascribed his change of heart to sexual
desire. However, during her years with Charles, Dorothy had proved
herself a capable actress in several roles that Charles had secured for
her. Moreover, the plight of Janice Elliot, who escapes one form of
unhappiness only to find something worse, must have struck a chord
with her after her experiences with James Knox.

The critics regarded the play as an artistic triumph, in part because of the subtle evocation of evil, in part because of the convincing characterisation of Edgar Caym. One highly regarded writer,
Trevor White, paid tribute to Dorothy's acting in a review that she
cut out and kept.

Dorothy's success was to be short-lived. In September 1926, an
associate of Charles offered her a major role in a play he was pro-
ducing. Rehearsals were due to begin in October. However, Charles,
returning unexpectedly from a business trip to Paris, discovered
Dorothy in bed with Martin Colehurst. I could easily reconstruct this
banal episode from the numerous versions I have encountered in
film and literature, but the poignancy Dorothy's diary expresses is
quite unattainable in art:

I found him in the lounge, sobbing and shaking like a leaf. I
laid my hand on his bulging neck and watched a trail of spittle
descend on to his trousers. Martin was laughing in the bedroom. He told me afterwards that it was because of Charles's
ludicrous appearance in the doorway, but I knew he was trying
to hide his humiliation. I have never loved Charles, I know,
but when I saw him like that I realised how much I had hurt
him. I am so weary of it all.

Charles threw Dorothy out of the flat and, using his influence in theatrical circles, ensured that she never acted in London again. She moved in with Martin Colehurst, but the relationship didn't last. Colehurst relished the aura of evil which had surrounded him since the success of his play, but in reality he was a neurotic dreamer with a drink problem, who was frightened of his own shadow. Like James before him, his awareness of his inadequacies turned him into a petty domestic bully. But experience had strengthened Dorothy and she found no difficulty in leaving him.

During the following six years, her fortunes went into decline. For a short time, she was employed as an artist's model. She then worked in a West End tearoom for a number of weeks, but she was fired when her employers discovered her scandalous past.

February 1933 found her posing nude in a seedy and draughty theatre in Soho and living in a rented room in Putney. Returning home one rainy night towards the end of the month, she found one of John McCluskie's shoe catalogues lying in a doorway where she had sought temporary shelter.

On the following morning, her neighbour – a solicitor's clerk who had been quietly in love with her for several months – discovered her lying fully clothed on her bed, perspiring and delirious. A doctor, grumbling at being called out on a Sunday to treat a prostitute, diagnosed pneumonia, didn't rate her chances and left the clerk with a useless prescription. The clerk sat with her for the rest of the day, happy beyond his dreams, squeezing her hand, wiping her forehead and praying for her deliverance in whispered fervour.

That evening, Dorothy's cry woke him from a troubled sleep in a cramped armchair. She was sitting bolt upright and staring at him. He groped around on her dresser for his glasses, upsetting a tumbler of water in the process. She began to speak, repeating the same words over and over: 'You must get John McCluskie.' He gently settled her under the covers again and then set about mopping up the water on the dresser. It was only then that he discovered the shoe catalogue.

Four days later, John McCluskie arrived at the house with an expert physician. While the doctor examined Dorothy, John explained to the distressed clerk that he had made arrangements for her to be taken to Scotland as soon as she was well enough to travel.

Chapter Three

In the summer of 1932, Katherine gave birth to another daughter, Anne, a fair-skinned child with red hair. John reckoned that she took after his Uncle Sam. Campbell, in his innocence, considered that his Uncle Fergus was a more likely candidate. Katherine flew into such a rage when he broached the subject with her that he never mentioned it again.

Campbell, then a swarthy child with thick black hair who scowled frequently, often pushed his mother beyond the limits of endurance with his attempts to grab her attention away from his numerous sisters. Obscenities he heard at school, or ludicrous stories, were his favoured means, but on one occasion, while she was changing Anne's nappy, he sat in a corner and held his breath until he fainted.

The arrival of Aunt Dorothy changed everything.

One sunny Saturday morning in March of 1933, a blackbird fell down the chimney and started to flap in awkward panic around the sitting room. All was in pandemonium. Joan was crying in terror. Their mother was shouting. Moira begged Campbell not to hurt the frightened creature when he managed to catch it, but the strange texture of its wings filled him with revulsion and he let it go almost immediately. It was their father who finally secured it in a shoebox with two holes pierced in one end. Afterwards, he carefully lifted a corner of the lid so that the children could peer in at the trembling bird, before he released it into the garden.

Later that day, Campbell witnessed his Aunt Dorothy's arrival. His father opened the front door and waited politely on the doorstep between her suitcases while she entered the hallway. She was wearing a light grey cloche hat with a shiny black band. Her skirt flared slightly below her knees. In one hand she was carrying a black Gladstone bag; in the other she held a wooden box pressed to her side. She walked straight up to Campbell, placed her bag on the floor and crouched in front of him.

'And you must be Campbell,' she said, squeezing his chin between thumb and forefinger.

There is strong reason to believe that this was the first of those 'moments of heightened awareness' which, as he later claimed, provided him with his artistic purpose and which are pursued by the central characters in all of his plays. Until his death, he could recall every detail of his aunt's arrival: her scent – a mixture of Chanel No. 5 and cigarette smoke – which never lost its erotic power for him; the glossy brightness of her lips; the tiny ladder in her left stocking just above her shoe strap; her black lace gloves; the deep orange sunlight slanting across the floor of the hall; his father in silhouette closing the door firmly behind him and standing there watching them for a moment before taking Dorothy's suitcases up to her bedroom in the attic.

In his ludicrous biography, Anthony Shaw maintained that Campbell underwent some kind of infantile orgasm when he met Dorothy. This is an absurd claim. Despite Shaw's insistent bleatings to the contrary, there was much more to McCluskie's aesthetics than mere sexual gratification. Years later, in an interview, Campbell said, 'There are moments in life which become highly focused in the mind, as if a circuit has suddenly been completed and the confusing impressions of the world attain a kind of order. At such times, I experience reality with an unusual intensity which I believe lies at the heart of creativity.'

I believe that this precisely expresses what Campbell felt when Dorothy stood up, patted his head and then followed his father upstairs, to the room in which she was to die almost two years later.

The house had a spacious attic that had been converted into a suite of guest rooms. Adjoining the bedroom (with its romantically sloping ceiling and arched windows) were a bathroom and a modest sitting room. Dorothy, who never fully recovered her health, would rise late, eat a light lunch with Katherine and then spend the afternoon reading. Unlike Katherine, she read Coleridge, Shelley and Byron and had recently taken a liking to D.H. Lawrence.

Dorothy confided her doubts about Katherine's marriage to her journal, which, despite its mysterious gaps, provides valuable insights into the McCluskie household. John was frequently absent on business. Dorothy noticed that Katherine and he were polite and respectful with one another but that they displayed few outward signs of affection. She also noticed inconsistencies in Katherine's relations with the children. Dorothy was convinced of the deep love that her sister felt for them, but she noted that this love was seldom expressed.

More often than not, Katherine was short-tempered with them and critical of their childish aspirations. Moreover, she avoided any kind of physical contact.

John, when he was there, was more outgoing with their daughters. He was always hugging and tickling them and sitting them on his lap. But he treated Campbell differently. As he said to Dorothy on more than one occasion, 'Campbell's at school now. You shouldnae coddle him so much, or he'll turn into a Jessie.' Ignoring this ludicrous advice, Dorothy did all in her power to provide Campbell with the affection he was lacking. She made a point of reading to him in bed every evening, and of taking him on outings when her health permitted. After an initial period of shyness, he began to respond eagerly to these overtures.

He particularly enjoyed Dorothy's tales of her time in London, which gave him a frisson of pleasurable fear. He pictured that city as a sinister, fog-bound place, and all the characters Dorothy mentioned were transformed in his mind into a gallery of grotesques. Most fearful of all was Jocky Widjin. Dorothy gave him the epithet of 'the absurd clown', and so he would occasionally enter Campbell's dreams in that guise, advancing inexorably through foggy, dimly lit streets towards him.

That summer, Campbell put on a play for Dorothy. A makeshift set was created on the back lawn using a clothes horse, Campbell's wooden toy box, the tiny cups and saucers of a dolls' tea set and several rugs. Campbell's sister Moira was the principal actress. The plot meandered for some twenty minutes until Campbell rescued her from an evil character, played by a school friend, who had kidnapped and bound her to the clothes horse.

Perhaps it was in order to offset Dorothy's influence that John devoted more time to Campbell that summer than he had before. There was one (not altogether successful) fishing trip, a boat ride to Dunoon and several walks in the Kilpatrick Hills. Campbell would later write of the wonderful views of Clydebank from those hills: 'For the first time, I could appreciate the pattern of the streets, and the way the town fitted into the world.'

One day towards the end of the school holidays, John took Campbell into Glasgow with the intention of going to the cinema. During the morning, there was a short and violent thunderstorm. They took shelter in John's shoe shop. While they sat in the office drinking tea, there was a knock on the door. In the doorway, Campbell saw a sales assistant and, just beyond her, a woman in a pale raincoat. He found himself placed under the supervision of the sales assistant while his father ushered the strange woman into the office.

Campbell soon became bored with the pretty assistant and the shoes lining the walls or gleaming on their modish podiums. Taking advantage of the distraction caused by the manageress returning from her lunch, he made his escape and burst into his father's office. The woman was leaning back in a chair near his father's desk, with her skirt hitched up and her legs apart. His father was kneeling in front of her with his head between her thighs. She was sighing and making strange noises.

There was a flurry of panic-stricken motion when his presence was discovered, which pleased Campbell enormously. John, red in the face and wiping his mouth with the back of his hand, led him out of the room and told him to remain there until the fitting was over.

Campbell went on to write, 'That afternoon, my father bought me a box of tin soldiers marching with shouldered rifles and swirling kilts. Then in a café, over a glass of lemonade and a cake, he asked me to mention nothing to mother about the fitting he had given to Lady Forsythe, because the conduct of his profession required absolute secrecy. I never told anyone what I had seen, but I didn't for a moment believe my father's explanation.'

The thunderclouds had dispersed when they returned to Clydebank without having gone to the cinema. As soon as he got in, Campbell dropped the box of soldiers on to his bed and then rushed out to see his Aunt Dorothy, who was reading in the garden. As he ran across the back lawn, he saw her sitting on the bench with her legs crossed twice. The shadow of the sycamore stretched out to dapple her pages with the late afternoon sunlight. She was gazing at the sky, lost in thought, but when she heard his approach she turned and smiled at him.

On another memorable occasion, Campbell found Dorothy sitting with a copy of Coleridge's poems (published in 1868 by Edward Moxon & Co.) lying on the arm of her chair. She looked up, smiling, when he burst in, and beckoned him over to sit on her lap. He remembered feeling the hard button of her cardigan against his cheek when he pressed his head between her breasts and listened to the dull beats of her heart. It was January 1935. An electric fire was glowing in the far corner of the room. At his request, she handed him the wooden box that was on the bookcase. He shifted his position on her lap and she began to stroke his closely cropped hair.

The box lid was (and still is) inlaid with five mother-of-pearl circles.

He opened it carefully and examined its treasures one by one: a photograph of Dorothy sitting on a couch wearing a black dress and an unusual pendant, with the cabinet of a gramophone just visible at the edge of the picture; a photograph of Katherine holding Campbell; a sixpenny bit with a hole in its centre; a faded newspaper cutting of a review of *Edgar Caym* by a well-known writer who had an affair with Dorothy after she left James Knox; a page from one of John McCluskie's shoe catalogues folded four times, with John's office address printed in one corner and four shoes pictured and described. One description is underlined in red ink by an unknown hand: 'Evening courts of silver, mauve and green brocade in a harlequin pattern; blunt-pointed toe, two-and-three-quarter inch "jewelled" heel, set with pastes and enamels.' He did not know what significance these things had for Dorothy. He merely liked to look at each in turn and then return it to the box.

Dorothy then read 'Kubla Khan' to him. It was a poem that one perceptive critic recently described as McCluskie's siren song. Campbell remembered that her reading was twice interrupted by a cough she had picked up earlier in the week.

Within a matter of days, Dorothy developed a virulent form of influenza. In her weakened state, her body was unable to deal with the virus and a number of complications ensued. She died on 26 February 1935. At a loss to explain her sudden turn for the worse, the doctor cited pneumonia as the cause of death.

Towards the end, Dorothy had begged Katherine to give her a notebook and pen so that she could write her memoirs before it was too late. She had scribbled furiously for several hours before losing consciousness. When the notebook was discovered under her bed shortly after her death, all proved to be gibberish save two ominous sentences: 'A clown with bloodied fists is steadily approaching me. Every night, I can hear his horrible laughter coming closer and closer.' These were followed by four repetitions of the words 'Sea Defile and White', of which no one could make any sense.

During the last month of Dorothy's life, Campbell only managed to see her once. Katherine, fearful that he would contract the unknown illness, had forbidden him to enter the sickroom. However, a week before Dorothy died, he managed to sneak in while Nurse Brady (who had been hired to help tend her) was having a bath.

Dorothy was awake but delirious. Campbell sat on her bed, holding her hand, until he noticed her copy of Coleridge's poems on her bedside cabinet. He carefully opened the book at 'Kubla Khan', which was marked by the photograph of an unknown man standing on a beach. The photograph fluttered to the floor. In an agony of suspense, he struggled to pronounce the words, but he was discovered by Nurse Brady, who, fearful of losing her job, dragged him out of the room more forcefully than she had intended. Campbell never forgave her. For all she had done to ease Dorothy's death pangs, his only comment on her was that she had the biggest bottom he had ever seen.

On the day of Dorothy's funeral, Campbell waited in the sitting room for the hearse to arrive. He had been told that Dorothy had gone to join God in Heaven, and he understood that she was not coming back. Uncomfortable in his grey flannel shorts and his black pullover, he whiled away the time by pulling at a loose thread on his sleeve.

Katherine paced up and down, twisting her damp handkerchief and occasionally dabbing her eyes. Aunt Margaret sat on the settee. Uncle Fergus was staring out of the window with his hands in his pockets. The telephone rang suddenly, startling everyone. Katherine went out to answer it, but she didn't close the door properly and it swung open after her. Campbell heard her say, 'No ... I'm afraid she passed away two days ago ...... Who is this? ...... No, of course I'm not. What do you take me for? ...... You are quite mad.' He heard her slam down the receiver. He heard her sobbing on the stairs. He heard his father shouting from the bathroom.

Margaret struggled out of the settee and marched into the hallway. This time the door was firmly closed. Uncle Fergus walked over to Campbell, cupped his head in one massive hand and said, 'Oh son, I'm so sorry.' He scratched one of his thick red sideburns and added, 'Not long now, sonny.'

One wet and windy night towards the end of 1988, I visited Lawrence Gardiner, one of Campbell's old school friends. During that visit, Lawrence inadvertently gave me a clue as to how profound Dorothy's influence had been on Campbell. My journey involved taking a bus to Bearsden and walking about a mile through unfamiliar streets, using the directions Lawrence had given me over the phone. I recall the dull yellow glare of the lights in the bus; my brooding reflection in the window; the blurred street lights beyond the glass, which provided little indication of my whereabouts; the asthmatic breathing of the man sharing my seat. Inevitably, I got off the bus at the wrong stop.

By the time I found the street leading to Lawrence's bungalow, the wind had blown my umbrella inside out, snapping one of the wire struts, and I had abandoned it. My life was as chaotic as the elements. My belongings were piled haphazardly in my new bed-sit. My father was suffering dementia in a private nursing home. The house I had lived in since childhood had just been sold. I reached my destination wet and miserable.

Then things took an unexpected turn for the better. The door was opened by Lawrence's daughter, Fiona, whom I had never met before. She was a beautiful girl in her late teens (blond hair, full lips, pale skin) wearing an open-necked blouse, black jumper and mini-skirt. She relieved me of my coat and led me into the sitting room to meet her parents.

Lawrence suggested that I have a cup of tea with the family before we got down to the business of the evening. I readily agreed and slumped in the chair near the television. Mrs Gardiner was knitting in the other chair, her mouth twitching slightly as she inwardly tallied the stitches. Lawrence went off to make the tea. Fiona sat on the couch with her legs drawn up underneath her. The family dog, a golden retriever called Candy, watched Lawrence leaving the room and then, sighing, placed its head between its paws.

Fiona said, 'It must be interesting, writing the biography. Campbell was a fascinating man.' I felt a stab of envy of the late playwright, which passed away when she asked me more questions about my work. All too soon, the tea was finished, Fiona went to her bedroom and Lawrence led me to his study.

In the room were an antique desk and two sets of bookshelves. Lighting was provided by an anglepoise lamp. I sat on the extra chair that Lawrence had brought in for me, and took my tape recorder and notebook out of my briefcase.

Lawrence leaned back, smiling. 'I think you might be interested in this,' he said, pushing a photograph into the circle of light.

Campbell and Lawrence were pictured on a motorcycle. A fence was visible in the distance, together with a Union Jack on a flagpole, a set of goal posts and the blurred figures of two women. Lawrence was wearing a flying jacket and a pair of waterproof trousers. His hair was swept back and shaved at the sides. Campbell, riding pillion, was wearing a dark suit. His hair was shaved well above his ears and was brushed back and to the left. His eyes were so deeply set that at first I mistook their shadows for thick eyebrows.

'We were very close then,' said Lawrence. 'We must have been about seventeen. But you know, the funny thing is, I cannae remember where it was taken, or who took it, for that matter. I remember the bike, of course. It was my first and it hardly ever worked.'

Lawrence continued in his rich baritone. The tape recorder quietly whirred. I found myself looking at the marquetry on the desktop – a border pattern of pine diamonds joined end to end against a dark background of mahogany with pine beading. He spoke of their long friendship; of how, when they had been caught stealing apples, he had rescued Campbell's school bag while leaving his own, and of how he had been called to the police station to reclaim it. He told me of Campbell's difficulties in adapting to life in the high school, and of his later success with girls.

When I asked him about Campbell's Aunt Dorothy, he told me that he had only met her once and he remembered being frightened of her. Her behaviour had seemed odd to him. The meeting had left him with the curious notion that she was a witch. He was completely unaware of how important she was to Campbell.

Shortly before Campbell enlisted in June 1943, Lawrence and he had gone on holiday to the Isle of Skye. During the night they spent in Kyle of Lochalsh, there had been a tremendous thunderstorm. Campbell had been greatly amused by a woman in the adjoining room shouting, 'No, Donald; you'll make me swallow my dentures!' They had crossed over to Skye on the following morning.

After a week of walking round the island, the pair had rested in the Broadford Hotel for two days before returning to Kyle. On the first evening, after several whiskies in the hotel bar, they had passed through the lounge on the way to their room. A newly wedded couple were having tea near the fireplace. The man was a soldier; the woman was very attractive, with black hair, high cheekbones and a dark complexion.

Lawrence had reason to remember the episode. He had left his tobacco in the bar and when he caught up with Campbell outside their room he had found him crying. Lawrence went on, 'I was really shocked. I had never seen Campbell cry. He said, "Not a word to anyone about this, Lawrence. Do you hear me? That woman in the lounge reminded me of someone who was very close to me. One day I'm going to do something she would have been proud of." I'm sure that's what he said. I wrote it down in my diary that night. I didn't know who he was talking about, but you may be right. It might well have been his Aunt Dorothy. Anyway, after that holiday Campbell seemed to avoid me and I never saw him again after he enlisted.'

44

I pressed the stop button on my tape recorder and closed my notebook.

'Now, Ian, why don't you spend the night here? We have a spare room.'

The bed was narrow. The mattress was too soft. The room was over-heated. I heaved and groaned all night on those creaking springs. The following morning, I caught sight of Fiona walking to the bathroom dressed only in a tee shirt. I shuffled back to my room, blushing, but I still managed a sly look at her bare legs and partially exposed buttocks. In dreams I see them still.

From Lawrence's descriptions I can picture Campbell striding along a desolate road, dressed in a sweater, with his trousers tucked into thick woollen socks, and a haversack on his back. A peat bog stretches away towards the west. He turns, opens out his arms, grins and shouts, 'Isn't it magnificent? I want it all.' Or I can picture him in the hallway of a small hotel, talking to a beautiful, dark-haired woman. He leans towards her, brushes her neck with his lips and winks at Lawrence over her shoulder. However, more frequently I picture him as a young boy, sitting alone on his bed, clutching a wooden box inlaid with mother-of-pearl and bawling his eyes out.

Chapter Four

Of his Aunt Dorothy's funeral, Campbell would later recall the parallel spade marks on the grave's earthen walls, and the stepped gables of the mist-enshrouded lodge house by the cemetery gates. Afterwards, the routine of school, the onset of spring and the passing of his tenth birthday lost some of their reassuring certainty. He learned that man is born of dust; that the seasons are caused by the Earth's revolution around the Sun; that black children in Africa would chew on the ends of sticks to make their toothbrushes; that his father still hated the Germans; that another baby was growing in his mother's tummy. All the while, a spurt of growth was imperceptibly transforming his view of the world.

By the time the midwife arrived one Saturday morning in October, Campbell had become a tall, gangly and rather stubborn child. He refused to go into town with his father and sisters. The brisk, rather abrupt manner of the midwife had put him in mind of Nurse Brady. In his imagination, she joined the nurse in an evil conspiracy that had destroyed his aunt and now threatened his mother.

Temporarily banned from the house, he ran to a grassy hollow at the end of the garden, where he kicked at the piled leaves and tried to see what was going on in his mother's bedroom, beyond the reflections of the sycamore tree and the louring sky.

At half past twelve, the home help, Jessie Connolly, appeared at the back door and called Campbell in for lunch. He ran across the grass, scattered with branches and leaves from a recent storm, and then threw his mackintosh and wellingtons on the washroom floor. In the kitchen, Jessie was ladling soup into a bowl while the midwife placed a tray of metal instruments into a pot of boiling water. Campbell sat down at the table and began to eat, holding the large spoon in his fist. He kept spilling soup down his chin because he was staring at the midwife in growing apprehension. He noticed that she had on her cheek a large mole, which had a wiry hair curling from its centre. Jessie slapped him once on the back of the head, jarring his teeth on the edge of his spoon, and said, 'Mind your own business, Campbell.'

He tried to get to his mother's room later in the afternoon, but he was prevented by his Aunt Margaret, who was staying with them until after the birth. Thwarted, he ran out of the house before anyone could see that he was crying. The clouds had dispersed and the setting sun coated one side of the sycamore tree with its orange glow. Campbell remembered his Aunt Dorothy as he ran towards it. His mother began to squeal in short searing bursts that were barely muffled by the bedroom window.

He sat down with his back against the tree trunk, pressed his hands against his ears and screwed his eyes shut. His face was wet with tears. Spittle bubbled out of his mouth. His nose began to run. That evening, when John took him in to see his mother, he was surprised to find her still alive. She was sitting up in bed with the baby in her arms.

'We're going to name her Dorothy,' she said.

Campbell looked at the baby with its dark hair and bruised temples, but could see nothing reminiscent of his aunt.

Five days later, Campbell returned from school to find his mother in the lounge with his Aunt Margaret, who was sitting with her legs crossed at the ankles, crocheting part of a table cover. He sat on the couch and started flicking through the newspaper that had been draped over one arm. A cartoon caught his attention, of Adolf Hitler, dressed as a clown, doing somersaults in front of a giant Mussolini wearing the top hat and tailcoat of a ringmaster. With an involuntary shiver Campbell remembered his Aunt Dorothy's tales about the sinister Jocky Widjin.

The story printed beneath the cartoon served only to enhance his sense of foreboding. I myself experienced an almost metaphysical dread when I found the cutting in Campbell's notebook. Malcolm Thompson, a teenager described by the reporter as being 'simple in the head', had been savagely murdered in the grounds of an orphanage near Lennoxtown. Another orphan, Ingram Farqueson, was reported to have narrowly escaped the murderer and was found wandering the woods nearby, shocked and covered in his friend's blood. The description of the killer given by Farqueson tallied with that of a tramp who had been seen in the vicinity by several people. While Campbell folded up the paper, his mother stood up slowly and went to close the curtains.

'Here, I'll get them,' said Margaret.

'I'm all right, Margaret,' Katherine replied, switching on the standard lamp. As she pulled on the tasselled cord to close the curtains, she suddenly bent over and blood began to flow down her legs. Margaret struggled out of her chair. Katherine began to moan.

'Campbell, quick, phone for a doctor,' said Margaret. Campbell ran to the hall, while she helped his mother to the couch.

'No, no, I'll get blood on the cushions,' said Katherine.

Campbell stood frozen in front of the telephone with the receiver in his hand until his aunt came out.

'I don't know the number. I don't know the number,' he said, fighting back the tears. He noticed that Margeret had blood on her hands. Within an hour, Katherine was rushed to the Western Infirmary, where she underwent an emergency hysterectomy.

Katherine was ill for nearly a year after the operation, so John employed a live-in maid to attend to the housework and look after the children. May Cameron was the daughter of one of John's employees. She was a slight young lady with red hair and freckles, who became something of a heart-throb among Campbell's school friends.

Time passed slowly for Campbell. He read voraciously outside of school, outstripping the other pupils in his class, and so was easily bored during lessons. His teacher also noticed a certain coldness in him; a refusal to give himself away or admit to any weakness. It was true that these qualities inspired devotion in other children, but she witnessed Campbell on several occasions being cruel to those who were closest to him. As she told his mother, she considered that Campbell would change for the better when he went to the high school later that year, as he would no longer be able to lord it over everyone there.

Katherine confessed that she was worried about his move to the high school. His father had told her out of the blue that he would be sailing to the Argentine that summer, to cement a deal with a tannery owner named Luis Lonnrot. It was unlikely that John would be back before the start of the next academic year. The teacher assured her that Campbell was a bright boy who would soon adapt to life in the new school.

Neither the teacher nor Katherine knew that, since Katherine's haemorrhage, Campbell had become convinced that he was the focus of a dimly perceived conspiracy that was linked in some manner to his Aunt Dorothy's lover, James Knox a.k.a. Jocky Widjin. I have read somewhere that such paranoid delusions are common in creatively talented people with inflated self-opinions. Nevertheless, a shiver runs down my spine when I think about a gangster named Ingram breathing heavily and sweating as he stands near the wall of the goods station by Kelvinbridge on a hot June night in 1954. Is it possible that Campbell could have foreseen this scene in all its stray details: the flapping sound of a poorly secured tarpaulin in the station; the thin man with different-coloured eyes carefully wiping with his handkerchief the handle of a steak knife, which is engraved with the name of a restaurant; his anxious companion pushing his greasy hair away from his face, while a limping dog steadily approaches like a portent from one of Campbell's plays.

In the event, Campbell did have problems adjusting to life at high school, which were exacerbated by his gawky appearance. He towered above his classmates, but his body had not yet filled out. In response to the ridicule he received at this time, he developed a sharp wit and a talent for mimicry. History and English were the only subjects in which he excelled. His indifference to science was viewed as wilful laziness by his Chemistry teacher, Dr Farqueson (no relation), and he was frequently belted.

On his return from the Argentine, John started to mechanise his workshop and expand his warehouse. He seemed unusually tense during the following months, but he said nothing about his plans until the spring of 1938. At dinner one evening, he announced to the whole family that, through the intercession of a civil servant with whom he had served in the Great War, he had secured a contract to supply the army with boots. He then dragged Katherine to her feet and waltzed round the room with her. She remained stiff and complaining throughout. Campbell, his face in his hand, idly pushed mince about his plate with his fork.

To celebrate his business success, John booked the family into the Royal Hotel in Portree on the Isle of Skye for their summer holiday. On a wet and overcast day in July, they piled noisily into two taxis and headed into Glasgow. The station was crowded with holidaymakers. John, wearing a tweed overcoat and with a pipe clenched between his teeth, led the way to the Mallaig train, closely followed by a porter with a heavily laden trolley. Katherine kept a close eye on the luggage. Campbell, Moira, Joan and Anne followed in Indian file. May came last, holding Dorothy by the hand.

There was a mix-up over their reservations. John, shouting at the conductor, disappeared into the carriage. Katherine followed them in, making reconciliatory noises. The porter pushed his cap up, twisted his left middle finger in his ear, withdrew it, examined its tip and then lit up a cigarette. May let go of Dorothy and tried to remove an insect from her canthus with a handkerchief-covered finger.

Sleepy-eyed Dorothy wandered away rubbing her nose with her tasselled blanket. May didn't notice her absence until she had disappeared into the crowd. She left Campbell in charge of the others and ran down the platform looking for her. Meanwhile Anne slipped down her pants, squatted and widdled by the carriage steps, a frown of concentration wrinkling her small forehead. Moira, annoyed at being passed over in favour of Campbell, poked him in the ribs and threatened to tell Daddy about Anne's behaviour. Campbell merely laughed as the puddle of urine began to drip over the edge of the platform. May reappeared with Dorothy. John leaned out of the carriage door and restored order with one gruff command.

Five minutes later, they were settled in a first-class compartment. Campbell, much to Moira's chagrin, sat next to the window. It was the first time he had visited the Western Highlands. Certain images from the journey remained with him until his death: the tree-covered shore of Loch Lomond; the desolate, boggy expanse of Rannoch Moor; the grey hills shrouded in mist. He also recalled the sudden appearance in the carriage corridor of a portly man wearing a deer-stalker and a tweed cape. His case appeared in the compartment window, then his large belly and finally his red face, shadowed by the brim of his hat and framed with woolly sideburns. Panting and wheezing, he peered in at them for a moment before continuing on his way. Campbell noticed the broken veins on his bulbous nose and a ticklish sensation ran down his back, as if someone had walked on his grave.

Campbell resented the fact that his parents lunched in the restaurant car while he was left with May and his sisters to eat sandwiches in the compartment. The train arrived in Mallaig in the late afternoon. The family ate their evening meal in a small hotel near the harbour, where they were to spend the night before catching the Armadale ferry.

Afterwards, John and Campbell took a walk to the harbour to see the fishing boats. It was no longer raining, but the clouds were still low in the sky. Campbell leaned over the harbour wall while his father strolled along the front. He noticed the corpse of a seagull floating in a cross-current between two boats. Its eye was missing and its head was twisted back on to its wing. It spiralled sluggishly towards the harbour wall, trailing a strand of seaweed behind it, until it wedged itself between the hull of one of the boats and a tyre that was being used as a buffer.

Campbell looked up and saw his father about fifty yards away talking to a young woman. She was wearing a light-coloured raincoat which seemed luminous in the twilight. She passed something to John, who bent down to kiss her forehead, and then she walked away into the town. John rejoined Campbell by the harbour wall and said, 'We'd best be getting back.' Campbell took one last look over the wall at where the grey sheen of the water still outlined the tail feathers of the dead bird, and then they walked back to the hotel in silence.

The crossing to Skye was turbulent. Joan was sick. Campbell experienced an unpleasant pressure at the back of his neck, but managed to keep his breakfast down. The hotel had sent out two cars to meet them off the ferry. Campbell was allowed to sit next to the driver of the second car. Named Euan MacDonald, he was a hard-drinking crofter in mud-encrusted Wellington boots. He had owned the car for several years and operated a taxi service to supplement his meagre income. Campbell's parents went in the first car with Moira and Anne. This was a sleek black Bentley with the hotel livery painted on the door, and a uniformed chauffeur.

The hotel stood on a hill on the outskirts of Portree. Its grounds were separated from the road by a small plantation of Scots pines. Beyond the trees the driveway skirted a steeply sloping lawn before opening into a parking area that was bordered on three sides by a stone balustrade. In one corner a mechanic was bending over the open bonnet of a Rolls Royce. The car that had brought Campbell's parents was parked nearby. The chauffeur was leaning against it chatting to the mechanic. Euan MacDonald deposited the cases by the door and drove away in a spray of gravel after getting his money from the chauffeur.

In the lobby, crossed swords and a buckler were mounted on the wall above the fireplace. Opposite them was the obligatory stag's head on its wooden plaque. A staircase rose beyond the reception desk, behind which sat a woman whose greying hair was pulled back into a tight bun. A gold chain descended from the arms of her spectacles to rest on her shoulders. She looked up when May approached, and said with surprising tenderness, 'Mr McCluskie has already registered and is taking tea in the lounge.'

It was in the lounge that Campbell first saw Emily Frost. She looked around the room, let her gaze rest on him for a moment and then turned round to see if her mother was coming. Emily had dark, wavy hair, slight shadows around her eyes and a somewhat pointed nose. As soon as he saw her, Campbell became conscious of the fact that his white Aran pullover was several sizes too big for him. He blushed and looked down at his egg sandwich. Small fragments of yoke dotted his plate. A portly man in a dark suit approached the table, rubbing his hands. Campbell noticed that the waistband of his trousers was digging into his stomach.

'I am so sorry, Mr McCluskie,' he said. 'The Rolls broke down this morning and I had to call Mr MacDonald out at very short notice. I hope you weren't too put out by his appearance. He came straight from his field, you see. Now if there is anything – and I mean anything – that you require, please do not hesitate to ask Jaqueline at the desk.' Campbell stopped listening and twisted his neck to watch Emily leaving the room on the arm of a tall woman in a pale grey satin dress.

Within three days, Campbell had overcome his shyness and discovered Emily's name. He learned that she was fourteen-and-a-half; that her father had died when she was eight; that her mother was an alcoholic who paid little heed to her.

Girls' names: Margaret Ridley; Annabelle Ingram; Dorothy Fulton; Marion MacDonald. These names conjure up so much for me – trembling excitement; pain; humiliation. Sitting behind my graffitied desk, always too cramped, sticky with desire, looking askance at their cheeks, their light-filled eyes, the hems of their skirts, their pale thighs. Only Dorothy Fulton spoke to me with kindness, but then at the school dance, when I tried to kiss her, she averted her face, broke free of my grasp and upset a glass of cola on the table behind her.

On the sixth day of the holiday, John left the hotel at 6.00 a.m. to go on a fishing trip. Later that morning, Campbell informed his mother over breakfast that he planned to hire a bicycle for a day trip to Broadford.

'You're just like your father,' she replied with a twisted smile. 'We women shall just have to make our own entertainment.'

After breakfast, he ordered a packed lunch for two and bathed himself carefully. As he lay in the murky bath water, he noted with pride the hair that was beginning to appear around his well-developed genitals. He crunched down the driveway shortly after ten o'clock, swinging his knapsack, dressed in a billowing white shirt, grey flannel trousers and scuffed hiking boots. Emily was waiting for him on a bench situated in the dappled shade near the gateway. As he approached her, he had a sudden vision of a poetry book lying open in a cotton-draped lap.

They walked to a hardware shop in the town, which hired out bicycles. The shopkeeper patted Emily lightly on the bottom as he directed her to her machine. He had a squint and thick red hair that stood out at odd angles. He said something that Campbell could not understand and underlined it with a gesture whose meaning was all too clear. Campbell was grateful that Emily hadn't seen it and alarmed by the strange complicity he felt with the man.

According to Campbell's journal, they took the southbound road out of Portree and cycled for about half an hour before leaving their bicycles at the edge of a narrow farm track. Then they hiked for an hour over the moors until they came to a fast-flowing stream that had cut a deep gorge into the cliffside they were trying to circumvent. On the near bank, a short distance up the gorge, they found a platform of grass sheltered by twisted shrubs, beside which a waterfall had hollowed out a deep pool. They stopped there to eat their lunch.

Campbell had little appetite for the ham sandwiches he had brought. His heart was beating loudly. He felt aroused by Emily's accent, which he had seldom heard except on the BBC, and by the fact that she sounded nervous. He did not trust himself to say too much, in case his own fear showed. The skirt of her dress flared out around her legs, but the bodice was tight. When she leaned forward for her drink, the paler skin of her breasts became visible.

She finished her drink in one gulp and suddenly kissed him full on the mouth. He was unprepared. Her lower lip pressed against his chin for a moment before connecting with his lip. He found himself slipping down beneath her and, struggling to regain his balance, he groped for the buttons on the front of her dress. She let her hand fall on to his crotch. His hand moved blindly over her breasts. She stretched out beside him. His hand moved down. He tried, not altogether successfully, to keep his lips pressed against hers throughout, but she pulled back her head for breath. Then she leaned on her elbows with her head thrown back and her throat exposed, as she had once seen Greta Garbo posing in a photograph. Campbell, leaning on his right elbow, attempted to slide his left hand under the waistband of her knickers. He was surprised by the coarse texture of her pubic hair. The pressure of her knickers' elastic strained his wrist. He pressed his middle finger against something soft. She grimaced and pulled his hand free.

53

'That's enough for now,' she whispered. He drooped. 'Tonight in your room,' she added.

Campbell was the only one in the family to have a room of his own. It overlooked the car park. Unlike their other rooms, its walls were panelled with light blue wooden planks. There was a dormer window. There was a sink. There was a wardrobe. There were brass balls on the bedstead. There was an incongruous print of yachts racing at Cowes. He lay on his back, wide awake, eagerly listening for Emily's approach. A drop of water elongated and fell from the tap. She didn't come. He finally fell asleep at four o'clock in the morning.

He dreamed he was searching for Emily through all the rooms in the hotel. In the first, a woman in a light-coloured raincoat, whose face he could not see, was standing by the window holding a fishing rod. In the next, a red-haired man with his father's features was wringing the neck of a seagull. After trying five more doors that were locked, he opened the last one. Sunlight flooded the room. His Aunt Dorothy was sitting on a bench with her legs crossed twice. The floorboards were bare. Somewhere a tap dripped. Dorothy beckoned him over and placed his left hand inside her blouse on her bare breast. He woke with semen drying on his pyjama trousers.

PART TWO

Chapter One

Human sexual development always puts me in mind of the messy metamorphosis of some disgusting insect. During my embarrassing and somewhat protracted puberty, I contrived to remain aloof from the other boys in my class. I had no time for their sordid discussions about sex, which seemed to me to sully my unfulfilled romantic urges, and I looked instead to literature for examples of loving relationships.

I can still recall the stomach-churning despair I felt when I saw Annabelle Ingram in the bicycle shed with one of those moustachioed lotharios from 4S who was merely counting the days until he could leave school. It seemed to be a betrayal of all my hopes. Annabelle was bright and vivacious; far too clever for that oaf. From my hiding place, I watched them share a cigarette. Then they started to kiss. He tried several times to run his hand up her skirt, but she kept pushing it away. Finally, he contented himself with pulling her blouse free from her waistband and groping her breasts while he fed on her beautiful, pale throat.

It would appear that Campbell did not share my belief in the ennobling virtues of literature. When he returned to school after his holiday in Skye, he lost no time in coaxing girls into the bicycle sheds. Haunted by memories of Emily Frost, he hoped that he might persuade someone to finish what she had started. But all that resulted were a few love bites (with which girls would taunt their rivals), occasional tears and some colourful schoolgirl gossip.

Other distractions were provided by the war, which was bringing the McCluskies more wealth than they had ever had before. Despite this, Campbell's father could not suppress his rage at the German victories. After listening to evening news reports on the wireless, his shouts would reach the attic where Campbell would escape to read, or to write his journal.

Like most of his friends, Campbell remained impervious to the gravity of the situation facing Britain after the fall of France. He would adopt a cynical pose whenever his classmates tried to share their excitement about events. Unless there were any girls about. Then he would grow suddenly serious and talk about the terrible slaughter of the Great War, before announcing his intention to enlist as soon as he was old enough.

In March 1941, when the sirens heralded the first night of the Clydebank Blitz, John McCluskie found himself stranded in Glasgow. After wandering in desperation around the city centre for nearly an hour, he was persuaded by an air raid warden to take shelter in the St Enoch underground station, where he spent an uncomfortable night between an hysterical shorthand typist and a retired fitter. Two days were to pass before he was able to rejoin his family.

Meanwhile, back in Albert Road, Katherine and May led the girls down into the cellar, which had been furnished with camp beds and oil lamps for just such an eventuality. Grabbing the nearest book, Campbell followed them down. He felt a profound uneasiness when he realised the book was his Aunt Dorothy's copy of Coleridge's poems, especially when it fell open at 'Kubla Khan'. Turning instead to 'The Rime of the Ancient Mariner', he started reading aloud to distract everyone from the sounds of the explosions outside, until Moira told him to shut up.

When they emerged the following morning, they found the house undamaged. However, a large, still-smoking crater was visible at the foot of the garden. The sycamore tree had been uprooted by the blast. Its upper branches were rustling in the light breeze, some ten yards from the back door. The garden bench lay splintered beneath its trunk. Scattered pieces of masonry from the garden wall had fallen just short of the house, but had more or less destroyed Mr Shaw's greenhouse in the neighbouring garden.

After breakfast, Katherine asked Campbell to look in on Mrs Shaw to check that she was all right, since her husband had been called out to the naval base at Rosyth to do some emergency work.

Nora Shaw was then twenty-eight years old. Campbell had met her a few times when she had come to have tea with his mother. He had described her in his journal following two such meetings, using the lurid but hackneyed imagery that was then characteristic of his descriptions of young women. Only in certain details do we see the acute observations that were later to give his plays their immediacy – the bulge of a suspender outlined by the material of her skirt; the fluttering motion of her painted fingernails as she dropped some cake crumbs on to her plate; the sound of her stockings rubbing as she uncrossed her legs.

Nora had spent the night lying on cushions underneath the dining table, convinced that she was going to die. When Campbell arrived, she was sitting in the kitchen drinking tea, wearing a dark blue silk dressing gown. He noticed that her eyes were dark from lack of sleep and that her hands were shaking. She said that she had just boiled some water on her paraffin stove, and offered him a cup of tea. He declined. She looked out of the window at the shattered greenhouse and the thick pall of smoke rising beyond the garden and burst into tears.

'Jack's tomatoes,' she said. Campbell felt embarrassed. He looked away. He had just turned sixteen. His body had filled out.

'Are you all right, Mrs Shaw?' he said. His recently broken voice rose unexpectedly as he said 'Shaw'. She laughed and approached him, wiping her eyes on her sleeve.

'It's just the shock, I suppose. I'm fine. Anyway, I hate his bloody tomatoes.' She put her arms round him and pressed her head against his chest. She was about six inches shorter than him. He felt awkward. He felt the pressure of her breasts against his stomach. He realised that she wasn't wearing anything under her dressing gown and found himself becoming aroused.

What followed is described in detail in Campbell's journal. She began to unbutton his shirt and to kiss his gradually exposed chest. His stomach took a sudden inward dive as she reached his trouser belt, by which time she was kneeling on the floor. I am sure that hidden by the adolescent posturing of McCluskie's description is the reality of a shy and clumsy lover embarrassed by the exposure of his penis and mortified by an ejaculation that covered the lower half of Nora's face with semen.

I am also certain that it was Nora who later led Campbell to her bedroom to continue their lovemaking, and not the implausibly masterful teenager portrayed in Campbell's journal. Just before they had sex, she wriggled free from his embrace and went to fetch a contraceptive from the chest of drawers, where, rather disconcertingly, a framed photograph of Mr Shaw was angled towards the bed. Campbell averted his eyes from it and watched Nora slipping out of her dressing gown. He noticed her abundant pubic hair and the diamond-shaped birthmark on her left shin, which had a little line of speckles trailing from its lower corner. She pushed him on to his back and, sitting astride his legs, unrolled the contraceptive over his penis. Then she lowered herself on to him.

Once again, McCluskie's immature prose gives him away. He

cannot convey the mixed emotions he felt as he entered her. The writing verges on the poetic hyperbole that he later deplored, before slipping into clichés: 'I drove myself into her again and again', etc. etc. There are several indices that suggest that Nora was dissatisfied with his lovemaking.

Over the next four weeks, Campbell spent only two mornings with her. Judging by his journal, she occupied all his waking thoughts. It is curious to observe the way he sheds the affected cynicism, occasional brilliance and absurd deceptions of his writing, to become a rather conventional lovesick adolescent. After their second tryst, he barely discusses the physical side of their meeting, dwelling instead on the 'rapture I felt when I was inside her' and 'the meaning which our love has given my life'.

After their third meeting, Nora informed him that their affair was at an end. He pleaded with her. He wrote to her several times. One sunny morning, he even followed her when she went out. Blossoms still covered the road. He noticed the squashed corpse of a baby bird in the gutter beside a crumpled cigarette packet. Nora was wearing a light blue dress with a very broad white belt. When she reached the street corner, a man in blue overalls approached, kissed her lightly on the lips and then they walked arm in arm along Janetta Street. Campbell's stomach began to churn and he threw up his breakfast on the dusty pavement.

For several weeks after this, his journal takes on an embittered tone, with which Campbell usurps Mr Shaw's role as a betrayed lover whose ideals have been destroyed by 'an evil, manipulative temptress'. It is quite clear that Campbell knew nothing of Nora's feelings. I imagine that she was attracted by his initial attentions but that she quickly grew tired of his poetic effusions and lack of sexual experience.

I was surprised, given Campbell's concern for his image, that he hadn't destroyed the journal in which this affair is recorded. Perhaps he kept it as a salutary example of the kind of writing he should avoid. Whatever the reason, it survived his death and was given to me by his sister, Dorothy, in January 1989.

Despite the grey streaks in her hair, Dorothy bore an uncanny resemblance to her aunt and namesake. As I sat in her sunny sitting room, I could understand why Campbell had stayed in touch with her alone of all his family. She was kind and considerate. She was widely read. And she was remarkably attractive.

Outside, a sparrow was precariously perched on a wire basket of nuts. A small avalanche of thawing snow startled it into flight. I lapsed into silence and sipped at my tea while Dorothy read through my dissertation on Campbell McCluskie.

After finishing it, she agreed to give me all the papers she had relating to her brother. She even allowed me to copy out certain passages of her diary which she had shown to no one else. I noticed that there were tears in her eyes when the time came for me to leave. I assured her that I would send her a copy of the finished biography before it was published, and that I would return all the papers to her when I had completed my task.

Those papers threw up as many questions as they answered. One of the journals revealed that a marked improvement had occurred in Campbell's prose style during the latter half of 1941. Also, I found tucked inside it an extraordinary poem entitled, 'Dalmuidy'. In it, Campbell draws together with consummate skill and humour his love for his Aunt Dorothy, his affair with Nora Shaw and the preoccupation with gangland violence which was to figure so largely in his mature writing.

None of Campbell's sisters could recall anything significant happening in that year to account for these dramatic developments, and so I decided to contact Lawrence Gardiner again. By a happy coincidence, Lawrence had been contemplating getting in touch with me. His daughter, Fiona, was going to study English Literature at Glasgow University, and he thought that I might be able to offer her more advice about the reading list. I told him I would be more than happy to help her. A date was made. I was invited over for lunch and dinner. I was to spend the afternoon with Fiona and the evening with Lawrence.

When the day arrived, I was surprised to discover that Fiona was in the house alone with the dog.

'Mum works for an estate agent's in Milngavie,' she said as she took my jacket and briefcase. The golden retriever pressed its nose into my crotch. I was conscious that my palms were sweating, and I rubbed them surreptitiously on the seat of my trousers as she led me into the kitchen, where the table had been laid for lunch. 'I've only made something light,' she said. 'Mum's planning something more substantial for this evening.' I could see the lacy pattern of her bra through her blouse. I blushed. I played with my cutlery. She ladled out two bowls of homemade soup and set one down in front of me.

I avoided looking at her while we ate. The kitchen units had fake marble surfaces. Among the white tiles that covered the wall above the sink were scattered tiles with sepia diamond-shaped illustrations of rural scenes: a man reaping corn with a scythe; a sower; a comely milk maid. A plastic butterfly magnet held a note of the week's menus to the door of the fridge. I tried not to slurp my soup. She asked me if I enjoyed cooking. I replied that I only had a Baby Belling, which limited my scope.

Her self-confidence made me feel less anxious. Smiles came readily to her and dimpled her cheeks. Casting odd glances at her voluptuous lips, I became all too painfully aware that I was a corpulent, middle-aged lecturer who would never sleep with her, but I foolishly allowed myself to hope.

After lunch, we went through to the sitting room. The golden retriever was lying near the door, lolling its tongue and panting in the heat. Fiona handed me her reading list. As I scanned through it, I was able finally to set aside my anxiety. I was in my element. I discussed style and metre; form and content; the historical context. I drew her attention to the best books of criticism. I warned her about Professor Williams, who was still creating difficulties for me. I told her about the prejudices and idiosyncrasies of the other members of staff.

'And what about your prejudices, Mr McDuffy?'

I suddenly realised that I had been speaking for some time without being aware of her presence. She was leaning towards me with a peculiar expression on her face, the meaning of which eluded me.

'Me? Oh, I suppose I have my obsession with Campbell McCluskie. That's what everyone ribs me about.'

'That's a quaint way of putting it,' she said, smiling. 'Would you like a cup of tea?'

When Fiona had finished making the tea, she asked me about my biography. I fetched my briefcase and began to go through my notebooks with her. Once again I got carried away by my theme, and I started to tell her about the difficulties and complexities of my research. After a few minutes, I feared that I had lost her and that she was bored with my conversation. My confidence evaporated and I stopped speaking. It was Fiona who broke the silence by saying, 'You know, I love Campbell's plays.'

It was an unusual situation for me to be sharing a passion with a beautiful girl. She ran upstairs and returned with a paperback edition of *The Complete Plays of Campbell McCluskie*, which she had annotated extensively.

'I haven't told my Dad about it,' she said. 'I don't think he would approve.' It was then that I told her about the poem 'Dalmuidy'. She became extremely animated when I informed her that I had a photocopy of Campbell's original manuscript in my briefcase. She begged me to let her see it. I confess that her enthusiasm disheartened me. It struck me that it had been Campbell who had interested her all along. However, I couldn't deny her the pleasure of seeing the poem. She read it avidly, as I had done when I discovered it, and she blushed when she reached the sex scene that closes the first part. I told her that she could keep the copy, as I had another with me. I even offered to show her the original sometime.

At that moment, a key turned in the front door. The dog struggled to her feet and began to wag her tail furiously. Fiona slipped the poem between the pages of her book of McCluskie's plays and hid that beneath the pile of books and papers on the coffee table. Mrs Gardiner entered and began to pat the excited dog. I felt guilty, as if she had interrupted an embarrassing intimacy. Fiona picked up her books and papers and said, 'Mr McDuffy's been very helpful, Mum. I'll just put these away and make you a cup of tea. Would you like another one, Mr McDuffy?'

When we finished our meal that evening, Fiona went up to her room with her mug of tea. She reappeared in the sitting room later, dressed up for a date. From my position on the couch, I had to twist my neck painfully in order to see her alluring kohl-lined eyes.

'I'll see you in the lecture room,' she joked, and then rushed out.

'See and be back by 11.30,' shouted Lawrence in a voice that would brook no argument.

'Cheerio,' she replied, closing the front door with a slam.

'Teenagers – what would you do with them, Ian?'

I smiled nervously, not knowing how to reply.

Once we were settled in his study, Lawrence told me that he wasn't sure what fresh information he could give me, since he had covered most of the ground at our last meeting. I gave him copies of the passages from Campbell's journal which related to Nora Shaw, and also a copy of 'Dalmuidy'.

'That's pretty hot stuff,' he said after perusing the journal extracts. 'I didn't know anything about that; although, it probably explains the rumour about Campbell and Moira Skelley. That would have been in the summer of 1941. Moira had a bit of a reputation for being loose. After Campbell went out with her one night, a rumour spread round the school that she had performed fellatio on him.'

Lawrence then turned his attention to the poem.

'Christ – Dalmuidy!' he said. 'I'd completely forgotten about that little gobshite. I don't think Campbell knew him that well, but he [Campbell] had one of those personalities. He had a way with words. Dalmuidy took a shine to him. It was just after the Blitz. We had a bit of a break from school and Dalmuidy had already left. Christ knows how he avoided being called up. He was a real spiv. Maybe Campbell admired him in some way. Anyway, Dalmuidy got involved with a really bad crowd and he was knifed to death. It was just like Campbell to make him the winner in his poem. He [Campbell] was a big softy at heart. It's funny; just seeing Dalmuidy's name brought it all back.'

I then asked Lawrence if he could think of any reason why Campbell's writing might have improved during 1941.

'I never knew anything about Campbell's writing until the success of his plays. I seem to recall that he became quite chummy with our English teacher, Mr Hogg, at around that time, but he kept the friendship close to his chest. He got good marks, but he had a reputation for being tough and was careful to keep his distance from the teachers. I remember seeing Mr Hogg coming out of Campbell's house on one occasion. I asked Campbell about it, but he said Mr Hogg had been visiting the house at his mother's request; that she wanted to borrow some books from him.'

That's all that Lawrence could tell me that evening. When I left, I had the strange feeling that he was eager to see the back of me, but I was under a lot of strain at the time and I may have been imagining things.

Police records reveal that McCluskie was with Dalmuidy on the evening of his murder, but there was no evidence to link Campbell with the crime. That said, it is clear that Campbell's involvement with Dalmuidy went deeper than Lawrence had led me to believe.

Dalmuidy was in a gang led by a man known as Johnny Nelson (because he had lost an eye in a razor fight). The police believed that another gang had been trying to muscle in on Johnny's patch and that Dalmuidy had been caught selling them information. They were unable to pin anything on Johnny and the crime went unpunished. Johnny Nelson himself was murdered at the end of 1945 by an unidentified assailant, wearing a black hat with a white silk band, whom the police concluded was a professional hit man.

As for Campbell's English teacher: I learned from his daughter that he died in action in Italy in 1944. She had never heard him mention Campbell McCluskie.

And so I am left with the poem, 'Dalmuidy'. I suspect that the mystery behind its composition will never be solved. Aside from the journals, it is the only piece of McCluskie's juvenilia to have survived and it is quite clearly a parody of Coleridge. Campbell tells the story of a gang war between Dalmuidy and the narrator, which has arisen over their shared passion for a woman.

The first part ends with the narrator being seduced in the heroine's kitchenette:

> The shadow of my dome of pleasure
> Did fall across her eyes,
> While I took in the mingled measure
> Of her tongue and lips and thighs.
> It was a miracle of rare device,
> This sunny kitchenette; her secret vice.

However, it is in the closing sequence, with its mixture of fact and fiction, that we have the first hints of what was to follow:

> A woman sitting reading
> In a garden once I saw,
> With dappled light upon her head,
> In leafy shade the book she read,
> Which told of Nora Shaw.
>
> Could I revive the picture
> Of Nora's lovely face;
> Those parted lips whose tincture
> The woman's tongue did trace;
> Then I would build my dome in air;
> My pleasure dome; her secret vice.
> But all too late, Dalmuidy's here,
> And those around me cry, 'Beware
> His flashing eyes; his Brylcreemed hair;
> The blade he weaves around you thrice;
> And close your eyes in holy dread,
> For he on agony has fed
> And sent McLean to paradise.'

Chapter Two

There is a widely held misconception that Campbell never intended to enlist in the army in 1943; that his pledge to do so was merely a ploy to help him to seduce girls, which had gone wrong when one of his rivals called his bluff. Again we have Anthony Shaw's biography to thank for this calumny.

In reality, Campbell's motives were varied and complicated. In the journal he was keeping at the outbreak of war, he imagined his role in the conflict as a heroic one. Like a medieval knight, he would sacrifice himself to the memory of his Aunt Dorothy, as if Hitler was merely a larger and more violent version of Jocky Widjin. Shortly thereafter, he told his mother that he wanted to join his father's regiment, the Royal Scots Fusiliers, to prove himself his father's equal. (I picture her smiling her agreement while secretly hoping the war would be over before he was old enough to fight.)

A year before his murder, he gave his lover, Helen Miriam, yet another reason for his decision: namely, that by consciously putting himself into danger he hoped to dispel the dreadful conspiracy that he discerned beneath the surface details of his life. He was drunk when he told her this, and immediately retracted what he had said, muttering that it had only been a childish fancy.

He did not remain in the Royal Scots Fusiliers for long. The prospect of escaping the drudgery of life in the infantry made him volunteer for the parachutists. At the end of August 1943, he was sent to Hardwick Hall, near Chesterfield, for selective training.

An army report made at the end of the selection process commended him on his physical prowess and his ability to get on well with men of all ranks. It was considered, however, that he didn't always pay due respect to officers and regulations. Despite these quibbles, he was duly graded as A1 plus. Parachute training took place at Ringway near Manchester and by the end of the year he was assigned to the 8th Parachute Battalion.

It has been argued that Campbell's plays derive their almost metaphysical anguish from his wartime experiences. Seen from an ordinary soldier's perspective, the preparations for D-Day appeared frighteningly arbitrary as he was moved about the south of England for purposes he could only dimly apprehend. Intervals of endless drilling were interrupted by brief periods of leave. These were characterised by casual sex, heavy drinking and bouts of violence with soldiers from other regiments.

Campbell described one such fight outside a pub in Devon. The full moon cast an eerie silver light on events. Campbell was sitting on a wall, smoking a cigarette and looking up at the sky. A horse-drawn cart laden with hay disappeared round a corner with a tortured creaking sound. The door to the pub opened behind him, sending a triangle of light across the yard. Two Scottish soldiers paused in the doorway to continue a heated religious argument. One of them had different-coloured eyes, deeply set in a thin face. At almost the same moment, they and Campbell noticed a couple, caught in the light from the doorway, having sex in a corner of the yard. The man, an American soldier with his buttocks partially exposed, twisted his head and shouted at the two soldiers to close the door. The woman attempted to bury her face in the American's shoulder.

'Here is that no Lillian?' said the man with different-coloured eyes, drawing a switchblade from his pocket. Campbell put on his beret and started walking down the road, pausing only to stamp out his discarded cigarette. His last view of the incident was of the American standing with both hands held out in front of him, his trousers round his knees and his semi-erect penis swinging ludicrously from side to side.

It was not until a week before D-Day that Campbell was able to make sense of all these months of preparation and waiting, when his battalion was briefed about its part in the invasion. They were to be dropped in Normandy near a village called Touffreville. Their objective was to destroy the bridges over the River Dives, to the east of the village, and thereby to help secure the left flank of the landings.

The importance of the two-and-a-half days he was to spend in Normandy is attested by the (posthumously published) memoir he would write in Glasgow the year after the war ended. It commences with a description of him boarding a Dakota aircraft with twenty-three other parachutists, shortly before midnight on 5 June. To give the reader some idea of what it was like, he provides a full list of the equipment he had had with him:

Helmet; boots; gloves; main parachute; reserve parachute; Sten gun; six magazines; five hand grenades; entrenching tool; two knives; a first aid kit; two morphine needles; a gas mask; emergency rations; cigarettes; a box of matches; some French currency; a copy of *The Dubliners* sent to me on my 19th birthday by my mother.

As events were to prove, McCluskie was fortunate to find himself next to the door. Private Hughes was sitting on his left. Opposite them were a sergeant and another private nicknamed Chalky because of a white patch in his otherwise black hair, a fact that didn't prevent McCluskie from writing to his mother, 'Why is there always somebody nicknamed Chalky in this damned army?'

Campbell described the strained silence of the men; the excitement he felt; the smell of the burnt cork with which he had blackened his face; the steady drone of the engines. By twisting awkwardly, he was able to look out of a window and, for a moment, through a break in the cloud, he saw the invasion fleet spread out on the sea below.

German anti-aircraft fire started almost as soon as the Dakota reached the Normandy coast. The plane began to climb and then banked to the left, throwing Campbell against the fuselage. As it straightened out, he saw the captain in charge ('a thin man with a thin moustache and a propensity for patriotic gibberish') move towards the cockpit and begin shouting at the pilot. The plane banked to the right. McCluskie managed to remain on the bench, but Private Hughes grabbed his arm, leaned forward and vomited. Campbell saw flashes in the sky around the plane. The captain drew his pistol and pointed it into the cockpit. The plane banked to the left and began to descend again.

'What the fuck's going on?' shouted Chalky.

Campbell cricked his neck as he turned to see a pale ribbon of water bisecting the ground beneath the window. The plane straightened out again. Glowing tracer bullets tore through the floor between the two rows of men. They all pulled in their feet. Suddenly, an explosion ripped holes in the fuselage opposite Campbell. Chalky was thrown forwards with a piece of hot metal protruding from his nape. The sergeant's left arm was blown off and he was thrown to the side. Campbell was cut below his right eye and he heard a number of metal fragments strike his helmet. Later, he would find a piece of shrapnel embedded in the bag that was slung over his stomach.

Another blast struck the front of the plane. Campbell pulled Hughes's arm and pointed at the door, but when he turned to look at him he realised that Hughes was dead. His staring eyes against his blackened face reminded Campbell of Al Jolson.

Everything was in pandemonium. I realised the plane was losing height. I grabbed Hughes' Sten gun and fired a burst at the catches on the door. Then, placing a hand on either side, I swung my feet against the door and pushed myself out in one movement. The jolt of the parachute, as it opened, uncricked my neck with a painful wrench, and then, carried by the strong wind, I landed in a field somewhere to the east. As I descended, I saw the plane spinning towards the ground on my right, but no other parachute appeared.

When he landed, his parachute draped itself over a number of surprised cows, who began to bellow and stumble among its folds. His first instinct was to get as far away from the parachute as possible. The field sloped up to a thick hedgerow beyond which was a copse of trees. When he reached the hedgerow, he realised that a sunken lane separated it from the trees. He was about to cut his way through the hedge, when he heard an engine approaching. Through the tangle of branches, he saw a German motorcycle and sidecar moving along the lane towards the west. The soldier in the sidecar was pointing at the sky and shouting something at his companion.

After they had passed, McCluskie used his entrenching tool to hack his way through to the road. He abandoned his reserve parachute and prepared to crawl through the hole. The moon was not full, but the sky was clear and McCluskie was able to see first one cow then another struggle free from his parachute.

He walked through the copse and continued to the summit of the hill. From there he was able to see a patchwork of fields descending towards the coast. Inland, the ground dipped before rising again to a higher hill. In the shallow valley he could see a field of corn with more woodland beyond it and a farm on the opposite slope. He looked at his watch, but the face was cracked and it had stopped at five past one. He began walking towards the farm.

As he walked he experienced a curious sense of detachment. He began to entertain the notion that he had dreamed the entire landscape and that he was still sleeping in the transit camp in England. When he reached the woodland, he slung the gun over his shoulder and lit a cigarette. Before he moved on, he kneeled down, clawed up a handful of earth and raised it to his nose. More than anything else, it was the rich odour of that soil that brought home to him the danger of his situation.

The approach road to the farm initially wound its way between trees before crossing an open stretch planted with rows of vegetables. Buildings ran along three sides of the courtyard, but the wall that had formed the fourth side had been destroyed by an Allied bomb. McCluskie hesitated at the door of the farmhouse, fearful that the place might be occupied by Germans, but, nevertheless, he knocked loudly. From the west, he could still hear the drone of planes and the sound of gunfire. He waited. He knocked again with the butt of the gun. A thin line of light appeared under the door. A voice shouted something in French. McCluskie knocked again. The door opened.

He found himself staring down the barrels of a shotgun. Beyond, he could see a face: hair cut very high at the sides; thick moustache trailing over lips; eyebrows lowered in anger; forehead furrowed. Beyond that, he could see a beautiful dark-haired woman standing in a doorway, pulling together the lapels of her dressing gown.

'Écossais! Écossais!' he yelled, but the man merely pulled back the hammers and raised the gun to his shoulder.

Campbell turned and ran across the uneven cobbled yard towards the barn while the farmer shouted something he couldn't understand. He opened the barn door and jumped inside, scattering some chickens. He heard a horse neighing in a stall at the far end. Finally, he found a large pile of straw and lay down on it, exhausted. He could still hear raised voices coming from the farmhouse, but he simply closed his eyes and fell asleep.

He dreamed he was back on the plane. Through the window, he could see drifting cloud formations that occasionally parted to reveal a stretch of coastland. He felt that the clouds were hiding something of significance to him, but he was distracted by the fluttering wings of a blackbird that he was trying to hold in his hands. It escaped and began to fly around the plane in panic, banging its beak on the windows and fuselage, until his captain shot it dead with his pistol. Campbell suddenly found himself in a sunlit field. His Aunt Dorothy was standing in the shade of a tree at the far end. She raised her hand to her mouth, as if frightened by the sound of the shot. He tried to shout to reassure her, but he had caught the sleeve of his pullover in the hedge that bordered the field. He began to cry when he realised that the wool on his sleeve had started to unravel. Private Hughes was sitting on the road beyond, trying to place a magazine in his Sten gun. He turned towards Campbell and said, 'Not long now, sonny.' Campbell felt a dull blow strike his chest, then another, and then he woke up.

The young woman from the farmhouse was bending over him with an oil lamp and tapping his chest. A tankard of milk, covered with a plate of bread and pâté, had been placed on the ground beside him. She was speaking quickly in French. Campbell, still dazed, could understand little of what she said. It was still dark outside.

She crouched nearby watching him while he greedily ate and drank. He tried to recall something associated with his dream, but it eluded him. She had placed the lamp on the ground between them and had pulled the back hem of her skirt up between her thighs to cover her crotch as she squatted there.

Her name was Geneviève Morel. She explained with difficulty that her father's sister had been killed the previous week during an Allied air attack and she begged Campbell not to think badly of him. He was a loyal or honourable Frenchman who hated the Germans. Campbell, speaking loudly and slowly, tried to explain that he wanted to rejoin his unit in Touffreville, if possible before sunrise. She laughed at his garbled pronunciation of the town.

With heart-rending accuracy, Campbell was able in 1946 to reconstruct her efforts to dissuade him from such a dangerous enterprise. She told him he would be safe in their barn until the following night, but he would not listen. She then insisted on accompanying him some of the way. It was beginning to get light when they set out.

She led him across open fields, but he hid behind the hedge at each gate while she checked that the lanes were clear of Germans. On the western extremity of her father's land, they took advantage of another stretch of woodland to stop and rest. Once again she begged him to return to the farm with her. Once again he refused. He told her to go home, but she said that she was in no danger and that she would accompany him to the edge of the wood. As they made their way among the trees in the early morning light, they heard the opening rumble of the naval bombardment to the west and north. Geneviève, alarmed at the noise, covered her mouth with one hand and pushed her hair away from her eyes with the other.

Reminded of his dream, Campbell realised with a stab of excitement that she resembled his Aunt Dorothy. He walked towards her. She said in heavily accented English that she would go back, and then, speaking slowly in French, she explained that the road that was just visible between the trees led to Touffreville. Finally, using gestures as well as words, she tried to explain that the road was bordered by hedges beyond the woods, although he only learned afterwards that this was what she was trying to convey.

McCluskie then kissed her. Her lips parted for his tongue. His hand slid down her back and cradled her left buttock for a moment before she pulled away.

'Je returnerai,' he said with an ill-disguised Scottish accent, and then slowly, 'I will return.'

She smiled, said, 'Au revoir,' shifted her weight from foot to foot, as if embarrassed, gave him a shy wave and walked away.

McCluskie made his way carefully through the undergrowth to the edge of the wood. Across a dirt track was a gate to a field bordered by a hedgerow that followed the gentle curve of the road. He was about to run across the track, when he saw a bicycle wheel appear around the bend in the road. He dived for cover as three German soldiers followed the bicycle wheel into view. Campbell would never forget them.

The soldier pushing the bicycle was in the centre. He looked as if he was in his early forties. He had a determined expression that was emphasised by the lines on his face. A rifle was slung over his right shoulder. Beside him, and closest to Campbell, was a younger soldier. The skin of his face was stretched tightly over the bones and was slightly discoloured in places as if he had suffered burns. He was holding a machine gun in his right hand and looking at his watch. He appeared anxious. The third man had a very bad scar running across his face and a goatee beard. His helmet was pushed back and he had shouldered his rifle. It was only when they were in full view that McCluskie noticed that there was a smooth-haired mongrel with them, which had a diamond-shaped splash on its chest.

The dog ran to the edge of the road and started to bark and snarl. The man with the bony face pointed his machine gun in McCluskie's direction. A wood pigeon suddenly flapped through the branches above him. The two other soldiers laughed and began to chant some doggerel to their companion, of which McCluskie could only distinguish the name 'Gretchen'. The younger soldier blushed red where his face wasn't scarred, but he remained looking anxiously about him.

McCluskie lay still until they were out of sight. He thought that five minutes must have elapsed when he heard the dog barking again. There was a burst of gunfire. He began to run towards the

71

sound without thinking. He tripped over a root, scraping his cheek on the trunk of an elm tree. He heard German voices shouting. He heard a woman screaming, not constantly, but in searing bursts, as if the pain was timed with her breathing. As he ran he realised that he had heard a similar sound before, but he couldn't place it. He was too conscious of the woods jolting around him; the weight of his equipment; the burning sensation in his throat.

He came to a clearing. At its farther edge a screen of bushes and ferns bordered the road. Geneviève was lying on her back near the edge of the clearing, surrounded by broken branches and scattered leaves. The bone-faced German was kneeling beside her, supporting her head and trying to give her water from his bottle. His gun was lying on the ground beside him.

The scar-faced soldier, who was standing near them, raised his rifle and fired when Campbell burst into the clearing, shouting. Campbell fired his Sten gun without aiming. Branches fell to the left of the scar-faced German. The bone-faced one dropped Geneviève's head and picked up his gun. The third soldier ran into the clearing. Campbell heard a bullet whistle by his ear. He stopped and fired another burst. The bone-faced German raised his gun, but four or five bullets struck his chest, flinging his contorted body backwards through the bushes. The scar-faced man fell back clutching his throat. The third dropped his rifle and ran towards the road. The dog followed him, yelping, with its head down and its tail between its legs.

Campbell shouted, 'Geneviève!' and rushed over to her. She was still screaming. Blood was soaking through her jacket in three places. He dropped his gun and searched frantically for his first aid kit and morphine needles. He rolled up her sleeve, squeezed her skin to raise a vein and jabbed her arm with each needle in turn. After a while, she stopped screaming and began to whimper softly. Shaking, he raised her and carefully removed her jacket. The bodice of her dress was drenched in blood. Her breathing was becoming laboured. He pulled off his helmet and attempted to give her mouth-to-mouth resuscitation, but she literally died in his arms.

As he gently lowered her head, he noticed the burnt cork smudges around her mouth and on her cheek, but he did not recognise the marks he had made when kissing her earlier.

McCluskie would make no record of what he did with Geneviève's body. Having discarded all but his book, his Sten gun, magazines, knife, rations, grenades and grief, he resumed his journey, crawling painfully along the hedgerows towards the sound of gunfire. At one point, a French farmer who was herding some cattle paused to watch his tortuous progress along the length of his field, before waving at him conspicuously and shouting, 'Vive la France!' As Campbell moved further west, he had to hide more and more frequently from German troops who were also heading towards the River Dives.

He was captured while hiding out in a copse of trees. A squad of German infantry, escorting some twenty captured parachutists, stumbled upon him when they were taking cover from British aircraft. Campbell, who had been dozing, gave in without a fight. He recalled that one of the German soldiers gave him a cigarette; a tall, slim man with eyes set close together and a pointed chin, he explained quietly in broken English that he was a Polish prisoner of war who had been pressed into service. He was about to say something else when the officer in charge shouted at him in German.

The prisoners were then pushed into line and marched along the road, with two German soldiers on either side. Two more took the rear, and the officer marched at the front with the remaining two. McCluskie learned from whispered snatches of conversation with his neighbour, Alan Bullock (well built, pale blue eyes, fair lashes and a recently broken nose) that there were in addition to the Pole two Ukrainians and one melancholic Cossack among their captors, who were merely waiting for an opportunity to give themselves up. After about an hour, they crossed a river by an old stone bridge and then passed through a tiny village. There was a row of grey, shuttered houses and a small tabac with a tattered Michelin advertisement on its gable end. Campbell noticed the wrinkled face of an old woman emerging from the shadows and peering at them through a window of the tabac. Then they found themselves once more walking along a sunken lane bordered by hedgerows. It was late afternoon. By the angle of the sun, Campbell estimated they were heading southwest, but he didn't know where they were going.

As they approached yet another stretch of woodland, he saw a German staff car manoeuvring into the shelter of the trees. An officer was standing up on the passenger side beside the driver, gripping the window frame to keep his balance. When he caught sight of the column of prisoners, he motioned to the driver to stop and then he dismounted and marched up to the officer in charge of the escort. Through a gate on the right, McCluskie could see a low line of hills with the sun glaring above them. The prisoners stood around in small groups, whispering. Campbell remembered a frenzied cloud of midges caught in the orange light at the edge of the wood; a German tank parked in the dappled shade with two soldiers on the turret sharing a water bottle; another two tanks parked beyond it; the blackened corpse of a frog squashed flat on to the road. He licked his parched lips. The Polish soldier handed him another cigarette and smiled nervously. An argument was taking place between the two German officers. A British officer approached them, waving a bloodstained white handkerchief, and addressed them in German with a clipped English accent.

McCluskie understood nothing of the exchange, but the Polish soldier informed him that the officer from the Panzer regiment was ordering their officer to shoot the prisoners. Their officer was insisting that he had orders to march them to Vimont for transportation to Caen. McCluskie once again felt a sense of detachment, as if the argument was of no concern to him. He drew on the cigarette and turned towards Alan Bullock. Bullock shrugged his shoulders and said quite clearly, 'I think we're fucked, Jock.'

There was a distant sound of aircraft. McCluskie looked up, shielding his eyes with his right hand. He saw five planes approaching from the south. The leader dipped its wing to the right and began to descend. The German officers stopped speaking. Everyone looked up at the sky. The Panzer officer took out his Lugar, shot the British officer in the head and then ran back to the staff car, shouting. The back wheel on the near side began to spin in the ditch as it tried to gain a purchase on the grassy bank. McCluskie flicked his cigarette away and turned. The Polish soldier's face suddenly exploded, scattering blood, bone and tissue, and then Campbell heard a screaming sound. He retained a surprisingly vivid image of himself 'crouching and running while bullets drilled into the road surface on either side. I kept running. I heard machine gun fire; explosions; shouts; screams.' The memoir ends here.

No one knows how Campbell managed to get back to British lines in the early hours of 7 June. At first light, he was seen by a group of parachutists from his battalion, running across a field towards them and yelling that he was Scottish. He was hit in the back by a German sniper on the very brink of safety. Luckily, the bullet passed under his right shoulder blade, through his right lung and between his ribs. He fell beside a slit trench containing two of his comrades, one of whom recognised him. Two medics risked the sniper fire to drag him behind the cover of a hedge and administer morphine.

So ended Campbell's war; by the evening of 7 June, his wounds were being treated in a hospital ship off the coast of Normandy. He subsequently remained in hospital in England for six weeks, owing to complications with his lung. In late August, he returned home to recuperate. Following his recovery, he rejoined his battalion in Germany for two months after the European War ended, before being demobilised.

Chapter Three

I wonder, does our planet occupy the same stretch of space each time a particular date comes around? How many miles does it travel during the course of twenty-four hours? No doubt, these are questions that an astronomer could answer with comparative ease. More difficult to explain are the movements of the tiny individuals on the planet surface, where each day closes in a riot of sun-dusted clouds and the stately progression of shadows around a lamp post lends order to a muddled life.

Let us suppose that on 16 June 1954 three men have a fatal scuffle in a cobbled side street, while in the city's maternity hospital a woman approaches the climax of an agonising childbirth. Now, if I take the whole wobbling and spinning globe back through eight orbits, we find the same woman smiling with happiness and pulling her reluctant dog towards the entrance of her close, while across town Campbell McCluskie appends the date – 16 June 1946 – to the final copy of his war memoir.

It was his habit to sign and date every piece of work on its completion, and so the date is still there, somewhat faded, at the foot of the page. I imagine him writing it, utterly oblivious of its future significance, in the bed-sitting room in Belmont Crescent which he was renting from an elderly widow. He would have been sitting at his desk by the window. The last of the sunlight would have been illuminating the chimneys of the houses opposite. He would have laid aside his pen and pressed a sheet of blotting paper to the foot of the page. Then he would have gathered together the sheaf of papers and placed it in the pale yellow folder, where it was to remain unread until the folder was sent to his sister Dorothy shortly after his murder.

Partly because Campbell had come so close to dying in the war, his father had decided to give him a monthly allowance of fifty pounds until he completed his university degree. Consequently, the playwright was able to devote the better part of that summer to writing his first play, *Shona of Lismore*. He would later refer to this time as 'the sunny period of my life'.

His journal bears witness to his intellectual ferment during those months. It is filled with descriptions of people and places, snatches of overheard conversations, and ideas for plays and stories. There is 'an elderly woman with a hooked nose, whose back is bent over so far that she can only see the ground immediately in front of her'. After which, Campbell (rather callously) wrote, 'How does she get dressed? Idea for a one act play.' And further on: 'In the semi-circular garden beneath my window, a plump boy chases his slimmer and more agile friend, whose frequent shouts of "Come on, Fatso!" provide the scene with a shrill commentary.'

However, Campbell's thoughts kept returning to his experiences in Normandy. The first draft of *Shona of Lismore*, which he completed towards the end of August, reveals quite clearly that its inspiration lay in the death of the French girl Geneviève Morel. Angus, the captain of a small puffer, shelters from a storm on the Isle of Lismore. There he undergoes a number of strange adventures that bring him at length to the Laird's house. He meets and falls in love with the Laird's daughter, Shona, who accidently drowns before they can consummate their love, and he continues on his journey to Glasgow.

By the time Campbell finished revising the play, shortly after starting university, he had removed most of the autobiographical elements, thereby setting the pattern for much of his later work. His plays, with their formal games and hidden devices, were to be fashioned like pearls around the detritus of his life.

Aside from the interruptions caused by visits to or from his family, Campbell adopted a strict daily routine. His landlady, Mrs Stuart, would bring him his breakfast on a tray every morning, weekends included, at seven o'clock. She would then fold her arms over her prominent bosom and discuss the weather, or fill him in on the neighbourhood gossip, while he, dipping his toast in his yolk or eating a mouthful of porridge, would take in the details of her face and body and try to memorise this or that turn of phrase. She had an elaborate scar on her elbow, legacy of a childhood fall. She had the habit of finishing his sentences. She had beautiful green eyes.

After breakfast, he would wash and dress with a self-conscious regard for appearance which never left him. Then he would write straight through until lunchtime. After spending a couple of hours in a nearby pub or café, he would return to his room and work until six o'clock, when he would take his evening meal with Mrs Stuart and the other lodger, 'a middle aged clerk from the labour exchange with a button nose, thick glasses and a perpetual expression of surprise'. Afterwards, he would go out to the pub.

Things continued in this manner until the last Sunday in August. A detailed record that Campbell made of the events of that day reveals the chance meeting that initiated a new phase in his life.

I left to catch a tram on the Great Western Road at a little after 11 o'clock in the morning. The air smelled autumnal for the first time this year. It was sunny, but the sky last night had been clear and it was still quite cool when I reached the tram stop.

While I was waiting, the girl from Gucci's café happened by. I greeted her and she stopped to speak to me. Her name is Rowena. She works in the box office of the Pavilion Theatre. She asked me the title of the book I had with me. I held it up for her to look at. She smiled, but said nothing.

'He's a Czech writer,' I volunteered and then changed the subject by asking if she had been to church. That made her laugh.

'Of course not,' she said. 'I'm an atheist.'

The skin under her eyes looked slightly bruised. Her nose was slim but it had a rounded end. Her hair was quite thick, light brown in colour and done up in a pony tail. She was wearing a sleeveless white blouse and a flared skirt which emphasised her slim waist. Her jacket was draped over her right arm, which she held, rather defensively, in front of her. As she raised her hand to push back a stray hair, I caught sight of the light brown tuft in her armpit, which I found very arousing. She looked away.

'There's a tram coming,' she said. 'That always makes me think of the Arabian Nights,' she added, pointing at the corner turret of a tenement block further down the road.

'Will you be in Gucci's this Tuesday lunchtime,' I asked, casual as you like. She smiled. 'About half past twelve,' I added.

'I might be,' she said as I jumped on to the platform of the tram. She was still standing, looking at me from the pavement with her hands clasped under her jacket, when the tram shuddered into motion.

The conductor swaggered along the aisle towards me, and leaned against the back of the seat diagonally opposite with his legs apart. When he took my fare, I noticed that one of his front teeth was chipped. There was something deeply satisfying about the sound the ticket machine made as he turned the handle to feed out my ticket.

The tenements moving past on the left made me think of pompous dowagers drawing in their shadowy skirts at the tram's approach. On the right, the soot stained buildings gave way to a park, and then to a classical terrace which had been built above the level of the road behind wooded gardens. The sight of the dappled shade under the trees made me feel an almost unbearable sense of loss.

Sharing my compartment on the train to Clydebank were a plump fellow in a dark suit and a woman with her son. The boy looked rather uncomfortable in his school uniform. There was a diamond shaped badge on his blazer pocket, in the centre of which was embroidered a bear's head with a grey chain hanging between its neck and its muzzled snout. The boy had large, brown eyes which he averted when he realised I was watching him. It was only then that I noticed his white gloves.

'On account of his eczema,' his mother said, leaning forward and twisting her mouth on one side. 'They keep him from scratching,' she added and then busied herself in her handbag. The boy squirmed in his seat, blushed and gazed out the window, as if looking for some means of escape.

The plump man raised one pale hand and squeezed a sliver of dirt from his thumbnail. An indefinable, queasy sensation settled on my stomach and remained with me for the rest of the day.

I arrived at my parents' house at quarter to one. Dorothy opened the door while I was still only halfway up the drive, and then watched me from the entrance with a finger on her chin, her dark hair slipping out of her Kirby grips and her socks crumpled about her ankles. I ran the last few yards and, with a deep giant's laugh, I whisked her off her feet. Then I clasped her to my chest with one arm and tickled her until she struggled free. As she ran through the hallway, she collided with Joan, who was just emerging from the sitting room with a precariously balanced pile of cups and saucers. The top cup rocked for a moment, fell, bounced off the floor and shattered on the corner of the grandfather clock. Joan, struggling to retain her hold on the remaining cups, shouted, 'You stupid child.'

'My fault entirely,' I said and bent to retrieve the broken pieces. Dorothy ran, sobbing, up the stairs. I looked round the door jamb and saw my other sisters in the sitting room.

Moira, sitting cross-legged on the chair, said, 'I might have known you were behind it.' While Anne looked shyly back at me, as if she feared that she was partly to blame.

The smell of roasting lamb permeated the house. Joan, one heel angrily tapping on the varnished margin of the floor, strode towards the kitchen. My mother appeared in the kitchen doorway and I approached her with the broken china in my cupped hands.

'Still the same old Campbell,' she said with a rueful smile. Then she lightly brushed my cheek with her lips and suffered me to follow her into the kitchen.

At the dining table, red eyed Dorothy sits beside me. Moira, opposite, restricts herself to making the odd sarcastic jibe. Joan mimics Moira; both now aloof young ladies, resisting my charms. Anne, very quiet, allows her thick, red hair to cover her face. Mother says little and sits, unsmiling, in the chair nearest the door. Father is at the head of the table. He seems subdued. No doubt a mistress has finished with him. As he places his fork and knife on his empty plate, he says, 'Have you started your course reading yet, Campbell?'

'I'm writing a play,' I reply.

He rubs his eyes, looks out the window and says, 'I don't think I'll bother with dessert, Katie.' Everyone passes their plate along to mother. Father excuses himself, but turns to me from the doorway and adds, 'Mind what happened to your Aunt Dorothy.' Then he pulls the door firmly to behind him.

Campbell did meet up with Rowena at Gucci's on the following Tuesday. After lunch, they relaxed over a leisurely coffee. The owner stood behind the counter, staring at Rowena and squeezing his lower lip. Sunlight gleamed on the espresso machine. As Campbell swept away a bluebottle that was exploring some sugar grains near the table edge, his fingers brushed her arm. She blushed and looked away. He noticed the hollow at the base of her throat; her shadowy cleavage; a small area of stomach flesh where her blouse arched between two buttons. Aching to possess her, he asked if she could get next Saturday off so they could go to the Locarno. There was an excited catch in her throat when she said that she could.

Campbell particularly enjoyed dancing the jitterbug, which, to judge from his description of that Saturday evening, he did with some proficiency. And so we can see them: Campbell in his zoot suit, swinging Rowena to either side of him, his hands on her waist; she in a patterned dress (which she had made for herself out of curtain material) and white, lace-fringed gloves, wrapping her legs around him for a moment before swinging away again. We see the band on the podium; the saxophone soloist half closing his eyes; the trumpeters raising their horns and inflating their cheeks; the conductor – insouciant, slim and balding; the tables and chairs round the edge of the hall; the faces peering over the ornate balcony; the couples crowding the dance floor. We take in the mixed smells of sweat and cheap perfume. All faded away in Campbell's mind to the momentary sensation of Rowena's warm crotch pressing against him.

In his journal, after the description of the dance, she is described in terms of 'her glossy lips; her white teeth; the sweep of her eyelashes; her dilated pupils'. Then there is 'the pale curve of her breast, with its tracery of blue veins and its small mole and its nipple hardening under my thumb, while I press my tongue between her lips and feel in my mouth her excited intake of breath'. She is reduced after a period of awkward fumbling in a darkened close 'to an incomparable scent on the middle finger of my right hand'. And finally: 'In a park at dusk, she leaves a trace of blood on the lining of my coat when I make my first, painful, entry; my hands on either side of her head bearing the weight of my raised torso, a sound akin to a deep sob breaking from my throat and a black something flitting in front of a distant street lamp.' There are no subsequent references to her.

McCluskie started university in early October. He mentions 'the lines of students queuing up for matriculation, while sunlight picks out columns of floating dust and cracked portraits grimace from the wall and I gaze in futile rage at the hateful neck in front'. Not surprisingly, he avoided the company of his fellow first-year students, who by and large struck him as immature. He also avoided the small clique of ex-servicemen among their number because, as he wrote in a letter home, 'I cannae abide their spurious air of superiority.' Consequently, for the first couple of weeks, he kept himself to himself in university, while outside he put the final polish on *Shona of Lismore*.

The discipline of organised study did not appeal to Campbell. On crisp autumn mornings he preferred to 'stroll round the neo-Gothic quadrangles of the university building with three or four unsampled books under my arm, and vague notions of literary fame floating through my head, while Professor Stevens delivered his lectures on Anglo-Saxon literature with tiresome enthusiasm in a freezing lecture hall'.

He considered that university had nothing to offer him, until he saw Megan Stuart walking along Kelvin Way. Accompanying her were a skinny fellow with a severe limp and a plainer and more ample female. Megan was tall with dark hair. The cold air brought colour to her otherwise pale face. Her round cheeks contrasted pleasingly with her jaw, which was strong without being pointed. There was a small, sickle-shaped scar above her upper lip. When they drew level with Campbell, she raised one eyebrow and smiled in his direction. He noticed that she was carrying a book, but he was unable to read its title. The skinny fellow was reciting Keats to her in a declamatory style that did not go with his thin voice. He blushed when he caught Campbell's eye, but he continued with his recitation. Campbell felt sorry for their companion. The effort of keeping up with them was showing on her face and she was inexpertly trying to place some hair back into a clip as she walked. Surprisingly enough, he found her more attractive close to.

You can imagine my surprise and delight when, at the outset of the 1989 autumn term, I discovered that Fiona Gardiner was in my first-year seminar group. It occurred to me that for once Fate had been kind. I can still picture the first seminar vividly. My room at the university is situated in the attic of the departmental building. The walls are lined with bookshelves. There is a table of dark wood, round which are placed a number of disparate chairs. My students were already chattering quietly among themselves when I entered with my briefcase under my arm.

I first of all noticed Fiona's neighbour, Stephen Pendle. He would prove to be a precociously brilliant student whose work was marred by arrogance and laziness. He alone did not turn to look at me when I entered, because his gaze was fixed on Fiona, who was caught in the late afternoon sunlight. Her hair was blond then, cut in a bob. Her mouth was slightly open. The tiny window reflected in each of her eyes made me think of a Flemish Madonna. It did not strike me as an inappropriate comparison, because I believed that Fate had shown its hand; that Fiona would in some way redeem my life.

For all the precision of my memory, I find it hard to recapture the optimism I felt then. The street outside looks almost like a stage set. Two young boys are squatting down near a lamp post, playing some game with a bent twig. If I lean forward, I can see the point further along the road where the shadow of the lamp post escapes that of the tenement opposite. The fact that I can predict where these shadows will fall reassures me. With Fiona, I am all at sea.

There is no evidence that Campbell devoted any further thought to Megan Stuart (whose name he did not yet know), until a couple of weeks later in the offices of the student newspaper, when he met Archiebald Williams, the future head of the English Department at the university. Archiebald was indulging in some tiresome sniping at the newspaper editor, and it took several minutes before Campbell recognised him as the man who had been reciting poetry to the beautiful girl on Kelvin Way; whereupon, he invited Archie out for a drink.

Darkness was falling. I imagine Williams, hands in pockets, muffled up in his scarf, accompanying Campbell down the hill towards Byres Road. I picture the evenly spaced street lamps, each with its blurred aura. I picture the lights from the shop windows reflecting off the wet pavements. I picture the playwright waxing eloquent, making voluble arm gestures as he walks. Later, we find a drunken Archie, rather red in the face, sitting across from McCluskie. He leans towards the playwright, drawing in his chin and burping as he does so, and in a confidential tone informs him about his literary group, 'The Pleasure Dome'.

'After Coleridge?' asks the sober Campbell, smiling. 'And who else is in this group?'

Chapter Four

Archiebald Williams had been the driving force behind the formation of the literary group, pretentiously styled 'The Pleasure Dome' because it had been founded in the distinctive glass and iron structure that dominates the Botanical Gardens. The other members were: Donald Fraser, who had been spared the war when a reaping machine on his father's farm had deprived him of an arm; Megan Stuart, with whom Archiebald was hopelessly in love; and Anne Comrie, whom Archie would later marry.

When I spoke to her in 1990, Megan could still recall the first time McCluskie had attended the group. He had walked straight up to Donald and begun to shake vigorously with both hands the space where Donald's right hand should have been, while everyone else looked on in open-mouthed embarrassment. After a moment, Donald joined in the fiction and, laughing, grasped Campbell's shoulder with his remaining hand.

Campbell found the meeting to be an 'insufferable affair', which he would happily have avoided if it hadn't been for his overriding desire for Megan. The venue was a stuffy room in the English Department furnished with an oil-filled radiator, a table, chairs and foxed engravings of William Shakespeare and Ben Jonson. On the wall to the left of these engravings, a rectangle of unfaded paint revealed that a third picture had recently been removed.

Before they got started, Donald and Anne took some milk and sugar to a small room down the corridor, where there were facilities for making tea. Archiebald sat at the head of the table and, taking a copy of Pope's *Poetical Works* out of his briefcase, he told Campbell that he was going to read Epistle I of the poet's 'Essay on Man'. The playwright merely nodded and looked over at Megan, trying to gauge what brought her to these meetings and what was the nature of her friendship with Archiebald. He could not bring himself to regard Williams as a serious rival, with his limp, his hopelessly affected voice and his irritating pedantry.

While Archiebald read the poem, Campbell found his mind wandering. He tried to picture what Megan looked like naked. He was careful not to stare at her, building up her image instead through a series of sly glances.

Campbell dominated the discussion that followed. Portraying himself as the kind of rebel angel denounced by Pope, he claimed that the world should not be accepted for what it is, but should be prised open, like a nervous virgin, until all its secrets were laid bare; that only by rebelling against our condition could anything be achieved. As he continued, his argument proved too slippery for the others to grapple with. It kept twisting into contradictions, jokes, irony; the whole bravura performance being nothing more than a smokescreen to hide his lust for Megan.

During the next fortnight, Campbell was unable to make any progress with her. He became convinced that she would deliberately lead him on, only to cool suddenly towards him. Then she would play up to Archiebald. It was Campbell's opinion that 'polio had turned Williams into a devoted dog that would lap up any crumbs of affection which Megan deigned to throw at him'.

Given its inner tensions, it is surprising that the group held together for as long as it did. After the last meeting in November, Campbell suggested they go to a local hotel for a drink. That occasion was brought vividly to life for me by Megan. Anne, sitting at the end of the table between Campbell and Donald, nursed her drink, barely paying attention to Donald's soft monologue. By her own account, Megan sat beside Campbell, taunting him by frequently crossing and uncrossing her legs. Meanwhile, driven by a desperate need to impress her, Archiebald's conversation achieved a certain transient beauty, to which Campbell responded by sinking into ominous silence until he suddenly turned to Anne and said, 'For Christ's sake, will you stop kicking my foot.' Anne burst into tears. Donald lost his temper. And it took all Campbell's wit and charm to restore the situation.

When they next met, Campbell handed Anne two pairs of black-market nylons. Eyes sparkling with emotion, she moved her fingertips slowly over the packages. Before she could say anything, Campbell took out another two pairs and walked over to Megan, who was standing by the radiator, shaking snow from her coat and stamping her feet.

In early December, Donald Fraser threw a small party at his flat. Campbell went to it, secretly hoping that afterwards he might persuade Megan to come back to Belmont Crescent with him. In the event, she didn't turn up, sending a message through Archie that she was going home to her parents' to nurse a bad cold. Williams left early after getting into an argument about one of his poems with McCluskie. And so, by nine o'clock, only Campbell, Donald and Anne were left. Unusually, Donald had been in a bad mood all evening, probably because he had realised that Anne was still infatuated with Campbell. They all had too much to drink, but Donald drank more than the other two. At around midnight, he made a half-hearted lunge at McCluskie and passed out.

After dragging him through to his bed, Anne and Campbell returned to the sitting room, where they talked and drank some more. Then Campbell found himself stretched out on the floor, kissing her and sliding his hand up her stockinged leg until he felt a cool band of flesh. Murmuring softly, she lay back and turned her face away from him. With a surge of exultation, he realised the power he had over her. He hesitated for a moment and then began to remove her underwear. A window sash rattled. Campbell thought of the curious pad of skin on Donald's stump as he unrolled a contraceptive over his penis.

When the business was over, he wanted nothing more than to leave her, to forget her pain and her inexplicable happiness, but she pressed her face into his chest and hugged him so insistently that he could only lie on his back with his hand poised rather embarrassingly above her tousled hair, as if he wasn't quite sure what to do.

Speaking of parties, it was my habit, soon after the start of each academic year, to throw a small party for my first-year seminar group. Usually, the most interesting students found some excuse to stay away, leaving me with a residue of shy individuals who either had no other plans or feared that not to come might prejudice me against them. However, all the students from Fiona Gardiner's group came to the party I threw that year. Fiona arrived a bit late, with Stephen Pendle and two other students whose names now escape me.

I fancied that the red light bulb I had put in set off my room to its best advantage. Music had been carefully selected that might appeal to young people. An arrangement of raw vegetables, dips and nibbles added a sophisticated touch. I was liberal with alcohol.

To be sure, things were a trifle cramped. Some of the students were nervous. I clearly recall one unfortunate girl with a complex about her height, standing by the wardrobe, pushing her glasses up her nose, spilling a blob of mayonnaise into her cupped hand and looking around in confusion and embarrassment.

As the host, I had to wander about refilling glasses and handing out food, but all the while I was painfully aware of Fiona's presence. She sat on my bed talking to Stephen Pendle for a while. Then she looked at my books. She was wearing a long skirt of a deep, shimmering purple (which looked darker in the red light) and a pair of Doc Martin's. Several times, I noticed her pushing her hair behind her ear. Most of the young men gravitated towards her at one time or another, except for Stephen (who remained sitting on the bed, smirking) and myself.

I was fairly certain that he had only come along because of Fiona, but he was a master of ironical detachment. My situation was altogether different. It was fear that made me avoid Fiona whenever possible.

Towards the end of the party, she came up to me and asked why I had been neglecting her all evening. The remaining guests were by that stage gathered on the bed around Stephen, holding an animated discussion about the future of literature. I was clearing away the remains of the food. Fiona stood beside me stacking the empty dishes. Words cannot convey the beautiful, complex movements of her arms and hands. Dry-mouthed, I let my gaze travel over the ribbed top she was wearing under her cardigan, along the twisting tendons of her neck, to her wonderfully candid eyes. She asked if she might help me with my research for Campbell's biography; that was, if I didn't already have a more qualified assistant.

I was so choked with emotion that I could not answer her immediately. A hurt expression crossed her face, which disappeared when I impulsively grabbed her hand and told her that I would be grateful for any help she could offer. A cauliflower floret rolled on to the table cover from the plate I was absent-mindedly holding. I must have been squeezing her hand too hard because I felt it squirming in my grasp.

Later, I watched her through my window, talking and laughing with Stephen on the street below. I felt happier than I have felt before or since. The sky was spangled with stars. Above the rooftops opposite, I could see the silhouetted cranes of the shipyards and the line of hills in the background. Everything struck me as being harmonious and beautiful. Fate had cast aside its cloak and scythe, turning out after all to be a ravishing handmaiden with dimpled cheeks and blond, bobbed hair.

Now wiser, I sit at my desk looking out over the same view, on an overcast day in spring, trying to evoke Campbell McCluskie reading *Shona of Lismore* at the final meeting of Archiebald Williams's literary group. The others were arranged in a loose semicircle around him. Donald, sitting on the only chair with arms, was leaning on his callused elbow and looking glumly at the window. Williams had placed himself between the two women. I imagine him sneaking a cursory glance at Megan's be-nyloned calves as he settled himself in his chair.

Campbell began to read, sweeping his audience democratically with his dark eyes and gesticulating. Anne directed an imploring look at him whenever he chanced to catch her eye, but he did not respond to it. He did not ignore her exactly; he merely refused to acknowledge the meaning of her look. As he wound up the reading, she rushed out of the room, stifling a sob. Donald ran out after her. Archie sat staring at the open door until McCluskie said, 'Why don't you go and see what all the fuss is about, Archie? You're good at that kind of thing.'

Left alone with Campbell, Megan allowed him to kiss her for the first time. He was beginning to unbutton her blouse when she caught sight of Archie watching them from the doorway. She believed that it was seeing them there together that prompted Archie to transfer his affections to Anne. Whatever the truth of that assertion, I see in these tangled relations the cause of both Professor Williams's hatred of the playwright and his antipathy towards myself.

I was sitting with Megan in her cottage in Blanefield when she told me of these things. Tilting her head and smiling, she continued, 'Campbell was a beautiful man and I wanted to sleep with him as soon as I saw him. But of course I didn't let him lay a finger on me, until he read *Shona of Lismore* at that last meeting. It was a mediocre play, but it gave him away, you see. I realised he had based the heroine on me. I was flattered, naturally, but I also felt that I had him in my power.'

'You seem shocked,' she added after a pause, pressing my knee and allowing her fingernails to linger for a second on the trouser material as she removed her hand. A husky laugh. 'You know, he had exactly the same expression when we slept together for the first time. That would have been at Christmas 1946; in this house, in fact. He was standing in his pants and socks, searching through his pockets for his contraceptives. I lay on bed watching him become more and more desperate, until I relented and told him I was wearing my Dutch cap. He made a face just like you did then, and shouted,

"Your what?" I told him to keep quiet or he'd wake my parents. He didn't like the idea at all; such an egotist. I think he was expecting me to be as innocent as that fool Anne Comrie had been.'

Megan was mistaken in thinking she was the inspiration behind *Shona of Lismore*, which Campbell had completed before he met her. It opens in a Glasgow bed-sitting room. A young man, described in the dramatis personae as 'The Author', sits stage left, at a desk piled with papers. A beautiful woman, Vanessa, enters. He puts down his pen and pushes back his chair. She runs her fingers along his shoulder and sits down on his lap. Then she picks up some pages and begins to read.

> *Music is heard from off-stage: a haunting Celtic lament. The light over the desk dims. A deep red light illuminates the right side of the stage, revealing a painted backdrop of distant hills with a natural harbour in the foreground. A boat is anchored in the harbour. A man stands on the stage with his back to the audience, looking out over the water.* VANESSA*'s voice is heard recounting the story of Angus: the sudden deaths of his close family; his decision to sail to Glasgow to start a new life; the storm which brought him to Lismore. She stops reading.*
>
> VANESSA: So where's the romantic interest?
> *The red light fades. The desk reappears.*
> THE AUTHOR: What do you mean, 'romantic interest'?
> *He puts his arm around her waist.*

And so the play continues; 'the author' outlines his plot to Vanessa. He wants to send Angus to Glasgow. Great things await him there. He alludes to 'violent events', 'tortuous machinations'. The storm was not part of the original plan. It had arisen during the writing and now he doesn't quite know how to proceed. Vanessa suggests a woman.

> VANESSA: Let her be called Shona. Let her be wealthy; a dead laird's daughter perhaps. She could repair Angus's vessel.
> *They kiss. The light on the desk fades. Once again, we see the distant hills, the water, the boat and the man. He turns to face the audience. He is well built and handsome. A young woman walks on to the stage. She is beautiful with long, black hair.*
> ANGUS: My boat's taken a bit of a pounding.
> *They stand for a moment looking awkward. He wipes his hand on his trouser leg and reaches out to shake her hand.*

ANGUS: I'm Angus.
SHONA: I'm Shona.

From there, events lead inexorably to the play's tragic conclusion. Angus decides to resume his journey. Shona, distraught and mentally unbalanced, commits suicide.

All things considered, *Shona of Lismore* is the least satisfying of Campbell's plays. I believe that he created 'the author' and his muse, Vanessa, to attain an ironical detachment from the narrative. However, the melodramatic ending does not fit with the rest of the play and so the whole is somewhat less than the sum of its parts. Nevertheless, during the sixties and seventies, it was the play that was revived more frequently than any of the others. Possibly, this owed to the fact that people saw it as a precursor of Beckett's metaphysical explorations.

Certainly, the 1969 production, adapted by Christopher Marriat, owed something to Beckett. The parts of 'the author' and Vanessa were taken by two cowled figures, Wight and Homm, who stumbled about on the margins of the set, mumbling a garbled commentary on the action.

Later still, Simon Wilde adapted *Shona of Lismore* for the stage in San Francisco. He replaced Vanessa with a young man named Martin Ganymead and turned the play into a witty comedy on heterosexual mores.

Despite its failings, it has some noteworthy aspects. In Campbell's willingness to experiment we can see prefigured some of the radical techniques he was to bring to perfection in his later works. More significantly, it would appear that the plot of Campbell's next play is adumbrated in the 'violent events' and 'tortuous events' that await Angus in Glasgow.

An ominous passage in Campbell's notebook also provides hints of what was to come:

A stretch of wasteland scattered with debris: a rusting car propped up on bricks, with three upended bricks standing near one wheel in a curious arrangement that recalls the Needles on the Isle of Wight; the carriage of a child's toy pram; some scraps of clothing. There are tenements on three sides; a quiet side street on the fourth. A van is parked on the grass with its back doors open wide. Two men pass me out various items: eggs; bacon; nylons. One is small with grey stubble and grey wisps of hair; the other is tall and much younger – black hair, Brylcreemed. I am about to pay for my purchases when a car screeches to a halt behind me.

'Jesus, it's Nick,' says the tall man. Sounds of doors slamming; segs clicking on tarmac; I am pushed aside roughly. A broad-shouldered man in a black pinstriped suit and a white banded hat, pulled low, he grabs the small man.

'Here, take the money,' says the small man, pulling out a wad of notes and stuffing them into the newcomer's hand.

'Too late, Jimmy,' he replies, pocketing the money. Flash of metal. A flap of skin slips down the small man's cheek, revealing a raw, red muscle. His hand moves to his face. The newcomer turns to me. I can only see his jaw moving below the brim of his hat. A brown paper bag, containing eggs, dangles uselessly in front of my chest.

'You huvnae seen anythin',' he says, punching the bag.

PART THREE

Chapter One

Campbell's stay in Belmont Crescent came to an abrupt end when his landlady discovered him in bed with Megan. The next day, his father came out to collect him and his belongings. His landlady stood in the hallway in her slippers, keeping a close eye on what he was taking and making comments about him to his father, who seemed highly entertained by the whole business.

Although she had her suspicions, Katherine was not told why Campbell had been evicted. Consequently, he felt that he had been drawn unwillingly into collusion with his father. When they took Campbell's things up to the attic room where his Aunt Dorothy had died, John clasped Campbell's shoulder and said, 'You're a chip off the old block.'

During the five weeks Campbell stayed there, Megan only came to see him once. They were ostensibly looking after Anne and Dorothy while his parents were out at a dinner dance. Before Megan arrived, he had extracted a promise from both sisters that they would go to their beds early. However, Megan spent most of the evening talking to them, while he sat a little apart, nursing his wrath with glass after glass of whisky. When they were finally alone, he was in a state of frustration bordering on madness. He joined Megan on the couch and, without preamble, thrust his hand clumsily up between her legs. A chipped nail snagged on her stocking.

'Christ, Campbell, you've laddered it!' she said, pushing his hand away. Just then, a pair of headlights arced round the room as his father manoeuvred the car into the driveway.

In the small hours, Campbell, creeping slowly over creaking boards, made his way to the bedroom where Megan was sleeping; a journey he would make again and again in his dreams that night, with nightmare accretions at each attempt and a numbing sense of irrevocable loss. The door was locked and there was no response to his quiet knock.

Unexpectedly, Megan phoned him several days later to tell him

94

about a flat that an artist friend, Daniel Hargreaves, was trying to rent out. She said that if he was interested he could meet Daniel to discuss it at a party the following weekend. To Campbell's request that she go out with him before then, she replied that it wouldn't be a good idea. A tinkling female laugh filled the silence that followed.

Then Megan added, 'I'll see you on Saturday then.' After giving him the address and time, she hung up halfway through his disgruntled 'Cheerio'.

He returned to the attic room and his interrupted reading of Dorothy's journal. A gale was blowing in gusts outside, shaking the windows and ruffling the velvet curtains. As his reading progressed, he gradually forgot his anger at Megan. For Jocky Widjin began to stride purposefully through his thoughts, fists bloodied by a prostitute's split lip and broken nose, trailing after him Campbell's adolescent fear of a deadly conspiracy; the horrific night-time screams of the playwright's dying sister, Mary; his last view of his Aunt Dorothy lying in her sick bed – the slackness of her perspiring face, her irises all but disappearing beneath the upper eyelids – as Nurse Brady grabbed his collar and pushed him out the room with her implacably moving thigh.

That night, Campbell decided to exorcise his fears by writing a new play. He would turn Jocky Widjin into a Glasgow gangster – a sadistic thug obsessed by his appearance. A beautiful woman with an unnatural taste for danger would be ensnared by his good looks and reputation. The play would chart their relationship's inevitable slide into violence and horror. However, the woman's intelligence and inner strength would prevail. She would leave the thug writhing like a clown in his own vicious circles.

So enthusiastic was Campbell about the project that it was only with reluctance that he left his desk to go to the party on Saturday night. Everything there seemed off-key: the large villa with its classically pillared porch; the ostentatious décor; the smooching couples; the jazz records; that thin-lipped redhead in the fur-collared dress, slitting her eyes at him and exhaling cigarette smoke from the corner of her mouth.

He discovered Megan with a group of young men in a snug sitting room adjoining the kitchen. 'They were listening to a corpulent older man (in a Panama hat, baggy, linen suit and silk cravat) recounting an essentially dull, and probably fictitious, anecdote about a meeting with Matisse in the South of France.' Megan was wearing a clinging red dress that left most of her back exposed. Campbell responded coolly to her smile, but nevertheless joined her on the couch. He had half a mind to tell her that he wanted nothing more to do with her or her bloody friends, but then the corpulent man turned to him and said, 'You must be Campbell McCluskie. Let me introduce myself: Daniel Hargreaves. Megan has told me so much about you.' Campbell took the proffered hand. 'These young men are my acolytes,' Hargreaves added. 'They flatter me with both their admiration and their rebellious animosity.'

He then drew Campbell aside, poured him a stiff drink and proceeded to describe in detail the property he wanted to rent out, which was situated above his own flat in Cranby Terrace. Campbell looked at the golden eagle engraved on his glass. He would tell the artist to stuff his flat, he decided, peering through the doorway at the copper pots hanging on the kitchen wall. Barely concealing his exasperation, he turned and saw Megan leaving the room with one of the young men. The movements of her shoulder blades brought vividly to mind a memory of her kneeling on all fours on his bed, which made the seclusion of Hargreaves's flat appear suddenly desirable.

He asked the artist what the rent would be and when he could move in. Hargreaves stroked his jowls, sipped some whisky, rolled his eyes upwards and moved his lips as if inwardly calculating. The playwright, eager to go in search of Megan, gazed in mute frustration at a painting hanging by the door: a gloomy cottage interior in which a distressed peasant girl sat praying by a tiny casement, light catching on her creamy shoulders.

'Sentimental tosh,' said Hargreaves, adding after a pause, 'I would want twelve pound per calendar month and you can move in whenever you like.'

Throughout his subsequent search for Megan, Campbell experienced a curious sense of déjà vu. The first door he came to opened into a narrow cloakroom with a stained glass window at its far end. Some fishing rods (dismantled and wrapped in their canvas covers) were leaning in a corner. On the right-hand wall was a row of hooks from which jackets and coats were hanging. Partially hidden by a light-coloured raincoat on the end hook, a young woman stood with her face buried in her hands, sobbing. Campbell quietly closed the door and headed up a narrow staircase opposite. Passing through another door at the top, he found himself on a sumptuously carpeted landing, where the people chatting in scattered groups resembled pieces in a mysterious board game.

Campbell went to the nearest door that led into a bedroom. The thin-lipped redhead he had seen earlier was sitting on a chair by the wardrobe, smoothing down her dress, while (reflected in the oval glass of the wardrobe door) a man immediately in front of her was in the process of standing up and stuffing some lacy item into his jacket pocket. Above the marble fireplace on the other side of the room was a large painting of a village sea front, with a stylised seagull standing on a wall in the foreground. Campbell murmured an apology and shut the door.

After trying five more doors that were all locked, he descended the main staircase to an enormous lounge in which two men were rolling up a rug to clear the floor for dancing. Campbell took in the varnished floorboards; the oak bookshelves; a fallen glass that had circled a coffee table until its stem had caught under an ashtray and which was at that moment releasing with infinite patience a clear droplet of wine. Then he heard Hargreaves declaiming in a loud, ironical voice that he could immortalise somebody's beauty.

Two weeks later, on the morning Campbell arrived at Cranby Terrace, he could still clearly picture Megan sitting in that room with her legs crossed twice, smiling up at the artist, and the way she had avoided his eye shortly afterwards when he had told her that he considered Hargreaves to be a rather pathetic person, with his pendulous belly and his rubicund Latin features. By way of reply, she had said that she would see Campbell on the evening he moved into the artist's flat, and then she had left the party complaining of a headache.

Campbell stood at the entrance to the close in Cranby Terrace, holding his typewriter, a folder under his arm and a suitcase. On the street behind him, his father was struggling to pull another suitcase out of the car. The breeze carried the scent of the white blossoms in the garden on the right. Through the bay window overlooking the garden, Campbell could see a young woman holding up a string of pearls which she was apparently sucking. He looked back, sighed and headed into the close.

His father caught up with him on the landing of the fourth floor, just as Hargreaves opened the door to his flat. The artist was wearing a Paisley dressing gown. Hanging on the wall behind him was a framed drawing by Picasso. Through the doorway next to the drawing, Campbell could see a canvas on an easel and a woman's bare legs stretching across a dusty chaise longue.

'Jesus, I forgot you were coming this morning,' said Daniel. Then he turned and shouted, 'Tessa, make yoursel' decent. We've got visitors.' The legs disappeared from view. Daniel ushered them in. Leaving their luggage in the hall, they followed him into the main room. Canvases were leaning against the wall. There were two armchairs near the bay window with a small blue table in between. It had a hexagonal-shaped top decorated with carved arabesques. Tessa was sitting on the chaise longue in a plain white dressing gown. Her thick brown hair was pushed behind her ear but curled round to a point on her right cheek.

Campbell and his father sat down in the armchairs while Daniel poured them whisky.

'I'll have a gin and tonic,' said Tessa, leaning over to pick up a packet of cigarettes and a lighter from the floor. Campbell stared at her breasts which were fully visible down the opening of her gown. When she straightened up, he noticed that her eyeliner was more thickly applied at the outer edges of her eyes. He noticed that her nails were filed to points. He noticed a small nick on her recently shaved and glistening shins. Ignoring him completely, she flicked open the lighter, half closed her eyes and drew the blue flame to the end of her cigarette.

An acute sense of excitement filled Campbell. He was about to enjoy a degree of independence he had never known before. He was going to see Megan that night. His new play was still in its ecstatic early stages, but all that faded to insignificance compared with the life revealed to him in Daniel's flat.

In fact, the ten minutes they stayed there were rather awkward. Campbell's father bristled at the Bohemian trappings, perhaps, as Campbell maintained, because he envied the lack of restraint in the artist's lifestyle. Tessa treated Campbell with a coldness that he had seldom encountered before and which intrigued him enormously. The only person who seemed entirely at ease was Daniel, who recounted the same dull story about Matisse which Campbell had heard him tell at the party.

Complaining all the way about his ill health, Hargreaves led Campbell and his father up to the attic flat that was to be Campbell's home for the next year and a half. It consisted of one large room with a dormer window that commanded a fine view of the city, a kitchenette and a bathroom with a WC awkwardly placed under the slope of the roof.

Having deposited all of his son's belongings, Campbell's father treated him to lunch in a nearby pub, after which he patted the playwright once on the back and left. Campbell leisurely finished his pint, and he too was about to leave when he noticed the familiar scarred face of a man at the adjoining table. After buying the man a drink, the pair of them went to the toilets, where Campbell bought two pairs of nylons the man had hidden in the lining of his jacket. By now slightly tipsy, the playwright headed into Byres Road, where he purchased a bottle of whisky and some food.

Back in the flat, Campbell enjoyed the luxury of a hot bath. A fresh breeze came through the open window while he relaxed in the grey, soapy water, sipping whisky and looking out at the clear blue sky. A jazz record played on the portable record player his parents had given him for his birthday. He felt a fluttering in his stomach when he thought about Megan. After draining the whisky, he pulled the plug and stood up, letting the water drip off him for a moment before rubbing himself vigorously with a towel. He tried not to think about the hours remaining before she arrived.

As the afternoon wore on, he grew more impatient. He poured himself another whisky and began in a desultory manner to unpack his belongings. Occasionally, he would stop to look out of the window. Beyond the tenement opposite, he could see the buildings of Park Terrace rising above the leafy foliage of Kelvingrove. Caught in the evening sunlight, the view presented him with such complex and subtle gradations of shadow and colour that he experienced an intense pleasure bordering on anguish.

The sound of Megan's staccato footsteps on the stairs outside held the illusory promise of a resolution for these contradictory feelings, which in the event was unfulfilled. The light blue dress and broad white belt she was wearing made a disagreeable impression on Campbell. She was ill at ease. She drank some whisky. She would not sit down. Campbell sat looking up at her with his forearms resting on his thighs, compressing his whisky glass with an almost simian fury.

'It's difficult for me to say this, Campbell,' she said, 'but I'd rather say it to your face.' She fell silent and stood with her back to him for a moment. Then she turned round and added, 'There's no more to be said.' Campbell did not reply. She went up to him and laid her hand lightly on his. He pulled his hand away. She turned and walked out of the room. After a moment, he threw his whisky glass at the door.

It appeared to Campbell that only by thoroughly exhausting himself would he be able to endure the spoiled dregs of that evening. He left the flat and began walking quickly and aimlessly through the streets, aware of nothing beyond his own racing thoughts, until he found himself on Park Road outside a pub called The Doublet.

Greedily lapping up the palliative it offered, he ended up at a table by a pillar, expressing maudlin sentiments to a beautiful stranger. She asked him his profession. He told her he owned a shoe shop and then kissed her full on the lips. She responded by pressing her tongue into his mouth and stroking his cheek, and after he returned to his seat she looked over at him from time to time. He saw her leaving when he was heading to the loo.

While relieving himself in a blocked and overflowing urinal, he felt a sudden, urgent desire to see her again. He stumbled out of the pub and caught up with her about fifty yards down the street. She was talking to a man, but she left him to go over to Campbell. They embraced and kissed again. The man approached and said, 'Hey pal; that's enough.' He had a deeply lined face and greased hair and displayed no signs of anger or jealousy. Campbell looked down at the woman's face. She was smiling. Her body felt warm. He pulled two pounds from his pocket and slipped them into the man's hand. He smiled but held out his hand for more. Campbell slipped him another three pounds. The man pocketed them, handed the original two pounds to the woman and walked away.

She led Campbell into a nearby close, to a dingy room on the third floor. He looked around it, wondering if she lived there and, if so, what significance the few objects scattered about had for her. Her platinum hair had dark brown roots. She took off her clothes and sat on the bed. He removed his clothes. She stretched across to the bedside cabinet for a contraceptive and then took his penis in her hand. After a few strokes, she unrolled the contraceptive on to it and lay on her back with her knees raised and parted.

As he entered her he was filled with a familiar sensation, as of something unfurling in his chest. He buried his face in the pillow by her head, but it smelled of hair lotion, so he raised himself on his hands. Her head was tilted back and she was staring at the headboard. Campbell attempted to kiss her, but she averted her face. The sky in the east was grey when he made his way home. It occurred to him that he had disappointed her.

For the rest of the month, Campbell was so busy working on his new play that he barely attended his university classes. His poor examination results prompted a visit from his father. John reminded Campbell that his generous allowance was to help him through university 'and not to subsidise a dissolute life'. Campbell apparently took note. He abandoned his play unfinished, curtailed his social life and began to save money.

In fact, Campbell had abandoned the play because he was dissatisfied by its obvious connections to his aunt's life and by the clumsy exposition of its plot. Moreover, he had the unpleasant feeling that its psychopathic anti-hero was escaping his artistic control and he needed a more subtle narrative device to constrain the character. Realising that his father would never accept his literary ambitions, he started saving money in preparation for the inevitable loss of his allowance.

At this critical stage in his life, Campbell came to rely quite heavily on Hargreaves's friendship. The artist seemed to enjoy his company, and Campbell soon felt able to drop in on him at any time.

Although his model, Tessa, was never friendly towards the playwright, she grew to tolerate his presence while she was sitting. Campbell, for his part, was surprised to discover that he no longer found her desirable. He was also surprised to discover that she wasn't sleeping with Hargreaves. Initially, Campbell, like his father, had considered the artist to be the quintessential Bohemian. As he got to know him better, Campbell became convinced that his hackneyed lifestyle was a front and that the key to Hargreaves's talent lay elsewhere.

Day after day, Hargreaves would obsessively paint studies of Tessa, breaking her body up into lines and planes; setting it against different backgrounds; experimenting with different colours and styles. Campbell experienced a profound sense of peace when he was with them. Birdsong and the distant sounds of the city would drift into the room. Periodically, Tessa would change her position. Daniel's eyes would dart constantly from her naked body to the painting and back again while he covered the canvas with swift, confident brushstrokes. Campbell would watch him carefully, convinced that the artist would present him with the revelation he was seeking.

If Campbell called upon him during the evening, Hargreaves would pour them both a whisky and tell Campbell about his childhood; about life in Paris and the South of France during the twenties; about his return to Scotland shortly before the Nazi invasion. He never alluded to his art until he finished the painting of Tessa.

One afternoon towards the end of April, Campbell dropped in to find the artist alone, standing by his easel cleaning a brush.

'Good to see you, Campbell,' he said. 'I was just going to invite you down for a celebratory drink.' While the artist wandered away in search of glasses, the playwright looked at the finished painting. It was an abstract work, but he could make out several unique features that identified Tessa's reclining figure, the hexagonal-topped table and a colourful Persian rug that had been draped over the chaise longue. To Campbell's eye, it appeared as if the scene had been distorted in a quite arbitrary manner. He was startled when Hargreaves came up behind him and pushed a glass of whisky into his hand.

'You see, Campbell, it's patterns and repetitions that interest me.' He then proceeded to point out the patterns and repetitions that Campbell had failed to notice. While the artist spoke, Campbell experienced a sensation of mounting euphoria. His mind began to whirl with ideas.

Two days later, he started writing a new and quite different version of the play. After an evening of drinking and exultation, he wrote the title – *The Irresistible Rise of Tam McLean* – at the top of a clean sheet of paper. Within two weeks, he had dropped out of university, lost his allowance and written the first act. By the end of May, he had finished the play.

He celebrated by drinking the better part of a bottle of whisky, and then he 'rushed out into the delirious night'. During his wanderings, he met a prostitute who called herself Lulu. For ten shillings she took him into the nearest close and they had sex up against a wall. When Campbell came, she struck his shoulder several times with her fists, but whether from pleasure or anger he neither knew nor cared.

Chapter Two

And so we come to Campbell's first masterpiece, *The Irresistible Rise of Tam McLean*. It is a play for which I have a special fondness. So much of the happiness I have experienced is tied up with it. Even now, when I read it, I sense behind Tam McLean's ebullient rise an appetite for life which fear has always prevented me from expressing. Despite its violence and the tragedy of its ending, there is something about the play that makes me dream of another mode of being, in which opportunities could be seized and desires acted upon.

Watching Fiona Gardiner kneeling by my filing cabinet, putting my scattered notes and files in order, I would notice the different shades running through her hair; the arrangement of freckles on the back of her hand; the sudden revelation of a bra strap on the smooth skin of her shoulder; the slight curves of her upper thighs stretching the material of her skirt. And yet I was always aware that there stood between us an invisible barrier, like that useless stage prop that had once obscured an actress's breasts.

It is to Campbell's credit that in a play about a violent gangster he has managed to convey a breadth of emotion which can even encompass my own anguished yearnings.

At first, we see Tam through the eyes of his enemies in the Calton Mob. To them, McLean, a small-time crook who has been extorting money from people under their protection, is nothing more than an annoying insect that they will easily crush.

The scene shifts to a Glasgow pub, where Tam, accompanied by his sidekick, Wully Pollock, is chatting up a young woman named Lynette. At first, she is cool towards him, but the intensity of feeling underlying his charm and wit draw her to him, almost despite herself. In these and in later scenes with Lynette, Campbell offers us glimpses of powerful emotions that go far beyond the sexual obsession of which he is so frequently accused.

It is at this point that the hoodlum from the Calton Mob arrives to deal with Tam. McLean's subsequent transformation from smooth-talking joker to frenzied killer is so shockingly unexpected that within seconds the hoodlum is in his power. However, instead of delivering the fatal blow, Tam merely produces a playing card from his pocket and says, 'That's the sign of ma friendship. Frae now on, a'll kill anyone who so much as looks at you the wrong way.'

After that, Tam's rise proceeds apace. Having gained control of the Calton Mob, he turns his attention to Big Davie Docherty of Parkhead. Docherty hopes to trick McLean, but it is he who is tricked and slain in front of his wife, Rowena. In her grief, she rips open her blouse and plunges Docherty's knife into her bare breast. The act ends with McLean marrying Lynette and thereby gaining the support of her father, who holds sway in the Gorbals.

The remainder of the play revolves around Docherty's son's desire for revenge. He first of all seeks help from the Possilpark Fleet. However, McLean brutally murders their gang leader outside one of his own pubs and calmly adds Possilpark to his growing empire.

It is now that Fate delivers McLean his first serious blow. Lynette contracts diphtheria and dies. Enraged by his impotence to save her, Tam's treatment of his enemies reaches new depths of cruelty.

In a desperate final attempt on McLean's life, Docherty's son hires a notorious hit man. The attempt fails and Tam seduces the hit man's callous but beautiful wife in the abattoir while the poor man is hanging from a meat hook and painfully dying.

It seems that nothing can defeat Tam McLean, who now dominates the stage with his egocentric pronouncements and megalomania. But a lung haemorrhage interrupts his final speech in the penultimate scene. The play ends with Tam on his deathbed. His old confederate, Wully Pollock, is with him:

At Tam's request, Wully collects two playing cards from Tam's bedside cabinet. Painfully and slowly, Tam shuffles the cards several times, and then he asks Wully to take one.

TAM: What is it, the Queen of Spades or the Queen of Diamonds?

WULLY: The Queen of Diamonds.

TAM: Aye, I thought it would be.

TAM McLEAN *dies.*

The ending infuriated some reviewers when the play was first performed on the public stage. Those who followed the play more closely noticed that McLean shows a playing card to each one of his rivals before he kills them. He also shows a playing card as a sign of friendship to those who come over to his side.

It is only during McLean's final exchange with Wully that we learn what the playing cards are. In this manner the playwright very subtly reveals Tam's inverted standards to the audience. For McLean, the black queen symbolises life, while the red queen symbolises death. Moreover, to the best of my knowledge, no critic has mentioned the references to diamonds which occur on the occasions when Lynette and Tam fall ill.

Firstly, after leaving one of his rivals dead on a street in Possilpark, Tam returns to Lynette. She has taken to her bed with a fever. Despite her difficulty in speaking, she chides Tam for his unnecessary cruelty. He flies into a rage and, noticing a bracelet on her arm, he rips it off, scattering gold links about the floor.

'You're quite happy when I shower you wi' gold and diamonds, aren't you?' he shouts, before he becomes aware of her laboured breathing.

Then later, in the penultimate scene of the play:

Tam is on a street with two of his hoods. One is lighting the other's cigarette, while Tam stands a little apart, gazing at the sky.

TAM: A feel good. (*He turns towards them with hands outstretched.*) Naebody can touch me now. See here, lads; look at these windaes. Behind them you'll find yer wee people, livin' their wee, pokey lives. Yer printer's apprentice slavin' awa fer months, tae get his lassie a diamond nae bigger than a flea's arse. (*The hoods shift uncomfortably from foot to foot.*) But me, A'm laird of all a survey. (*He takes out his handkerchief and starts coughing violently. After a particularly deep cough, he looks at his hankie and then at the two men.*) Jesus, there's blood in ma hankie.

Thus, Tam McLean's plight becomes universal. His attempts to control his world have proved futile. He is merely part of a pattern he has failed to discern, and just as he is about to grasp the world, it slips away from him like the promise of a love denied.

The Irresistible Rise of Tam McLean was first performed on 19 July 1947 in The Basement, a private club in Otago Street. The club belonged to a friend of Daniel Hargreaves, Andy Davies, who shared a large villa just around the corner with his lover, Tom Lomond. Campbell had met the pair at one of Hargreaves's parties in March, when he had mentioned that he was working on a play.

At the beginning of June, he had shown it to Tom Lomond, who had enthused about it to Davies. After a show of reluctance, Andy had agreed to put it on. Plays were usually staged in the club at about three-month intervals. The rest of the time, it was host to avant-garde jazz bands, specialist revues and risqué cabarets.

Lomond, who looked after the creative side of the venture, offered the play to the Red Clydeside Theatre Co., a group that was trying to create a theatre of and for the working class. Fooled by the coarse language and violence, the director (and principal actor) of the group, Keiran Brody, hailed Campbell as a poet of the streets and agreed to stage the play.

It is clear that the twenty-two-year-old Campbell was a little in awe of Brody. He has left us with vivid descriptions of the actor, dressed in a torn, shapeless pullover and threadbare trousers, striding about the stage during rehearsals and swearing at the other actors and actresses; of his thick black hair; of the damaged eyelid that gave a peculiar slant to his right eye. There is a quality of admiration in these descriptions which is uncharacteristic of McCluskie and which he was later to contradict.

Something of the frenetic activity preceding the first performance is conveyed in a short passage by McCluskie which was discovered among the various drafts of the play:

The club was chilly, despite the heat outside. The owner was at the bar handing over some money to a man in a black pin-striped suit. Scattered lights illuminated odd corners of the room, multiplying shadows and catching the varnished surfaces of the tables and stacked chairs.

Keiran was pacing up and down the stage with his hat perched on the back of his head. He was frowning with concentration and hugging himself. Marie Seton [the actress playing Lynette] was standing at the edge of the stage, smoking a cigarette and watching him. Her smile made her look as if she was laughing at a private joke.

Voices were raised behind the stage. The band leader tapped his music stand with his baton and Keiran shouted, 'Is everybody ready?'

Nobody replied. He walked over to the lamp post which was standing at the left-hand side of the stage. 'Does this have tae go here, Campbell?' In replying, I revealed some of the anger

I felt at his continual and petty interference. Two spotlights went on suddenly, disclosing the inadequacies of the tenement building which was painted on to the backdrop. Somebody swore loudly and the lights were extinguished. 'Jesus Christ,' yelled Keiran. Marie dropped her cigarette and crushed it under the sole of her white patent shoe. Then she followed Brody offstage.

A black curtain descended from the lighting gantry to cover the backdrop. The band started to play an upbeat number. The lights on the stage dimmed. Men, dressed in pinstriped suits and moving in time to the music, carried props on to the stage – tables; chairs; two boxes with a board stretched between them to represent a bar. A barman strolled on, polishing a glass. Lynette took her place at one of the tables. Groups of men clustered around the other tables. The trumpeter stood up and raised his horn. Its brass rim glinted in the half-light. He played a short, haunting solo which ended on a sustained note. McLean walked on to the stage, brushing his lapels and looking from side to side. Wully followed him on.

Following a drink with the cast to celebrate the success of that first performance, the rather inebriated playwright attempted to walk the lead actress, Marie Seton, home. She turned to him on the pavement outside the pub and said, quite sharply, 'Where do you think you're going?' McCluskie, feeling unusually flustered, mumbled an apology and walked away.

It was a warm, clear night. He did not want to go home. As he headed down the hill towards the river, he counted his money. There were four crumpled pound notes and about six shillings in loose change. He pocketed the banknotes. Then he spread the coins across his right palm. They glinted for a moment in the light of a passing street lamp before he closed his fist and dropped them into the same pocket as the banknotes. He reflected that he was nearly down to his last twenty pounds.

After walking for about half an hour, he stopped beneath a railway bridge to light a cigarette, while a train passed above him in a flurry of steam. The noise was deafening as each truck created the same shuddering rhythm as the preceding one. After it had gone, he was able to hear a repetitive, metallic clanking from the direction of the river. In the gable end of the nearest tenement, beside a poster for Bovril, an open window betrayed a bitter domestic dispute.

Campbell inhaled his smoke and looked up and down the street. He saw a woman approaching in the distance. The short steps imposed on her by her tight pencil skirt reminded him of a Japanese geisha. Just as she reached the far side of the bridge, one of her heels got caught in a drain. When she lifted her foot, the edge of the drain rose and then the heel snapped off. Her handbag slipped off her shoulder and she stumbled forward, nearly losing her footing. Campbell flicked away his cigarette and ran over to her.

'Are you all right?' he said.

'Whit dae you fuckin' think, you stupit arsehole?' she replied in a shrill voice. Campbell retrieved the heel from the drain. The surface was scraped through to the wood in several places. He handed it to her. 'Oh Hell, these are ma best shoes!'

'Can you no get them repaired?'

'Are you fuckin' kiddin'? A cannae even pay ma fuckin' rent.'

While they talked, Campbell took in her sharp, freckled face, her black, straight hair and her stringy calves. He watched her drop the heel into her bag, take off her shoes and rub her right ankle bone. The stocking was worn through and bloody there. When she straightened up again, she pushed her hair out of her eyes and looked at him.

'Whit brings you tae these parts? Are you slummin' it?' she said.

Campbell shrugged his shoulders and offered her a cigarette. She shifted the shoes to her left hand and drew a cigarette from the packet. Campbell took one for himself and then cupped his hands round a match while he lit them. He had a sudden vivid recollection of his father dressed in uniform, which for a moment distracted him from what she was saying. They started to walk down the street together. As they walked she made her intentions apparent. Campbell analysed his feelings. He did not think she was attractive, but he felt aroused by the situation and by her musky scent. Finally, she named her price – two pounds. Campbell agreed, although he knew he could have bargained her down.

Her flat consisted of two rooms. The entrance door opened into a large room smelling of fried food, with curtains drawn across one end and a cooker and sink at the other end. A few odd bits of furniture were scattered about. A plaster statuette of the Virgin Mary stood on the mantelpiece between two candles.

A single bed and a wardrobe filled most of the available space in the other room. Campbell lay down with his hands behind his head and watched her wriggle out of her skirt. She then removed her blouse and pants and disappeared into the main room. She returned after a couple of minutes, wearing only her suspenders and stockings. With deft movements she unbuttoned Campbell's fly and took out his already erect penis. She scrutinised it carefully from several angles before saying, 'A never let ma clients go on top.' Campbell moved his hands down behind his neck and sighed as she sat astride him and drew his penis inside her. In the memoir of his sexual life that McCluskie compiled shortly before his murder, he describes the pleasurable pain he felt each time she thrust downwards. Later, as he made his way out of the flat, he caught sight of a little girl's face peering at him from between the curtains in the larger room. As he pulled the entrance door closed behind him, he heard the woman's shrill voice shouting, 'How many times dae a huv tae tell you?' followed by a loud smack.

The next day, Campbell went to The Basement in the early evening. When he entered, he saw a stranger sitting at a table near the stage talking to Keiran Brody. The actor beckoned Campbell over to them.

'Campbell, this is Mr Malquist. He's a literary agent,' said Keiran, rising from his chair. Malquist remained seated. He lowered his head slightly and held out his hand to the playwright. On that occasion, Campbell only took in Malquist's curious accent and the chalky appearance of his skin.

He was to have a clearer recollection of their next meeting, which took place three weeks later. Malquist was sitting opposite him with his head cocked. His hair was heavily lacquered and parted in the middle. His prominent but rather low cheekbones created unpleasant shadows under his eyes. He had a thin nose. Deep lines, descending from the outer curves of his nostrils, emphasised his full lips. Blue-grey shading on his jaw indicated that he had to shave frequently. Mastering his repugnance, Campbell began to read the contract that was spread out on the table between them.

'You won't regret it,' said Malquist, slowly unscrewing the lid of his burgundy-coloured fountain pen.

Chapter Three

McCluskie, shivering in the cold air, looked at his watch. The station was relatively quiet. He could see the London train standing at the platform, its engine shrouded in mist and steam. People were already boarding. Near the ticket gate a woman in a white bonnet was bending down to adjust her daughter's hood. Campbell smiled when he realised that they were partially obscuring an advertisement for his father's shop. The words 'I BOUGHT THEM AT McCLUSKIE'S' were written above a picture of two women, one of whom was raising her hand in admiration of the other's shoes. Campbell had recently heard a rumour that his father was having an affair with the model who had posed as the fortunate owner.

The playwright slapped his gloved hands together once or twice. He gazed at a young woman making her way to the tearoom, and had more or less decided to follow her, when he heard his name being called. Mouthing a silent curse, he turned to greet Malquist.

The agent looked even paler than usual in the grey morning light. He was carrying an attaché case. His suitcase was being carried for him by a bulky character with cropped hair. The pair came to a halt in front of the playwright. Campbell held out his hand to Malquist, but the agent hesitated before shaking it.

'This is my new driver, Baynes,' said Malquist, gesturing to his companion. Baynes put the suitcase down. He was wearing tight-fitting leather gloves that creaked when he straightened his fingers. He acknowledged the playwright with a smile. Campbell retained a vivid impression of the roll of bristly fat which formed at the back of Baynes's neck when he twisted his head to look up at a passing pigeon.

Malquist dismissed Baynes. Then he shifted his attaché case to his other hand and reached into his coat for the tickets, leaving McCluskie to carry the suitcase. The playwright would not readily forget the sense of humiliation he felt at that moment.

They had to share a compartment with two teenage lads, whom McCluskie took for students. One was tall and slim; the other was small with sharp features and very fine greasy hair. They fell silent when Malquist and Campbell entered. Malquist sat opposite them by the window. Campbell put the suitcase and bag on to the luggage rack, reached into his coat pocket for the novel he had bought at the station, threw his coat on to the seat and sat down a little apart from Malquist.

He felt a vague sense of unease as he watched Malquist settling in for the journey. While the train rattled across the river, the agent stood up and removed his coat and scarf. He folded each in turn and placed them on the end of the seat. Campbell thought that Malquist's hands, with their pallid skin, prominent knuckles and precise movements, resembled some unpleasant creature you might find on the ocean floor. Struggling to contain his disgust and rancour, he unwrapped his book and started to read.

The smaller of the two lads whispered something to his companion, who responded by grabbing his wrist with both hands and twisting the skin in opposite directions. Malquist smiled. Campbell tried to focus on his book, but he was distracted by the smaller lad climbing on to his seat and stretching up for a navy blue duffel bag. He could barely reach it and only succeeded in pulling it open. Then he slipped off the seat and banged his knees on the floor. The bag fell forward on to the front of the rack and a blue clothbound book fell at Campbell's feet. The playwright picked it up, dusted it off and read the title, *Sinister Street*. As he handed it back to the lad, he felt a sudden anxiety which arose for no apparent reason. In his notebook that night, he would ascribe it to the musty smell of the upholstery in the compartment, the scent of carbolic soap coming from one of the lads and his uncertainty about the prospects for his play.

Events had moved swiftly since Campbell had signed the contract with Malquist. The agent's first act had been to persuade the club owner, Andy Davies, to put on another performance of *The Irresistible Rise of Tam McLean* at the end of August. Malquist had then arranged for several journalists to be invited to that performance, one of whom was a known enemy of the agent. An article by that journalist subsequently appeared in the review pages of the *Glasgow Herald*, condemning the play for being violent and sexually explicit. Reference was made to the scene in which Rowena bared her breasts. Another journalist came to McCluskie's defence in a rival newspaper. Rumours were spread by the two hundred people who had actually seen the play. A prospective third performance was banned by the Corporation, pending an inquiry by the Lord Chamberlain's office.

By the middle of September, McCluskie's name was known throughout Glasgow.

It was then that Malquist sent a copy of the play together with some newspaper cuttings to James Hawkins, who owned the Pantheon Theatre in Charing Cross Road, London. Towards the end of the war, Malquist had obtained some black-market building materials for Hawkins, which had allowed the theatre owner to carry out emergency repairs after the theatre had been damaged by a doodlebug. In his covering letter, the agent reminded Hawkins of the favour and pointed out that the success of McCluskie's play would be to their mutual advantage.

So it was that Malquist and McCluskie booked into a hotel in Bloomsbury late one October afternoon in 1947. They had taken a taxi from the station. McCluskie described the freezing fog; the half-seen crowds; the muted shop lights.

After washing and changing, he met Malquist in the hotel bar. There were few other customers. A bored waitress leaned on the bar counter with her chin in her hand and her pinky in her mouth, scribbling on her order pad, while the barman, dressed in a short white jacket and a black bow tie, regarded her with an expression of sullen resentment.

Malquist, who had told Campbell very little about the impending meeting, produced a typescript of *The Irresistible Rise of Tam McLean* from his attaché case. The waitress ambled over and took an order from the agent for a whisky and a glass of wine, while Campbell flicked through the typescript. Many lines of dialogue and several stage directions had been circled in blue pencil.

After the waitress had gone, Malquist said, 'I had a lawyer look at your play and he has indicated anything that might be unacceptable to the Lord Chamberlain. You shall have to make changes if we are to get the play on to the London stage. Also, Hawkins has expressed some doubts about the dialect. You may have to tone it down if you want the play to be understood by an English audience.

The waitress returned with the drinks. Malquist paid. Campbell tried to ascertain what the likelihood was that Hawkins would stage the play, but Malquist seemed unwilling to commit himself either way. Campbell found his attention wandering to a young woman who had taken a seat at a nearby table. She was with an affluent-looking man in a blazer, but Campbell was convinced that she kept looking over at him.

The meeting with Hawkins took place on the following morning in a cluttered office in the Pantheon Theatre. Folios and manuscripts formed uneven piles on the floor. A stack of wire trays on the desk overflowed with invoices, receipts and ticket stubs. An American pin-up calendar, open at the month of July, was hanging on the wall. Sitting on a rock by a river was a smiling brunette with glistening legs, wearing a cowboy hat, a figure-hugging waistcoat, matching shorts and cowboy boots. A fishing rod was propped on the rock beside her. She was holding a frying pan containing two fish over an open fire. A single-bar electric fire roasted Campbell's back but failed to heat the room. A grimy window looked over the narrow alleyway leading to the stage door. The playwright would come to know this office very well during the following six weeks.

James Hawkins had a bloated face which was given an impish quality by his snub nose and thick, wiry hair. Campbell thought he looked a bit like a clown and was surprised by his tenacity during the financial negotiations. He offered McCluskie fifty pounds for sole rights to stage the play in London for the next three years. Malquist declined before Campbell had a chance to speak. There followed a lengthy discussion. Hawkins grew quite heated and began to wave his arms about in a dramatic fashion that sat oddly with his wheezy voice. Campbell was convinced that the play was going to be rejected outright. However, Malquist remained unperturbed throughout. For the first time, Campbell became conscious of the economy of gesture which made him appear so powerful.

At a certain moment, Malquist made a sign with his left hand which Campbell was unable to see. Hawkins did not complete his statement. A bewildered expression crossed his face and he agreed to the agent's terms without further argument. Campbell would receive five per cent of the ticket receipts. Hawkins would have sole rights only for the play's first run. McCluskie would stay at Hawkins's house in Highgate while he carried out the changes to the play, but Malquist would cover his board and other expenses during that time.

Later that day, Malquist took a train to Glasgow. He left McCluskie at the hotel with a two-hundred-pound advance (to be repaid with interest if the play flopped). The playwright, feeling a profound sense of relief at the agent's departure, spent the rest of the afternoon in the hotel bar.

In the early evening, he ate a meal in a restaurant near Leicester Square, where he noticed 'an elderly woman in an emerald cardigan pressing together the tips of her forefinger and thumb to retrieve a hair from amongst her peas'.

Afterwards, he strolled along the Mall. Moonlight picked out the bare branches of the trees in St James's Park. He turned left at Buckingham Palace and headed in a direction he thought would take him to the river. However, he lost his way and eventually found himself in an area of seedy terraces interspersed with bombed-out sites where wooden beams propped up the buildings on either side. He turned into a street lined with rows of brick houses, which had a pub at its far end. A little girl, in a dark woollen coat and a headscarf, ran past with a loaf of bread under her arm and disappeared into a nearby doorway. Feeling the chill, he dropped into the pub, which he later described in his notebook:

The place was crowded, mainly with men. A piano in the corner, with partially melted candles in its brass holders, raised the spectres of cockney sing-songs. The barmaid (lipstick stained teeth, freckly cleavage) shed an eyelash into my beer. I retired to a quiet corner, to spare her feelings, and removed it carefully with my forefinger and thumb, reflecting as I did so on the curious coincidence. Two young blokes were playing darts. I watched one place his cigarette on the rim of an ashtray and throw two darts into the triple twenty. The third hit the wire and bounced back on to the floor. An old man asked if he could join me, and we spent the remainder of the evening drinking together in a state of amiable and mutual incomprehension.

That night, McCluskie dreamed that he was correcting the typescript of his play at a desk that was standing on a grass platform beside a small waterfall. Every time he finished working on a page, and despite all his efforts, a breeze would carry it into the deep pool at the foot of the waterfall. On the other side, a shapely brunette with prominent, glowing cheeks was using a rod and line to fish out each sheet of paper as it fell. She was wearing a light-coloured raincoat and a pair of cowboy boots. Each time she raised her arm to cast the line, her coat would flap open to reveal her pubic triangle. Campbell tried to stand up, but his desk was so small that his thighs were jammed between his chair and the desktop and he could not move. He woke up among his tangled blankets, drenched in sweat which cooled rapidly in the freezing hotel room.

It was in the mid-afternoon of the following day that Campbell arrived at James Hawkins's house. Situated next to Highgate

Cemetery, it was a complicated, obsessively symmetrical structure with numerous gables. Its tall chimneys were ornamented with bricks of various colours which seemed to glow in the orange sunlight.

James's wife, Marjory, answered the door and showed Campbell to a room at the top of the house. Her frosty manner left him in little doubt that his presence would be a great inconvenience. As they mounted the stairs, he saw through the open lounge door a girl in her late teens patting a black Labrador which was lolling its tongue in pleasure. One of its ears was folded back on to its head, displaying a triangle of pink flesh speckled with brown. Mrs Hawkins was somewhat mollified when Campbell thanked her for going to so much trouble and handed her the forty-two pounds which her husband had agreed would cover his keep for six weeks.

The room was small, with a slanting roof and a dormer window overlooking the cemetery. A card table had been fitted into the window recess to serve as a desk. A portable typewriter in a black case had been put on an old place mat to protect the green baize of the table. Two towels had been draped over the end of the bed. Campbell finally gave in to the feeling of excited anticipation which he had held in check for the past two days. His hands trembled as he unpacked his clothes. He placed the typescript of his play on the table next to the typewriter. He located a bathroom and washed thoroughly his armpits, neck and face. Then he shaved, changed his clothes and descended the stairs to join Marjory and her daughter, Cynthia, for a glass of sherry.

McCluskie was to have a vivid memory of that afternoon drink when he was making love to Cynthia six weeks later. She was kneeling on the bed astride him, her body picked out here and there by a spectral light that had no obvious source. He was slightly drunk. His penis felt numb. Their prolonged, rhythmic movements were threatening to become ridiculous. He closed his eyes.

Initially, his frustration at not being able to come reminded him of the distressing rewrites of the past few weeks. He had had to dismantle his play and put it back together several times to satisfy the often contradictory requirements of the censor, Hawkins and the cast. When his orgasm finally approached, he had a sudden vision of that October afternoon: the orange sunlight flooding through the windows; the dog growling, baring its teeth and shifting its eyes from side to side when he attempted to pat it; Marjory handing him a glass of sherry and trebling her chin as she tried to locate a piece of fluff on her shoulder; Cynthia turning her head, chastising the dog and smiling at him.

He opened his eyes. Cynthia pushed down and let out a deep moan. He came, but the pleasure passed quickly, leaving him with an unpleasant sense of remorse. Cynthia, still in her own happier world, pushed her hair away from her eyes with both hands and looked up at the ceiling, smiling. Silver light burnished her right cheek. The whites of her raised eyes resembled crescent moons.

Two days later, a pallid, sanitised version of *The Irresistible Rise of Tam McLean* opened on the London stage. The audience and most of the critics, primed by a Malquist-inspired controversy, greeted it with rapture. McCluskie joined the cast on stage for the final curtain call. The applause quietened his doubts about the changes; about the dubious Scots accents; about the set designs. Catherine Black (the actress playing Lynette) squeezed his hand as they took their bow. She was a slim, dark-haired woman, whose expressive shoulder blades McCluskie had admired during the dress rehearsal.

There was a backstage party. Marjory Hawkins, dominating the conversation in one corner, told a group of ageing actors and actresses of her admiration for the playwright and her delight that he had chosen to stay in their house. Malquist was huddled in conversation with her husband. It was clear that the agent was angry. He stood at Hawkins's shoulder with a malevolent look in his eyes, a frown deepening the lines between his eyebrows. McCluskie took note of his expression and afterwards started referring to him in his notebooks as 'the Gargoyle'. Cynthia was standing by herself near the buffet, watching McCluskie talking to Catherine Black. When she finally caught the playwright's attention, she looked away and extinguished her cigarette by crushing it underfoot. Then she started speaking to the lead actor.

At the outset of the party, McCluskie had exerted his considerable charm on the more influential critics who were present. However, in his eagerness to talk to Catherine, he had unconsciously snubbed Swinbourne, who was then working for *The Times*. The critic's subsequent review of the play was full of backhanded compliments and snide remarks, which had little effect on its overwhelming success.

McCluskie slipped off with Catherine before the party finished. They passed a dozing janitor (dandruff-dusted waistcoat; sloping shoulders; square moustache) and made their way to a cramped storeroom. There, Catherine cleared a desk of various props: a plaster skull; a stiletto; a telephone; an Art Nouveau ink holder. Then they had sex.

Later, in his room in Hawkins's house, Campbell heard a soft knocking on the door. He did not respond. The knocking was repeated. Still he did not respond. Then the silence was broken only by the faint scratching of his fountain pen as he described Catherine bending over the desk, her buttocks and back partially exposed. Her head was resting in the crook of her arm. There was a dreamy expression on her face. Her eyes were closed.

'I felt as if I was on the brink of some revelation,' he wrote. 'I ran my fingers along the narrow furrow between her shoulder blades. I felt the skin over her vertebrae, the soft down rising before my fingers and, further up, the dampness of the sweat under her hair. I wanted to prolong the moment indefinitely, but all too soon the commonplace resolution came, trailing disappointment in its wake.'

I still have queasy recollections of the morning that I allowed Fiona to read this passage. She had dropped in unexpectedly to borrow one of my books. My feelings were mixed. As usual, her presence excited me, but it struck me forcibly that she only ever called on me socially when she needed something, and I wondered if she was using me. I offered her a cup of coffee. She was standing at the door, holding the beautiful edition of Poe's poems I was lending her. White tidemarks encircled her boots. I realised that she was hesitating about leaving, and I mentioned the passage as an inducement to keep her with me. Also, I was inflamed by the notion of showing her such sexually explicit material.

She settled into one of the armchairs, and I gave her the notebook to read while I made the coffee. My mouth was dry. I felt sure that she must hear my heart beating. I put her mug by her chair and sat down opposite her. She had taken off her boots and curled her legs under her. I watched her raise the mug to her glistening lips. She stopped reading and said, 'I think it's his unhappiness that I find so attractive.'

I was taken aback. I hadn't expected that. I looked over at my bed and then back at her, before blurting out, 'But are you appalled by the lack of affection … the dispassionate descriptions? I mean, he never mentions love or affection.'

It was her turn to look surprised. 'He was only twenty-two, Mr McDuffy. He was too young to be thinking about love.' She looked at her watch, put her mug down on the arm of the chair and started to put on her boots.

'Are you going so soon?'

'Yes. I'm meeting Stephen in the Curlers'.' On the landing, with the book under her arm, she turned to me from the top of the stairs and said, 'Oh, can you do without me next week? Stephen's taking me to the theatre.'

'Of course,' I replied, smiling. She disappeared. I returned to my room and thought about Stephen Pendle: his long eyelashes and slim build; his curious predilection for fifties clothes; the ham-fisted imitations of Kerouac which he had published in the university magazine. I found myself grinding my teeth and wondered if I had perhaps done too much reading in my life. Somewhere in the building a toilet was gustily flushed.

Chapter Four

McCluskie returned to Glasgow with Malquist shortly after the play opened. He did not tell Catherine that he was going. On the train, Malquist informed him that Hawkins intended to keep the play running for three months. The playwright was delighted. Malquist pointed out that, given its success, it would have been better to move the play quickly to a larger and more prestigious theatre. Campbell wondered why Malquist always made him feel a sense of futility.

Back in Glasgow, McCluskie was able to pay Daniel Hargreaves most of the rent he owed him. He hoped to have a rest so that he could prepare for his next play. However, Malquist was already arranging a production of *The Irresistible Rise of Tam McLean* in the Theatre Royal with Keiran Brodie and the Red Clydeside Theatre Co. Campbell was drawn unwillingly into the rehearsals. Two weeks before Christmas, he renewed his acquaintance with the actress Marie Seton.

On Christmas Eve, Keiran, Marie, and he went out for a drink in a West End pub. Campbell noticed the new suit Keiran was wearing and wondered what had happened to the actor's man-of-the-people stance. Marie unbuttoned the top two buttons of her jacket and pulled out her scarf. She placed her hands (the left one still trailing the scarf) on the edge of the seat on either side of her and leaned forwards so that she could see Keiran buying the drinks. After a moment, she looked at the playwright and smiled. Keiran returned with the drinks and sat down beside her. It occurred to Campbell that Keiran and Marie would make love later that night. As he pictured them together he experienced a twisting sensation in his stomach which he had not felt since his time in Normandy. As the evening progressed, his sense of bitterness expanded. He overheard a young man at an adjoining table accuse one of his companions of speaking Papish nonsense. McCluskie, a devout atheist, leaned over, tapped the man on the shoulder and said, 'Who are you calling a

Papist, you Proddy bastard?' It was only Keiran's intervention that prevented a fight. Marie insisted that they left, and refused to speak to Campbell while they waited for their separate taxis.

As he paid the driver outside his parents' house, Campbell remembered that he had left the family's presents at his flat. His mother answered the door in her dressing gown. She made him a cup of coffee in the kitchen and told him that he would have to share his room with Joan's fiancé. Before she went up, Katherine asked Campbell to go quietly to the camp bed she had made up for him. He replied that he wasn't tired, that he would stay up for a short while. She shook her head and slowly climbed the stairs. He winced when one of the steps creaked and then squeaked when she stepped off it.

After finishing his coffee, he started on his father's whisky. At three o'clock in the morning, his father, woken by his singing, came downstairs and found him stumbling about, waving an empty bottle. When Campbell became aware of his presence, he asked him why his mistress wasn't joining the festivities. John tried to take his arm, but Campbell pulled it away, stumbled back and fell among the presents that were piled under the Christmas tree.

When the playwright finally got out of bed late the following morning, he found Dorothy squatting, red-eyed, on the living-room floor. Joan's fiancé was kneeling at the coffee table, trying to repair a Chinese chess queen, part of an antique set that Campbell's father had bought Dorothy for Christmas.

'I know you didn't mean to do it, Campbell. I know you didn't mean it,' Dorothy said, and burst into tears. Campbell noticed the dexterity with which Joan's fiancé was applying glue to the queen's severed neck. Then he looked at his sister and strode out of the room, pressing his nails into his palms to keep himself from crying. There was frost on the ground, a clear sky, a pale, winter sun, but there was no sycamore tree and no dappled shade.

The Irresistible Rise of Tam McLean opened in the Theatre Royal at the end of January. To judge by his notebook, the playwright was still trying to begin work on a follow-up play. Once again, he had found inspiration in his Aunt Dorothy's life. He had become interested in the play *Edgar Caym* (in which his aunt had taken the part of Janice Elliott), having obtained a typescript of it while he was in London. Sometime after returning to Scotland, he drew the following diagram on a fresh page in his notebook:

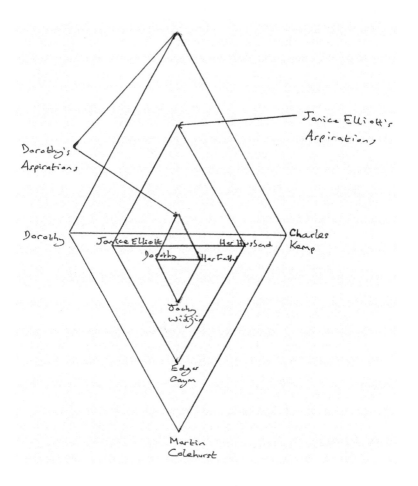

Janice Elliott's
Aspirations

Dorothy's
Aspirations

Dorothy

Janice Elliott   Her Husband

Dorothy   Her Father

Charles
Kemp

John
Widgin

Edgar
Caym

Martin
Colehurst

Underneath the diagram he has written, 'Idea for a play'. Unfortunately, the note appended to this caption is so abbreviated that its meaning is unclear. It would appear that Campbell saw some significance in the interplay between the plot of *Edgar Caym* and Dorothy's life. Dorothy twice escaped from unhappy situations only to find something worse, as does Janice in the play. McCluskie also seems to be suggesting that their aspirations lay entirely outside the triangular confines of their lives. One recent commentator has even gone as far as to posit Paradise and Hell at the highest and lowest points of each rhombus. However, such a reading takes no account of the playwright's avowed atheism.

How Campbell intended to fit this pattern into his play remains a mystery. For he himself became involved in a triangular relationship and abandoned the project before it was even begun.

During the week after Christmas, Marie Seton discovered that Keiran was having an affair with an actress who had recently joined the company. On Hogmanay, Campbell was just leaving his flat to go downstairs to Hargreaves's party, when he met Marie on the landing. She averted her eyes and asked him if she could have a word in private. He was tempted by the music and voices coming from Hargreaves's place, but he agreed to take her to his flat.

Once inside, she burst into tears and sat down, covering her face with her hands. Campbell felt embarrassed. Unsure of what to do, he laid a hand on her shoulder.

'Would you like a cup of tea?' he said, 'Or whisky?'

'Whisky; neat.' She sniffled and took the handkerchief he was holding out to her. As he poured the whisky, he looked at the etching that Hargreaves had given him for Christmas: a nude woman reclining on a couch with her arms behind her head and her legs slightly parted. He looked at the black line that had been traced between her thighs, licked his lips and then returned to Marie.

'Here,' he said. She wiped her right cheek with the back of her hand and smiled at him.

After she left in the early hours of New Year's Day, McCluskie confided his thoughts to his notebook. He tried several times to describe her, but each time he grew dissatisfied with the result and scored heavily through the words. He eventually gave up and wrote,

I sat opposite her, listening to her complaints about Keiran and trying to sympathise with her distress, but lust kept jabbering in my head like a lecherous uncle at a wedding feast. Now,

I feel the sadness of a missed opportunity, made all the worse by the sounds of revellers out in the street. Strangely enough, I could have sworn that I heard Megan's voice outside earlier.

During January, Campbell invited Marie out a few times. He also wrote her two letters, in which we find the curious mixture of egotism, tenderness and deception which characterised his dealings with women. There is also an awkwardness about them which we have not seen since his journal entries about Nora Shaw.

Initially, when they were together, she talked about Keiran or told Campbell unpleasant stories about Keiran's lover. The playwright would return from such evenings despondent and frustrated.

Occasionally, he would drop in on the artist, and they would talk late into the night. Hargreaves was putting the final touches to a painting that he had begun while Campbell was in London. He considered it to be his best work, but he refused to let Campbell see it until it was finished. If he was unable to rouse Hargreaves, as was the case more often than not, Campbell would return to his flat, make a few desultory stabs at writing and end up abusing himself in the bathroom.

Things changed. Marie and Campbell made love for the first time on 11 February. Unused to sharing a bed for the whole night, the playwright slept badly and woke early from ominous dreams.

During the next three weeks, they made love a further four times, but on the last two occasions Campbell sensed that something was wrong. His repeated attempts to find out what was the matter only served to irritate Marie. Shortly after, he received a letter from her. Keiran had split up with the other woman and Marie had started seeing him again. She was vague about dates and circumstances and concluded the letter with, as Campbell put it, 'a succession of conventional regrets which were quite inadequate for my needs'.

Writing in his notebook in early March, after a drinking bout that induced a mood of self-pity, McCluskie wondered,

What will I do with all those memories: Marie lying naked on my couch, smiling at me with her arms behind her head and one knee raised; the way she drew in her lips when she was angry; her large eyes; her fine hair; the reproduction of a painting of St. Catherine's martyrdom, which was hanging above her bed, and which she kept staring at on the one occasion we made love in my favourite position; the rose tinted highlight

123

which appeared on her cheek in a bar one evening, and which disappeared when I tried to kiss it.

Perhaps it was on that same March evening that he remembered the advertisement for his father's shoe shop which he had seen at the railway station on the day he had gone to London. It had struck him as ludicrous because of the look of religious fervour on the model's face and the tawdry materialism of the message.

After two months of frenzied writing, all was transformed by the alembic of McCluskie's genius into the pawnbroker auld Hughie Salter. Campbell's third play opened in the Criterion in London on Thursday 10 June. It was reviewed, together with *The Gioconda Smile* at the New Theatre and *The Winter's Tale* in Stratford, in the issue of *Punch* which was published on the following Wednesday. By an extraordinary chance, I discovered a copy of that very issue in a second-hand bookshop on Great Western Road. Even now, when I look at its cover, the date on the scroll that unfurls in front of the grotesque, hook-nosed Punch fills me with a sense of unease, for it was precisely six years before the playwright's murder and my own unfortunate birth. The reviewer's response was mixed:

> In *Auld Hughie Salter* at the Criterion, Mr McCluskie is evidently at pains to equal the success of his first play. Once again, we find the colourful language, the intricate plotting and criminal milieu of the earlier work, but the playwright has seen fit to burden this play with some heavy-handed satire, much to the detriment of its otherwise admirable effects.
>
> Hughie Salter is an irredeemable villain; a pawnbroker and fence, he lives in a dingy flat above his shop with his young step-daughter. Salter wishes to exact vengeance on a local hoodlum, McGlaig, who, he believes, has cheated him of money. To this end, the pawnbroker gets his step-daughter to cultivate McGlaig's affections, and then to betray him with a more powerful rival; a character named Dalmuidy, competently played by Mr Jonathon Sutton.
>
> Once again, Mr McCluskie glories in his exuberant and implausible plot. However, his characterisation of Salter is, perhaps, a trifle overdone. In his efforts to portray the hypocrisy of the man, he has expressed sentiments that might disconcert the small shopkeepers in his audience. Moreover, one wonders how long the novelty of his Scotch settings will retain their appeal amongst English theatre-goers.

Despite the reviewer's quibbles, the play went on to surpass the success of *The Irresistible Rise of Tam McLean*, By the end of July 1948, Campbell's plays had earned him a total of £3,358 6s & 6d, from which Malquist deducted £814 to cover his commission, his advance and sundry, inexplicable expenses.

Odd, that picture of St Catherine's martyrdom hanging above Marie Seton's bed.

PART FOUR

Chapter One

Outside, it is raining. The street is empty. I am tired. Everything seems unreal: the photograph of my mother and her dog; McCluskie's notebooks; the grey metal filing cabinet by my desk; the typewriter; my typescript. Water droplets chase each other down the window; moving slowly; suddenly gaining momentum; merging; tracing irregular lines on the glass. Two seagulls stand on the ridge of the roof opposite. The sky is dark. It is over a week since I last saw Fiona.

That sunny morning, I was at my desk early, trying to penetrate the mystery of Campbell's much publicised break with Hargreaves in September 1948, which was to form the opening of this chapter.

All kinds of things distracted me: the milky skin that kept forming on my coffee; the damp patch that had been spreading on the wall above my bookshelves; the heavy rock music thumping in the room below; a large winged insect on the window which had bright orange legs and was raising and lowering its abdomen in a threatening manner. I was conscious of a growing panic, which I initially ascribed to writer's block but which began to attach itself willy-nilly to these insignificant events, until I realised that its true source lay in my anxiety about Fiona.

During the five months since her split with Stephen Pendle, her visits had become less and less frequent. They ceased altogether last month, after she appeared at my bed-sit one morning with her hair dyed black and spiked, wearing thickly applied eyeliner, a tight black dress and stiletto-heeled boots. She was quite agitated, but I was too shocked by her appearance to fully appreciate her mood. While I put the kettle on, she sat in my armchair, picked at a worn place on the arm, stood up again and looked out of the window. When I brought over the tea things, she returned to the chair and leaned forward as if she was about to say something, but then she sat back and resumed picking at the chair arm, a distant expression on her face.

At that moment, just as she was crossing her legs, I inadvertently caught sight of the crotch of her pants and the milky flesh of her upper thighs. I felt as if someone had hollowed out my entire chest cavity. Dry-mouthed, I handed over her tea and offered her a chocolate digestive, which she rejected with a shake of her head as she took the mug in both hands.

Going over these events last weekend, I was shamed by the idea that I had been too preoccupied with my own desire, to take account of Fiona; of the new slang words with which she peppered her conversation; of her unprecedented lassitude; of her unhealthy pallor; of her strident avowal that she was perfectly happy with her life. However, even after three weeks, the clearest image I had retained of her visit was of the black lace pattern of her pants.

I decided that I had to see her, and without further consideration I pulled on my jacket and headed out. The breeze carried all kinds of pleasing scents. The streets were divided into clearly defined blocks of light and shade. Yet, for all their clarity, and despite the numerous people crowding their pavements, they seemed to me to be suddenly devoid of meaning.

There was a musty smell in the close of Fiona's building. I rattled her tarnished brass letterbox and, while I waited, chanced to look at the landing window, which was missing a diamond panel of blue glass. Fiona herself opened the door. She was wearing a dressing gown with a small hole over her right shoulder. Seeming neither pleased nor displeased to see me, she beckoned me in with a half-hearted gesture.

Through one of the doorways leading off the hall, I saw a muscular young man drinking tea in bed; clothes strewn on the floor; an abstract painting on an easel; a charcoal drawing of a nude pinned to the wall above the mantelpiece.

In the sitting room, a girl with hair dyed bright blue munched toast and Marmite. A record was playing too loudly for comfort. It was my first visit to that flat, and everything about it jarred with the image of Fiona I had so carefully nurtured. I stood for a moment looking out of the window at a tree-filled and quite irrelevant garden.

I longed to take Fiona's hands in mine; to explain quietly and forcefully that my love for her was almost spiritual; that I was not the kind of person who looked up girls' skirts; that if she could get beyond my physical shortcomings, there was a place of unequalled beauty reserved for her in my thoughts.

Instead, I found myself trying to talk to her about my biography over the noise of the stereo and my straining heart, while her attention kept drifting to the length of water-damaged cornice running

129

above the window.

The record finished; the girl with blue hair ambled out of the room, scratching her bottom. A deep voice could be heard from somewhere singing Puccini off-key. I tried to convince myself that Fiona would not pose naked for any artist, however talented or handsome he might be.

A week has dragged by since then, and the charcoal sketch still taunts me with the image of her lying naked on a bed, offering herself to the artist's gaze, her arms behind her head, the soles of her feet pressed together. And now, through the medium of Campbell's words, a September morning in 1948 emerges in all its stray details, like a charm against the horrors of my life.

The playwright wakes suddenly from bad dreams, tattered odds and ends of which bring vividly to mind the unpleasantness at his sister Joan's wedding. Joan (veil awry; tear-stained face; satin dress) helped their father on to his feet. Nearby was an overturned table, beside which a silver-plated salt cellar, shaped like a chess bishop, described a curve round a shattered champagne flute. The gentle bridegroom was leading Campbell's sisters, Dorothy and Anne, off the dance floor. The red-haired accordionist, legs bowed, continued to play for a moment after the rest of the band had stopped. A circle of shocked faces were looking at Campbell, bubbled spittle on his lower lip, his forehead gleaming, his fists clenched, a livid bruise forming round his knuckle. His mother approached him from the far end of the room, with the stiff motions forced on her by her damaged joints. Through the windows on the opposite wall, in another, calmer world, between rustling branches, the loch surface sparkled in the August sunlight.

Campbell opens his eyes just as Hargreaves enters the room. The playwright rubs his face and without embarrassment gets up and pulls on a pair of trousers and a jumper. Then he goes to put a pot of water on to boil. Hargreaves stands in the doorway, yawns and stretches, revealing the lower curve of his belly straining against his shirt.

'I've finished the painting,' he says. Through the kitchen window, the playwright can see the back wall of the tenement opposite. A man in a vest is putting breadcrumbs out on a window ledge. Roofs and chimneys stretch away towards the west. In the distance the lower slopes of the Kilpatrick Hills rise beneath a bank of cloud. Campbell drops two heaped spoonfuls of tea into the pot.

Half an hour later, we find him sitting by the window in the artist's living room. The canvas is mounted on the easel with a grey blanket draped over it. He looks at the artist's speckled grey pullover and grey slacks.

'You look like a fisherman,' Campbell says, thinking of the freshness of seaside air; the play of light on water; a seagull's floating corpse. 'Are you finally reconciled to life in Scotland then?'

Hargreaves responds in a slightly affected Scots accent which is meant to underline his contempt for his homeland. His words are dismissive. He expresses surprise that Campbell does not take advantage of his success and move south.

As Hargreaves pulls the blanket away from the canvas, his face no doubt bears the expression made famous by Tommy Farquar in his controversial portrait of the artist: the head tilted towards the viewer so that the upper rims of the pupils disappear behind the brows; the deep lines forming a shallow V on the bridge of his nose; the high cheekbones; the heavy jowls; the uncertain smile belying the confidence of the gaze. The whole effect was summed up rather neatly by one critic as 'that compound of arrogance and fear which marks the artist in decline'.

The scene has faded into idle speculation, as happens so often. Campbell left his carefully polished passage hanging on an unfinished sentence, as if thereby to express his contempt for the painting and its insignificance in the general scheme of things – note that (quite possibly fictitious) man feeding breadbrumbs to the birds. Neither was Hargreaves's high opinion of the painting shared by posterity. It now languishes in storage at the National Gallery in Edinburgh, where I saw it last summer.

It is an ambitious work in which Hargreaves took it upon himself to trace the history of art in the twentieth century. The left-hand side is dominated by a naked woman (filched from Picasso) who is sitting with her legs apart. Predictably, the entire composition focuses on the stylised oval of her genitals. Thin brushstrokes suggest her pubic hair. An elongated red diamond represents her inner labia and subtle gradations of colour draw the eye inwards to the entrance of her vagina.

One's attention is then drawn to the right side of the painting, to a rhombus-shaped window. Through it, can be seen a hilly landscape that might have been painted by Cezanne. A number of abstract shapes, suggesting various furnishings, carry our gaze back to the woman. She appears to be in the throes of sexual ecstasy. Her hands are joined above her head, which rests at an impossible angle on her left shoulder. Her eyes are raised. Her mouth is slightly open.

It was only on my second viewing that I noticed the small area below the model's extended right foot: a chaotic swirl of clashing shapes and colours, which Hargreaves boasted was the only true image of death ever to have been put on canvas.

Thinking about the painting now, I can finally understand the almost physical pain Campbell must have felt when he became aware of the sickle-shaped scar painted above the woman's mouth.

In the absence of any direct statement by McCluskie, we have only the artist's account of what occurred after he showed Campbell the painting. The playwright apparently fell silent as he struggled to contain his emotions.

I said, 'Megan's a lovely lass, Campbell, but, as usual, you only see the surface.'

'What do you mean?' he replied, outraged.

'You don't think for a minute that I failed to see my influence on your plays, do you?' I added, warming to my theme.

'I don't know what the Hell you're talking about.' I leave his expression to your imagination. I let him reach boiling point before delivering the coup de grâce.

'What upsets you, Campbell, is that a woman could jilt you and then give herself to an old man with "rubicund Latin features and a pendulous belly". But you cannae get beyond the surface. You cannae perceive the secret harmonies. You huvnae really grasped what I'm doing at all.'

As it happened, the painting (which is still listed in the National Gallery Catalogue as *Portrait of Megan*) did nothing to restore Hargreaves's already flagging reputation. The only time that Campbell ever referred to it was in an interview shortly after Hargreaves's death, when he said, 'Not since the time of Jesus has anyone attempted to invest so much significance in the portrait of a whore.'

A week after seeing the painting, Campbell underlined his break with Hargreaves by moving into a furnished flat in Clouston Street, which he described at length in his notebook:

The lounge looks on to the street. There is a wooden picture rail, below which the walls are covered with green and white striped wallpaper. There is an imposing wooden fire surround with a wally dug at either end. On the wall over the fireplace, in an ornate gilt frame is a faded reproduction of 'The Monarch of the Glen'. Hanging beside the door is an improbable leather harness with a brass horseshoe suspended from its centre.

The bedroom overlooks the back court. There is a brass bedstead; a bedside table; a wardrobe with a rotating, fucking tie rack. In the kitchen the cupboards are painted yellow with white drawers and doors. In one of the cupboards I found a flamenco dancer made out of shells, a broken electric kettle and an egg cup with 'The Isle of Wight' written on the side.

The man from the letting agency was small and unusually thin. His feet pointed inward and deep lines on either side of his nose imparted a sneer to his face. He indicated each item with a slight nod and an extended palm, and kept stressing the importance of avoiding stains on the carpets and rugs.

'The furnishings are unique,' I assured him, 'quite unique. I wouldn't dream of altering them.' A nervous expression crossed his face as he handed me the keys. I like to think that he heard my laughter from the close.

Quite what McCluskie found amusing is not clear.

True to his word, Campbell fitted his belongings around the furnishings that were already there, relishing the occasional absurdity of their juxtapositions. He placed his desk under the living-room window, so that he could look out on to the street while he was writing. He picked up an old Underwood typewriter with a black metal casing. 'The paint on the letter "e" was almost worn away, leaving a grey residue in its angular depression.' There were three different-coloured folders beside it – red, blue and yellow – containing the definitive versions of his plays. These would subsequently provide the texts for his collected works. An empty beige folder on the other side of the typewriter awaited his next project.

He hung a recently purchased lithograph by Matisse next to the harness and horseshoe. Hargreaves's engraving he relegated to the bathroom wall above the toilet. He gave the shell flamenco dancer pride of place on the mantelpiece and purchased a number of small brass ornaments to go with it: a cannon; a boot; a windmill. He also found a tiny pair of ceramic clogs, decorated in blue with Dutch scenes. He scoured flea markets for bric-a-brac: a worm-eaten folding cake stand; a Japanese lacquered screen with a badly damaged panel – its elaborate pavilion surrounded by trees poised over a void.

One senses in this obsessive recording of minutiae Campbell's response to Hargreaves's criticism. The surface reveals its own harmonies. McCluskie doesn't strain for profundity as does the artist through an obvious coupling of sex and death. However, I believe that something monstrous lurks in these descriptions: a kind of inhuman laughter at everything – at art, at love, at beauty, at the disposable objects that people cherish. Campbell peers out from behind his prose, like a goatish god sitting among the reeds, and laughs at the pathetic probing of an unattractive virgin.

Written in that same notebook is a tantalising reference to a novel that Campbell intended to start writing at the end of 1948. He states quite explicitly his belief that he had made a mistake in becoming a playwright and considered that his true talent lay in prose writing. Nothing else remains of that novel. Its composition was interrupted by the Scottish production of *Auld Hughie Salter* and by another tumultuous love affair.

Malquist surprised Campbell by suggesting that the comedian Tommy Skelton should play the role of Hughie Salter. The agent was worried that people in Scotland might have been alienated by his decision to open McCluskie's second play in London, and he considered that Skelton's popularity would assure the play's success. Campbell was dubious about the idea. When he saw Skelton playing morose straight man to his wisecracking partner, Bobby Docherty, he was reminded of Jocky Widjin and felt once again the creeping sense of doom he associated with that clown.

As it happened, Skelton was also reluctant to accept the offer and did not agree to take the part until he met McCluskie in the Grosvenor Hotel in early November. Tommy subsequently cherished fond memories of that meeting.

The evening started awkwardly. Both agents were present. Campbell noticed that Malquist's lips made a slight slapping sound every time he took a sip of whisky. Skelton's agent looked at the table while Malquist made his offer. Then he raised his head and stroked his throat for a moment, before suggesting that a higher fee would be in order. The negotiations continued for some fifteen minutes while Campbell sat back nursing his drink in silence. At a certain point, Skelton nodded to his agent. An agreement was reached, the forms were signed and the meeting broke up.

McCluskie was collecting his coat, when he felt a hand touch his shoulder and heard Tommy say in a hauntingly familiar baritone, 'Here, Campbell, d'you fancy goin' for a pint? We can wash some of that shite out of our systems.'

'It'll take more than a few drinks to wash Malquist out of your system,' replied the playwright, smiling. After the pub closed that night, Campbell invited the comedian over to his flat for a few more whiskies. The fire in the living room had burned low during his absence. McCluskie, swaying in its uncertain glow, shovelled in some more coal. Then he threw in a hastily bundled-up sheet of newspaper, which started to unfold as it caught fire and was sucked into the chimney. Tommy noticed the dark screen zigzagging across the room, its broken panel disclosing the legs of Campbell's desk beyond.

'Here, you've kitted this place out like a Parisian bordello,' he said.

McCluskie, on one knee poking the fire, replied, 'Aye, it makes me feel at home.'

They both sat in the flickering orange light, drinking and laughing at nothing until nearly four o'clock, when Skelton suddenly roused himself, pulled out his pocket watch and said, 'Jesus, Bella will kill me. I'll have to be going.'

Two weeks later, Campbell met Tommy and his wife in the City Halls, at the party that Malquist had organised to publicise both the Scottish production of *Auld Hughie Salter* (which was scheduled to open in the Theatre Royal at the end of January 1949) and the BBC broadcast of *The Irresistible Rise of Tam McLean* (scheduled for the Saturday before Christmas).

Tommy, stooping slightly in a manner characteristic of those who are self-conscious about their height, introduced Campbell to his wife, Bella, and the three of them took a table by the stage. Initially, Bella was a bit frosty towards the playwright. He noted, rather unkindly, that 'her face was too round and her lips were thin. She had a spot on her chin and was wearing a ludicrous silver brooch shaped like a ballerina standing on the tip of one foot.' Tommy was talking too much, in order to deflect Campbell's attention from his wife's annoyance. Increasingly bored, Campbell let his gaze wander round the crowded room until it fell on Malquist.

The Gargoyle was talking to a handsome man, who suddenly, in a refined English accent, called out, 'Helen!'

A woman walked over to them with her back to me. She had black hair and was wearing a stunning black ball-gown, which plunged in loose satin folds to the small of her back. With a proprietary air, Malquist put his arm about her and clasped her right hip with his grotesque, chalky hand.

The band started playing a waltz. Campbell asked Bella to dance.

She was too taken aback to refuse. As they circled the floor, he whispered that she looked ravishing. His breath was warm in her ear. She found herself smiling and saying, 'Away with you,' into his starched, shirt front.

The music stopped. They returned to their seats. Tommy became calmer and wittier. The playwright and he fell into the easy banter they had established on their first evening out. Campbell affected not to notice Keiran Brody walking past their table with Marie Seton. He did, however, experience a pang when he realised that the Englishman and the black-haired woman had both left.

After a while, Campbell went to the toilet. On his way back, he stopped off to talk to a poet from Malquist's agency, who at that time was slipping steadily into alcoholic obscurity. Campbell wanted to ask him what he thought about Malquist, but as soon as he mentioned the agent the poet changed the subject. The playwright wondered if the few royalties from his early successes really justified his contract with Malquist, or if the agent was keeping him on for some other purpose.

Malquist's amplified voice drew all eyes to the stage, where Skelton and his partner, Bobby Docherty, went on to entertain the audience with one of their more famous routines. Campbell headed for the bar.

He became aware of a discomfort that had been with him all evening. His dinner suit made him feel like a little boy forced into his best clothes for a church service. Fighting back a sensation of emptiness, bordering on self-disgust, he ordered another whisky. As the contents of the glass followed their burning course, he contemplated returning to the Skeltons' table, since Tommy and Docherty had finished their routine. Almost without thinking, he found himself calculating his chances of seducing the comedian's wife.

It was then that he noticed a young woman just beyond the end of the bar, sitting side on to a table with her legs crossed. Her jacket (of a deep red that matched her dress and shoes) was draped over her shoulders. She was searching around in the gaping handbag on her lap for, as it turned out, a small mirror to check her lipstick. As she raised it to catch the light from the bar, she saw the reflection of the playwright leaning on the counter and extinguishing a match in his mouth.

McCluskie would later imagine her looking in that mirror at her lips and the smooth, rounded point of her chin, in which little dents and dimples would appear when she was upset. It would occur to him that she could also see the future there. The impassioned rush up two flights to his rocking hallway, where she would find herself raised against the wall; a hand cupping each buttock; his rough chin burning and scratching her throat; the maddening pressure building on her silk-covered pubis. The sudden interruption as his foot knocked the wooden cake stand by the bathroom door, which folded and fell – dropping, in succession, an antique armillary sphere, an ebony elephant with a missing tusk, and a cut-glass ink bottle.

Then she would witness herself in a receding perspective, watching the playwright carefully packing up a Chinese chess set and wrapping it in Christmas paper. She would experience the acid burn of discovering the name 'Dorothy' written on the tag; the recriminations; the reassurances; the reconciliation; the pain of a clumsily inserted finger.

Smaller still, as if at the end of a long corridor, would be the anger and despair: Campbell walking beside her, patting her shoulder in an unbearable manner, as if dealing with a child, and carefully avoiding the accusation in her eyes, while the wind whips up leaves and presses a chocolate wrapper against a lamp post with a curiously human insistence.

Finally, in a blur of flesh, light and darkness, eternity would swing shut with the click of a clasp. She would drop the mirror back into her bag, smile at the approaching playwright and say, 'My name's Alison Drew. I'm pleased to meet you.'

We find the playwright in his flat. It is an overcast day in February 1949. The poor light fails to illuminate the far side of the room. Campbell, sitting with his back to the window, is reading a letter from his sister Dorothy. Her handwriting arouses a feeling of tenderness in him for which he can find no outlet.

She thanks him for the chess set, but says that he shouldn't have gone to so much expense. Then she goes on to write that their mother has severe pains in hips and legs, which make her constantly irritable; that their sister Joan is expecting a baby in July. At the end of the letter, her matter-of-fact tone slips to reveal her anguish. (Campbell remembers pulling back a piece of cotton, sticky with blood, to uncover three, surprisingly small, entry wounds.) She begs him to apologise to their father, saying that if he does so, things can return to normal.

Campbell puts down the letter, lowers his head and rubs his eyes. Then he goes to his desk. On top of the empty folder is a selection of reviews praising the new production of *Auld Hughie Salter*, a copy of a contract from Gaumont Pictures for a twelve-month option on *The Irresistible Rise of Tam McLean*, and a letter from Malquist reminding the playwright that the terms of their agreement oblige him to write seven plays.

Later that year, after his new play opened in Glasgow, Campbell told a journalist that it had started as an anagram. In an attempt to overcome a block, induced by various emotional pressures, he had borrowed an anthology of plays from the library. One afternoon in March, he had started making anagrams of one of the play titles in the anthology, chosen at random by closing his eyes and sticking a pin in the contents page. He had thus come up with the title *Deeds and the Crow*. When asked what the original title had been, Campbell leaned towards the journalist, winked and said, 'Now that would be telling.' Given McCluskie's reputation, the journalist concluded that the playwright was pulling his leg. In his finished article he pointed out that Campbell's (now public) breach with Hargreaves provided a more likely inspiration for the play.

I myself have tried to determine the truth of Campbell's claim. It was like looking for a needle in a haystack, since Campbell left no clear record of the anthology he used. I worked at the problem for a couple of hours one evening, but all I ended up with were a jumble of letters, a headache and a queasy sensation in the pit of my stomach.

Deeds and the Crow is set in an English country house. There are only four characters, none of whom is Scottish: Edward Deeds, a writer in his fifties; Charles Warwick, his agent; Pauline Gaveston, a young poet made famous by a poem entitled 'The Crow' – a parody of Poe's 'The Raven' – in which a dead woman complains to a crow about the neurotic lover whose overweening possessiveness has driven her to suicide; Reginald Spencer, a university student whose first novel has been accepted by a publisher, on condition that he makes certain changes.

In two creakily contrived acts, we are presented with the outline of the plot. For nearly two years, Deeds has been having an affair with Pauline. During that time, he has stopped writing his populist fiction, in the hope of making himself more attractive to her. However, the harder he tries to mould himself in her image, the less she likes him. Unbeknown to Deeds, his agent has become increasingly dependant on his success, since losing many of the writers whose reputations he has helped to launch. This mixture of failure and dependency has twisted Warwick inwardly, so that he harbours an almost pathological hatred of Pauline.

Neither Deeds nor Warwick is aware that Pauline is also having an affair with the young writer, Spencer, and that she has promised to marry him when his novel is published. Pauline has persuaded Deeds to invite Reginald to an intimate gathering at his house, hoping that Deeds and his agent might help to get Reginald's novel published. Warwick, ignorant of this arrangement, plans to murder Pauline.

The intricate, implausible plot, the upper-class English accents, the country house setting all prepare the audience for a farce with complicated bedroom scenes. However, at the start of the third act, Warwick joins the other three at the dinner table and announces that a crow has got into his bedroom. He then proceeds to pass around a feather that he has quite clearly taken from his pillow.

The play shifts into a darker mode. Inexplicable shadows appear in odd corners of rooms. The dialogue becomes peculiar as the actors emphasise their lines in a curious manner that changes the meaning of what they are saying. Finally, Reginald, divesting himself of his heroic role, runs screaming from the house and Warwick kills Pauline with a viciousness that nothing in the play has prepared us for. While he carries out the act, the flickering shadows projected on the set take on the appearance of a giant crow flapping its wings. They are still there after Pauline is dead. Warwick starts gibbering. His distorted logic tells him that the crow emanates from Deeds. As he slowly mounts the stairs, he swears that he will send the writer to Hell.

By Campbell's standards, the play was not a success. Few critics realised that the last three acts are seen through the eyes of the madman, Warwick. It was to be another six years before it found its audience, when a sensitive French translation brought it to the attention of the practitioners of the Nouveau Roman.

Strangely enough, Malquist liked the play. In his crabbed handwriting, reminiscent of medieval legal documents, he wrote to Campbell, 'It is an amusing and perceptive piece, but, as you are no doubt aware, it is doomed to failure. Of course, you realise this changes nothing.'

Chapter Two

A moonless night: narrow streets; worn steps leading up to ill-fitting doors; broken windowpanes stuffed with material; light from the street lamps reflecting off the damp cobblestones; in the distance, shots and screams can be heard; a man in a long, black leather coat stands on a street corner with his hands behind his back. Nearby, a soldier in a black uniform aims his rifle at a young woman who is kneeling on the road, trying to cover herself with the torn remnants of her blouse. The body of a young man lies in the gutter beside her.

In the auditorium a woman in the fourth row, whose neck and shoulders stand out in the darkness, raises a gloved hand to her mouth and quietly clears her throat before releasing the cough that has been tickling her for the past few minutes. A portly man behind her alters his position on his groaning chair. The material of his trousers catches on the numbered white plaque that has been fixed to the seat in front with two small screws. Three rows behind him an accounts clerk in an ill-fitting suit lets his hand fall naturally on to the chair and then, after a series of barely perceptible movements, brings his knuckles into contact with the thigh of the shorthand typist who is sitting on his left with her hands clasped on her lap. She expresses her distaste at the developments on the stage by making a sharp tutting sound. The clerk, in panic, withdraws his hand.

The balcony above them is decorated with plaster mouldings and gilt paint. In a box on the right-hand side of the auditorium, Campbell McCluskie sits beside a young woman. Malquist sits in the semi-darkness behind them. It is the opening night of Campbell's fifth play, *The Massacre*. The playwright, however, is not looking at the stage, but at the audience. The woman has a slim, slightly hooked nose. She is bored. The play strikes her as being needlessly obscure.

McCluskie seduced her three weeks earlier, after a dinner dance at a hotel just north of Glasgow. It was a mild evening. They were walking together in the hotel grounds. The moon was visible through a circular opening in the clouds, its craters and blue shaded seas clearly delineated against its white surface. Light striking the cloud patterns within the opening created curious striated shadows that resembled rock formations.

'It's like the inside of a cone,' said Campbell, gesturing to the moon and the clouds. Then he put his arm around her waist. His attentive, sympathetic expression made her think that he was really interested in her. She told him about the novel she was editing at Coultt's and complained of difficulties with her colleagues. In the lower reaches of the grounds the path swung to the right, following a line of trees. Between the branches, it was just possible to make out the lower slopes of the Campsie Fells. She found herself tolerating caresses that, under the circumstances, she would not normally have permitted. 'It was', she later reasoned, 'a momentary delirium with an unpleasant aftermath.'

Although McCluskie would go on to describe the marks she left on his neck and the way she crossed her legs on his back when she came, her most enduring memory was of the playwright standing up as soon as they were finished, removing the used and repulsive contraceptive, vigorously wiping his penis with his handkerchief and then buttoning up his trousers.

Sitting in the box in the Theatre Royal, she is angry at herself for having got involved with him and wonders why she didn't realise how insecure he was. She feels a mounting revulsion as she watches him gazing fearfully around the auditorium, trying to gauge the reaction to his play.

However, McCluskie was merely subjecting the audience to his cold, cynical gaze. He recorded in his notebook a number of cruel and salacious observations, most of which must have been imaginary given the darkness in the auditorium. When the lights came up for the interval, he noticed 'a beautiful woman, resembling Greta Garbo, who was sitting in the front row of the circle. The fat, balding man beside her must have fallen asleep during the performance, and was at that moment blinking and looking about him like an agitated goldfish.'

McCluskie had finished the play some two months before it opened. It is set in an unnamed city and revolves around the massacre of a minority religious sect (also unidentified), which has been instigated by a sinister and powerful individual named Guise.

He was dissatisfied with that first production. He felt that the black uniforms worn by the soldiers carrying out the massacre led to the mistaken belief that he was writing about the Holocaust. He subsequently told one interviewer that the inspiration for the play came from much closer to home, but, as usual, he made no effort to clarify his meaning. Whatever Campbell intended, the play owed its success to that misapprehension.

In fact, the revolutionary aspects of the play have never been fully appreciated. Reviewers praised its apposite political message, its ambitious, 'McCluskian' central character and its strong plot. Audiences relished its earthiness, its humour and its pace. Everyone regarded it as a return to form after the incomprehensible *Deeds and the Crow*.

During the first act,

GUISE *and his soldiers burst in on the philosopher,* RAMUS, *as he sits in his book-lined study, observing the complicated motions of an armillary sphere.* GUISE *wanders about, pulls a book from a shelf, looks at its opening page and then hurls it across the room. He pauses before the reproduction of an anatomical engraving which is mounted on the wall. Then he turns to look at* RAMUS, *who is apparently indifferent to their presence.*

GUISE: You're a crusty old fool, Ramus. Maybe you should have spent your time chasing real women. They offer more pleasures than mouldy engravings.

RAMUS: I am working, Guise. Please leave me alone. There is nothing here of any interest to you.

GUISE: Ah yes; your precious work. I have read your books with their absurd refutations and conceits. Surely you can understand that such arguments threaten our Faith.

RAMUS: I have made no reference to politics, sex or money. Now please call off your brutes. Religion is of as much concern to me as a child inscribing patterns in the dirt with a bent twig.

GUISE: You cannot escape from your family or your name, Ramus. You cannot ignore History. And you cannot refute this. *(Guise draws his gun and shoots Ramus in the head.)*

As the play proceeds, Guise sheds various masks: religious zealot, homicidal sadist, Machiavellian conspirator, demagogue, betrayed husband and, finally, powerless fugitive. The two opposing religions (which it transpires are separated only by minor points of ritual and belief) offer momentary consolation to their adherents and justification for the various atrocities that ensue. As systems of belief, they cannot account for Guise's increasingly erratic behaviour or the disordered city that McCluskie has created.

Now, when I read the play, I perceive the subtle pattern that Campbell has woven through it, like the child's patterns invoked by Ramus. There is a painting on the wall in Guise's wife's bedroom, of Venus standing in her shell, which we see when Guise discovers her writing to her lover. Later, while Guise and the lover duel, a blind beggar sits at the corner of the stage, holding a seashell that is surely invisible to most of the audience.

Many such instances, scattered through the play, go to make the secret pattern that to the best of my knowledge I was the first to discover. In the process of my search I was reduced to a kind of referential mania which left me exhausted and feverish. But still I could find no trace of a pattern in McCluskie's life. Everything seemed contingent, even Ingram Farqueson, that psychopath with different-coloured eyes, who had paused to light a cigarette in the entrance to a close one sunny June morning in 1954.

As for my own life, it has been a shambles from the start. I recall the occasion I first told Fiona of my mother's death. It was February 1990. By then Fiona was coming over to my bed-sit on a weekly basis to help me with the biography. It is strange now to think of the hopes I entertained then. The novelty of having Fiona in my room had not yet given way to the quiet despair I would later feel in her presence.

She would kneel on a cushion with my disordered papers spread around her, or she would sit at my desk, displaying the prominent bone at the base of her nape as she bent over a list of references she was methodically placing in alphabetical order. Meanwhile I would bundle about the room making tea or coffee, or sit in my armchair, a book spread ostentatiously in my lap, a finger at my pursed lips, harbouring a preternatural awareness of her every movement.

On that particular February afternoon, I was heating up some soup. Debussy's *Prélude à l'après-midi d'un faune* was playing on my stereo, but it was more or less drowned out by a neighbour's television blaring out the *Grandstand* theme.

As Fiona cleared my desk to make room for the lunch things, she came across the photograph of my mother and her dog.

'Is that your mother?' she asked, wiping dust from the glass with her sleeve. Over lunch, I told her the whole sorry story. Fiona was sitting along from me on an old swivel chair I had obtained from the university. Side on to the desk, her legs crossed, she reached over to take my hand. She was wearing thick woollen tights on which tiny bobbles had formed, a short skirt and a loose turtleneck pullover which disclosed her clavicles when she leaned forward. Everything about her belied the bloody events unfolding in my glib narrative. It now strikes me that I betrayed my mother's memory; for I was aching with desire for Fiona, too preoccupied with how I might cross the gap separating us, to concentrate on what I was saying, or on Fiona's assurances that I was not to blame; that my mother would have died happy in the knowledge of my safe delivery; that it is futile to impose a moral on chance occurrences. Only when she suggested that I visit my parents' honeymoon cottage in Kyleakin did I emerge from my reverie. She let go of my arm and, gathering the dishes together, she brightly (too brightly?) offered to make another cup of tea.

Later that year, as I slowly climbed a hill outside Kyleakin, rain drumming on my umbrella, I wondered how I could have believed it possible that Fiona might join me on that futile pilgrimage. Trying not to picture what she was doing with Stephen Pendle in the abstract Greek landscapes my jealousy conjured, I gazed at the dry stone wall running alongside me to disappear into the mist ahead. In my pocket was a scrap of paper on which was written the strange Gaelic name I had gleaned from one of my father's postcards.

Eventually, I came upon a gaunt man in a black oilskin coat and a peaked cap. He had thick red sideburns and a roll-up hanging from the corner of his mouth. Beside him sat a bedraggled collie which kept shifting its eyes from side to side and sniffing the air. I showed the man my scrap of paper. He looked at it, looked at me, looked back at it and then pointed over the wall to where a rectangle of grey stones on the ground marked the outline of a cottage. I tried to remonstrate with him. I told him that that could not possibly be the cottage my parents had stayed in, but he merely flicked his roll-up over the wall, whistled to his dog and walked away, his coat flapping about his legs. I turned and headed back down the hill.

Dimly lit hotel lounge. Cheddar cheese and oatcakes arranged upon a plate. View through the casement of a bank of cloud obscuring the mainland. A frantic fly repeatedly striking the glass. Me, sitting with my round back to the room. Floral upholstery on the chair opposite, assuming every shade and nuance of my despair.

Now I find in my fruitless quest a curious echo of the trip that McCluskie took to France at the end of the summer of 1950. But what purpose might lie in this duplication I cannot tell.

It was a particularly radiant August. Campbell, flush from the success of *The Massacre*, bought himself a car in Calais with his smuggled cash and headed to Normandy in search of Geneviève

Morel's farm. After five frustrating days, he gave up on the ghost and drove to Paris.

On arriving there, he found a room in a hotel in the rue de Navarin. Having breakfasted in its dim, little dining room, he would walk around the streets until he stumbled on a familiar landmark. His French was appalling, and so eating out proved to be a hit or miss affair, until he met up with a young woman called Brigitte Louvet, in a chic café overlooking the Luxembourg Gardens.

The inebriated playwright, being rather free with his money, had gathered an odd little group about him, none of whom could speak any English. Of that group, he would subsequently recall only one – a spindly young man in a dark suit and polo-neck jumper, who for some odd reason kept patting the side of his nose with his bony forefinger and whispering, 'Un coup de dés jamais n'abolira le hasard,' over and over in his ear, until Campbell managed to repeat it correctly back to him. Whereupon the curious fellow lost interest and poured himself another wine.

Brigitte, seeing her opportunity, drew Campbell aside as he made his way back from the toilet. She led him out of the café before anyone noticed his absence and took him to her tiny apartment, where, shortly afterwards, Campbell passed out.

When he woke up on the following morning, she was sitting up in bed beside him drinking coffee. He immediately noticed her small, slightly upturned nose, her blond hair, her full lips and the rosy edge of her areola that was visible above the blanket. Campbell, still in his clothes, was lying on top of the blanket with his left arm twisted under him. She smiled at him. He looked around the room.

Just at that moment, a key turned in a lock and one of the doors opposite the bed swung inwards. A tall, handsome (yet hesitant) man appeared in the doorway. He looked from Campbell to Brigitte and back to Campbell again. Brigitte suddenly jumped up, spilling coffee all over the place, and, beating the bed with both hands, started screaming at the top of her voice, 'Jamais! Jamais! Jamais! Jamais! Jamais!' A smile flickered on the man's face. He raised his hat, revealing a completely bald head, bowed and quietly left.

During the next two weeks, Brigitte applied herself assiduously to spending Campbell's money. Only once, at the end of that period, did she allow him to have sex with her. They were on the floor of his hotel room. He was disconcerted by her refusal to let him touch her nipples and by her indifference to his foreplay. As he reached his climax, she merely twisted her head in order to look at a pigeon that was cooing and strutting about on the windowsill.

Afterwards, he watched her from his hotel window walking along the rue de Navarin in her lemon two-piece suit. Her hair as usual was inexpertly held in place with a large tortoiseshell clip and had begun unravelling as soon as she got out on the street. Unaccountably, Campbell confessed to his notebook that he wept when he saw her hands making those familiar darting motions as she tried to rearrange her hair while she walked. He had to sell his car in order to settle his hotel bill and pay his fare home.

Of his last day in Paris, Campbell would later remember the thick smell of urine on the streets, a man in grey overalls and a grey hat hosing down the gutters at the end of the rue de Navarin, and the die he discovered between the seat cushions while the train stood at the platform in the Gare du Nord.

Back in Scotland, he retired to his flat and refused to see or speak to anyone, except the woman he employed to bring in his food and do his cleaning. She told a concerned Tommy Skelton that Campbell was forever reading but that she never once saw him write anything.

That is how things remained until the evening of 20 November 1950, when Bella Skelton answered an insistent knocking on the door to find McCluskie with a bottle of whisky in one hand and a box of chocolates in the other. He stayed up talking with Tommy after she went to bed, and she heard his voice booming through the floor for a good half-hour before she managed to fall asleep. She dreamed that Campbell arrived uninvited at a dinner party she had organized for her dead parents. He sat down next to her and started to scratch his name on the table with a steak knife while doing something unmentionable to her with his left hand. Bella was surprised and a little upset when Tommy said in a harsh voice, 'I bet you enjoyed that.'

Malquist had been busy during Campbell's absence and was furious that the playwright had made no attempt to answer his letters. A critically acclaimed production of *The Massacre* which had been staged off Broadway had attracted the attention of a New York producer, who wanted to see more of Campbell's work. Malquist had posted *The Irresistible Rise of Tam McLean* out to him. The producer had been enthusiastic about the play but had asked for Campbell's permission to adapt it to a New York setting. He had subsequently cabled the agent to tell him that he had a writer in mind, Joe Valdarena, and that he was willing to pay McCluskie to come to America to explain some of the obscurities of the Glaswegian dialect.

146

Malquist was mollified by Campbell's immediate agreement to the New York proposal and by the finished play *Shona of Lismore*, which Campbell now showed him for the first time.

It would be the spring of 1951 before Campbell would fly to America. Joe Valdarena met him at the airport. He was a small Italian with curly black hair, whose acerbic wit initially got on Campbell's nerves. It was clear that Joe resented both the playwright's presence and the job he had been given of showing Campbell round the city. Their first port of call was the producer's office. Campbell wrote,

> I could tell that he was a slippery customer as soon as I saw him; a man just like the Gargoyle but thinner and older. He gave me the briefest handshake courtesy allowed and then gestured to a leather swivel chair. Apparently, Joe was meant to stand.
>
> 'I bow to Joe in all matters relating to dialect,' I said after the preliminaries had been dispensed with, 'but I will not have the plot tampered with.'
>
> 'I see; and is there anything else?'
>
> 'Yes, the title has to be "Louie Diamond".'

Campbell would subsequently describe his time in New York as being 'like those sequences in Hollywood movies when a person's success is conveyed through a succession of images – upturned faces, neon lights, theatre façades, glittering skyscrapers – all shot at crazy angles, as if time is compressed and the entire city is collapsing about you'.

The only calm he experienced in the two weeks he stayed there was the sunny morning he spent strolling round Greenwich Village with Joe, during which he purchased the novel *Bend Sinister*, by Vladimir Nabokov, from a second-hand bookseller. Afterwards, over a beer, Joe suggested that in view of their slow progress on the play it might be an idea to stay with his sister, Grazia, in Baltimore, so that they could escape the distractions of Manhattan and devote more time to writing.

The journey in Joe's ageing Packard took two leisurely days. The two writers had by then come to an understanding that, if it did not lead to a meeting of minds, did allow them to tolerate each other's company. Campbell sat in the back with his legs stretched across a plaid rug, reading *Bend Sinister* and jotting notes. He now used a sturdy notebook with waterproof covers. Occasionally, Joe, looking at Campbell in his rear-view mirror, would extol the virtues of his sister's cooking, or bad-mouth his brother-in-law.

It gives me a peculiar thrill to read the notes taken on that journey. The odd strokes, shaky lines and deviations in Campbell's handwriting record the unforeseen jolts and turns of the car. As I struggle to decipher the words, I feel as if I am accompanying McCluskie to that river in New Jersey, with the meadow beyond and the horse standing in the dappled shade on the far bank; to that diner, with its circular stools lining the counter and its surly waitress frying burgers on a griddle; to that industrial city on the Chesapeake which so reminded Campbell of Glasgow.

Grazia's husband, William Brady, taught literature in Johns Hopkins University. They lived in a two-storey brick-row house. Grazia was on the porch when they arrived. Leaning on the balustrade with one arm of her sunglasses in her mouth, she watched them unload their bags. William pushed open the front door and the screen and approached them with both hands held out in greeting.

That evening, they dined on chicken and tomato risotto and drank wine late into the night. Joe and William began an old argument about the atomic bombs in Japan. As it grew more heated, Campbell wandered into the kitchen, where Grazia was preparing coffee. She apologised for the behaviour of her husband and brother. Campbell shrugged and told her it didn't bother him. Then he looked over her shoulder at the window. The entire room was reflected against the darkness outside, only a nearby street lamp showing through. Grazia, a full-figured woman in her early thirties with olive skin and dark, shoulder-length hair, was leaning over the table to load a tray with the coffee things. Campbell noticed that she was wearing a silver bracelet with an amethyst setting. Joe's loud Brooklyn accent could be heard from the lounge. Shaking her head, Grazia mimicked him and then smiled at Campbell's reflection in the window. As she grasped the edge of the tray, Campbell placed his hand lightly on hers and said that he would carry it through.

Owing to William's sterility, the house had two spare bedrooms. Campbell took one, just above the kitchen and with the same view of a busy intersection; Joe took the other. During the day, they worked on the play in William's book-lined study. In the evenings, they talked with William and Grazia.

McCluskie found the job of translating the play dull and mechanical. He would have been bored senseless were it not for

148

Joe's persistent attempts to meddle with the plot. After three weeks, they had completed four acts.

It was then that the producer phoned to tell them he had assembled a director and cast, and insisted that rehearsals start the following week. Joe hired a typist (a thin, sallow girl with sinus problems) to type four copies of the acts they had so far completed. Then he drove to Manhattan to deliver three copies to the director.

Joe subsequently phoned McCluskie to tell him that he would be delayed for a few days while he checked the proofs of his latest novel (*Death Occurred Last Night*, the fourth to feature hard-boiled private eye Joe D'Allessandro).

On the weekend Joe left, William invited Campbell to a small party organised by one of his friends in the Faculty. Shortly after they arrived at the elegant apartment on Saint Paul's where the party was being held, Campbell started talking to an attractive woman in a black dress. It transpired that she was married to an eminent mathematician called Kolowski, whose piercing brown eyes and thick eyebrows were just visible over William Brady's shoulder. Campbell was not able to speak to Jean Kolowski for long. People crowded around him to listen to his accent. Some among them proudly traced their ancestry back to Scotland. The playwright laughed and drank, enjoying the attention; flirted with various women; found his thoughts returning more and more frequently to Grazia; and ended up, by the by, with the mathematician in a small sitting room cum study that the man of the house used as a den.

Kolowski was drunk. He invited Campbell to join him on the sofa. A standard lamp nearby created an atmosphere of warm intimacy. The open door framed a view that took in part of the hallway and the open doorway to the lounge, where Grazia was talking to Kolowski's wife.

Kolowski refilled Campbell's glass with Southern Comfort from a crystal decanter which left a sticky square on the small table beside the sofa.

'So you are a playwright then,' said Kolowski. His accent bore traces of his European origins (Silesia, Berlin, Danzig). He took a sip of his drink before continuing. 'I think you will find that yours is a dying art. Mathematics is the language of the future. Elegant equations will soon replace all this confusion, this babble. We have already described forces powerful enough to destroy a city. Soon we will have equations that will explain everything, even the beautiful curve of my wife's cheek. Let me add, in parenthesis, that if you so much as lay a finger on her I will crush you with my bare, but quite powerful, hands.'

Before Campbell could reply, William Brady's congenial bald head appeared in the doorway.

'A little man's talk in the den; that's what I like,' he said, and lowered his rangy frame into the chair. Kolowski made his excuses and left. Campbell remained, but paid little attention to what Brady said.

Certain connections were forming in the playwright's head: Hiroshima; a mathematician; a jealous husband; a crime of passion. These were the first stirrings of *The Life and Death of Doctor Frost*.

The title came to him five days later. Campbell wrote it down in his notebook, together with a rough outline of the play. Then, in a sudden access of emotion, he rushed to the kitchen where Grazia was making her morning coffee. He lifted her off the floor and planted a kiss on her mouth. She responded. He slipped his hands under her buttocks. She wrapped her legs about his hips. Her skirt rode up. Her hands moved down between her thighs and began to unbutton his fly. Knocking one of the chairs on to the floor, he deposited her on to the kitchen table and pulled her blouse clear of her waistband. Impatiently he began to undo the buttons. One flew off and rolled under the cooker. He began to kiss her throat, her clavicle, her dark brown nipples. She lay back on the table and pulled aside her pants. He caught a glimpse of pink flesh amidst the black hair down there.

Just before they came simultaneously, a taxi collided with a car at the intersection below. Grazia's flailing arms knocked a plastic cruet set off the table. The taxi driver started hitting the bonnet of the car and swearing. Steam rose from the taxi's broken radiator. A delivery boy from the shop across the street looked on, whistled and rubbed his shoe up and down his calf. Then he leaned his bicycle against the shopfront and disappeared into the shop. Another car pulled up, just short of the intersection, and a young woman in sunglasses got out on the driver's side. Campbell's flaccid penis slipped harmlessly out. Semen dripped on the table. That evening, William asked Grazia what had happened to the table cloth.

'I spilled mustard on it,' she replied, and put his food down in front of him.

Joe returned two days later. Campbell had no further opportunity of seeing Grazia alone. When, after another week's work, the still snivelling typist delivered copies of the final act, William suggested a small celebration.

Grazia cooked her special pasta sauce. William caused a scene by suggesting that it wasn't up to her usual standards. Joe flared up at him. Grazia fled the room. Campbell had to restrain Joe from hitting William, who just smiled and drank his wine. After a while, Joe calmed down. He asked Campbell to join him for a drink, but the playwright declined.

McCluskie then found himself alone with William. Brady made no effort to voice his suspicions. Nevertheless, a fierce argument rose up between them. They raged at each other for nearly an hour, before Campbell announced that he was going to bed. Later that night, Campbell could hear William arguing with Grazia through the wall. The playwright lay with his hands behind his head, smiling at the wedge of light cast on the ceiling by a nearby street lamp.

Chapter Three

It occurred to Campbell, as he sat listening to the young woman, that there was something sickly about that proscenium arch with its scallop-shaped lampshades. He was in the theatre bar beside the low partition separating it from the stalls. *Shona of Lismore* was due to open later that evening. The actress playing Shona was on stage under a spotlight, one foot tilted back on its stiletto heel, talking to the director. An usherette was walking up the aisle, buttoning her maroon jacket, a torch tucked under one arm. The young journalist sitting opposite Campbell had just asked him for his impressions of the *Louie Diamond* opening in New York. He toyed with the idea of describing the romantic view of Manhattan from his hotel window, thinking it might make the journalist raise those exquisitely shaped eyebrows, but the back alley reality of rusting fire escapes and his drunken debauch with a prostitute clouded his thoughts. Moreover, he had more or less decided that he would seduce the lead actress after the show.

The journalist, Mary Ryder, would subsequently be Campbell's sole female biographer. Just as she was winding up the interview, Robert Colwan, the actor playing Angus, entered the bar. Campbell experienced an all too familiar pang when he saw how eager Mary was to speak to him. Consoling himself with the knowledge that Colwan's sexual tastes didn't stretch to young women, Campbell made a conspicuous show of taking out his copy of Coleridge's poems while Mary went off to speak to the actor. So busy was he observing Colwan brush something from his garish Paisley scarf that he didn't notice the photograph slipping out from between the pages of his book.

Mary was quick to conclude that the small piece of dirt Colwan was so assiduously cleaning from his scarf was none other than herself. She decided to leave with as much dignity as she could muster. But, on her way to the cloakroom to collect her raincoat, she noticed the photograph under Campbell's table.

'Oh, it's Trevor White, the writer,' she said, handing it to him.

'I didn't realise,' he replied. 'It belonged to my aunt.' Looking into Campbell's eyes at that moment, Mary discerned a profound sadness that belied his taciturn self-confidence.

Two days later, she told herself that it was because of that sadness, and because of the careful manner with which he had replaced the photograph in the book, that she now found herself with Campbell on a train bound for Exeter. Night was falling on the speeding landscape. Campbell closed all the blinds in the compartment and kneeled down in front of her.

'Someone's bound to come in,' said Mary, trying to push his hands back down her legs. His thumbs described circles on her inner thighs. Mary slid forwards on her seat. Campbell worked her pants down over her suspenders, raising her leg and freeing her left foot from the silk garment, which came to rest around her right ankle in a series of concentric folds, each with its own highlight and shadow. Campbell looked at these for a moment and then pressed his face between her legs. Mary, sighing, began to enjoy the danger of interruption and gave herself over to pleasure. However, a quite inappropriate anxiety had taken hold of Campbell, which deprived him of any pleasure in her eventual orgasm.

On the following morning, they took a bus north along the River Exe. Campbell tried 'to focus on the beautiful, wooded scenery; on our fellow passengers (that old woman clutching a brown paper bag, on which was a circular inscription in faded red ink – David Lapiner's Pharmacy); on the purple ear of the driver; on the vibrating gear stick. By mid-morning, the sun had risen above the hills on our right. Mary was reading, but she would periodically look up from her book and smile. Crescent shaped dimples formed about the raised ends of her lips.'

They parted with the bus at Dunster and eventually managed to hitch a lift to Porlock. Once there, Campbell lost no time in booking them into the Seaview Hotel. As a joke, he registered them as Samuel and Theresa Coleridge, but the allusion was lost on the receptionist.

Over the next two days, they only left their room 'to eat and to excrete'. They had sex repeatedly. In between times, Mary would read, while Campbell stood looking through the window at the harbour; at the grey sky; at the ever-changing, foam-flecked sea. As the hours progressed, Mary wondered why she was so attracted to the playwright, but she failed to rationalise her feelings. On the third night, she dreamed that [she] was standing at the seashore. Campbell was further down the beach, dragging a rowing boat towards the shoreline. A little girl nearby was playing a dulcimer. Campbell suddenly shouted, 'Mary!' and I was about to approach him, when I noticed he was addressing the girl. The girl, a sickly-looking child, stopped playing and skipped over to him. The pair of them attempted without success to fit the dulcimer into the boat. Eventually, she clambered aboard, leaving the dulcimer on the beach, and Campbell dragged the boat into the water.

At this point, I began to run towards them shouting Campbell's name, but he merely waved me back and pointed at an island that was visible across the water. Undeterred, I continued to run after them. As I drew near, Campbell leaned over the side of the boat and spat a diamond into the water. I noticed that he had a cut over his right eye, and then I woke to find myself alone in the bed.

Seized by a terrible panic, I groped for the light switch. Campbell's clothes and bag were gone. The wardrobe door was open. I could see my dress hanging inside. My clothes were still scattered where Campbell had thrown them in his passion. My book was on the bedside table with the flap of its dust wrapper still marking my place. Beside it was a wooden box with a pattern of inlaid wood on its lid. In the centre were four diamonds, one within the other, in contrasting shades. However, the inlay of the central diamond was missing. The box was empty, save for a single cufflink engraved with the letter 'I'.

I quote from the foreword of Mary Ryder's (highly subjective) biography of the playwright. She claimed that, at the time of the dream, she had no knowledge of Campbell's older sister; a claim I can't take seriously. However, I am more troubled by the fact that she never learned the true identity of Campbell's murderer and so could have had no reason to invent the detail of that cufflink.

After leaving Porlock, McCluskie spent a week in London. He would return day after day to the same warren of damp streets to visit the same flea markets and antiquarian bookshops, 'each with its ancient, long fingered proprietor brewing tea, or reading in the half-light at the back of the shop'. Campbell would search desperately through dusty portfolios and books ('like a dog chasing its own tail') until he finally rooted out a set of stills from *The Cabinet of Doctor Caligari*, an old leather-bound volume and a collection of stories by an obscure follower of Poe named Arthur Smythe.

The books were still in the McCluskie museum when I visited it. The Smythe collection, *Bella Donna and Other Stories*, was published in New York in 1904. Facing its title page, behind a sheet of tissue paper, was the engraving of a woman (who strongly resembled Campbell's Aunt Dorothy) standing in a city street beneath a lamp post, half turning to look at the viewer. The other book was an altogether stranger affair. On its title page, within a border decorated with terrifying demonic creatures, was written

'The Necronomicon'

of

Abdul Alhazred

Made English by James Hasolle, Esquire

(Qui est Mercuriophilus Anglicus)

London

Printed by J. Flesher for Richard Mynne

At the Sign of St. Paul, in Little Britain

1650

On returning to Clouston Street in late September 1951, Campbell hung the Caligari film stills mounted and framed on either side of the window so that he could see them while he was writing. He read and re-read the title story of the Smythe collection and he studied in depth the section of *The Necronomicon* dealing with demonology. Then he started writing *The Life and Death of Doctor Frost*.

His life now entered a period of stability he had not enjoyed since he lived in Belmont Crescent. After a day spent writing, he would socialise with the Skeltons and their circle. He made his peace with Keiran Brody and Marie Seton, who had recently married. He was also to be seen on a number of occasions drinking with members of the backstage crew from the Theatre Royal.

Once again, it is difficult to comprehend why Campbell changed his life at this particular time. Perhaps he recognised that things had been running out of control. Perhaps he merely felt the need to recuperate. Mary Ryder believed that it was because of the strong, barely admissible, feelings that she had aroused in him. However, she is a decidedly unreliable witness.

Anthony Shaw, rooting around in the gutter as usual, suggests that Campbell was smitten with Anne Powheid, the young woman Malquist had recently employed as an assistant; a quite ludicrous suggestion, given the role she was to play in Campbell's unfolding tragedy.

When I interviewed her, Anne told me of how she had met Malquist at a lecture given by Campbell on the future of Scottish drama. She had asked a question that had angered the playwright.

'Campbell didn't like it when people disagreed with him,' she said. 'And I had asked him why he didn't write plays that addressed Scotland's many social ills. I don't know what came over me. I had never liked socially committed literature. I suppose that I was merely playing Devil's advocate.'

Anne went on to tell me that Malquist had introduced himself after the lecture. The agent had displayed an uncanny awareness of what she wanted from life. The job he had offered her was exactly what she had been looking for, and resolved a number of family problems that were preoccupying her at the time.

Although the job had proved to be interesting and unusually well paid, she confessed that she had grown terrified of Malquist. He was, so far as she could tell, an intelligent man, but he had no interest in literature. He received frequent visits from an unsavoury character named Nicholas Skeres. Often, there were telephone calls from hard-voiced men who refused to give their names. She occasionally found it difficult to match up writers' royalties with the agency's income. But she understood the dangers of probing too deeply into these matters.

By the time Campbell started working on his new play, Malquist was leaving most of the important decisions to Anne. She read the manuscripts and took on the new authors. Campbell may have hoped that, since this was the case, he would have no further dealings with Malquist. If so, he was sorely mistaken. Malquist retained full control over McCluskie's work.

I would suggest that the clue to Campbell's sense of well-being lies in a note he made in his hotel room on the night before his return to Glasgow. The books and the Caligari stills seem to have offered him the solution he had failed to find with Mary in Porlock. For on that evening in London all the elements of his most autobiographical play came together. He wrote, 'A demon's contract; a femme fatale; Life, Death & Fate are mine to juggle. I have laid my ghosts to rest.'

It was to take Campbell eight months to complete *The Life and Death of Doctor Frost*, which, if it is now largely forgotten, was greeted at the time as a masterpiece. Sad to relate, Campbell's ghosts did not remain at rest for long.

For myself, the play is now bound up for ever with the image of Fiona as she was in the early months of our collaboration. It was a Saturday. We had spent much of the afternoon discussing the playwright's work and, although I cannot recall everything we said, I believe that I was closer to Fiona then than I have been to anyone before or since.

I do not remember which one of us suggested having a takeaway meal. It seemed the natural thing to do. And so I found myself walking back to the bed-sit on that increasingly blustery evening, with four or five foil containers in a carrier bag and two bottles of wine in another, while Fiona waited for me. I stopped on the street below, looking up at the patchy sunset reflected in my window while torn clouds scurried overhead.

After the meal, we drank more wine and I searched out my whisky. Fiona took the copy of Campbell's play from its place on the shelf. She sat in my armchair and crossed her legs. She drank some whisky, laughed in an odd manner and, pressing a hand to the opening of her blouse, she began to read *The Life and Death of Doctor Frost*.

I was lying on the floor in front of her, my head propped up on my elbow, my glass forgotten on the floor, while my gaze travelled the length of her body. The top two buttons of her blouse were undone. When she pushed her hair behind her ear, I could see the creamy skin of her breasts in the opening. Her tights were honey coloured. My eyes followed the lower curve of her raised thigh to the seductive angle it formed with her tensed calf.

Meanwhile, she read aloud without inhibition words familiar to her from years of study. The cynical and disaffected Frost, having gained a doctorate in mathematics, sets out on a dissolute life, financed by betting on the horses and other games of chance. It transpires that, during his researches, he has stumbled upon a 'Law of Improbability' which allows him to predict the outcome of such games with extraordinary accuracy.

Fiona uncrossed her legs and flicked through the following scenes, which revolve around Frost's adulterous affair with the wife of a physically repellent but wealthy industrialist.

'Too obvious,' she said. 'That broad farce. It's nothing but sleight of hand. Campbell's only trying to divert attention away from the husband; from his anger and humiliation. This is more like it,' turning to the second act, where Frost meets the improbably named Stephen Asmodeus at a race meeting. She leaned forward in her chair, while I lay back on a cushion and looked at her through the V of my raised legs. Her breasts were revealed in the opening of her blouse to the lacy cups of her bra. Her thighs, now pressed together, were slightly flattened where they rested on the front of the chair.

She continued reading through the next scene, in which Asmodeus makes his bargain with Frost. Elegantly gesturing with her hand, she adopted the sinister, raspy tones that have since fixed my image of Asmodeus. He says, 'What do you say, Frost? Do you want to grow old and settle down with some cosy little hausfrau? Or do you want to lead a short, exciting life, full of incident and colour?' Frost smiles, believing that this is one of his friend's jokes. Asmodeus then reaches inside his coat for a battered black notebook. Holding it with mock reverence, he offers it to Frost on condition that he signs a receipt, 'in blood, dear chap. It wouldn't be right if it wasn't in blood.'

The notebook contains equations that by themselves are meaningless, but which, when combined with certain of Frost's discoveries, suggest the possibility of a weapon so powerful that its possessor could rule the world unopposed. In order to defer accusations of lunacy, Frost fabricates a prototype of the weapon 'from ordinary household objects deranged and reconstituted in the alembic of nightmares'. He proves its efficacy by blasting an open stretch of heath. During the test, a young woman is accidently killed.

At this point, Fiona burst into tears and put the book down. She confessed that she was unhappy about Stephen Pendle. She had fallen in love with him, but was unsure whether he shared her feelings.

You must understand how unhappy this confession made me. I began to think that the passages she had read held some hidden significance for her in her relationship with Stephen. I sat down on the arm of the chair and began to stroke her head. Little shudders passed through her. To distract her, as I try to distract myself now, I took up the play.

Frost has gained the power and wealth he sought from the government, when Asmodeus makes his third appearance. He recommends that Frost enjoy his power while he can, for time is short.

'Death will be preceded by eight portents,' he tells the arrogant mathematician. What he doesn't tell him is that four of these portents (which he duly lists) have already occurred. 'A hound baying in the night will be the last,' he says, and slopes off.

All this was merely the idle chatter of a conjuror, or a dentist administering gas, for I was with great stealth slipping my hand down Fiona's back under her blouse towards her bra strap. And then, quite simply, she rested her head on my thigh and placed a hand on my knee. This manoeuvre carried my still questing hand to the small of her back, but it quite unmanned me. I withdrew my hand and let it rest on her silky hair for a moment, before removing it to the neutrality of the chair's arm. The evening ended with a perfunctory and clumsy embrace, and then Fiona left without looking me in the eye.

Now, when I think about how close I came to consummating my relationship with Fiona, I have some real insight into the desperation felt by Doctor Frost. True, he is able to pile up wealth, to seduce beautiful women, to collect valuable artworks, but all the time he knows that his power is steadily slipping through his fingers.

It is then that Asmodeus, making his fourth and final appearance, introduces him to a beautiful woman named Lilith, whereupon Frost decides to build a mansion for them both. Surely, like Fiona to me, Lilith represents the elusive woman Campbell had been seeking all his life.

The fifth and final act is set entirely in the mansion and covers a twenty-four-hour period. Frost and Lilith are alone together. He grows suspicious of her and increasingly paranoid about events outside. Confirmation has reached him that a foreign power has tested a weapon similar to his own. He realises that his power is all but gone and he waits feverishly for the first portent – 'The gift of a hundred heads' – to announce his impending doom.

As the hour approaches midnight, Frost hears a sound like a hound baying in the night. With the force of a revelation, he recalls the hundred pounds he won at the races shortly before he met Asmodeus for the first time. Everything falls into place. Frost draws the curtains on the moonlit landscape visible through the window. A young man walks on to the stage and stabs him as the clock starts to chime midnight.

At a deeper level, however, the play tells another story. An industrialist, cuckolded by Frost, seeks vengeance for his humiliation. He bides his time. After a while, he is able to enlist the help of a young man whose fiancée has been killed while walking on a stretch of innocent moorland. Finally, Frost is betrayed by a government for whom he has outlived his use, and a duplicitous lover. This story is conveyed through odd hints and allusions, not least of which is the note that Campbell appended to the programme of his own production:

> Finally, although most commentators agree that Asmodeus is the Demon of Lust, Ahbdul Alhazred in his 'Necronomicon' referred to him as 'the Prince of Vengeance'.

Chapter Four

I should like to make it known here that I met Anne Powheid on 29 February this year, shortly before I began writing the final draft of my biography. I say this because there are those, including Anne Powheid herself, who might try to deny that any such meeting took place.

I understand Anne's feelings. The following events do not show her in a good light, but I should like to assure her that in relating them I intend no malice towards her. If she ever reads this biography, she will realise that I am merely serving truth, and truth is a harsh mistress.

Anne insisted on holding our meeting in a situation of absolute secrecy. Consequently, she arranged to collect me from a coffee shop in Milngavie, but gave me no hint of our final destination until she pulled into a muddy track on the edge of Mugdock Wood. As we walked along the path towards Mugdockbank Castle, she started to tell me about her tormenting and tormented relationship with the playwright.

That day still haunts me with its reed-fringed loch and its ruined castle. Anne's words put flesh on my playwright. For the first time, I could picture him as a living, breathing man entering Malquist's offices in June 1952 with the typescript of *The Life and Death of Doctor Frost* under one arm. Anne sensed 'an excitement in him which was unnatural in its intensity'. When I asked her to explain what she meant, she went on to say, 'It's something I have noticed in other writers. It's as if they aren't quite there, if you get my meaning. I can still remember Campbell so clearly. He had such a lot of energy. He was only standing in front of my desk, asking if Malquist was in, but it was as if he was restraining himself; as if at any moment he might dash about the office. And his eyes (he had such piercing, blue eyes), his eyes looked as if they were focusing on something beyond the room.' It is obvious that she was hopelessly in love with the playwright.

As it happened, Malquist was in a meeting and did not have time to speak to Campbell. He merely popped his head around the door, smiled unpleasantly in the playwright's direction and took the type-script from Anne. Through the open doorway, McCluskie could see a corner of Malquist's desk upon which there was a black hat with a white silk band. He could also see someone's leg extending beyond the edge of the door. A ribbon of hirsute flesh was visible between the trouser hem and a black and white Argyle sock. Malquist closed the door. Anne offered Campbell a cup of coffee, but he seemed lost in thought and did not reply immediately. After a moment, he said, 'Curiously familiar hat,' and then, as if recollecting himself, 'No, no thank you, em …'

'Anne,' she said.

'I know. I know. I was just following a train of thought.'

On the following afternoon, she had just finished typing a letter, when she heard Malquist in his office, laughing in a very peculiar manner. Shortly after, the agent emerged, a wide grin distending the lower half of his face and etching a series of lines in his cheeks.

'What a brilliant idea. The man's a genius,' he said, and then, with barely a pause, he added, 'Anne, would you be good enough to find me the telephone number of Lawrence Minton's Model Agency in London.'

Anne fell silent. My wandering gaze swept over her legs; the sky and some branches reflected in a puddle on the path; a rook stand-ing on one of the castle battlements. Mesmerised by all these inci-dental details, I did not immediately grasp the significance of what she had told me.

'It's funny how some things stick in your mind for years,' I said, or words to that effect. Our path wound between disconsolate trees towards the castle and to further revelations.

Campbell's more illustrious path led him, in early September 1952, to a charity reading from *The Irresistible Rise of Tam McLean*. A perspicacious bookseller had organised the event to raise money for the British soldiers fighting in Korea. A ten-pound ticket paid for readings by several greater and lesser authors, followed by a drink (in an anteroom where books were displayed and sold) and a dinner-dance.

By all accounts, Campbell's reading was an unqualified success. He strode up and down the podium performing each part in character. His Tam McLean was considered by one critic 'to be a revelation'. Over drinks afterwards, the prominent display of the playwright's books ensured that he profited quite as much from the evening as did the soldiers in Korea. Then it was back to the main hall for the dinner-dance.

Although Anne Powheid had gone to great lengths to have herself placed next to Campbell during dinner, he paid little attention to what she said and, when he did finally acknowledge her, she became unsettled and spilled wine down her chin. His gaze quickly resumed its avaricious flicker about the room, leaving her to the humiliating solitude of her passion.

So depressed was she by the end of the meal that she was hardly aware of the sudden interest aroused in Campbell by the sight of Madelaine Milverton crossing the room in a low-cut dress with a fringed skirt. He wondered why he hadn't noticed her earlier and lost no time in asking her to dance a waltz.

I imagine Campbell holding Madelaine close to him. As they move around the floor, his left hand presses the small of her back. She rests her head against his shoulder and laughs quietly.

'I have spent the past four years engendering monsters in my sleep,' he whispers into her hair. His meaning eludes her, but she finds the sound of his voice strangely reassuring. She feels the pressure of his erection against her stomach and her heart begins to beat faster. She doesn't want the dance to end.

They escape the throng. Hand in hand, they hurry along Sauchiehall Street for a short distance. Madelaine is convinced that Campbell can hear her heart beating. They turn on to a side street to get away from curious passers-by. Reason banished, they have sex up against the wall of a close on Garnet Hill.

Afterwards, remorse; emptiness; awkwardness. Campbell stands smoking on the street for a few minutes before following her in. She hopes that no one will notice the crumpled silk of her dress. She worries about being pregnant. She worries that he won't want to see her again.

They meet up ten minutes later by the bar. Campbell finds her changed. She strikes him as being shallow and affected. They exchange addresses and phone numbers. She tells him he can contact her only on Wednesday afternoons before four o'clock. Her husband, Colin, is asleep in his armchair when she gets home.

Four days later, past and present come together on Campbell's doormat in the shape of two letters. One was from Grazia, telling him of a complicated miscarriage she had had to keep hidden from her husband. The other was from Madelaine, inviting him to meet up in a hotel on Saturday and raising the possibility that she might smuggle him into her house later.

Campbell tore Grazia's letter methodically into eight pieces before sitting down to write an acceptance letter to Madelaine. Of that hastily penned reply, nothing now remains. Madelaine would later imply to Inspector Greig that her husband had discovered this undated letter on the eve of McCluskie's murder. By then the letter had almost certainly been destroyed and Greig could not confirm her statement.

So here we see Campbell at his desk, writing, oblivious of the complex machinery he is setting in motion; a bit cranky at first, but soon it will run smoothly, with only the shadow of a rope to distract us from its glittering movements.

Despite his written assurance, Campbell was not able to meet Madelaine on Saturday after all. Malquist insisted that he travel to London on the Friday evening, to sort out a crisis with the play. While waiting for his train he wrote in his notebook:

Today, I strolled over to see Madelaine. The walk through Kelvingrove was glorious – the endless variety of the autumn colours filled me with the vague images of future projects. When I arrived at Kensington Gate, I saw her husband putting bags into his car. He is a fat little man; his chin, a gleaming hemisphere, haphazardly placed; his hair, thinning. I sat on a bench in a small park across the road, while he led a small plump boy and a pretty girl to the car. The girl reminded me of my sister, Dorothy. I stood outside the house for a couple of minutes after they had gone, but I made no attempt to see if she was in. Instead, I left a message in the hotel where she had arranged to meet. It was only when I got to the station that I realised the coin was missing. All evening, I have been trying to rid myself of the feeling that my luck has gone with it.

What coin, for Christ's sake? What coin?

In the event, Campbell was detained in London until *The Life and Death of Doctor Frost* opened. It was premiered in the Royal Court Theatre in the presence of the Duchess of Rutland, who was then twelfth in line to the throne. Although no great fan of royalty, Campbell had been taken with the Duchess's creamy shoulders and pale blue eyes. On being presented to her at the party after the play, he had given her a lingering kiss on the hand, in which his tongue had played a fleeting part.

It was the first time Campbell had ever seen Malquist look flus-

163

tered. He led the playwright away from the smiling Duchess and her grim consort. The evening then settled into the usual routine for such events. Campbell found himself 'exchanging idle chit-chat with elderly widows, nodding vigorously at the inevitable cleric and leering at the occasional debutante'. That is, until Malquist approached with a beautiful, dark-haired woman. The agent was grinning and pressing her lightly in the small of her back while making subtle gestures with his other hand. He introduced her to Campbell as Helen Miriam. After a short interval, the still grinning agent left them alone together.

Helen's resemblance to Campbell's Aunt Dorothy was slight, but it was sufficient to charge the remainder of the evening with an intolerable frisson for the playwright. He hoped that by talking he might draw attention away from his discomfiture. As they strolled over to the punch bowl, Helen looked around, smiling occasionally at a passing acquaintance, until, as she waited for a steward to refill her glass (from a silver ladle with a long curved handle), she said, 'Do you always talk so much?'

After that, Campbell was more successful in hiding his unfamiliar excitement, but its jagged edge surfaced later when she waved at a distinguished-looking man who was talking to Malquist.

'Who's that?' he said abruptly.

'Oh, it's only my agent, Lawrence Minton,' she replied.

Things then took a turn for the better. Campbell became more relaxed. He found he enjoyed talking to her. At the end of the evening, she took a note of his hotel and room number. After permitting him to kiss her cheek, she told him that she was going to Paris the following morning on an assignment, but that she would meet him in London in a week's time.

Campbell, feeling frustrated and angry with himself, took a taxi across town, secured the services of a prostitute and spent two hours with her in a seedy hotel. That night, he dreamed of Helen. She was sitting in an attic room with her legs crossed twice, reading from a blue clothbound book. He felt cold and went to warm himself by the electric fire in the corner, but it kept getting further away. Helen started reading louder, but he could not make out the words. Through the window behind her he could see an impossibly large fleet spread out on a moonlit sea. A photograph slipped out from between the pages of the book. He woke up. During the night, his blankets had slipped off the bed.

Campbell waited obediently for Helen to return from Paris. They went out for dinner together at an intimate Italian restaurant off Charing Cross Road. Helen, who knew the owner and most of the staff, kept speaking to them in Italian. Campbell inwardly fumed. Everything seemed jaded and second-rate – the fat-bellied bottle with its basket and irregular layers of candle wax; the crackly tenor singing Puccini in his circular Hell; the theatrical gestures of the waiters; the affable owner; the red chequered table covers; the surreptitious glances cast at Helen's naked shoulders.

'What do you do when you're not modelling, or fraternising with the Cosa Nostra?' he said, pushing his plate away and lighting a cigarette.

'I give the papers something to write about,' she replied.

Campbell ordered more wine. They drank and talked some more. As they stood outside after the meal, Campbell said, 'And how do you know Malquist?' It was a question he had been mulling over since meeting her.

'It was my agent who knew him,' she said.

They took a taxi to her flat near Swiss Cottage. While she made him coffee, he looked around her sitting room. Shelved alcoves were situated on either side of the fireplace. In the right-hand one, he noticed some books, two African statuettes and a small charcoal sketch of Helen sitting naked with her back to the viewer and her face in profile above her left shoulder. He tried vainly to decipher the signature.

After they finished coffee, she suggested in a matter-of-fact voice that they go to bed. Campbell felt a strange disquiet. She led him into her bedroom. Its tall windows looked on to a tree-lined street where a man in a raincoat was trying to pull his dog away from a pile of leaves. Helen closed the curtains using a tasselled cord.

Once in bed, he tried to remove her pants, but she stopped him. 'Not yet,' she said. He lay back. She began kissing his stomach. He recalled a sunny kitchen in a different decade.

Two days later, Campbell returned to Glasgow. When he got round to reading his mail on the following morning, he discovered a letter from Madelaine. It took him a moment to remember who she was. That evening, he met Tommy Skelton for a drink. Skelton would later tell his wife that Campbell had seemed preoccupied and unusually excitable. However, the playwright made no mention of Helen Miriam.

On leaving Tommy, I went for a walk along Great Western Road. The sky was clear. It was cold. I passed an old lady in a long, black coat and woolly hat. Almost by force of habit, I consigned odd details of her clothing to memory – the corner of a pocket curling over; the one red button amongst the black ones on her coat; the flapping sole of her right boot. I leaned on the parapet of Kelvinbridge and looked across the goods yard towards the backs of the Park Road tenements. I noticed that a tarpaulin, which had been tied over a pile of coal in the goods yard, was folded back at one corner. 'Just like the old lady's pocket,' I thought.

The reflections of lights rippled on the surface of the river, but appeared to descend into its depths. I remembered Helen lying on the bed with her arm curved round her head. Her armpit had been stippled with dark hairs. Her right breast had been raised slightly. The outline of her ribcage had been visible. I cannot understand why I find so intolerable the idea of never seeing her again.

When he returned to his flat, he re-read Madelaine's letter, sketched on the back of it the outline of a story and drank several whiskies to settle his mind before bed.

Campbell makes his next appearance in a grainy newspaper photograph taken at the launch party for the publication of *The Life and Death of Doctor Frost*. He is making an emphatic gesture with his right arm, while Helen looks on, her lips smudged and oddly askew.

With an eye to the Christmas market, Coultts had published the play in a de luxe illustrated edition. On its dust wrapper is an etching of Doctor Frost, dressed in a black suit, standing in a cramped room. On the floor is a pentangle inscribed within a circle. A young woman sits on the beds, looking at him with her arms and head resting on her knees. Campbell has provided the play with an uncredited epigraph:

> The fool who speculates on things is like some animal
> on a dry heath, led by an evil fiend in endless circles.

The quotation would prove disturbingly relevant to the Christmas and New Year holiday that Campbell subsequently spent with Helen in London.

They attended a number of parties at which Campbell wandered around upsetting people with his sarcasm. He kept wondering which, if any, of the other men present had been Helen's lovers. He was only really happy during their exhausting bouts of lovemaking.

On Hogmanay, they ended up at a party somewhere in Ladbroke Grove. They sneaked off to someone's bedroom before the bells and had sex three times in a bed hung with satin curtains. The next morning, they woke to find a corpulent man, partially covered by a quilted house coat, snoring in an armchair near the bed.

Just over a year later, we find Campbell in his house in Park Terrace, sitting brooding in his study. On the wall above his desk is a framed print by Dürer: *The Knight, Death and the Devil.* Beside it is a photograph of Helen taken by Campbell in the Glasgow Necropolis the previous summer. His notebook lies open in front of him. A photographic postcard of the Pyramids is propped against the wall beyond it. On the postcard is a short message from Helen. Her father is dying. His mistress is making life intolerable for her. She cannot understand why Campbell refused to come to Egypt with her.

The record that Campbell made that night includes all this incidental detail. It opens with an observation on the Egyptian origins of the obelisk beside which Helen had posed in the Necropolis. Campbell had deliberately photographed her beside that obelisk, as an allusion to her origins. Her father had been an English diplomat working in Cairo. Her mother, a Greek Cypriot, had died there of typhoid fever when Helen was sixteen. Helen's dreams were still haunted by the image of her mother crying out and clutching her stomach while a nurse struggled to rearrange the sheet over her rose-spotted torso.

Campbell also knew that Helen had lost her virginity to a young English officer, on the shaded eastern side of a sand dune, only weeks before he stepped on a German land mine near El Alamein. The playwright reacted so badly to this anecdote that she was loath to share anymore of her past with him.

On that cold January evening in 1954, Campbell reflected on the adverse turn his fortunes had taken. Early in 1953, a major Hollywood producer had paid a sum in excess of ten thousand pounds for the rights to *The Life and Death of Doctor Frost.* At that time, the playwright was in the process of negotiating for a mortgage on a house in Park Terrace. His career was at its zenith. But then he started work on the ruinously expensive Scottish production of the play.

Collaborating with Angus Deacon, a theatre designer of genius, Campbell poured much money and time into perfecting the sets, particularly the interior of Doctor Frost's mansion which provides the setting for the entire final act. Judging by photographs, the mansion was a curious blend of the Gothic and the Expressionist, which owed a lot to the architecture of the Glasgow Necropolis and Campbell's stills of *The Cabinet of Doctor Caligari*. However, when I first saw its strangely angled columns and arches, I was reminded of nothing so much as the Glasgow skyline as seen from the hills to the north.

The right-hand side of the backdrop was dominated by a diamond-shaped window. In contrast to the brooding atmosphere of the mansion, McCluskie had wanted the view through that window to represent 'an unattainable but cliché paradise; very English, with rolling hills and scattered copses, somewhat in the manner of a railway advertisement'. However, the final act is divided into four scenes, each of which is set at a different time of the day. To achieve this effect, Deacon painted four different versions of the landscape around a circular board that was mounted on an axle behind the backdrop. At the end of each scene, the board could be turned to place the appropriate view in the window.

The resulting production was visually stunning, but it did not impress the critics. One wrote that it 'left the audience with a vague sense of nausea, as if it had feasted on too much rich food'. Most concluded that Campbell had overreached himself. A journalist from the *Glasgow Herald* made the mistake of asking Campbell if Lilith was based on Helen Miriam.

'I'm not a bloody prophet!' was Campbell's furious response. In private, he confided to his notebook, 'I'm sick of these greasepaint charades. Language is my medium.' The play's limited run did not come anywhere near recouping its costs.

Malquist was angry that McCluskie was making no effort to write a new play. He sent Nicholas Skeres to see Campbell in his new house; a meeting of which Campbell made a careful record:

Wooden packing cases shedding straw on the carpet. My dented armillary sphere caught in angled sunlight on the sideboard. Metal clicks of segs on the pavement outside. I put down the framed photograph of Helen I am cleaning and answer the door. Skeres is silhouetted on the doorstep.

He enters, takes off his hat and sits on a packing case in the lounge, in an unpleasant fug of Brylcreem, stale sweat and decaying molar.

'Malquist tell't me tae drop by. Wanted tae know how yer gettin' on wi' the new play.'

'Tell him he's been taking my plays too much to heart. If it's all the same to him, I'd like to keep my work quite separate from whatever shady transactions you pair are involved in.'

Skeres stands up, pauses, carefully reshapes his hat and then, just as he is about to leave, gestures with the hat at the picture of Helen.

'A very pretty lady,' he says. 'Let's you and me see that she stays that way.'

'You should be in the movies, pal,' I reply.

He disappears, leaving his fetid trace on the air like a promise of Hell. Something oddly familiar about this whole, grotesque scene; it is still two weeks before Helen arrives.

Helen had agreed to move to Glasgow in much the same casual manner as she had decided to sail to England at the close of the Second World War. It is clear that Campbell still harboured unusual anxieties about the relationship, but he hoped that these would disappear once they started living together in Park Terrace.

Anthony Shaw would have us believe that he interviewed one of Helen's friends from this period, who told him of the secret doubts about Campbell that lay behind Helen's breezy optimism. If this woman is not a fabrication of Shaw's, then she was clearly one of those 'soi disant friends' who appear at times of tragedy, trying to cover their mediocrity with the mantle of an assumed intimacy. And so she pirouettes for a moment in the limelight. Step by step, Shaw cobbles together his argument from the tales and testimonies of similar figments, until on the final page of his odious biography he concludes that Campbell McCluskie was nothing more than a fraud and a charlatan, incapable of loving or understanding anyone other than himself. But if this is true, what then are we to make of the beauty of his art? Must I accept that my life has amounted to nothing more than a slime trail of blood, lust and shame?

I prefer not to think of the petty arguments that arose after Helen moved in; about the demands Campbell made on her time. Or of the interference from others that made Campbell seek solace, first of all in compiling a shameless inventory of his past love affairs, then in the arms of his best friend's wife, before finally following a prostitute into a pub.

Rather, I try to think of them in a secluded corner of a Victorian cemetery in August 1953. They have just made love and are lying together, naked, on the grass. Campbell is contented. He has not the urge to leave that he usually has after sex. He desires nothing more than to lie there on his back, stroking her head – which is resting on his chest – and gazing into the blue infinity of the sky.

But no; in the office of an agency of which Campbell is growing ever more suspicious, during a winter of increasing creative, emotional and financial difficulties, pretty but diminutive Anne Powheid, possessed of an almost Shakespearian jealousy, whispers in the playwright's ear that in October 1952, shortly before the premier of *The Life and Death of Doctor Frost*, she had overheard Malquist on the telephone suggesting to Helen Miriam that he had a proposal that it would be very much to her advantage to consider.

Campbell never confronted Helen with this piece of information. Therefore, it was not until several weeks after his death that she finally understood why he had stormed out of the house impotent, angry and drunk, on that sunny morning of 16 June 1954.

When she wandered into his study later that morning, all that she found on his desk was a travel brochure for the Isle of Wight, lying open at Bembridge. Campbell had circled in red ink an engraving advertising a holiday cottage, in which was portrayed a man in a suit and fedora bending to unlock the front door. Beneath it, in Campbell's now rather shaky hand, was written, 'Here is where it began.'

BOOK TWO

THE DEATH OF
CAMPBELL MCCLUSKIE

PART ONE

Chapter One

In Colin Milverton's final testimony, he said that he had felt ill on waking up on 16 June 1954, but that he had got out of bed nevertheless to get his children ready for school. His twelve-year-old daughter, Anne, sat in sulky silence, while his son, James, showed him his homework – a short essay outlining their plans to visit the Isle of Wight during the holidays, with some interesting facts about the island. Below, James had drawn a crude map of the island with the places at its four cardinal points named and underlined in red.

'It's Bembridge with a "d",' Colin corrected him, and returned the jotter to the disappointed child. Then Colin experienced an acid rush of anxiety as he recalled the contents of a terrible letter he had burned on the previous evening.

His wife, Madelaine, recollected through the haze of sleep and time that he had looked in on her before he left the house that morning. He had mumbled something about not feeling well and going for a walk, had responded with an affirmative grunt when she asked if the children had gone to school and then he had left without saying anything else. During the brief period of wakefulness that followed, she reflected that such behaviour was out of character. Then she went back to sleep.

She had a startlingly vivid dream of an island rendezvous with a grim-looking fellow wearing a dark cloak, who underwent two transformations. First, he changed into a handsome, unshaven stranger with high cheekbones and different-coloured eyes, who was lighting a cigarette in the entrance to a close. Then he assumed the guise of a young man, named Charles, whom she had loved passionately for four terrible years but who had recently turned into a repulsive and impoverished blackmailer with rotten teeth.

Later that morning, James's schoolteacher informed Madelaine that James had burst into tears during 'news time' when he said he had seen his father crying in the bathroom. Madelaine replied that James had an over-active imagination, but a worried frown remained on her face after she replaced the receiver in its cradle. That is how I imagine the scene. The phone stands on her dressing table. Madelaine, sitting on the bed, languidly crosses her legs and smooths the ruffled material of her nightdress as she reflects on this turn of events. She searches her husband's bedroom for clues. A large ashtray on his well-ordered dresser contains a curled leaf of grey ash which crumbles at her touch. 'Burnt paper,' she thinks, pressing a forefinger to her lips. Then she returns to her room, gets dressed and goes downstairs to make a cup of coffee.

The day was already warm when Colin left that morning, without wearing a tie for the first time in years. Across the road was a small private park in which several species of birds were trilling. There were trees and a path laid out in a triangle. It all seemed pointless now. He turned left, turned left again at the corner and, panting slightly, emerged on to Great Western Road.

The thoroughfare has changed very little in the intervening years. Colin would have seen the same terrace stretching gracefully towards Byres Road with its attendant row of trees. A slight breeze ruffled the branches and their shadows. Colin, leaning against the nearest trunk, lowered his face, his jowls shaking in suppressed emotion. A tram rattled past. He rushed awkwardly across the road, hiding his tears, and headed to the Botanic Gardens 'to collect his thoughts', as he was later to put it to Inspector Greig.

He wandered past the glittering dome of the Kibble Palace and made his way to a wooded bank of the River Kelvin, where he settled himself in the leafy shade with a hip flask of malt whisky. He took a gulp and swilled it around his mouth before swallowing it.

'You remember that night in Perth in 1941? Your wife couldn't sleep. Can you remember that? You were snoring like a hog. Madelaine went out for a breath of air.' At first, Colin had tried to convince himself that the letter was a hoax, but the writer had known too many intimate details. Why had she told him all those things? Colin clawed up a handful of twigs and soil. Dirt collected under his fingernails. Tiny insects darted hither and thither. He took another mouthful of whisky. 'Snoring like a hog,' he said as he let the soil slip through his fingers. Then he tossed the remnants away.

Only much later would he tell Inspector Greig that he had received a letter the previous day, informing him of his wife's infidelity and bringing into question the paternity of his children.

Colin wept. He shouted. He drank. He had no idea how much time elapsed before he brushed himself down and headed to the main entrance of the gardens. A young boy, who had been hiding nearby, threw a stone at him and called him a 'big wean'. However, when he left the park, he had recovered sufficiently to pass unnoticed by the few morning strollers.

Colin also told Greig that he had bumped into the playwright just by the park entrance. But he insisted that he had never met McCluskie before and that he didn't encounter him again until he found him lying unconscious in South Woodside Road at about half past ten that evening. Colin remembered that McCluskie was reading a letter as he walked, which he dropped when the pair of them collided. Colin, apologising, retrieved it, but McCluskie neither thanked nor acknowledged him. When pressed to describe the letter he had picked up, Colin said there was bold handwriting on it, which he hadn't read.

Colin weighed sixteen stone. He was five feet seven inches tall. His hair was thinning at the front. His chin was a gleaming hemisphere, haphazardly placed. He kept his eyes to the ground as he bustled through the shoppers on Byres Road. The day was growing uncomfortably hot. Damp patches were forming under his arms. He had no clear idea of where he was going. He felt as if he was suffocating.

Under pressure, he found it difficult to collect his thoughts.

'When did you decide to visit your lawyer?' repeated Inspector Greig. (Detective Cairncross was taking notes.)

'I don't know. I was standing near the Art Galleries. A tram stopped and I climbed aboard without thinking.'

The tram was nearly empty, but it was hot and stuffy inside. Colin got off at the end of Sauchiehall Street and headed down Renfield Street towards the premises of his solicitor, Donald Usher.

Colin felt a short-lived surge of relief as he made his way into the office with its oak cabinets and leather-bound volumes. The loudly ticking clock announced it was quarter to eleven. Usher sat behind the desk, wearing a grey suit and a look of professional concern. Colin, feeling rumpled and awkward in the presence of the younger and more attractive man, informed him that he believed Madelaine had been unfaithful. Donald offered him a cigarette from a silver case, which Colin declined.

'So you want to divorce your wife, Mr Milverton?' said the solicitor, reflecting on the beauty of the woman in question and how much she reminded him of Greta Garbo.

Milverton refused to give Donald any details of his wife's infidelities. He merely reiterated his belief that she had been unfaithful, stated that he would begin divorce proceedings in due course and then broke down and began to sob. Usher stood up, laid a hand on his client's shoulder and said, 'I shall get Doreen to make us a pot of tea, old man. You just calm yourself.'

While Doreen poured the tea, Colin apologised for his outburst. He said that he wanted to spend some time by himself and that he would probably find a room in a hotel for the night, because he didn't feel up to seeing Madelaine. Usher sat across from him, anxiously twisting the signet ring he wore on his right index finger. Milverton wiped his face with his handkerchief and then fell silent.

Donald said, 'Let's not be hasty, Colin. Are you quite certain your wife has been unfaithful? It would be a shame to allow a foolish suspicion to destroy your marriage.'

Milverton scrutinised his nails, which were black with dirt. 'Snoring like a hog,' he thought. Tears welled up in his eyes again. 'Oh, I'm quite certain,' he said. 'Would it be all right if I used your bathroom to clean myself up?'

'Why, of course, old man.'

On his way to the bathroom, Milverton heard Doreen asking Donald what the date was. Colin turned to see her standing in the entrance to the office, holding a sheet of paper in front of her, which was bent over at the top and resting on her chin. Her face bore a pleasant expression of bewilderment.

'I can never remember what day it is,' she said by way of apology. True to her word, in her brief interview with Inspector Greig five weeks later, she would not be able to confirm the date of Milverton's meeting with Usher.

And now I imagine a telephone ringing in the lounge of Milverton's house. Sunshine floods the room. The gramophone needle crackles inconclusively about the centre of a Caruso recording. Madelaine, who is smoking a cigarette through a gold holder engraved with arabesques, answers the phone with an irritated, 'Yes?'

'Madelaine? It's me, Donald. Colin was just here. I think he suspects something.'

'What gives you that impression?'

'Look, I really can't talk now. Can I come over and see you? This is the cleaner's day off isn't it?'

'Where's Colin now? I mean, if he's not at work, he might come back at any time.'

'I shouldn't think he'll be back for a while. That's what I have to talk to you about.'

'All right. Can you get here in about an hour?'

Some such conversation must have taken place while Colin Milverton stepped out of Usher's office and into the lunchtime crowds on Renfield Street. As he stood on the steps leading down to the pavement, wiping his neck with his handkerchief, he saw Isobel, one of his shorthand typists, walking down the street. Unfortunately for Milverton, she didn't see him turn and make off in the opposite direction.

Fearful of seeing anyone else he knew, Milverton walked quickly to a nearby pub that he had never been to before. In its dark interior, he found respite from the sun and the crowds. The atmosphere was smoky. A short, bald man, wearing a white shirt, black waistcoat and tartan bow tie, was serving a pint of beer to a seedy looking-man with a black moustache and a side parting.

'A pint of 80 Shillings,' said Milverton, avoiding the barman's eyes, 'and a malt whisky.'

The seedy man sidled up, wiping foam from his moustache. 'The heat fair dries you out, does it not?' he said.

Milverton did not reply. He remained leaning on the counter and gazing into his pint.

'It does that and no mistake,' said the barman, raising his eyebrows in futile expectation.

'The name's Frank Connolly,' said the seedy man, holding out a hand to Colin.

'Pleased to meet you,' replied Milverton.

Connolly took his hand and shook it three times, vigorously.

'I'm in finance.'

'Banking?' asked Milverton, looking about for some means of escape.

'In a manner of speaking,' replied Connolly. 'Things are a bit tight at the moment.'

The garrulous stranger spent the next twenty minutes extracting two drinks from Milverton and recounting his life: his arrival in Glasgow at the age of ten; the honours he received at school; his numerous and varied sexual exploits. Then he rushed away to close an important deal with two of Milverton's pound notes safely stashed in his pocket.

Meanwhile, Milverton sat down at a table in a corner. Nearby, an old man with surprisingly white teeth was sitting with his hands clasped across his belly, humming 'Danny Boy'. Milverton gradually became aware of another man sitting two tables along from him.

He was wearing a dirty beige linen suit that had seen better days. His hair was thick and black with strands of grey running through it. He was unshaven. His teeth were rotten and yellow. Milverton thought that he was younger than he looked. He was drinking beer and smoking a cheroot which he held between his index and middle fingers, his thumb raised and his other fingers curled in a curious manner. Milverton, sipping the last of his beer, became conscious that the strange man was staring at him. Unsettled, he decided to leave the pub immediately.

At the entrance, he pushed his hand into the inside pocket of his jacket and pulled out three crumpled ten-pound notes. In a trouser pocket he had a further £2 8s & 3d.

'Parsimony', that was her favourite word, he thought. He felt angry as he considered Madelaine's financial acumen. He recalled his mother's cruel words: 'Take a look at yourself, Colin. Why would anyone that beautiful want to marry you, if not for money?'

'She was always very good with money,' he muttered as he walked away from the pub, stuffing the banknotes into his trouser pocket, oblivious of the strange looks people were giving him. 'So bloody good with my money. "Our little nest egg," she'd call it; our little bloody nest egg.' Milverton tried to control his emotions, but memories kept coming as he turned into West Regent Street. He was beginning to feel sick. He took off his jacket. Damp patches were clearly visible beneath his armpits, but he made no effort to hide them. Another queasy memory came to him.

Two weeks after their holiday in Perth in 1941, he had been poring over ledgers in his study. Madelaine had been in a strange mood throughout the previous month. A week earlier, she had demanded a bedroom of her own because her back was playing up. Sex had been out of the question. Was he really so insensitive and selfish? He had given in to all her demands. She was so beautiful that he could deny her nothing. Moreover, when he had considered it, he had mainly felt a sense of relief at the decline of their physical relations. (All this was haltingly expressed by Milverton, taken down by Cairncross and later paraphrased by me.) But, on that evening, Madelaine had entered the study wearing only her dressing gown. She had switched on the desk lamp and drawn the blackout curtains. She had knelt down by his chair.

'All very interesting, but why did you go to Laing's Restaurant after you left the pub?' asked the inspector, exasperated (from his third interrogation, dated 16 August 1954, in Cairncross's hand).

179

'But don't you see? It's important,' said Milverton. 'She seduced me that evening so that I would believe that Anne was my daughter.'

'Why do you persist in this fantasy?' replied the inspector. He moved the perpetual calendar that was standing on the corner of his desk, inadvertently turning the date towards Milverton as he did so. Then he sat down on that corner and crossed his right leg over his left. 'Besides, Mr Milverton, your solicitor denies meeting you on the sixteenth. His secretary has no recollection of you being there. And we have not been able to find any trace of a bank employee named Frank Connolly.'

'Perhaps he worked for a building society,' said Milverton.

'Or perhaps he doesn't exist,' said the inspector, removing a piece of fluff from his trouser leg.

I recall a cheese and wine evening I took Fiona to shortly after Stephen Pendle dropped her. I realise now that it was a mistake to take her there, but at the time I thought it would cheer her up, bring her out of herself. I don't know how I managed to let her out of my sight, but I got involved in a discussion with a group of colleagues about the nature of biography. I had, perhaps, drunk too much wine, for I foolishly started talking about Campbell McCluskie. My listeners began to pull faces. There were some suppressed titters, but I continued regardless. I wanted to prove my point that biography could be a form of imaginative recreation.

I noticed, by the by, that Professor Williams's wife had joined our group, drawn perhaps by the animated discussion. At the first opportunity, I asked her what her opinion had been of Campbell McCluskie. She looked at me with a pained expression.

'Whatever do you mean, Dr McDuffy?'

'I merely wondered if you could shed any light on the playwright's character from your own experiences.'

'But I never knew the playwright,' she replied. Colin Milverton must have felt something of the vertigo I experienced then when Inspector Greig questioned the veracity of his memories. At least the inspector was trying to get at the truth. Professor Williams's wife (née Anne Comrie) was merely intent on drawing my attention away from her husband, who was talking to Fiona in the far corner of the room. I saw him whispering to her and pointing over at me. God knows what poisonous yarns he was spinning.

Laing's Restaurant had an elegant Art Deco façade which was to remain its hallmark until it was destroyed by fire in September 1958. Milverton had to go to Sauchiehall Street to buy a tie in order to fulfil the strict dress code of the place. Drink had induced an un-characteristic determination in him when he was denied entrance by the head waiter. Instead of his usual meek response, he stated firmly that he would return as soon as he had purchased a tie. He felt quite proud of himself and even managed to smile at the pretty cloakroom attendant. She reminded him of Botticelli's *Birth of Venus*, a repro-duction of which was hanging on Madelaine's bedroom wall. The association reduced his self-confidence but not his resolve. He re-turned to the restaurant at ten to one, dressed in a new shirt and tie, with his jacket draped neatly over his arm.

Before taking his seat, he went to the lavatory. There were three cubicles with black doors, a line of urinals, chromium towel rails and three sinks with overly attentive mirrors above them. At the sight of his gleaming fat face, something crumpled up inside him. He floun-dered into one of the cubicles and threw up into the toilet several times while painful memories swept through his head with renewed vigour.

He recalled the groping embarrassment of his sex life and that one bright moment when Madelaine had kneeled beside him in the study and unfastened his trousers. He remembered the churning feeling he had had in his stomach when she had taken his still flaccid penis into her mouth. Then, for the first and last time, she had al-lowed him to see her naked body as she lay on the floor of the study with her legs apart. It occurred to him, as he spat out a trailing residue of bile, that she had been less circumspect with other, more virile lovers.

Chapter Two

We shall never know what went through Campbell's mind as he made his way through Kelvingrove Park on that morning in June. The sky was cloudless. The air was still. The sun was just rising above Park Terrace. The shadows of the trees slanted across the parched grass towards the river. Campbell, clearly preoccupied, trod on the paw of a smooth-haired mongrel that had sidled over to investigate his numerous scents. His heavy brogue must have hurt the dog quite badly, for it limped away, yelping, with its tail between its legs.

I don't believe Campbell knew where he was going. As he turned into Eldon Street he noticed a man in a grey suit and hat crossing the road, but unwisely he paid no heed to him. At the end of Gibson Street, Campbell turned left into University Avenue. I imagine him standing at the corner of University Avenue and Byres Road unsure of which way to turn. After some reflection, he headed south past sooty, red sandstone tenements.

Turning into Dumbarton Road, he passed the window of a dental repair shop. Dentures grinned out at him from dusty glass shelves. Further along, a large woman was scrubbing the wall of a close. Two men in overalls crossed the road and disappeared down Keith Street. Dirt and rubbish had gathered in the baked gutters. A dustbin awaiting collection outside a greengrocer's exuded a sickly smell of rotting fruit. Wasps buzzed energetically around its tilted lid. On the right, just before the railway bridge, was Jock Taylor's café. Campbell peered in at the sun-faded menu before entering.

An espresso coffee machine and chromium urn were visible beyond the counter. Jock, dressed in a grimy shirt with his sleeves rolled up, was frying sausage, bacon and eggs on a blackened griddle. Lizzie Jamieson was leaning over the counter, scoring through rationing coupons, the light material of her dress stretched across her massive buttocks. An elderly man sat by the window as he did every morning; eyebrows raised expectantly, fingers trembling. Another, younger man in oil-stained overalls finished his tea, dropped a six-penny bit on to the table and left. Campbell sat at a table near the door, cleared the surface of crumbs and flattened two sheets of paper on to the table. His appearance was unkempt despite the high quality of his clothes. A whisky bottle poked out of his pocket and his breath smelled of alcohol. He ordered a full cooked breakfast.

According to Lizzie, he sat staring into space and occasionally writing until half an hour later, when he ordered a fresh pot of tea.

'His pen was green,' she remembers, 'quite flashy with a gold nib.'

Inspector Greig stands with his back to her, stroking his moustache and looking out of the window. Detective Cairncross scribbles away in his notebook. Lizzie stands in front of the counter, supporting her elbow with her left hand, while her right hand cups her sagging chins, fingers fanning upwards. It is one week after McCluskie's death. Rain streaks the grimy window. A woman dressed in black walks past holding an umbrella. The inspector thinks he recognises her.

'That will be all for now, Lizzie. If you remember anything, you know where to find me.'

A black car waits for them outside. The detective holds open the passenger door for Greig. The brim of the inspector's hat catches on the car roof and flips back. Cairncross tries to catch it, but merely knocks it into the gutter, where it floats towards a drain, a damp patch spreading up to join its silk band. Muffled curses are heard from the car. The detective retrieves the hat. Three minutes later, the car completes an awkward U-turn and, shuddering into gear, makes its way along Dumbarton Road to the foot of Hyndland Street. Cairncross parks outside a small second-hand bookshop. The inspector makes a dash across the pavement and into the shop, leaving the detective to lock the car doors.

The shop is small and cramped. Several books are piled on the fly-strewn window ledge. By the entrance is a table on which are scattered a number of old movie magazines. The owner, Ronald Cluny, sits behind his desk at the back of the shop, lighting a pipe, with a newspaper spread out in front of him. He is a thin man with sloping shoulders, wearing a brown sleeveless pullover and a green and white striped shirt. Grey and black hairs are visible in the opening of the shirt. A mug of tea stands next to the newspaper on top of a black ledger book. A malodorous paraffin heater stands beside the desk.

'Can I help you?' Cluny addresses the inspector in a refined Scottish accent as Cairncross enters the shop. The constable comes to a

183

halt two paces behind the inspector and takes out his notebook and pen.

'Maybe you can,' replies the inspector, reaching inside his coat. 'I wonder if you can remember selling this book last week.' He hands Cluny a book with a torn red dust wrapper.

'*The Real Life of Sebastian Knight*?' says Ronald. 'Of course I remember selling it.'

'Why are you so certain, Mr Cluny?' says the inspector.

'I didn't think I'd ever see the back of it. It was part of a library that I took out of kindness from a bereaved friend four years ago. I finally sold it last week. On Wednesday, I think. Quite a handsome man, I recall; but drunk. He seemed very pleased to have found it.'

'Can you remember what time it was?'

'It couldn't have been long after I opened. I remember thinking it strange that someone would have been drinking that early in the morning. I said he could have it for sixpence, but he insisted on giving me two shillings. How did you come by it?'

'He left it at his agent's office.'

'It's funny, you know. I thought he was an actor. I get to know these things in my line of business.'

'The man was a writer, Mr Cluny. He wrote plays.'

Cluny turns the book over. Cairncross notices that he has spatulate fingers. Greig has stressed the importance of observation in crime detection.

'Was anyone with him, Mr Cluny?' says the inspector.

'Not that I recall. He left as soon as he had made his purchase.'

Out in the car, the inspector reads through Cairncross's notes.

'"Spatulate fingers"?' he says. 'What in God's name do you mean by that?'

Campbell had never really liked the summer. He would have found the heat of that morning oppressive. The women standing gossiping in the closes, the tired children sitting on the kerb beside their abandoned football, the reddish dust on the pavements would all have contributed to his malaise.

In the summer of 1989, I spent a morning wandering around the streets of Partick, Hyndland and Dowanside, trying to guess what route Campbell had taken to the Botanic Gardens. I imagined him walking through Dowanside with its elegant Victorian terraces, its trees and its gardens. He would have relished the dappled shade under the trees. But all we know for certain is that he phoned his agent from a public call box.

After his encounter with Milverton in the Botanic Gardens, several people saw him sitting on a bench, writing. The head keeper was willing to overlook the occasional swig of whisky that McCluskie took, but he was later compelled to take action. Shortly before ten thirty, two elderly women made comments about the playwright as they walked past and Campbell shouted, 'Mind your own business, you fucking philistines!' The keeper sought out the gardener and his young assistant to help escort McCluskie from the gardens. Campbell apologised for his outburst as soon as they approached, but he was not allowed to stay.

The playwright stood at the park entrance for a moment, scratching his stubbly chin and looking at the church across the road. He took the bottle out of his pocket and drained the whisky in one gulp. Passers-by gave him a wide berth. He walked along Great Western Road until he came to Ruskin Terrace. He paused at the roadside and, shielding his eyes with his hand, looked to right and left. After waiting for a car to pass, he dashed across the road in front of a swaying tram and, wheezing slightly, entered the wine merchant's on the corner of Hillhead Street.

As the door let out a startled ring, the assistant was bending down to retrieve a half-crown that had rolled between the two halves of the counter. With some difficulty he had managed to move one section of the counter far enough over to make a narrow opening for his hand. Scraping his knuckles on the poorly finished wood, he felt the coin touching the tip of his finger, before it rolled further out of reach. Sweat beaded his forehead and glistened on his pointed nose. His boss would not be pleased. The assistant stood up, pressing his hands into the small of his back.

'Can I have some service here?' said McCluskie testily. The assistant, hiding his anger, sold the playwright a half-bottle of whisky with practised contempt. (When he described to the inspector and Cairncross in minute and bitter detail the events of their short exchange, he could barely hide his satisfaction at having heard the news of McCluskie's death.) As McCluskie turned to leave, he took the empty bottle from his pocket, said, 'Here, could you dispose of this for me?' and tossed it over the counter. The bottle slipped out of the assistant's grasp, struck the till drawer and shattered on the floorboards.

Jack Logan, known as 'Jackie' to his friends, was the conductor on the tram that took Campbell into the town centre after he left the wine merchant's. Inspector Grieg encountered some difficulty in finding out which tram McCluskie had taken, and so it took him more than a week to track Logan down to the tenement in Dennistoun which he shared with his elderly mother. Jack could offer him no information about the playwright. The only passenger he could remember from that morning was a beautiful young woman, wearing a light blue striped dress, who resembled Vivien Leigh. She had been sitting on a side seat near the front of the tram.

I imagine McCluskie sitting nearby so that he could have a clear view of her. Jackie would have stood in the aisle near the door with his blackened hands resting on his change bag and his ticket machine. His legs would have been parted for stability. It would have been a matter of pride for him to walk up and down dispensing tickets and giving change without recourse to a handrail. However, few passengers would have noticed his poise, or his skill in operating the ticket machine.

The young woman would have been sitting with her legs crossed. Her dress would have had white lapels, and a string of pearls would have been resting on her collarbones. She would have been holding a white clutch bag. Her breasts would have been fashionably pointed. McCluskie would have taken in every detail. She would have noticed his stubble, his whisky smell and the alarming candour of his gaze.

Campbell left the tram at Sauchiehall Street. The time was approaching half past eleven. The pavements were crowded with shoppers. Parked cars lined the edges of the road. Campbell drew his fingers through his hair (a characteristic gesture) and then headed unsteadily in the direction of Charing Cross until he came to a shop with an Art Deco frontage. Above the window the words 'McCluskie's Footwear' were written in red on a cream background. The façade looked a bit dowdy and in need of a clean. The door squeaked slightly as Campbell entered.

A young sales assistant approached him, thought better of it and disappeared hurriedly through a door marked 'Staff Only'. Shortly afterwards, the shop manager, William Leucher, appeared in the doorway; a small thin man in a dark blue suit.

'Oh, Mr McCluskie, what are we to do with you? You know your father told you not to come back here.' The man made quick, nervous movements with his hands, scratched his head and, holding Campbell's sleeve, led him through to his office.

The office was spacious. There was a desk, a chair, a cocktail cabinet and a leather couch. Campbell slumped on the couch.

'I'm drunk, Willie. I'm drunk,' he said.

William opened the door and shouted, 'Glenys, Glenys dear, could you make a cup of black coffee?' He looked back at Campbell. 'Oh, make that two cups. I think I'm going to need one too.'

As he closed the door again, Campbell lurched through the other door and into the lavatory. He threw up in the toilet and then stood bent over the sink, clutching his head and supporting his elbows on the brass taps. After a few minutes, he was sick again. Then he sat on the floor with his back against the toilet bowl and his head bowed.

'Look at the state of you,' said William from the doorway.

Glenys appeared behind him, holding a tray and straining her neck to see what was happening. 'Can I be of any assistance, Mr Leucher?'

'No, no, Glenys. I'll deal with this.' William slapped Campbell several times on the face. Then, groaning with the effort, he dragged Campbell back on to his feet. A dark trace of hair dye appeared on William's neck.

'You'll be the death of me yet, Campbell. If your father knew you were here, I'd lose my job for sure.'

Campbell slept on the couch in William's office for nearly an hour. During that time, Maureen, the youngest sales assistant, sneaked in to have a look at him while William was buying him a collar, two collar studs, a tie, a toothbrush and a tube of toothpaste.

At twenty to one, McCluskie washed himself as thoroughly as circumstances permitted. He brushed his teeth. He put on the collar and tie and neatly rolled up his shirtsleeves before putting on his jacket. Mr Leucher was sitting at his desk, perusing a ledger book.

'I'm really sorry, Willie,' said Campbell.

'You know there was blood in your vomit, Campbell. How much did you have to drink?'

'Not much; it was only a hair of the dog.' Campbell's hands were shaking. 'I'll be fine after I've eaten something. I've started writing again, Willie.'

'And what about Helen?'

'I'll see her later. I've got a meeting with Malquist this afternoon. God, my head's killing me.'

'I'm surprised you can even walk. Your powers of recuperation are a mystery to me, Campbell.'

McCluskie left the shop and made his way to Laing's Restaurant in Hope Street. On entering, he winked at the girl in the cloakroom, who was checking her lipstick using the mirror in her shell-shaped compact. A waiter approached, addressed him by name and led him to a table by the window. Campbell tapped the bottle that was still lying snug in his pocket, and then started to read *Bend Sinister*. The waiter returned with a menu. McCluskie gave it a cursory glance and ordered a medium rare steak, carrots and potatoes together with a carafe of water. As he did so, he noticed a rhomboid gravy stain on the waiter's towel, which made him think of an island, a dark-skinned girl, Helen's naked body and a skeleton lying against an old sea chest. Then he resumed his reading.

Until the end, Colin Milverton insisted to anyone who would listen that he had not seen Campbell sitting there while he was shown to a table in an out-of-the-way corner and handed a menu and a wine list. The waiter made no effort to hide his contempt. Milverton felt as if an incredible weight was crushing his chest. He tried to think about work: the consignment of bricks that had gone astray between Kirkintilloch and Stirling; an unfortunate typing error on an invoice to McTeague's Building Contractors. What would Madelaine have to say about that as she lay by the Rhône with the writer of that disgusting letter pressing his face between her legs, just as she had tried to get Colin to do one night in the habitual darkness of their lovemaking? And what about that time near the Loire when he had driven her through France on their honeymoon on the eve of the war? She had disappeared behind some bushes to relieve herself and been gone for a suspicious length of time, maybe fifteen minutes, only to return with a badly twisted ankle and an inappropriate smile. Every wine-growing region on the list seemed to tabulate his wife's infidelities with a painful, geographic precision.

A waiter approached his table with a tray.

'Medium rare steak, carrots and potatoes with a carafe of water, sir?'

Milverton, startled, 'I haven't ordered yet.'

Waiter, drawing a slip of paper from under the plate, 'Sorry, sir. It's for table six.'

Another waiter came, took his order and left. Milverton sweated freely in his new shirt and, looking down, noticed he had stained his new tie while he was being sick. He tried to remove the dried matter with his thumbnail, in which was still lodged a tiny wedge of dirt.

Chapter Three

It was not until two days after Campbell's murder that Inspector Greig made his first visit to the scene of the crime. On South Woodside Road, McCluskie had stopped to pee at the back of some tenements. The pavement was covered with debris: pieces of glass; an old shoe lace; a tram ticket; a chocolate wrapper. Some tufts of grass were growing between the cobbles at the edge of the road, but all that remained of Campbell was a small bloodstain and an unseen fragment of material from his jacket.

Detective Cairncross leaned against the wall separating the road from the goods station. Greig was peering at the ground where the playwright had fallen.

'Has anyone reported seeing Milverton in the pub?' he said suddenly.

'You surely don't think Milverton did it?' replied the detective.

'At present, I don't think anything.' The inspector kept peering at the ground.

'No one in the pub is saying anything. If you ask me, they're scared,' said Cairncross, turning towards the goods station.

The inspector stood with his arms crossed, still staring at the ground. 'I can't see anything here.' He turned to look at Kelvin Bridge and then at the detective. Cairncross took off his hat and smoothed back his hair. He began to twirl the hat around his right index finger until it suddenly flew off over the wall. Greig put his hands on his hips and shook his head slowly from side to side.

'You bloody eejit,' he said. 'When you've finished acting the goat, maybe you can call out some of the lads to go over this area with a fine toothcomb. This place should have been cordoned off right away.'

'Och, inspector, it was an ordinary pub brawl. He probably started something with one of the local toughs and everyone's too frightened to come forward.'

'Would a local tough, as you put it, have used a steak knife with a silver-plated handle?'

Without replying, Cairncross set off to retrieve his hat from where it had fallen among the shattered remains of a beer bottle.

Neither policeman ever knew my mother; the impact of her drama was scarcely felt beyond the room and kitchen she shared with my father in Ruchill. What did she feel on that morning of 16 June after enduring nearly thirty-six hours of labour? Terms like 'contractions' and 'dilation' mean little to me. They merely serve to intensify the mystery. Beyond the fact that I was the cause of those contractions, I really know nothing of her experience; of her pain.

Consider also Fiona Gardiner walking across my room in the short skirt she used to favour, while I watched breathlessly, focusing all my attention on the movements of her hem against the backs of her thighs. As if those few inches of flapping material contained all the mysteries.

Inspector Greig, for all his obsessions with plots and motives, could have had no intimation of the hidden links between Fiona, me, the playwright, my mother's painful delivery and the flat in Eldon Street where Molly Damart was curled up in bed on that June morning in 1954.

Screwing up her face, she pulled a blanket over her head.

'Gonnae shut those fuckin' curtains?' she said to the tall, slim man who was fastening his tie in front of the open wardrobe door. He smelled of carbolic soap and stale tobacco in equal measure. His hair was shaved at the back and sides, but was longer on top, slicked back from his forehead and shiny with Brylcreem. His eyes were different colours: the right was brown; the left was dark green flecked with yellow. His face was unshaven. He had high cheekbones and hollow cheeks. Molly's head appeared above the blankets. Her beautiful face was marred by a bruised eye and her upper lip was swollen.

'Go and make ma fuckin' breakfast,' said the man as he retrieved his watch from the dressing table.

The room was squalid but expensively furnished. Molly looked at the clock on the bedside table and asked him why he had got up so early. He told her to mind her own business and get his breakfast, or else. He picked up the black-hilted switchblade that was lying on the dressing table. It was inlaid near the pommel with an ivory eagle. At the click of a switch the shining blade swung out and the man pointed it at her.

She got up, still grumbling, and pulled on a dressing gown and a pair of slippers. Then she shuffled through to the kitchen to cook some bacon and eggs. The man retracted the blade and put the knife in the pocket of the jacket that was hanging over the chair in front of the dressing table.

The pair ate in silence. The man carefully sliced his bacon and dipped it into his yolk before taking a mouthful. Molly pushed away her food half finished and sat back in her chair watching him.

'You shoodnae huv done it, Ingram,' she said suddenly.

'A warned ye. A tell't ye a'd hud enough. Ye jist widnae shu'up.' Ingram pointed at her with his fork as he spoke.

Such is my tentative reconstruction of what passed between them that morning. We know that Ingram Farqueson beat Molly up on the evening of 15 June. They had shared the flat in Eldon Street for almost a year. Ingram was a well-to-do thug, employed by Johnny Meikle, an extortionist, black marketeer, illegal bookie and loan shark who held sway in an area extending from Kelvinbridge to Anniesland, bordered by Maryhill to the north and the river to the south. Johnny, who lived with his family in a large villa in Pollockshields, had, by that time, established himself as a respectable citizen and Ingram was one of the men he paid to do his dirty work.

That morning, Ingram was seen leaving the flat at seven thirty wearing a grey double-breasted suit and fedora. He paused in the entrance of the close to light a cigarette. Then he started walking in the direction of Gibson Street. As he crossed the road near the public convenience beyond the terrace, an unkempt man in a green tweed suit emerged from Kelvingrove Park. Ingram drew heavily on his cigarette to mask the pungent smell rising from the river. He looked over at the goods station by Kelvinbridge, where there was already considerable activity, but he could see no trace of future events. The sky was virtually cloudless. The long shadows of the Park Road tenements stretched towards the Kelvin. Muttering to himself, he made his way along the north side of Gibson Street.

I know this street well. Along its length you will find three Indian restaurants, an Italian restaurant, an antique shop, an expensive clothes shop and an off-licence. In my student days, there was also a dusty window at street level, in which were displayed, for no apparent reason, two massive tins of virgin olive oil.

I do not know what shops were there in 1954. Ingram would have been too preoccupied with his own anger to pay them any attention. As he walked he periodically thrust forward his head, pulling back his shoulders as he did so; a mannerism betraying a dangerous

191

combination of neurosis and aggression. Before Ingram committed acts of violence for Johnny, he would look down, gripping his nose between finger and thumb. Then he would raise his eyes heavenwards while he carried out the act. By and large, his victims were weak, scared individuals who were deeply in debt to Johnny Meikle. These acts did nothing to relieve Ingram's anger, which remained with him throughout his waking hours like a dull pain.

Towards the top of the hill, Ingram stopped and looked northwards along Southpark Avenue. He flicked his cigarette stub on to the road and swore loudly. He remained at that intersection of Gibson Street and Southpark Avenue for nearly an hour. A housewife, peeking round her lace curtains, observed a rough-looking individual making his unsteady way along Southpark Avenue towards him. She reported that Ingram grabbed the newcomer by his lapels and shouted something like, 'Where the "effing" "h" have you been?' followed shortly after by, 'You're still drunk you "effing" "b".' He then punched the newcomer on the side of the face, knocking him to the ground. After more shouting and swearing, the two men headed off towards University Avenue. The policeman to whom the housewife made this complaint duly noted down the details but did not pursue the matter.

Ingram's companion was named Robert Pollock. Robert was unshaven, his clothes were dishevelled and he smelled of alcohol. He was a short but wiry individual with sharp features and very fine hair. As they made their way along University Avenue, Robert dabbed the cut on his cheek with a dirty handkerchief. He told Ingram that his late arrival had been entirely due to McGuigan, who 'had tampered wi' ma alarm while a wis sleeping aff the drink'.

'McGuigan,' said Ingram in a soft voice, his anger barely under control. Paul McGuigan had joined Johnny Meikle's organisation two years earlier. He was responsible for Meikle's loans in the poorer area around Maryhill, where the takings were smaller and harder to collect. He was a charmer and a lady's man, and a sharp dresser like Ingram. Meikle admired him for his skill in squeezing money from his territory without resorting to unnecessary violence. As he fell into step with Pollock, Ingram recalled with some bitterness the first time Molly had met McGuigan: her animation and excitement. It had been the first time he had hit her. Across the road, students stood around in groups, while a small, smooth-coated mongrel with a white diamond splash on its chest limped among them, whimpering.

The two gangsters walked to a terraced house halfway along

Ashton Road. A brass plate beside the door described it as the surgery of Dr K. W. White. Ingram rang the bell and the door was opened shortly afterwards by Nurse Helen MacIntyre. Her keen sense of propriety was immediately offended by Ingram's vicious demeanour and the shabby clothes of his companion. She frowned. Ingram announced that Dr White was expecting them. She admitted him to the hallway while she consulted the appointments book on the reception desk. Her frown deepened. She informed him that she had no record of any such appointment. Ingram, looking at the floor, told her to tell Dr White that he was there or else. He began to finger his hidden switchblade. The nurse, too angry to realise her danger, strode through to the surgery.

When she entered, the doctor was accepting payment from a frail old woman wearing a fox fur wrap. He looked disapprovingly over his glasses at Helen as he completed the transaction. The outraged nurse informed him that a Mr Farqueson was outside demanding to see him, and then she led the patient out before he could respond.

Alone in the surgery, Dr White pushed his glasses back on to the bridge of his nose and pressed his hands together as if in prayer. Shortly afterwards, he wandered through his waiting room (assuring his next patient that he would be with her shortly) and into the hallway, where Ingram and Pollock were waiting. To Helen's surprise and disgust, he ushered the two men through another door to his private quarters. Shaking her head in exasperation, she scuttled through to the waiting room to apologise to the patient for the unforeseen delay.

In contrast to the surgery, the doctor's lounge betrayed signs of neglect. The hearth rug was threadbare in places. The surfaces were thick with dust. Several John Buchan novels, in cheap editions with torn dust wrappers, were piled by the couch. A plate with a half-eaten fried-egg sandwich rested on top of them. Three ebony elephants of decreasing size were arranged in a line on the mantelpiece. The doctor scratched the back of his head and looked first at Ingram then at Pollock.

'McGuigan has collected the money already,' he said in a whisper.

'Who?' shouted Ingram. He gripped the bridge of his nose and looked down. The doctor, a tall but stooped man, moved closer to Ingram and repeated the name. His glasses slipped down his nose. There was a hesitant knock on the door.

'Dr White, Dr White, Mrs Campbell is still waiting to see you.' Helen's voice had lost its assurance.

Robert opened the door a crack and said, 'The doctor'll no be seein' any mair patients today.'

Ingram told the doctor to make them a cup of tea while he conferred with his partner. The doctor replied that he would do so as soon as he had spoken to his nurse. She was sitting at the reception desk when he emerged. She told him that Mrs Campbell had got fed up of waiting. He apologised for the morning's events. He assured her that the gentlemen would be gone before Mr Hegarty arrived at eleven o'clock to have his boil lanced. By way of explanation, he told her that he had treated one of them for an injury several weeks before, when he had encountered them after a fight; had done so because he could not bear to see a human being suffer, whatever the reason. The nurse was not convinced.

Dr White went through to his kitchen, rinsed three cups and put the kettle on to boil. As soon as Ingram heard the water shuddering through the pipes, he drew his blade on Robert, who was scrutinising one of the ebony elephants and shuffling from foot to foot.

'Now what the fuck's goin' on wi' McGuigan?' said Ingram, holding the tip of his knife at Robert's throat.

'A swear, a dinnae know,' replied Robert, sweating. We jist hud a bevy last night. He came back tae ma place.' The elephant fell on to the tiled fireplace, shedding an ivory tusk.

In the kitchen, the doctor could hear every word. It took five minutes for Ingram to piece together the events of the previous evening. McGuigan and Pollock had gone to Robert's local and then McGuigan had invited himself back to Pollock's flat. McGuigan had professed an interest in Ingram's methods for collecting money, because Meikle was on his back to speed up collections. Robert assured Ingram that he hadn't given McGuigan any details about the collections. He had merely outlined some of Ingram's methods for dealing with non-payments: the trick with Morgan's fingers; the slashings; the assault on McDermott's wife. He remembered asking McGuigan to set his alarm clock for him because he had to get up early, but after that he could recall nothing. McGuigan was gone when Pollock woke up that morning lying fully clothed on his couch.

Ingram retracted the blade and placed his fedora on the arm of the settee. Robert sat down on the chair nearest the fireplace and began to rub his throat.

'Johnny Meikle's the only other person who knows aw the details of ma collections,' said Ingram as he too sat down. 'A dinnae like this at aw.'

Dr White entered carrying a tray. He set the tray on the floor between the two men and retreated to the far end of the couch.

'Did a ever tell ye whit a did tae Malcolm Thompson?' said Farqueson, nursing his cup in both hands and looking at the floor. The doctor and Robert were unsure to whom he was talking. Ingram did not continue. He remembered the forbidding mansion where he had spent six years of his adolescence. He remembered its wooded grounds. He remembered the freckled face of Malcolm Thompson. Without warning, he threw his cup against the opposite wall, stood up, dragged the doctor off the couch and kicked him hard in the chest. The doctor fell back against the pile of John Buchan novels. The books, plate and egg sandwich scattered over the floor. Ingram knelt down beside him, took hold of his left hand, raised his eyes to the ceiling and snapped the doctor's pinky with one sharp movement of his right hand.

'Now you listen here. Next time, you'd be'er keep the money till a come; or am gonnae rip oot yer tongue wi' ma bare hauns.'

Chapter Four

Ingram and Robert left Dr White's surgery at just after ten o'clock. Neither of them spoke as they made their way along Ashton Road. They turned right into Byres Road and walked to a nearby barber's shop. The shopfront was still in shadow. The proprietor's name, J. Bailey, was painted in cream lettering on the dark green window sash. Ingram peered through the window. Jim Bailey was married to one of Johnny Meikle's sisters. Johnny had given him the money to set up the barber's shop as a wedding gift. Occasionally, Jim acted as a middleman in setting up loans for desperate punters.

'We'll see Matthews la'er,' said Farqueson. 'Am jist gonnae huv a wee word wi' Jimmy, as he's no busy.'

'Am right behind ye, Ingram,' replied Pollock. Ingram straightened his jacket. Robert put his hands in his pockets.

A bell rattled as Ingram pushed the door open. Four chairs were ranged in front of the mirror that dominated the right-hand wall. On the left was a bench for waiting customers. A stocky man with Brylcreemed black hair was wrapping towels around a customer's face.

'Is Mr Bailey in, Tommy?' said Ingram.

'Aye, he's oot back, Mr Farqueson.'

In the back room, Jim Bailey was sitting with his forearms resting on his thighs, emptying his pipe by striking the bowl repeatedly on the rim of a metal bucket. His white jacket was draped over the back of the chair, his braces were hanging down on either side and he was wearing a grey simet. A saucepan was heating up on a two-ring electric cooker. A teapot was standing ready on the windowsill. Through the open door beyond him his head barber, Archie Donnolly, could be seen standing in the backyard smoking a cigarette and staring up at the sky.

'Hello, Jimmy,' said Farqueson.

'A didnae expect tae see you roond here, Ingram,' replied Jim, drawing his hand through his remaining hair. 'McGuigan wis in earlier; said he's doin' the collectin' noo.'

'Am gonnae kill that fuckin' toe rag when a get ma hauns on him.'

'Oh, here, go easy, Ingram. Meikle wants him tae dae it, or so a heard. Yid be'er be careful, if ye know whit's guid fer ye.'

'Johnny's no tellt me onythin aboot it. Whit uv you heard then?'

'Och, jist whit McGuigan tellt me this mornin'. He reckoned it hud come frae above Johnny.'

'Whit dae ye mean, "above Johnny"? There's naebody above Johnny.'

'Look, am only tellin' ye whit he said.' The water in the saucepan began to boil. Jimmy offered them both a cup of tea, which they declined. Throughout the conversation, Robert stayed just behind Ingram, leaning on the door jamb with his hands in his pockets.

Ingram turned to him. 'Right, we're gonnae go tae Matthews's hoose.'

'McGuigan'll huv been there long since,' said Jimmy, pouring the water into the teapot; 'if your collectin' frae Matthews.'

'Look here, Jimmy, a think you're ge'in tae know too much aboot whit goes on roond here. It 'ill take mair than yon scrawny bastard tae get rid of me.'

'Aw hey, Ingram, why don't a get Archie tae gie ye a shave?'

On the head barber's right forearm there was a tattoo of a blue anchor, around which a narrow red ribbon, fringed with yellow, unfurled the word '*Invincible*', the name of a Royal Navy destroyer. It shifted from side to side as Archie brushed the soap into a lather. Ingram was leaning back in the high barber's chair with his head on the rest, his prominent Adam's apple exposed for the razor. He sat stiffly (conscious of the barber's proximity) and watched two flies overhead that were buzzing in frenzied convolutions about one another. The soap felt warm as Archie applied it with practised strokes to his face and throat. Nobody spoke. The other barber, Tommy, was leaning on his broom, watching Archie take Ingram's cut-throat razor from its hook on the wall above the mirror. A silver 'I' was set in its mother-of-pearl handle. Archie began to whet the blade on his leather strap. Ingram painfully raised his neck to watch him. There were reddish lines of exposed scalp between the grey strokes of Archie's heavily lacquered hair. Ingram grabbed his arm just above the tattoo.

'You be careful, or else,' he said and lowered his head again. There could be no peace for Ingram; no lowering of his defences; no relaxation.

Who does Meikle take his orders frae? he thought. Archie began

197

to scrape hair from under his chin. Ingram recalled the dark corridors of McCreadie's orphanage, through which he had been chased by Malcolm Thompson; a child's pale face, eyes wide with fear, peering at him from the doorway to one of the dormitories; the lumber room where Malcolm Thompson had held him bent over an old vaulting horse. From somewhere behind him he had heard McCreadie's voice: 'You're an absurd clown, Farqueson; always will be.' Then he had heard the sounds of high heels clicking across the floorboards. The matron had leaned over and giggled in his ear, before pulling down his trousers and pants. McCreadie had started to sing, 'The Old Rugged Cross'. Ingram's legs had been roughly parted. Finally, he had felt the searing pain in his anus.

Archie slapped lime water on his face. Jim Bailey appeared in the doorway, buttoning his white jacket, with Pollock behind him. Ingram stood up. Archie handed him his hat and jacket.

'This wan's on me, Ingram,' said Jim. Then he watched them from the doorway as they stepped beyond the shadow of the building and headed diagonally across the road towards the entrance of a close.

Stephen Matthews's flat was on the third floor. It comprised two rooms and the kitchen and bathroom. Stephen was fortunate in having a kindly and forgetful landlady who never pressed him for the rent he owed her. His wife, Beth, worked six days a week in a greengrocer's while Stephen looked after their baby boy and tinkered with a play he had been writing for three years. Much of his wife's income was swallowed up by his gambling debts and his drinking.

It was dark on the landing of the close after the brightness outside. Ingram knocked twice on the door, while Pollock leaned on the wall beside it. As soon as Matthews saw Ingram, he attempted to push the door to, but Robert swung his foot into the opening while Ingram reached through the gap and grabbed Matthew's shirt. One of the buttons was torn free and fell between the edge of the carpet and the skirting board.

'I've already given the money to McGuigan,' said Matthews in a querulous tone. Ingram pushed the door further open with his left hand. Robert withdrew his foot and followed Ingram into the hallway.

Stephen was at least three inches shorter than Ingram. His rather flat cheekbones gave his face a doleful appearance and he spoke with a slight lisp. Ingram felt an overpowering sense of revulsion when he noticed the damp patches on Stephen's shirt, the stains on his trousers and the dirt between his toes. He pushed him twice between his shoulder blades and the three of them made their way into the main room.

A dining table stood against the wall beside the door. On it were a typewriter, a bundle of typewritten pages and a copy of *Moby Dick*. Two tall windows on the opposite wall overlooked Byres Road. Stephen's baby son was crawling on the hearth rug, wearing only a nappy and a chocolate-stained vest. Ingram tossed his hat on to the table and took out his switchblade, while Robert grabbed Stephen's wrists from behind and began to push them up against his upper back.

'So you gave the money tae McGuigan,' said Ingram, releasing the blade. He pulled back Stephen's head by the hair and pressed the tip of the knife against the puffy skin beneath his right eye. 'Now you listen good. Next month, you haud on tae the money till a get here, or am gonnae slice aff yer son's twinkie and feed it tae ye raw.

Ingram straightened up and retracted the blade. 'Let him go, Rab,' he said, taking out a cigarette. He walked over to the window, patting himself all over until he found his matches in his trouser pocket. Stephen moved towards his son, rubbing his shoulders. Robert sat on the chair in front of the typewriter and laboriously typed out the word 'fuck' with his right forefinger.

Ingram took a drag of his cigarette, thrust his head forward and blew the smoke out slowly. 'A think we'll stay here fer a bite tae eat, Rab.' He sat down in the armchair by the fireplace, carefully pulling up his trousers as he did so, so they wouldn't go baggy at the knees. Pollock came over and sat near him on the end of the couch.

'What's yer plan, Ingram?' he said.

'Well, a think Stephen's gonnae make us some food while a consider the possibilities.' The baby began to cry. 'For Christ's sake shut that wain up!'

Stephen carried the child through to the bedroom. After settling him in his cot, he returned to the sitting room and said, 'There's a pot of broth in the kitchen I could heat up for you.'

Half an hour later, Ingram and Pollock were sitting at the table, eating bread and soup. Ingram's jacket was hanging over the back of the chair. The brim of his hat partially covered *Moby Dick*. The typewriter had been thrown on to the couch. Stephen was sitting beside it, gazing towards the windows and chewing his nails.

'If we get tae MacLure's place before McGuigan, we can deal wi' him there and get the money,' said Ingram.

Robert, wiping a crust round his bowl, replied, 'But whit if Jimmy was right? Whit if Meikle wants McGuigan tae dae the collectin'.'

At that moment, the door to the flat opened. The baby's muffled cries could be heard. The sitting-room door opened and a young woman appeared in the doorway. Her brown hair was held back from her temples with tortoiseshell combs. She was wearing a blue overall with the top two buttons undone.

'Have you seen the state of that wain?' she said, and then froze at the sight of the two men sitting at the dining table.

Stephen, straining to look at her over the back of the couch, said, 'Please don't make a fuss, Beth. They'll soon be gone.'

'Is that my broth they're eating?' she said. Ingram stood up, carefully wiping his mouth with a napkin, and retrieved his knife from his jacket. 'In God's name, who are these men, Stephen?' Ingram approached her with the closed knife resting in the palm of his hand.

'Rab, look efter Mr Matthews,' he said, releasing the blade. Then he pushed Beth out of the room at knifepoint. Stephen tried to get up, but Pollock pushed him back on to the couch.

'Please don't harm her!' said Stephen.

There was a sudden terrible scream from the bedroom. Ingram reappeared, wiping his blade on a scrap of material torn from Beth's overall. His face was flushed. His hands were shaking.

'Mind this, Matthews. Next time a'll no be so lenient. Let him see tae his wife, Rab.'

Stephen's eyes filled with tears. He gazed through them at the print above the sideboard, as if trying to make sense of it. The print is still in the flat. It is a hand-tinted steel engraving of a painting by Frederick Calvert, of the seaside town of Cowes on the Isle of Wight.

PART TWO

Chapter One

It was a bitterly cold day when I went to the grave of Colin Milverton's father in Sighthill Cemetery. The trees lining the central avenue were bare. The grass was white with frost. I had to clamber through a gap where a section of the wall had collapsed, because the main gate was chained shut. The grave was situated away from the path. Its headstone was surmounted by a conventional draped urn. As I read the inscription, I wondered about the complicated emotions that had brought Colin Milverton here on the day of McCluskie's murder.

At the time of his father's death, Colin had been staying in Oxford with a friend from his university days. He made no effort to return to Glasgow for the funeral, because he had set his heart on going to a party that had been organised in his honour.

In the event, he felt rather out of place there and spent much of the time standing in a corner, his fat face beaming, while people milled around him chatting awkwardly. At around ten o'clock, he was jokingly introduced to a late arrival as the son of a famous industrialist, which prompted him to rush away from the outstretched hand. He subsequently remained locked in the bathroom for ten minutes, hunched on the floor, sobbing inexplicably for a father he had never loved.

In 1954, as he walked through the entrance gates of Sighthill Cemetery, he would recall that bathroom with its Victorian bathtub and mouldy floorboards. He would recall his first visit to the grave with his mother. He would recall his first meeting with Madelaine.

Colin walked slowly up the path. The sun was by then past its zenith, but it was still unbearably hot. A gang of boys were running among the trees further up the hill, shattering the peace with their Red Indian whoops. When Colin reached his father's grave, he dropped his jacket on to the ground, drained his flask in one gulp and stood for a moment gazing at the inscription, lost in thought.

'Fatherhood.' A cultivated voice interrupted his reverie. He turned to see standing behind him a well-built man of medium height wearing a filthy beige suit. A half-smoked cheroot had been pushed behind his ear. His hair was shiny with grease. Colin recognised him as the man he had seen in the pub, because of the two fingers on his right hand which were curled round on to his palm. The man slipped the cheroot from behind his ear and lit it with a brass lighter, using only his left hand. Then he stepped forward. 'I take it that this is your father's grave.'

'Who are you?' said Milverton. 'What do you want?'

'It's funny, isn't it?' said the man, as if he hadn't heard him. 'A young woman (pretty, let's say) wiggles her tail at you one evening in Perth. Can you imagine that? On all fours, raising her bottom for you, and, lo and behold, twelve years later – a slim, young girl with dark pigtails, freckles and milky white thighs.'

'What do you mean?' Milverton, chin trembling, screwed the lid on his flask and continued to twist it.

'Of course, it wasn't planned. An embarrassing accident. The young woman was married to someone else. And now things have changed. My money has all gone. Loan sharks have humiliated and maimed me. I only asked for a little consideration. I would have spared you the truth, but, oh no, the bitch spurned me.'

'What do you want of me?' Picture Milverton: breathing heavily; squeezing the words out syllable by syllable.

'Just a little consideration. I'll leave you and your wife alone. I'll leave your reputation intact.'

Milverton swung out with all his strength and struck the man just below his right eye with the base of the flask. The man dropped his cheroot and raised his hand to protect his face from further blows. Then he backed away, cowering, repeating the words 'You bastard' in a voice broken by sobs.

Colin told Inspector Greig that after leaving the cemetery he went to a pub called the Keppoch Hill Vaults. The pub still occupies the remaining ground floor of a former tenement that it shares with two other pubs and a bookmaker's. Colin must have stood out like a sore thumb with his posh accent and lachrymose demeanour. He insisted that he had spent about half an hour drinking there and that he had been joined, after ten minutes or so, by a small man who looked as if he was in his late fifties. Milverton had started a drunken monologue about the treachery of women. When he finished, the man's face broke into a broad smile, revealing his sole remaining tooth, and he proceeded to tell Milverton some salacious anecdotes about his nights at the dance halls in the late thirties.

By the time Milverton got round to recounting these events to the inspector at his third interview, in August 1954, no one in the pub could remember Milverton being there on the day of McCluskie's death. Moreover, Inspector Greig did not trust Milverton's detailed description of the events in Sighthill Cemetery. He considered that there was something bogus in the elaboration of memories and details; as if Colin was too eager to establish the truth of what he said.

His suspicions are clearly laid out in his notebook. I have it in front of me. Its cheap blue cover makes it resemble the exercise books that I was issued at school. The margins have been drawn in by hand. Greig's writing is very small. The letters are well defined, but are not joined together and look as if they have been written by a conscientious schoolboy – anxious to please, careful and neat.

Since neither he nor Cairncross had been able to find any trace of Madelaine's ex-lover and alleged blackmailer, and since Madelaine persisted in denying his existence, Greig could only conclude that Milverton had invented the fellow, in a pathetic attempt to hide his knowledge of Madelaine's affair with Campbell and therefore his motive for killing the playwright.

Curiously enough, Professor Williams's handwriting is very similar to the inspector's. I have several notes from the professor dating from the period following Stephen Pendle's break with Fiona. They are full of distortions and misunderstandings. He insisted on describing Fiona's unhappiness as 'a nervous breakdown'. He saw fit to repeat slanderous rumours about my association with her and concluded that I was 'responsible for her drinking and drug taking'. I did not see fit to grace this nonsense with a reply. It is clear that he was merely trying to distract me from my biography. Nevertheless, his accusations hurt me. How could he link my spiritual love for Fiona with the desperate promiscuity to which Pendle's cruelty drove her?

The entry for 16 June in the recently discovered diary of Milverton's solicitor, Donald Usher, reveals that he arrived at Milverton's house at about quarter past one in the afternoon. Madelaine seemed anxious, but said nothing as he followed her into the house. Without asking, she poured him a whisky and soda and returned to the sofa and her large gin and tonic. Donald described her light green dress and her matching red lipstick and nail varnish. He was feeling agitated, having convinced himself that Colin had found out about their relationship. Madelaine, cupping her chin in her right hand, was tapping a front tooth with her fingernail and staring into space. Donald, pacing up and down, asked her what was wrong. She fished the sliver of lemon out of her drink and began to suck it. He drained his whisky, put down his glass, rubbed his hands.

'How did he find out?' he said, walking over to her. She dropped the lemon peel back into her glass. He grabbed her wrist and added, almost shouting, 'Did you tell him?'

She wriggled her arm free and stood up. 'He hasn't found out about us,' she said, swaying her hips from side to side. Then, spreading her fingers wide, she pressed her palm against his crotch. 'Now what are you and I going to do about it? If Colin divorces me, we'll have nothing.'

It is clear that Donald spent the time between leaving Madelaine at half past two and writing his diary that evening in thinking about what she had said. He wrote, 'Damn it, but it smarts. I can't stop picturing her with this man, Charles. If he is in touch with her husband, as she says, it will take a miracle to avoid a messy divorce. No chance of getting at the old man's money now. A great pity: lovely body, smooth haunches and those hollows which appear in her cheeks when she' ... Unaccountably, the entry ends here.

During the week following McCluskie's murder, Greig and Cairncross called on Madelaine while her husband was at work. The detective felt uncomfortably hot. He was embarrassed by the inspector's rudeness in wandering about the room examining books and ornaments. Madelaine sat opposite him, smiling, as she recounted a bizarre dream she had had on the morning of 16 June.

'I often have strange dreams,' she added, as if that fact would make her more attractive to the shy Cairncross.

Inspector Greig looked up from the maple-leaf ashtray he had been scrutinising and said, 'I wonder if you would be so good as to give us a written statement, Mrs Milverton. Purely routine, you understand; just to support your husband's statement.'

Cairncross's sensitive and observant notes on the case reveal that in many ways he had a better grasp of events than the inspector. When they returned to the police station, he tried to voice his suspicions about Madelaine. But the inspector was too preoccupied with her written statement to take any notice.

Greig had a temporary office in the basement of the station while his own office was being redecorated. Its ceiling was criss-crossed by pipes which rattled and shuddered from time to time, loosening small flakes of paint from their mountings. There was a map of

Glasgow on each wall, with different-coloured pins representing the victims, witnesses and suspects in the four homicides he was then investigating. Several of the pins on the map of the McCluskie case were linked by different-coloured threads, but Cairncross never learned what these signified. In a letter to his future wife, shown to me by their son, he wrote, 'Greig is a bit of a charlatan, who indulges in cheap mystification to hide the inadequacy of his working methods.' He also criticised the inspector's obsession with details, which he thought obscured rather than clarified matters.

The inspector pulled a yellow folder out of his filing cabinet. On returning to his desk, he took out a sheet of paper and placed it beside Madelaine's statement.

'Look at these, Cairncross,' he said, pushing both sheets of paper towards the detective. 'That's the letter McCluskie had with him when he died.'

'It's the same handwriting,' said Cairncross.

'Milverton's fingerprints were on the letter.'

'Come on, inspector. Milverton told us that he had picked it up without reading it.'

'I think the meeting was arranged, Cairncross,' said the inspector, tapping his nose. 'I think the playwright showed him the letter for some as yet unknown reason.'

Greig decided to visit Madelaine once more before interviewing Milverton again. It was early July. Colin had cancelled the family holiday that had been booked for the Glasgow Fair fortnight. Madelaine betrayed some irritation when she told the inspector about the cancellation, as if she held him responsible for the change of plan. Greig handed her a photostat of her letter to Campbell. She crossed her legs away from him and leaned over to stub out her cigarette in the ashtray on the coffee table.

I can picture Cairncross, his long body folded into the chair opposite, writing in his notebook and looking at her from time to time. The inspector walked over to the window, put his hands behind his back and said, 'That letter was found on McCluskie's body. Your husband was at the scene of the crime.' Madelaine frowned, dropped the sheet of paper on to the table and proceeded to insert a fresh cigarette into her holder.

'Inspector, that affair ended over two years ago. You surely don't imagine ...'

The inspector turned towards her. 'Have there been any other affairs, Mrs Milverton?'

'What do you take me for? Of course, there haven't. The whole thing was a hideous mistake. We saw each other only once. I arranged to meet him again, by letter. His reply was full of the usual endearments, but, as you know, he was unable to make it. I never saw him again.'

'Your husband claims that he was ill on the morning of 16 June. What was wrong with him?'

'I was half asleep when he went out. I thought he had gone to work as usual. He has not spoken to me about his illness.' The inspector picked up the photostat and placed it in an inside pocket of his jacket. After a moment, she added, 'So Campbell was actually carrying my letter with him on the day he died?'

'I think that'll be all for the time being,' said Greig. Madelaine put her cigarette and holder on the table and stood up, smoothing her dress. Cairncross retrieved their hats from the coatstand in the hall and followed the inspector out. Madelaine was standing in the porch with her arms crossed when the inspector turned to her from the garden path and said, 'You're quite certain that you noticed nothing unusual in your husband's behaviour on the morning of the sixteenth?'

'As I said, I was half asleep when he left,' replied Madelaine, and then, after a short pause: 'Actually, my son's teacher did phone that morning. My son, James, was apparently upset because he'd seen his father crying in the bathroom. I didn't pay any attention to it at the time, because James has a tendency to make up stories.'

'I don't trust her,' said Cairncross as he started the car. 'She's had more lovers than that. Did you no see the way she was looking at me, inspector. She's a fast one.'

'Cairncross, Cairncross, are you always to be blinded by your ego?' replied the inspector, shaking his head.

Chapter Two

Four days have passed since Campbell's death. Inspector Greig is entering a tenement close in the Gallowgate. Cairncross observes him from behind as he slowly climbs the stairs. He notices that the inspector is clasping the three middle fingers of his right hand behind his back. They both lower their eyes at each landing because of the sudden glare of sunshine through the landing windows. There is nothing in Greig's measured gait or compact physique to betray the heart disease that will kill him in three years' time.

They stop at a glass-panelled door on the fourth floor, on which is engraved, 'Christopher Malquist, Esquire, Literary Agent'. The inspector presses the bell and the door is opened by a diminutive, platinum blonde woman in a light green pencil skirt. She looks at the inspector and then at Cairncross.

'We have an appointment with Mr Malquist,' says Greig.

They pass through a small room barely containing two chairs and a desk on which are arranged a typewriter, a rudimentary telephone switchboard and a pile of manuscripts. The young woman knocks once on the inner door before opening it. Christopher Malquist is talking on the telephone, but at the sight of the two policemen he immediately cuts short what he is saying and replaces the receiver.

He motions to them to sit down and says to the woman, 'Anne, will you be so kind as to make these gentlemen some coffee.' Cairncross assumes that English is not his native language. The man is wearing a black suit despite the heat.

Without any preamble, the inspector says, 'I understand that the playwright Campbell McCluskie came to see you on the afternoon before his death.'

'You are very well informed … ?'

'Inspector Greig. And this is Detective Cairncross.'

'Well, Inspector Grieg, Mr McCluskie did come here on that afternoon. He was trying to interest me in an idea he had for a novel.'

'And how did he appear to you, Mr Malquist?'

'How should I say it? Campbell was not a happy man. He drank heavily. He had written nothing for two years.'

'Did he mention anything unusual? Did he appear anxious?'

'It was a short meeting and we did not part on good terms. I had to be blunt with him. Writers are by nature disinclined to listen to criticism. I explained to him that I was not in a position to place a novel. He was, after all, known as a playwright. He was angry. All in all, it was a very unpleasant scene. He was so agitated that he left behind a book that he had just bought.' Malquist reaches across his desk for the book in question, which is still wrapped in a brown paper bag. 'Execrable nonsense, inspector. I gave up trying to read it after five pages.' On the inside front flap, there is a small white label printed with the name and address of a second-hand book dealer.

Anne returns with the coffee. Cairncross wonders where the kitchen is located, shakes his head at the offered sugar and takes the opportunity to look at her legs as she hands the inspector his cup. When he looks at Malquist again he has the unpleasant sensation that the agent knows everything that has passed through his mind.

Greig did not follow up this visit to Malquist, and it was clear that he saw no reason to doubt Malquist's version of events. Cairncross, on the contrary, was adamant that further investigations should be made into Malquist's activities. They had a violent disagreement back at the station. The inspector believed that the detective was solely interested in renewing his acquaintance with Anne Powheid; an accusation that is borne out by the detective's notes on the meeting. Cairncross conceded that he had found her attractive, but he vehemently denied that this had affected his judgement. He told Greig that he had heard rumours that Malquist was using the agency to launder money. The inspector, pressing his sternum, said that rumours and feelings had no place in a murder inquiry.

Anne Powheid gave me a completely different account of that meeting between Campbell and Malquist. When I travelled with her to Mugdockbank Castle, and when she was quite certain we were alone, she handed me a letter that she had written to Inspector Greig shortly after McCluskie's murder, but which she had been too scared to send.

During the weeks leading up to McCluskie's death, Malquist had been growing angry at the playwright's continued silence. The agent feared that McCluskie would throw away everything that he, Malquist, had worked so hard to achieve. He had written several times to the playwright asking him to come to meetings to discuss his difficulties. It was part of Anne's job to type these letters. She could sense the threats underlying the words. McCluskie had responded to three of the letters, but Anne had seen only one of his replies. It was a shaky, handwritten scrawl, quite unlike McCluskie's usual hand, in which he asked to be left in peace.

Surprisingly enough, it was McCluskie who made the appointment to see Malquist on 16 June. He phoned from a public call box at around half past nine that morning. Anne answered the phone. He was slurring his words, but she thought he sounded very excited. He asked to speak to Malquist, but, as he was out of the office, it was Anne who made the appointment for half past two.

Malquist did not get back until a quarter past two. Nicholas Skeres was with him. While Anne told Malquist about the appointment with Campbell, Skeres sat down on the edge of her desk. He was dressed, as usual, in a black pinstriped suit with wide lapels and a broad-brimmed hat with a white silk band. He tipped the brim up, so that the hat rested on the back of his head, and stared at Anne while he lit a cigarette.

McCluskie arrived about half an hour later. Anne noticed that his hands were shaking and there were shadows under his eyes. However, his air of barely suppressed excitement reminded her of the time that he had delivered the typescript of *The Life and Death of Doctor Frost*.

Anne studiously worked on a manuscript while the playwright and Malquist were in Malquist's office. Skeres stood behind her, looking out of the window. For several minutes, she heard nothing but soft murmurs of voices from the neighbouring office. Then Campbell suddenly shouted, 'What do you mean, you won't take it?'

Malquist, losing his habitual composure, shouted back. 'Your time is up, Campbell. There's nothing else I can do for you.'

'Call yourself a literary agent!' responded Campbell.

'What do you mean by that?' Malquist replied.

'We'll see what I mean. I'll take this to someone who knows about literature!' McCluskie swept through Anne's office, avoiding her gaze, and slammed the outer door behind him. She felt Skeres's clammy breath on her nape.

'Dinnae trouble yer pretty heed aboot him.' His unpleasant hairy hands grasped her shoulders.

Malquist, appearing in the doorway, said, 'Skeres, leave her alone. I want you to follow him. We don't want him getting drunk and garrulous, do we?'

'Aye. awright, but whit aboot the other business?'

'If Meikle says that he's dealing with it, then he is dealing with it.'

I stopped reading the letter at this point and looked at Anne. 'Are you quite sure this conversation took place?' I said.

I realised immediately that my doubts were foolish. Her face expressed everything: her fear of Malquist; her guilt at not informing Inspector Greig; her implication in the death of an innocent man.

'I want you to use the letter in your biography. If Malquist was involved in Campbell's death, then it's time it was made known. I have kept silent for too long.'

'But why are you so afraid of Malquist?' I said. 'He's not been seen for over thirty years.' Her explanation made me fear for her sanity, but she ended up by infecting me with some of her terror.

'Now you might think me a weak person, Mr McDuffy, if I tell you that in March 1956 I married a boorish man who despised literature, but if you had met Christopher Malquist then you would understand why I wanted to leave that world behind me. McCluskie's death and the murder trial that followed it made me realise that everything has its price. You cannot imagine my relief when I heard in October 1958 that Malquist had disappeared on the Isle of Wight. But the whole thing was staged so that he could escape a police investigation. I have reason to believe he has returned to Glasgow. So by all means make the facts known, but please don't mention my involvement.'

As we headed back to the car, I began to straighten out the pages of her letter, which had been disarranged by the breeze. One of the sheets slipped out of my grasp and fluttered to the ground. It may have been my imagination, but I was sure that the wind suddenly picked up at that moment and began to whip it along the path in a sequence of flapping jumps. I broke into an ungainly run to try to catch it. How I hate running! My torso wobbles in an unpredictable manner. My glasses joggle about. I was out of breath when I reached a tall man in a leather jacket who was bending to pick up the elusive page. His companion (a young woman with dyed blond hair and too much make-up, who was wearing a short leather jacket, black mini-skirt and fishnet stockings) was openly laughing at me. His pale and skeletal fingers brushed my hand as he gave me the paper.

'You ought to be careful,' he said with ominous significance, and then they walked away towards the castle.

Anne caught up with me and we returned to the car. She held the door open while I squeezed into the passenger seat. I couldn't help staring at her legs when she climbed in. She was wearing a pair of honey-coloured stockings. My heart jumped when her skirt rode up to reveal a length of pale skin. She pulled down the hem with both hands, put on her seat belt and then drove me home. I did not tell her the details of my encounter with the strange couple. In fact, we hardly spoke throughout the return journey. She declined my invitation to come in for a cup of coffee and barely acknowledged my wave as she sped away.

I made several attempts to meet her again, to discuss aspects of my biography, but she refused every time. Eventually, her husband phoned me and told me never to attempt any further communication with her. I would like to make it known here that I did not intend to touch her in the car. I had merely reached down to pick up something that had fallen down the side of my seat.

I do not understand why my motives are always found to be suspect. Why is the attraction I feel towards women always greeted with hostility or indifference? Only four weeks ago, as I was returning from the supermarket with some shopping, I chanced to see Fiona walking down the street with her artist flatmate. He was wearing a shapeless, filthy pullover. His jeans were slashed at the knees, paint stained and tucked behind the tongues of his boots. Fiona was wearing a long pencil skirt and a worn leather jacket. She was jutting her jaw out to raise a cigarette to the flame of her lighter, her hips swaying dreamily from side to side. Without warning, he grabbed her buttock and squeezed it hard. Yet she displayed neither embarrassment nor revulsion. She calmly took out her cigarette, smiled and planted a kiss full on his lips. The pink flesh of her tongue appeared momentarily in the closing gap between them.

The handle of my carrier bag snapped suddenly. A carton of milk hit the pavement and burst open. Four potatoes broke free and began rolling in awkward circles. The artist looked back at me over Fiona's shoulder as I crouched down to gather them together. He pressed his lips to hers again, to prevent her looking back, while he stretched out his arm and thrust up his middle finger; a gesture with which I am sure Fiona is all too familiar. Painful visions; evil thoughts: I wonder if somewhere, in Heaven or Hell, Campbell is aware of his pathetic fat satellite.

Chapter Three

On the first anniversary of Campbell McCluskie's murder, Coultts Publishing House brought out a short novel, *The Death of Liam*, which was written by a young writer named George Chapman, ostensibly as a tribute to the late playwright. In the preface to that novel, Chapman described the circumstances that led him to write it.

On the day of Campbell's murder, Chapman had taken his fiancée to lunch in order to celebrate the publication by Coultts of his first novel, *The Songs of Summer*. He went on to write that they had had an argument and that he had stormed out of the restaurant.

> During the course of that afternoon, I fell into a profound melancholia (such as is often experienced by artists and writers after the completion of some difficult opus) and I wandered the streets at random until I found myself at the main entrance to the Necropolis. It is clear to me now that Destiny guided my steps to that secluded area of the cemetery beneath the Monteith Mausoleum, where I found Campbell McCluskie reclining against a memorial plaque, taking swigs from a half-empty whisky bottle.
>
> How vividly I can still picture that scene: the open stretch of grass in the shadow at the foot of the hill; the sunlight coming through the branches above; Campbell sitting with his left arm resting on his raised knee, like God on the ceiling of the Sistine Chapel. When I approached the playwright, his first concern was that I was trying to 'cadge some of his whisky', but when I expressed my admiration of his work he screwed the lid back on his bottle and said forcibly, 'Nobody understands my work. Nobody.' I thought that I should leave, but he detained me by grabbing my arm. 'Listen here,' he continued. 'I accidently stood on a dog's paw this morning. It was a skinny black mongrel with a white diamond splash on its chest. Now, suppose that I get knocked down by a tram this evening,

and that same dog comes up and licks my face while I'm dying; that's what I'm trying to achieve with my new novel.' He then went on to curse his agent, Christopher Malquist, in the foulest terms imaginable.

To distract him, I asked him if it was going to be a novel about a dog, but he replied that it would be about a love affair and a death; that its hero, Liam, would drown while rowing to an island to steal his lover away from her husband; that the whole novel would take place inside Liam's head during his dying moments.

Chapman then portrays himself suggesting alterations and refinements to the playwright's idea. 'Sadly', he wrote, 'the McCluskie who created *The Life and Death of Doctor Frost* was no more. The plot of his projected novel was sketchy and flawed. However, he approved of my humble suggestions, and my only regret is that he did not live to see his battered vessel repaired and made seaworthy.' To continue Chapman's metaphor, *The Death of Liam* may be seaworthy, but it is a dreadnought battleship compared with the racing yacht of Campbell's original fragment. Absent is that 'light-fingered, mischievous fate' described by one critic in an early review of *The Life and Death of Doctor Frost*. Chapman's clunky prose delivers his condemnation of adultery with all the subtlety of a twelve-inch naval gun. It is clear that Chapman's novel owes more to the fact that his fiancée abandoned him for a dissolute actor than it does to Campbell's projected fiction.

The statement that Chapman made to the police in August 1954 differs dramatically from what he wrote in that preface. He told Cairncross that McCluskie had grown excited when he talked about his novel and had seemed to forget that Chapman was there at all. The playwright paced around the area of grass, developing his theme and waving his hands about. Chapman watched him in fascination, barely comprehending what he said, until Campbell saw something in the bushes nearby and stopped speaking. When Chapman turned to look in that direction, he saw the bushes moving and caught a brief glimpse of a man's face.

'Don't worry about him,' said Campbell. 'I've got the measure of that bastard.' He settled down on the ground again, took out a pen and two sheets of paper and scored out something that was written there. Then he put the paper back in his pocket and he was about to put his pen away, when he said, 'What do you do yourself?'

Chapman, taken by surprise, took a moment to reply. 'Actually, I've just had a novel published by Coultts.'

'What? You're a fucking writer?' said Campbell, rising to his feet. 'You fucking bastard! You come here like some sneak thief and then tell me you're a fucking writer. Well, what's this novel about then?'

'It's called *The Songs of Summer*,' replied Chapman, backing away towards the bushes at the foot of the hill.

'"The Songs of Fucking Summer", eh? "The Songs of Fucking Summer". Here, I'll give you a song for summer.' So saying, McCluskie threw his pen at Chapman. The younger writer raised his hand to protect his face, and the nib stuck for a moment in the palm before falling to the ground. A small bubble of ink-stained blood appeared on the skin, and then Chapman started to run towards the path. He heard the playwright laughing. After running for about a hundred yards, he looked back and saw McCluskie hurling the empty whisky bottle high into the air. At a certain point in its ascent, the bottle began to glitter in the sunlight. Then it descended into the shadow of the hill once again and shattered on a gravestone hidden among the bushes. Having watched its descent, McCluskie walked away in the opposite direction.

After the interview, the inspector and Cairncross searched the Necropolis for anything that might corroborate Chapman's statement. The detective watched Greig sifting through the detritus that had gathered under the bushes near where Chapman had encountered the playwright.

'I've found it,' Grieg shouted. Holding up a fountain pen by its clip, he approached Cairncross. The inspector unfurled his handkerchief with his other hand and placed the pen upon it to present it for Cairncross's scrutiny, before then wrapping it in the handkerchief and putting it in his jacket pocket. Cairncross looked at the dark clouds gathering behind the mausoleum and a shiver ran down his back.

'Can we go back to the station now?' he said. 'I have to do some work on the McGuigan case.'

'I just want to check something else.' The inspector pushed his way through the bushes on the other side of the path. Cairncross followed him. They came upon a small stone obelisk surmounted by an angel whose face had crumbled away. Shards of glass were scattered around it. There was small clearing beyond this, fringed with cypresses and a rhododendron bush. One of the thicker branches of the bush had been broken off. Its damaged end was dark, suggesting that it had been exposed for some months.

'What do you make of that?' said the inspector.

'Looks like it was broken by a strong man. I mean, those branches are quite supple and it's broken clean through.' While Cairncross spoke, Greig fingered the broken end of the branch and looked back across the clearing at the stone angel.

'Or perhaps a very heavy man fell against it while he was trying to avoid being hit by that bottle,' he replied.

McCluskie left no trace of his movements between leaving Chapman in the Necropolis and meeting the stagehand George Pringle an hour and a half later in the Theatre Vaults.

Campbell particularly admired Pringle, who had been working for over thirty years among the gantries, ropes and pulleys of the Theatre Royal stage. A man of medium height, his face was dominated by deep-set, piercing eyes and eyebrows that were thick and curly towards the bridge of his nose but tapered away to nothing at his temples. When the playwright arrived, Pringle was leaning on the bar, drinking the double measure of single malt whisky which he took every evening before starting work. The place was stuffy and dark after the brightness outside. At first, George didn't recognise Campbell, who was silhouetted in the open doorway against the daylight.

I imagine Campbell swaying slightly as he took in the deep red upholstery of the chairs; the wall-mounted lamps with their red shades fringed with tassels; the framed engravings of famous actors; the gleaming brass taps; George Pringle standing at the bar, raising his glass to his mouth.

'George, it's me, Campbell,' he called as he walked towards him. George smiled, nodded and ordered another whisky. 'It's good to see you, George,' Campbell added, patting Pringle's shoulder.

'Aye, it's been a long time, Campbell,' replied George, pushing the whisky towards him. 'And how are things with you?'

'I'll confess they've been better. Look, why don't we sit down and have a wee chat?'

'Aye, awright, but remember I have tae start work in ten minutes.'

They sat down at a table near the door.

'I heard they made a film of yon play of yours,' said George. 'Weren't Fred MacMurray and Barbara Stanwyck in it?'

'No, you must be thinking of another film, George. Orson Welles was up to play the part of Doctor Frost, but they didn't offer him enough money. Anyway, the bastards butchered my play.'

Pringle winced and finished his whisky. 'Here, look at the time, Campbell. I'll have tae be goin'.'

McCluskie suddenly grabbed his arm and said, 'Please wait a minute, George. Can you read this? I've had this idea for a novel. I'd like to know what you think.'

George later described the meeting to Cairncross in the Theatre Royal. A man on a ladder was painting a backdrop. A group of men were arguing about how best to carry a heavy bureau on to the stage.

'Gonnae keep the noise down!' shouted Pringle. 'I cannae hear masell think over here.' Then, in a quieter voice, he said to Cairncross, 'I feel bad about it now. I mean I wasn't tae know he was gonnae get himsel' killed, but what could I say? I told him I'd never read a novel in my life. I mean I liked the man 'n' aw that. I couldnae tell him to his face that I didnae like his plays. If I'd known he was gonnae die, I'd have said I liked the idea, but, to be honest, I couldnae make head nor tail of it. He got pretty angry when I suggested he should stick to writing plays.'

Before he left, Cairncross asked Pringle why he didn't like Campbell's plays. The stagehand replied, 'I think Campbell was too clever for his ain good. The audiences loved his plays, but I felt there was mair goin' on in them than met the eye. I liked the man, but I felt that he wis laughin' at us all.'

Chapter Four

Stephen Matthews, looking over his shoulder as he walked out of the sitting room, saw Ingram and Robert standing in huddled conversation by the table. He would never forget them: Ingram stooping to whisper in Robert's ear with the slender fingers of his right hand spread fanwise, while Robert, chuckling and nodding, gouged a fragment of bread from the loaf on the table and rolled it into a pellet between his forefinger and thumb.

Shortly afterwards, Ingram directed Pollock to close the living-room door, 'to shut oot that awfu' din'. From the bedroom, the baby's crying was punctuated by Stephen's guttural sobs and an unsettling sound between a moan and a whimper, which made Pollock wince as he pushed the door to. Then there were only the sounds from the street and the whine of a neighbour's vacuum cleaner to disturb Ingram.

Stephen heard nothing from the other room but the soft murmur of their voices, until half an hour later Ingram suddenly shouted, 'A'm gonnae kill that fuckin' bastard, d'ye hear? A'm gonnae kill 'um.' At one o'clock, Stephen heard them urinating noisily, one after the other, and then the door to the flat was slammed shut.

Once outside, Ingram and Pollock turned into Dowanside Road. In the entrance to a close on the opposite side of the road, a frail old lady had unlocked the door and was struggling to remove her key from the lock. Ingram tapped Pollock's arm twice and ran across the road. Robert followed him. The old lady was attached to the key by a cheap metal chain. Her eyesight was bad. Her hands were shaking as she wrestled with the stiff lock and tried to retain a hold on her handbag. She heard Ingram's ringing footsteps, echoed by Robert's, but before she could turn to look at them Ingram had pushed her against the jamb. Her slender chain snapped. Her glasses slipped off as she fell back down the step, both hands instinctively clutching her bag.

'Get the door, Rab! Get the door!' The door was slammed shut and the two blurred figures ran, laughing, through the echoing close.

In the back court, a woman was hanging a white sheet out to dry. Her son, a tiny toddler, stood nearby on uncertain legs, wearing only a nappy and a short vest. I picture the raised crescent of flesh outlining his navel; the wispy golden curls on his head; the chipped blue enamel covers on the safety pins holding his nappy together. His mother held a peg in her mouth while she pushed another one on to the line. A beatific look came over her son's face as he began to fill his nappy. Then two men ran into the court.

She told the police that she had seen below the sheet only the grey upturned trousers and shiny brogues of the first man. She spat out the peg, but he pushed the sheet over her head before she could say anything. The two men then began to spin her round. As they wrapped the sheet tightly around her face and body, she heard each peg flying off the line with a wooden click. She heard the sheet flapping. One of the men smelled of sweat and whisky; the other of carbolic soap and stale tobacco. When they reached the end of the sheet, they continued to spin her round, until she lost her balance and fell on to the grass by the midden.

I imagine the toddler stepping from foot to foot, his smile breaking into an anguished yowl as he falls on to his bottom. I imagine the bright white linen on the line; the clearly defined border of shadow running along two edges of the court; the network of fences, paths, middens and grass which breaks up the space; Ingram and Robert running and jumping to the narrow alley between two blocks of tenements which connects with Highburgh Road.

At about the time they emerged on to Highburgh Road, a cantankerous midwife in a phone box near my parents' flat was calling an ambulance out for my mother. My parents were then living in a tenement in Ruchill. My mother had gone into labour two days earlier and the midwife had been called out. My father described her as a 'fat woman with varicose veins and a face like a nippy sweetie'. As soon as she had seen my mother, she had turned to him and said, 'Your wife is not screaming, Mr McDuffy. She is not in labour. Kindly do not disturb me again until her waters have broken.'

My mother knew that she was in labour and that something was amiss. In fact, my head was in the wrong position and the umbilical cord was caught round my neck. My mother endured a painful, sleepless night. The midwife came out again the following afternoon; this time with a student nurse. The nurse examined my mother and concluded that she was in deep labour. The midwife accused her of incompetence and refused to make any further examination.

It was not until a quarter to one on 16 June that the midwife finally examined my mother. I imagine her palpating my mother's belly with her capable hands, frowning and drawing in her lips, while my father paces the hall, chewing his cuticles. He hears her through the door, speaking harshly to my doomed mother: 'Don't push an inch or you'll kill your baby.'

I have a vivid recollection of my father describing this scene to me. I had returned home late one evening, to find him slumped in his armchair drinking whisky. The firelight made his bald head gleam. He was wearing a shabby cardigan with the sleeves rolled up. His eyes were red and puffy from crying. He cleared his throat noisily several times, as if trying to dislodge his grief, and then offered me a whisky. As he spoke, I sat looking into my drink and occasionally glanced at the photograph of my mother on the mantelpiece. It had been taken in the summer of 1948. She was kneeling to pat her Border collie. She was a beautiful, plump woman with a compassionate smile, dressed in a tartan skirt and light-coloured pullover. My father continued, 'Can you believe that? The bitch actually used those words: "Don't push an inch or you'll kill your baby."' I must have betrayed my emotion at the painful irony of these words, for he suddenly stopped speaking and looked away. I felt once again the burden of my ill-fitting life. My father tried to change the subject by asking about my studies, but he didn't listen to my reply. He never again referred to the events of my birth.

Last winter, armed with my camera, I followed the route taken by Ingram and Robert to Dumbarton Road. The cloud cover was high, giving a light grey cast to the day. A cool westerly breeze freshened the air, but the tenements were colourless and oppressive. When the two hoodlums passed this way in 1954 there was no breeze. The façades of the tenements would have offered rich patterns of red, cream and black. The tarmac would have been softening in the intense heat and giving off that heavy odour which for me destroys the charm of summer days in the city.

A policeman, who was walking along the road at that time, noticed two suspicious characters approaching from the direction of Byres Road. He was reminded of a comedy duo. The taller of the two was wearing a grey suit and walking quickly, looking to left and right. His companion struggled to keep up with him, stepping on and off the pavement, gesticulating and talking all the while. As soon as they caught sight of the policeman, they crossed the road and headed down Ellie Street. The constable was too hot to give chase, and contented himself with watching their curious progress until they turned right into Lawrence Street.

Pollock later told the police that, during the course of that afternoon, 'Ingram seemed tae lose the place completely.' Pollock was scared throughout the interrogation because of the serious offence he had been charged with; because he feared Johnny Meikle's power; because Ingram had escaped custody by seriously injuring a policeman. Nevertheless, he was very forthcoming.

When I look at my plan of Glasgow, the zany route they took from Lawrence Street to Dumbarton Road (Lawrence Street – Dowanhill Street – White Street – Hyndland Street – Chancellor Street – Lawrie Street – Gardiner Street – Dumbarton Road) resembles the indentations of a stretch of coastline. Ingram feared that the policeman might follow them. His hands were shaking. Sweat beaded his forehead. His lips were tightly compressed. As Pollock and he approached the junction with Dumbarton Road, Ingram thrust his head forward, pulling back his shoulders as he did so, stuck his finger into Pollock's arm and said, 'Naebody's gonnae push me around, d'ye hear? Naw Meikle; naw McGuigan; naebody.'

I have my photographs of their route. They are black and white. The first shows Highburgh Road towards Byres Road. You can just make out the alleyway that they ran through. A woman, heavily laden with bags, is stepping on to the pavement in the lower left-hand corner. She would have been a teenager when Campbell died. I wonder if she has ever heard of him.

The second photograph shows the intersection of Ellie Street and Lawrence Street. There is a church on the corner; more tenements. The Western Infirmary can be seen in the background. It is strange to think of Ingram passing here, his thoughts full of murder, unaware as yet of who McCluskie is.

The third photograph shows the church on White Street. Two young boys are in the frame. One of them said, 'Hey mister, are you takin' a photae of Glasgow culture?'

'No, son, I'm trying to recapture the past.'

'Whit dae ye want tae dae that fer?'

'I'm trying to understand why a woman died,' I replied, smiling bitterly as I replaced my lens cap. They ran off, laughing and twisting their fingers into their temples.

The fourth photograph, taken at the corner of Gardiner Street and Dumbarton Road, shows a corner of the pub where I had several drinks to relieve the weight of my despair.

Ingram and Pollock turned right into Dumbarton Road, and then, beyond the railway bridge, they headed down Hayburn Street. Red sandstone tenements (recently cleaned) still line Hayburn Street, but the third-floor flat in Beith Street (to which they were heading) has gone. It looked on to the junction with Boseville Road where children were enjoying a rowdy playtime in the local primary school.

Inside the flat, Patrick MacLure was reading a postcard from his mother, who was living in comfortable retirement in the south of England. There was a knock on the door. Patrick looked at his watch and scratched his head. Then there was a very loud crack, as if someone had kicked the door. He dropped the card on to the table and went to open it. Ingram was standing on the landing with his legs apart, his jacket unbuttoned and his hands in his trouser pockets. Robert was leaning on the wall by the jamb.

A photograph, taken by the police, shows that Patrick was a handsome man with high cheekbones and an aquiline nose, whose deep-set eyes radiated laughter lines. He appears curiously happy for someone who has just lost his job as a waiter and is in debt to Johnny Meikle to the tune of £150.

The flat consisted of one large room and a tiny kitchenette. A glass-fronted oak cabinet contained the few books and ornaments he owned. Newspapers were scattered everywhere. A notebook on the table was filled with figures and calculations relating to odds and careful notes detailing the form of various horses. Also on the table were an old wireless set and an ashtray (stolen from a local pub) that was overflowing with cigarette stubs. There was in addition a bed, an armchair and two wooden chairs. His spare clothes were slung over hangers that were suspended from a hook on the door. The hangers swung from side to side when Ingram pushed the door to.

'I wasn't expecting you for another hour yet,' said Patrick.

'A dinnae care when ye were expectin' us, ye filthy bastard,' said Ingram. You jist be'er have the fuckin' money.'

Robert held out his hand while Patrick pulled two folded and greasy banknotes from his pocket.

Ingram sat in the armchair and took off his hat. 'Right, MacLure, a want ye tae go oot an' fetch us some beer. Then a want ye tae skedaddle; a dinnae care where ye go; jist dinnae come back here fir at least three hours. D'ye understand?' Ingram reached into his jacket for his cigarettes, lit one and added, 'Oh, 'n' wha'ever happens, we huvnae been here. Dae a make masell clear? You huvnae seen us.'

*

There was a painting on my father's bedroom wall, which had been painted by a cousin of his called Alan, or Sam, or something. Throughout my childhood and early teens it was mounted above the fireplace between two brass candlesticks. It showed two men sitting at a table in a room. Two half-empty bottles of beer and two glasses were standing on the table. Framed in the window between the two men was a view of tenements beneath a blue sky scattered with clouds. The windows of those tenements were bright with the glare of reflected sunlight. In contrast, the room was rendered in a limited range of dull tones. The taller of the two men was apparently my father's uncle. To judge by the painting, he was a slim man with high cheekbones. The other man was small and thin. Whether by accident or design, the perspective had been skewed to unsettling effect.

As with so many things in my father's life, I never learned what significance the painting had for him, or why he gave it away to a charity shop when I was sixteen. However, during the time it remained in that room, I was frequently drawn to it by a fascination mingled with dread. Now, when I try to imagine Ingram and Pollock in MacLure's flat, waiting for McGuigan, it is that painting which comes to mind. That distorted room begins to fill with the various odours of dirty clothes, alcohol, cigarettes, stale sweat and carbolic soap. Ingram reaches for one of the bottles and pours more beer into his glass.

'Whit a dump,' he says, looking at the damp stained wall.

'A've stayed in worse places,' replies Pollock. He finishes his drink and wipes his mouth with the back of his hand. He stands up, looks into the glass-fronted cabinet and continues, 'Hey, look, Ingram; should ye no speak tae Johnny before ye dae anythin' tae McGuigan? A mean, mibbe Johnny's got somethin' in mind fer you.'

'We've earned oor cut, Rab. Naebody's gonnae take it away frae us.'

Pollock opens the doors of the cabinet. Inside, there is a small wooden box containing two antique ink bottles. On the shelf next to it are four or five books. He takes one out and slowly reads aloud its title: '*S-i-n-i-s-t-e-r Street*. Aye, a like tha'; *Sinister Street*.'

Ingram has taken off his jacket. His dark grey and red striped braces form a Y shape on his back. His shirt billows out slightly around his shoulder blades.

'Shu'up, Rab,' he says. 'A'm tryin' tae think.' Pollock settles himself in the armchair with the book. He tries to read the first page, flicks through it and then flings it across the room, exasperated. Ingram stands up. 'A tell't ye tae keep quiet!' he shouts. A strand of

223

hair has slipped forward and is hanging by his right temple. He tries to push it back, but it slowly springs forward again. 'Jesus fuckin' Christ.' He walks over to the window.

'Will a pit on the wireless, Ingram?'

Ingram strides over to the table, picks up the wireless set and hurls it against the glass-fronted cabinet. One pane is shattered. The lead strips around it buckle inwards, but the wireless falls to the floor, its casing intact. The light in the dial flickers on for a moment. A brief phrase of music comes from the speaker. And then the light dies. Ingram, his hands shaking, takes out a cigarette, lights it, but stamps it out on the carpet after taking one drag.

'A dinnae want any noise. D'ye hear? No' a fuckin' sound.'

Pollock, half-rising from the chair, is about to say something, but he thinks better of it and settles down again. Farqueson returns to his chair. He takes a sip of beer and then carefully removes his cufflinks. They are oval in shape, black with silver borders, and each has a silver 'I' set in its centre. He drops them in a pocket of his jacket, which is draped over the back of his chair, and rolls up his sleeves. He removes his watch and puts it in another pocket. Then he takes out his switchblade and lays it on the table in front of him. Finally, he places his hands, palms down, on either side of the knife and spreads his fingers. On his right forearm there is a tattoo of a naked girl with bluish black hair. She is holding her hands behind her head and thrusting her hips out provocatively. The tattooist has taken advantage of a tiny freckle on Ingram's arm to represent her left nipple. Ingram looks at the tattoo for a moment and then closes his eyes.

I wonder what he was thinking as he sat there in MacLure's room with his eyes closed. For, according to Pollock, he did sit there with his eyes closed. It is possible that he was thinking of Molly Damart, or perhaps he was thinking of Malcolm Thompson and McCreadie's orphanage. Certainly, he still remembered Malcolm Thompson in 1973, when he was interviewed for a BBC radio series, *Violent Lives*. None of the programmes has been preserved, but I was able to find a copy of the interview in an old edition of *The Listener*.

Ingram described how the sight of Malcolm Thompson's mutilated body filled him with a sense of calm which he had never experienced before and which he was never to experience again. The feeling lasted only a moment. Memories soon crowded back, bringing with them their burden of anxiety and anger. One thinks of the gesture that Doctor Frost makes during the final act of McCluskie's play, when, on the stroke of midnight, he draws the curtains on the beautiful moonlit view.

Through my window I can see the tops of the cranes in the ship-yards, shimmering in the evening sunlight. A Jack Russell on the street below is wagging its tail and standing up on its hind legs to beg a scrap of fish from a man in a Glasgow Rangers football shirt.

I am certain that hidden among the events of Campbell's life is the key that could explain everything: that dog; that man bending to feed it; the salmon pink vapour streaks crossing the sky; a woman's waters breaking in a Glasgow hospital room, while across the city McGuigan approached the back entrance of a pub in Dumbarton Road.

Crates of empty beer bottles were piled on the right, a foul-smelling dustbin shedding its contents beyond them. He knocked on the door. A bolt was drawn back. A key was turned and a man (wearing a white shirt, a black bow tie and a stained apron over black trousers) ushered him in. They made their way to the darkened lounge bar.

Johnny Meikle was sitting at a table with his jacket draped over his shoulders. A glass of whisky and ice stood on the table in front of him. His two bodyguards, Welsh and Grogan, were leaning against the bar, drinking beer and talking in hushed tones. Welsh was a monumental man with hastily sketched features and pitted skin, while Grogan was overweight with thinning hair. Out of vanity, the latter always wore jackets that were one size too small for him. They turned to look at McGuigan when he entered, but turned away immediately as if to underline his insignificance.

Meikle, his elbows resting on the table, brought the tips of his short, hairy fingers together and said, 'So you've come, McGuigan. I'll confess that I didnae expect to see you.' He gestured to one of the thugs. 'Give the man a whisky, Welsh. Mibbe it'll loosen his tongue.'

'Whit d'ye mean?' said McGuigan, taking a seat opposite Meikle. McGuigan placed his hat on the table. Welsh slammed the drink down in front of him and returned to the bar.

'Do you think am soft in the heid, McGuigan? Do you think a've got nothin' be'er tae dae wi' ma time?'

'Eh?'

'Picture me this morning, sittin' on ma arse for an hour, a whole fuckin' hour, waitin' fir Farqueson and Pollock. So, as a wis in the area, a thought a'd call on Jim Bailey. That wis a very enlightening visit.' Meikle stood up, gripping the table with both hands, and continued in a louder voice. 'Now don't you fuck wi' me, ye wee gobshite, or a will kill ye, do you understand?'

'Look, Meikle, a hud it frae Skeres. He tell't me that Ingram wis oot of control, so if the Big Yin wants rid'uv Farqueson, then that's fine by me. The man's a fuckin' lunatic. A'll gladly dae his collections.'

Meikle pulled McGuigan's arm towards him and pushed his head on to the table.

'Never underestimate me, McGuigan. As far as you are concerned, a am the Big Yin. If anythin' happens tae Farqueson, it happens wi' ma say so; no Malquie's.' Meikle released him and snapped his fingers. Welsh and Grogan moved over behind McGuigan, who sat rubbing his wrist. 'Okay, McGuigan; gie us the money.' Meikle moved his fingers back and forth as if encouraging a recalcitrant child. Welsh and Grogan moved closer, each with his right hand in his jacket pocket. McGuigan pulled a creased brown envelope from his jacket and handed it to Meikle, who took out the money and began to count it note by note on to the table. He counted it again.

'Three hundred and seventy-five pounds,' he said, after a pause. Then he counted out thirty pounds and gave them to McGuigan.

'The deal wis twen'y percent,' said McGuigan, his voice taking on a hard, stubborn edge. He attempted to stand up, but Welsh pushed him back into his chair.

'You've got ten pounds coming frae MacLure. Just think yoursel' lucky a didnae rearrange your face.'

The two thugs stepped away from McGuigan. He stood up, made a show of brushing down his lapels and picked up his hat. Then he was escorted out. I picture Johnny Meikle sitting there, watching him go; a stout, swarthy man with unruly black hair and a wart on his left cheek.

McGuigan met his girlfriend, Heather Torrance, outside the pub. She would tell the police that she had been looking for him all afternoon and that the barber, Jim Bailey, had told her she would find him there. Curious how these shady matters conspired to give McGuigan an hour's reprieve. He spent it in the top-floor flat in White Street which Heather then shared with her mother.

Heather, now a sixty-year-old widow, still lives there. When I visited her last year, she showed me a photograph of herself, taken when she was twenty, during a holiday in Morecambe. She had been an attractive blonde with painted-on eyebrows and a pert nose, wearing a white blouse with the collar and two buttons undone. Her figure had been breathtaking.

'Aye, those were grand days,' she said, smiling at some memory.

'But ma pig of a husband destroyed aw ma photaes of McGuigan. He wis a right jealous bastard, tha' yin.' She sketched patterns with a fingertip on the arm of her chair. I noticed the purple line traced by a broken vein across her right shin.

McGuigan finally arrived at MacLure's at around half past five. There was a short struggle, but Ingram and Pollock were prepared. They had torn a bed sheet into strips to bind him to one of the chairs.

Ingram found the thirty pounds in McGuigan's jacket pocket. Pollock took no further part in proceedings. He stood in the background, staunching a cut on his hand with his dirty handkerchief. A note of desperation entered McGuigan's voice. He told Ingram about his meeting with Skeres in an attempt to deflect his anger.

'Who the fuck is Skeres?' said Ingram. 'A work fir Meikle.'

'But it wis Meikle who tell't me tae dae the collection. He tell't me.'

'You've been done, ya Fenian bastard,' said Ingram, rubbing his nose and looking at the surface of the table. In the BBC interview, he would describe a sound like static which filled his ears when he picked up the knife, and a postcard on the table, of which later he would retain a vivid memory: the message; the address; the wavy lines of the postmark. Pollock would swear to the police that he shouted, 'Naw, Ingram; dinnae dae it!' But Ingram ignored him. McGuigan would have smelled carbolic soap when Ingram grabbed him under the chin and pulled back his head. He would have seen Ingram's shirt and tie; the swelling of his Adam's apple; the outline of his jaw. He struggled against the bindings. Ingram looked at the ceiling and began to cut his throat. The edge of the blade was not that sharp. He had to press hard and use a sawing action to cut through the skin and muscle. The jugular vein and carotid artery were severed. Spurting blood reached the table three feet away. McGuigan's windpipe was cut. Blood bubbled around the wound and began to slide into his lungs. Three minutes later, he was dead. Last images? Perhaps Heather's swaying bottom preceding him up the stairs; Meikle sustaining an interminable and absurd monologue on the other side of a table which seems to get longer and longer; the square face, deceitful arms and golden numerals of a Westclox travel alarm slowly fading into the blackness?

According to the police report, a postcard was found at the scene of the crime, just as Ingram would later describe it. On it was a photograph of the chalk stacks, known as the Needles, which are situated at the eastern extremity of the Isle of Wight.

PART THREE

Chapter One

Ingram straightened up. McGuigan's head slumped forward. Pollock approached the corpse, saying, 'Whit the fuck huv ye done, ya bastard?' Ingram looked at his right hand. Three lines of blood were arrested in their flow towards his knuckles. They slowly turned on themselves and began to run towards his wrist.

'Am gonnae clean masel' up,' he said, and went into the kitchenette.

Pollock ran his fingers through his lank hair. He looked as if he was about to cry. He screwed up his eyes and opened his mouth. His face began to show its seams. 'Jesus Christ, Ingram. Whit are we gonnae dae?' He reached out a hand to support himself on the table. He felt some warm blood on his fingers. He swore and knocked over Ingram's beer bottle. It rolled into the corner and clunked on the skirting board.

From the kitchen there came a crash of falling crockery; then the sound of tap water. Ingram returned to the room, shaking his hands. 'MacLure's towels are fuckin' mingin'.'

'Whit are we gonnae dae, Ingram?'

'We're naw gonnae dae anythin', you stupit eejit.'

Pollock turned away and began to look through the window. In the street below, six or seven schoolboys were kicking a can about. Two men, dressed in dark blue overalls, were walking along together arguing. Everything outside seemed bright. Pollock pressed his forehead to the glass. It felt warm.

Ingram let out a curse and returned to the kitchenette for his knife. He wiped it dry on the sleeve of one of the jackets hanging on the entrance door. Then he closed the blade and slipped it back into a pocket of his jacket, retrieving his cufflinks and his watch as he did so. Finally, he took out his comb, wet it in the kitchenette and combed back his hair.

Pollock was about to say something else, but Ingram strode over to him, grabbed his arm and dragged him towards the body. 'Take a good look at this, pal. Ye're in this up tae yer neck, so fer Christ's sake shu' yer fuckin' mouth.' McGuigan's face was bluish white. The eyes were open. The head was slumped forward in an unnatural attitude. Deprived of support, the jaw had lost some of its definition. The blood around the wound looked black.

Ingram pushed Pollock against the wall beside the window. Then he sat down in the armchair and began to rub his temples with the thumb and forefinger of his right hand. A man returning from work could be heard talking to his wife on the landing. Somewhere in the building a woman was shouting, 'Jamie, if a huv tae tell you again, there's gonnae be trouble.' Ingram remembered the sizzling sound a cigarette end had made when Malcolm Thompson had pressed it on to his thigh.

At around half past six, Patrick MacLure turned into Boseville Street from Dumbarton Road. He felt uneasy and paused for a moment by the school gate. He checked the money in his trouser pocket. He wondered whether it was safe to return to his flat. He was still undecided when a car screeched past and pulled up sharply at the corner of Beith Street. He thought he recognised the two men who got out the front, but he couldn't place them until Johnny Meikle emerged from one of the rear doors. As soon as MacLure saw Meikle, he walked quickly away towards Dumbarton Road.

Pollock, still standing by the window, was chewing his nails. Ingram was staring at the fireplace with its iron grate and its mound of cigarette stubs.

'Ingram, it's Meikle.'

Ingram looked at Pollock as if he had just become aware of his presence. He joined him at the window. Meikle and his two bodyguards were crossing the street below in classic formation – Meikle looking straight ahead, while Welsh and Grogan followed, one on each side looking to left and right.

'Huv ye got a weapon?' said Ingram.

'Naw, Ingram.'

'Well, get a fuckin' knife frae the kitchen then.'

'We cannae fight them, Ingram.'

'Just get a fuckin' knife.'

Lying near the sink was a stolen steak knife with the word 'Laing's' engraved on its silver handle. Pollock grabbed it and followed Ingram. They heard footsteps echoing up the close.

'Right, take yer fuckin' shoes aff,' hissed Ingram as he knelt to untie his brogues. They pulled the door to and made their way upstairs to the next landing. There was a loud knocking below, followed by the cracking sound of MacLure's door being kicked in.

'Here, this door's no locked,' whispered Pollock. They slipped inside and slid the bolt across. The curtains were drawn. The room was dark save for a slim band of yellow light on the wall around the window curtain. There was a terrible smell. Pollock and Ingram, holding their breath, froze by the door in villainous attitudes as footsteps approached the landing outside. A voice called from below and the footsteps descended. When Pollock and Ingram breathed in again, the smell caught in the back of their throats, making them both retch.

'What in God's name is causing that smell?' said Pollock, bending to refasten his laces.

'Is that you, Hughie?' came a wavering voice from the bed. Pollock noticed some movements there among what he had taken to be a pile of rags. As he approached the bed, the smell grew worse. Ingram pulled back the curtain. Meikle's car was still parked on the corner of Boseville Street. A line of sunlight fell across the room, illuminating the knobbly wrist of an arm that was stretching towards Pollock. Pollock drew back. Once again the voice said, 'Is that you, Hughie?' A buzzing sound was coming from the kitchen. By now Pollock could discern the figure of an old woman lying on the bed. Her arm fell back on to the cover.

'Have you got Jessie's towel?' she said.

'Get her tae shu'up, Pollock.'

'The water's cold, Hughie. Jessie'll need her towel.' The old woman stopped speaking. A rasping sound came from her throat. Pollock, finding the smell unbearable, went to the window, but there was no draught to freshen the air. Ingram opened the door to the kitchenette. A wedge of sunlight fell across the bed. The old woman's mouth was open. Her jaw was slack. Her neck was all sinews and sagging flesh. Hundreds of tiny flies were buzzing around the kitchen. On the draining board, among cluttered crockery, a small mound crawled with maggots. Ingram slammed the door, but not before some of the flies had flown into the main room to investigate the smell.

'Jesus fuckin' Christ,' said Ingram. The old woman muttered something and then quite suddenly began to sing 'The Old Rugged Cross' in a creaky, high-pitched voice. Ingram made a curious strangled sound which unsettled Pollock.

Raised voices could be heard from the street outside. An abandoned can was kicked hard. A car's doors were opened and slammed. Its engine rattled into life. When Pollock was interviewed by the police several weeks later, he was still tormented by their short stay in the old woman's room.

'It was like Hell,' he told them.

Fiona, too, found the scene disturbing when she read my description of it. It was in the spring of 1991. I was making a cup of tea. She was kneeling on the floor in front of the grey metal filing cabinet by my desk, sorting out the papers relating to the police investigations. She was reading from a sheet of paper headed with the name 'Miss Elizabeth Copeland'.

'Why so much detail?' she said as I entered with the tray. 'I mean, what's Elizabeth Copeland got to do with Campbell?' I set down the tray beside her as she continued, 'It's like my own Granny. She died recently, but she was senile for years. When my Dad cleared out her house, he found all these photographs of friends and family in a rusty biscuit tin, but nobody knows who most of them are.'

I asked her to pass me the sheet of paper, both to hide my agitation at her question and to try to understand what had caused her to remember her grandmother.

Fiona poured the tea. 'The old woman's words made me think of a faded holiday snap,' she said.

I nodded, took a mouthful of tea and gazed down at Fiona's leg as if lost in thought. I wondered if she was wearing tights or stockings and why the skin of her legs looked so alluring through the dark nylon mesh. Then I looked up and said, 'My father's got Alzheimer's disease. He no longer recognises me.'

At the foot of the sheet of paper a short note reminded me that on the evening of 16 June Miss Copeland had been discovered in a critical condition by the police. She had been admitted to Gartnavel Hospital, where she died in November 1954. There were no surviving relatives. Her only brother, Hugh, had been killed at the Battle of Passchendaele exactly thirty-seven years earlier.

I remember the day when I uncovered the circumstances of his death. Warm spring sunshine; a local records office; a urine stain on the pavement by the entrance, trailing a fading archipelago; a dusty bureaucrat with curiously pointed yellow nails indicated the name, Hugh Copeland, followed by the date and place of death.

The office was stuffy. The man said something, but I felt too faint to understand him. He took his glasses off and raised his eyebrows. The sun highlighted tiny flakes of skin around his nose. My heightened senses were beginning to make me feel sick. I stood up rather too quickly. Everything went dark. A succession of images passed through my mind: a thin soldier with protruding ears; an old man holding a photograph; a young boy scribbling in an atlas with a wax crayon.

When I came to, a young woman was bending over me, holding a cone-shaped paper cup of water. The clerk who had been dealing with me hovered in the background. I noticed that he was wearing shoes of soft suede and that his trousers were too short. I gratefully drank the water, assured the woman that I was feeling better and left with as much dignity as I could muster.

I still have vivid recollections of my journey to the railway station: a small white mongrel with patches of black and brown raising its hind leg and spraying the base of a lamp post; a Ford Cortina covered with patches of filler, furry dice hanging from its mirror, pulling away from the kerb in a cloud of blue smoke; a row of shops with graffiti-covered gable ends; a sad old woman in her stocking soles pushing an empty pram; a small boy in a grey shirt furiously pedalling a tricycle along a path towards a tower block; a woman wearing bright lipstick and a royal blue suit, crouching down at the foot of the steps to the station, licking her handkerchief and wiping chocolate from the face of a toddler, who gazed at me with innocent, but disturbing, candour until I passed, whereupon I heard him say in a loud voice, 'He's a fat man, Mummy.'

When I got home, I rooted out the photograph of Campbell's father which had been taken during the Great War. In the foreground Hugh Copeland sat crosslegged with his hands resting on his knees. His neck was shaded on one side. His nose cast a shadow on his right cheek. The sun was shining from the left. It must have been taken in the late afternoon. I concluded that the camera had been pointing southeast. I thought of the words that Campbell had given to Doctor Frost in Act 2, Scene 1, after Frost wins a hundred pounds on a horse race: 'Luck? You must be joking. It's all down tae patterns and figures. If you can decipher them, the fuckin' Devil will dance tae your tune.'

I was unable to tell Fiona any of this. We drank our tea. She continued to sort the files. I took the empty cups into the kitchenette.

It is evening now. An ice cream van has stopped further down the street. Children cluster around it. Two boys run along the pavement opposite, heads down, shorts flapping around their skinny legs. Two women are talking in the entrance to a close. One of them is standing with her arm folded under her breasts, cupping her right elbow in her hand, as she taps the ash from her cigarette with her right forefinger. And I sit here, alone, trying to imagine two hoodlums running down the stairs of a tenement.

I picture them from the point of view of Jean Wilson, who was standing on the landing of MacLure's flat. Its door was open. The right jamb was splintered at the level of the lock. Jean had just seen McGuigan's body through the opening. Her husband was shouting at her from their flat. She heard footsteps on the stairs. Ingram was in front. He was leaning back, taking the steps two at a time. Before she had a chance to say anything, he landed a punch in her stomach. As she doubled up, gasping for breath, she heard her husband shouting, 'Jean, where's ma fuckin' tea?'

Once outside, the pair turned right and began to run along Beith Street. At the next close-mouth, Pollock collided with a corpulent young man named David Irvine. Despite his speed, the much lighter Pollock was spun on to his back by the impact. His right arm became entangled between his partner's legs, causing Ingram to stumble and swear vehemently. Irvine would later describe Pollock to the police as a well-built man of medium height.

Mrs Agnes Garton saw the pair through the window of her ground-floor flat. She told the police that it must have been seven o'clock, because she always fed her pet canary at seven o'clock. Sound of seeds falling into the tin basin on the floor of the cage; the tring of the cage door; sight of Pollock through the net curtains, grimacing with pain and clutching his elbow as he ran.

Beyond the intersection with Hayburn Street, Ingram and Pollock passed a public park. Theresa Henderson's fiancé was kissing her neck in the gateway. Over his shoulder, she saw Ingram reaching up to pull down the brim of his hat. She noticed that his legs looked very thin, outlined as they were against the front of his trousers as he ran. Pollock was a little way behind him, wheezing and red in the face. He spat out a thick globule of mucus as he drew level with her.

Craig Thompson was walking his dog along Merkland Street when he saw Pollock and Ingram under the railway bridge on the corner of Beith Street. Pollock was bending over with his hands on his knees. Ingram was shouting at him and pointing along Merkland Street. While his dog sniffed out an exciting scent, Craig watched Pollock giving Ingram a lift up on to the wall by the bridge. Once there, he pulled Pollock up after him. One after the other, the pair squeezed between the bridge and the billboard that was angled towards the crossroads. Then Craig saw them using clumps of coarse grass to pull themselves up the steep bank to the railway line before they finally disappeared behind the roof of an intervening tenement.

Chapter Two

For some reason, I imagine the actor Henry Irving's engraved image looking down at McCluskie as he sat drinking in the Theatre Vaults half an hour after George Pringle's departure. The playwright, no doubt bored with the red plush and lustre of his surroundings, turned his attention to the couple at an adjoining table. They were part of the touring company scheduled to perform *Othello* later that evening in the Theatre Royal. The man was prefacing a clumsy seduction by complaining about a rash on his face, which he maintained had been caused by his stage make-up. The woman, 'a beautiful and beguiling Desdemona', was looking about her with an irritated expression.

The barman, Eddie Gilchrist, priding himself on his memory, recalled that, while the actor was at the toilet, the playwright, by then very drunk, had leaned over towards the actress and asked her if she was enjoying herself. Not recognising the famous playwright in the drunken stranger, she responded sarcastically, 'I'm having a whale of a time.' McCluskie lurched to his feet, splashing whisky on the table as he did so, and settled himself in the chair next to her. I imagine her raising her hand protectively to her bared collarbone. I imagine the prominent bone on her wrist. How many times have I endured a similar look of distrust and repulsion?

'Look, why don't you dump that eejit and come wi' me tae the One-O-One Restaurant?'

She did not reply. She took a sip of gin and tonic and looked over at the barman. Before Gilchrist had a chance to intervene, the actor returned, dragged the playwright on to his feet and punched his face. McCluskie fell back. The actor, squeezing his wrist, moaned with pain and held up his broken finger for agonised inspection.

Gilchrist told Inspector Greig that the pub was usually quiet at that time of the evening and that there had only been four other witnesses to the fracas: a fat man with thinning hair (whom he hadn't seen before and who left before Eddie could get to

237

McCluskie), a tall man in a black suit and hat (whom he had seen on a couple of occasions) and a middle-aged married couple (regular theatregoers, who always arrived early).

The barman helped McCluskie to his feet, brushed some dust from his back with two sweeps of his powerful hand and said, 'Right, pal, a think it's about time you left.' He escorted the bruised playwright to the door, encouraging him up the steps by firmly pushing him in the small of the back.

At their second interview, one rainy afternoon in August 1954, the inspector presented Gilchrist with a photograph of Colin Milverton. The barman looked at it for a long time while Greig stroked his moustache and stared intently at Gilchrist's face. Cairncross, suppressing a yawn, let his eyes wander over the inverted bottles of spirits until they came to rest on an impressive array of single malts standing upright on a shelf towards the end of the bar. The Highland scene printed on one of the labels made him think of a fishing holiday he had taken the previous year (fresh air, purple heather, freedom).

'Was that the man who witnessed the fight?' said the inspector.

'I cannae be absolutely certain, inspector,' said Gilchrist, scratching his head.

'Anxiety prickling your scalp, eh, Eddie? I thought you prided yourself on your memory?'

'Aye, a dae, but it wis nearly two months ago.'

'Just take your time.'

Gilchrist held the photograph up to the light. Cairncross looked at his watch. He had a date that evening and he was hoping to finish early.

'Aye, a think it might well huv been him, right enough,' said Gilchrist.

'Would you swear to it, Eddie?'

After a pause, he replied, 'Aye, it wis definitely him.'

Eddie followed Cairncross and Greig over to one of the tables to write a statement. The three men signed it. An old woman with a scarf wrapped around her head emerged through a door at the end of the bar, dragging a Hoover. She greeted Eddie with a look of contempt and proceeded to unwind the flex immediately in front of their table. The following February, she appeared in one of Cairncross's nightmares, strangling his fiancée with the Hoover flex while he struggled hopelessly to reach them.

Nobody knows where McCluskie went in between leaving the Theatre Vaults and arriving at the One-O-One Restaurant half an hour later. It is probable that he had more to drink, because he could barely stand when he arrived there.

At that time, the One-O-One was Glasgow's most fashionable restaurant. To judge by photographs, it was sumptuously decorated. There were glittering chandeliers. There was a kidney-shaped dance floor and a stage for the house band. There was a team of impeccably dressed waiters. A young woman in a sequined gown, slit to the thigh, sold cigarettes from a tray.

When Campbell arrived, the head waiter was chatting to the cloakroom attendant in the foyer while they waited for the first diners. The playwright, moving around the axis of his left leg, reached for the door handle, missed and fell forwards. Fortunately, his hands took most of the force of the impact, but his balance was gone and, face pressed against the glass of the door, he slid ignominiously to the ground.

Jack Stirling, the head waiter, recognised him immediately and called out two waiters to assist him. While they struggled to help the playwright to his feet, a lad came through from the kitchen to wipe the door clean of Campbell's spittle. McCluskie struggled against his helpers, insisting that he was perfectly capable of looking after himself. Then he leaned forward and vomited on the pavement. The kitchen boy was dispatched to a get a bucket of soapy water and a mop.

'Get him upstairs quickly,' shouted Stirling.

'We should call out the police,' replied one of the straining waiters. A circle of onlookers was beginning to form.

'Just do as you're told. This man has been a good friend to me.'

The kitchen boy swept the pavement clean and poured water into the gutter to flush the reeking matter into the nearest drain. The excitement over, the passers-by continued on their way.

Campbell was taken to the room that was set aside for special parties. A basin and towel were brought to him. Jack sent up a young cashier to clean him up. The semiconscious playwright winced when she rubbed his swollen cheek with a flannel. She untied his tie and unfastened his collar stud. When she went to fetch him some coffee, she complained to the sous-chef about the imposition. She would subsequently tell the inspector, 'He was fast asleep when I left him with half a cup of good coffee going cold beside him. It was real coffee too. Christ knows what he did for Mr Stirling to get that kind of treatment.'

Shortly before eight o'clock, the comedian Tommy Skelton

dropped in to see him. Campbell was stretching and yawning, his collar sticking out on either side and his tie still trailing from each end, when Tommy entered.

'Jack told me you were here.' He closed the door and pulled up a chair next to the playwright. Campbell drew his fingers through his hair, licked his cracked lips and looked at the crystal whisky glass that Tommy had brought with him. There was an awkward silence.

'I had a bloody strange dream,' said Campbell finally. 'A gravy stain on a waiter's napkin turned into an island with hidden treasure. There was a chest full of gold doubloons with a skeleton leaning against it, and a naked woman lying beyond it, but I couldnae make out her face.'

'I didn't come here to talk about your dreams, Campbell,' Tommy replied. 'Helen phoned me this afternoon,' he added, clearing his throat.

'Did she?'

'Look, it's none of my business; but what happened …'

'Too right, it's none of your business,' said Campbell, raising his voice. Then in a more restrained and weary tone: 'I'll see her later.'

Tommy took a sip of whisky, made a whistling sound between his teeth and looked at the picture on the far wall – a fully antlered stag raising its nose towards the sky above Glencoe.

'Tommy, I've started writing again.' McCluskie fished two sheets of paper from his jacket, unfolded them and handed them to Skelton. He watched Tommy's face closely as he read. Tommy said nothing. He finished reading and glanced at the verso of the first page, sighing. He carefully refolded the sheets along the creases and gave them back to McCluskie.

'You're too full of yourself, Campbell. You know, that woman really loves you and you just don't give a damn, do you?'

The head waiter came in with two coffees that Tommy had ordered before coming up.

'So Jack told you I was drunk?' said Campbell after Stirling had gone. With some difficulty, he placed his forefinger in the handle of the espresso cup. 'It's like a bloody doll's cup,' he added to cover the rattling and spillage caused by his trembling fingers. He took a sip and wiped his chin with the back of his hand before continuing. 'Did you notice that Jack had cut himself shaving?'

'I can't say that I did, Campbell.'

'Did you no see the wee bubble of dried blood on his chin?' Tommy sipped his coffee and looked away. After a short silence,

Campbell added, 'Well, I noticed it. I wish I could keep my mind clear of all that irrelevant trash.'

Campbell spent the next ten minutes elaborating his plans for his novel, while Skelton finished his whisky and coffee. Tommy realised, with growing exasperation, that the playwright had ceased to pay any attention to him. McCluskie's hands shaped figures and patterns in the air as he spoke, and he gazed with feverish intensity into the middle distance. Tommy could restrain himself no longer.

'For Christ's sake, shut up, Campbell. I couldnae care less about your damn novel. It's Helen I'm worried about.'

At that moment, the restaurant manager entered with Christopher Malquist. The manager raised his hand in greeting. Tommy, still agitated, looked down at the table. Malquist stopped several paces behind the manager like a nervous bridegroom, looking at his nails, straightening out his lapels, freeing a pocket flap. Then he coughed quietly into his fist. Campbell stood up so abruptly that his chair fell back. Tommy would later tell the inspector that he had never seen the playwright looking so angry. Campbell pointed at his agent and said, 'Well, Tommy, if you're so keen on Helen, there's the man to set you up with a meeting. Acting the pimp is just one of his numerous talents.'

Campbell strode to the door, fists clenched. Malquist, apparently unperturbed, moved out of his way and spread his arms in a gesture that reminded Tommy of Leonardo's Christ.

'The man's drunk,' said Skelton after Campbell's departure. He did not acknowledge Malquist. 'Make sure his coffee is added to my bill,' he added from the doorway before he too left the room.

As he made his way downstairs, Tommy saw Campbell's tie, its middle section still sheathed in the collar, snaking down the wooden margin of three steps. Campbell approached him in the foyer and grabbed his arm.

'We've said enough for one night, Campbell. I'll meet you when you're sober.'

'I just wanted to apologise, Tommy.'

'Just go home to Helen.' Tommy pressed the playwright's hand between his own. He heard Malquist's voice from the foot of the stairs. A camera flashed.

At the time, the photographer did not realise the extent of his good fortune. He had received a tip that an extremely eminent person would be dining in the One-O-One that evening. That person had not turned up and the photographer did not expect that he would find a buyer for a photograph of Skelton and McCluskie, neither of whom had been in the news recently. Within two days, he was able to sell what proved to be the final photograph of McCluskie to the *Glasgow Herald*, the *Daily Express* and *Vogue*.

On Friday 18 June, readers of the *Glasgow Herald* would see the stooped figure of Skelton half turning to McCluskie and grasping the playwright's right hand. Campbell looks ill. His hair is shiny and ruffled. There is no collar on his shirt. His suit looks crumpled. Few readers would have paid any attention to the blurred figure of Malquist in the background, talking to a man with his back to the camera, although that man's white hat band (apparently emerging from Campbell's left shoulder) undermines the composition of the photograph.

Chapter Three

Colin Milverton would remember very little about the tram journey he took back to the city centre after leaving the Keppoch Hill Vaults. He got off near Queen Street Station and wandered around aimlessly in the vicinity of George Square until hunger pangs drove him to seek out a fish and chip shop near the bus station.

It was about a quarter to seven when he reached his company offices in G—— Street. They were on the first floor of a grim-looking building: sooty sandstone façade; smooth-faced caryatids; grooved pilasters; dusty windows with gold lettering – 'Milverton Brick Co.' The entrance was through a door on the landing. As Milverton struggled with the lock, the janitor waved to him from the stairs and said something which was lost in the echoing stairwell.

The premises were, thankfully, empty. A short passageway terminated at Colin's office. A glass partition on the left gave on to the typing pool, beyond which was the door to the manager's office. Three windows on the right shared the view of the building opposite. Its upper storeys were still coated with a wedge of evening sunlight. Milverton entered his office. The imposing desk was laid out neatly with two wire trays, a rectangular blotting pad, a telephone and an Art Nouveau pen holder.

Milverton dropped his newspaper-wrapped supper on to the desk and swung his jacket over the back of his chair. He sat down, unwrapped the food, leaned back with his feet on the desk and guzzled.

Afterwards, he made his way to the empty typing pool, licking the vinegar and grease from his fingers and swaying slightly. He slumped down at the desk of his favourite typist and buried his face in his hands, his entire frame racked by sobs. Shortly afterwards, he heard the sound of voices and laughter. The door to the typing pool clicked open. As he quickly stood up he caught a glimpse of his office manager, Robert Caldwell. A young woman was standing in the passageway behind him. Colin wiped his eyes with his handkerchief and turned to face the wall.

Robert cleared his throat twice and said, 'I'm sorry, Mr Milverton. I didnae expect to find you here.'

'That's all right, Caldwell.'

'I left something in my office,' Robert added. Milverton heard him go to and from his office. He heard staccato heels on the floor of the passageway. He heard the glass rattling in the main door. He went into the passage and looked out of one of the windows until he saw Caldwell and his companion emerging on to the street below. He also saw two waiters from the restaurant opposite struggling with a drunk man in a green tweed suit.

'Very clever, Mr Milverton,' said the inspector. '"A drunk man in a green tweed suit." Those were your words, were they not?'

Milverton looked at him and then at Cairncross. 'You asked me to tell you everything I could remember.' A sickly smell of paint filled the inspector's office. Four maps of Glasgow were mounted on the walls. Milverton could see the date – 16 August 1954 – through the little windows of the perpetual calendar (fashioned from silver-plated metal in the shape of a plinth surmounted by a golf ball) that was angled towards the front of the inspector's desk. Traffic noise came from outside. The glossy, beige-coloured pelmet above the room's only window slipped down suddenly on one side. Three heads turned to look at it. There was a moment's silence.

'Bloody decorators,' said the inspector. Then he added almost immediately, 'Cairncross, show him the letter his wife wrote to the playwright.' Cairncross avoided Milverton's eye as he handed him the two sheets of paper. The inspector, sighing loudly, walked over to the window with his hands behind his back. In a raised voice he said, 'We might be able to accept that your encounter with the playwright in the Botanic Gardens was a coincidence. But you subsequently ate in the same restaurant as him. You saw him again in the early evening. You found his body. And he was murdered with a knife from the restaurant where you both ate.'

'How many times do I have to tell you? I did not know McCluskie.' Milverton began to read the letter. Cairncross noted that at a certain point he pressed his hand to his sternum, his face reddened and he spluttered, 'This is outrageous; outrageous. What are you trying to do to me?'

'Get the man a cup of tea, Cairncross. I'm afraid, Mr Milverton, that our next meeting may not take place in such pleasant surroundings.'

While Cairncross was away getting the tea, the inspector, holding a couple of typewritten pages, approached Milverton. He grabbed

Milverton's face, squeezing his cheeks until his lips pouted like those of a fish, and pushed the papers towards him. 'See here, these are your words, Milverton. Can you remember the lies you spun in July?'

The interview to which Inspector Grieg referred had taken place in Milverton's office on 9 July. Greig had given him to believe that the interview was a routine matter, intended to clarify his movements on the day of McCluskie's murder.

Grieg thought that Milverton appeared listless and indifferent to the proceedings. He told the policeman that he had been ill on the morning of the sixteenth and had taken a stroll in the Botanic Gardens to clear his head. He ascribed his illness to business difficulties. He had then paid a visit to his solicitor's on a private matter, before eating lunch in Laing's Restaurant. In the afternoon, he had gone to Sighthill Cemetery to lay some flowers on his father's grave. From there he had gone to his office to attend to certain problems. He had unwisely dropped into the pub on his way home.

On that sunny evening of 16 June, Milverton watched the kitchen boy from the restaurant mopping the pavement clean of vomit while the drunk was taken into the restaurant and the small crowd of onlookers dispersed. It occurred to him that Caldwell, too, had slept with Madelaine. The manager's woman friend had left a trace of Chanel No. 5 in the passageway. It reminded Milverton of his first meeting with Madelaine at the Glasgow Building Suppliers' Christmas Dance in 1937. He had been twenty-nine. She had been seventeen. I picture tables with white covers placed round the edge of the hall, and a full jazz band on the stage, ranged in tiers behind white-painted boards.

Milverton was there with his mother and Robert Caldwell. Madelaine came with her father, Claude Dubois; a French Canadian who had emigrated to Scotland after the Great War to set up a timber import business. A curious childlike strain in Claude's character had led him to invest in a toy manufacturer, whom he supplied with wood. The toymaker went bust during the Depression and Claude spent the next four years fighting to save his own business. By 1937, he was facing ruin. His wife had refused to come to the Christmas Ball that year, because she couldn't bear the thought of meeting her elegantly gloating peers, and so he was accompanied solely by his beautiful daughter.

Madelaine was wearing a black organdie evening dress, decorated with curlicues of silver thread, which uncovered her shoulders and disclosed the haunting shadow between her breasts. She was dancing

245

a waltz when Milverton first caught sight of her. She had her back to him. He could see her nape and the rippling shadows between her shoulder blades. Then, as her partner swung her round, he saw her face.

A shiver ran down Milverton's back. He wondered if her broad-shouldered partner was an avatar of Fate itself. For Madelaine's face closely resembled that of a woman in a book illustration who had obsessed him during his lonely teenage years. *How clearly I imagine the potency of those onanistic reveries.*

The illustration was from a story entitled 'Bella Donna', in a collection of stories by Arthur Smythe, an obscure follower of Poe, which Milverton had discovered in his father's library. *It is a vertiginous piece of writing.*

The hero, a sickly youth, lives in a secluded Gothic manor. Because his health is so poor, his doting parents jealously guard his solitude, to the extent that even the servants are not permitted near him. Their doctor has told them that even a slight cold could have fatal consequences for their son.

The boy spends much of his time buried in his father's books. All goes well until he reaches the age of ten. His mother falls ill. Afraid that she will pass her illness on to her son, she forbids her husband to let the boy near her. When she dies, the boy feels betrayed by his father and henceforth lives as a total recluse in the library.

The story then takes a strange turn, when the boy discovers a book entitled *Bella Donna*. In it a man is led to his death by a heartless woman who is using him to win the love of his rival. Facing the title page is an illustration of a beautiful lady in a long black dress. She is standing near a lamp post, half turning towards the viewer. A dog crouches terrified nearby, light glittering in its eyes. At the sight of this picture, the boy experiences a sensation like the onset of a fever.

He imagines himself riding to a nearby city. Once there, he wanders the streets and avenues at random until, in a delirium of purple prose, he encounters that same woman, standing by a lamp post while nearby a dog yelps in terror. The following morning, the boy is found dead. Slanting light comes through the diamond window-panes. The book lies open in his hand.

I find this story very disquieting and that is why I have described it at such length. It is an unusual coincidence that Campbell should also have read this very story when writing his last play. However, there are elements in its plot (for example the illness that keeps the young hero from his dying mother) that are positively uncanny. It is true that I am in a state of unnatural euphoria and so may be reading too much into these matters. I have barely eaten anything since my chance meeting with Fiona yesterday on Kelvin Way.

Sunlight filtered through the trees and railings. She was turning on the spot with her hands clasped behind her back, gazing up at the sky and smiling. I smiled too, despite myself almost. At that moment, I forgot about the young men and the sociology tutor with whom her name had been linked since her artist friend had moved away to London. Once again, she was the innocent girl who made me soup for lunch and who blushed at reading Campbell's poem 'Dalmuidy'.

I called her name. She stopped turning, shrugged her shoulders and returned my smile. Next week, she is coming over for a meal. Next week, I shall see her again. The shadows of leaves flitted across her face as she approached me. I noticed the crack in her boot and the fair hairs on her shins and I realised that I was as hopelessly in love with her as ever. She said. 'Of course, I'll come. It will be lovely to see your wee bed-sit again; just like old times.'

I was ludicrously aware of my body and, in particular, of my hands. I didn't know where to put them. I kept moving them about while we talked. When we were about to part, she reached out, took one of them and held it for a moment. Against her elegant hand, my fingers resembled the puffy larvae of some disgusting insect. Nevertheless, I didn't want her ever to let them go. All too soon, she turned and walked away towards the Museum and Art Gallery, moving slowly through the striped and stippled shadows, as if in a dream.

Now, I am counting the hours until she comes. My excitement is intolerable. What else can I do with these wretched and unnecessary hours, but return to that Christmas dance in 1937? Madelaine, in her organdie dress, is twirled rapidly at the focal point of Milverton's gaze, while Milverton's martyred mother makes her way unnoticed to the powder room. Caldwell, his hot breath on Milverton's ear, whispers, 'She's a lovely girl, isn't she? But you dinnae stand a chance. She's too good for you. And rumour has it she's in love with an English eejit.'

'What's her name?' asks Milverton, in the nervous tone he always adopts when speaking to the people who work for him.

'Madelaine Dubois. That's her father over there.'

Seventeen years later, Milverton could still remember meeting Madelaine's father at that dance and being surprised that Claude

Dubois knew who he was. Claude offered him his daughter's chair, a fine cigar and a glass of wine. They sat together for some time, talking; or rather, Milverton spent most of the time listening to Claude, who scrupulously avoided talking business and instead regaled the young man with descriptions of his native Canada. Milverton's attention kept drifting as he followed Madelaine around the room with his eyes, wondering all the while why she would not return to her father's table. Claude did not take offence.

Milverton's last memory of that evening was of Madelaine twisting round to talk to someone in a doorway next to the stage while her father tried to evoke the splendour of the Niagara Falls with a mixture of French and Scottish superlatives. Milverton never learned the identity of the young man to whom Madelaine was talking. He was hidden save for his thick, dark hair and a bulging shoulder.

Milverton unlocked the filing cabinet in his office where he stashed the bottle of single malt he reserved for special customers. The cork made a satisfying noise when it was drawn clear. He took a gulp which caught in his throat. He slumped in his chair and swept the wire trays and the telephone off the desk, shouting, 'The bastard signed it with my own bloody initials.' He took another gulp. He screwed up his eyes, as if to cancel the world, but all he did was to picture the letter more clearly: the shaky handwriting with its hint of delirium tremens, the fantastical sexual descriptions, the crude vocabulary, the grotesque ending and that final insult – the capital 'C' and the capital 'M' beside it, trailing its bungled flourish.

After a moment, he bent down to pick up the telephone and the wire trays from the floor. With some difficulty, he put them back on the desk and then, feeling dizzy, he slumped back in the chair. 'A young woman (pretty, let's say) wiggles her tail at you one evening in Perth.' Recalling those words, Milverton could no longer deny that the unpleasant man he had encountered in Sighthill Cemetery had written the letter. He tried desperately to remember if he had seen the man during the holiday he had taken with Madelaine in Perth.

There had been immense difficulties with transport. Two trains had been cancelled without reason. Madelaine had argued with a guard. Milverton could not remember what she had been wearing, but for some reason he had a very vivid recollection of the unshaven guard shaking his head throughout her tirade. When she had fallen silent, the man had said, 'Thir's a bloody war on, ye stuppit bitch.' Then he had taken a yellowed toothpick out of his pocket, brushed some oose from its tip, pushed it into his mouth and walked away down the platform. Madelaine had remained agitated throughout the subsequent journey and had blamed Milverton for not complaining to someone about the guard.

Milverton could also recall the black and white chequered floor in the hallway of the hotel they stayed in. At a dinner dance there one evening, he had had a severe attack of dyspepsia. He had been sitting self-consciously in his straining waistcoat, spinning his knife and belching periodically. The dance floor had been partially obscured by the foliage of a potted plant. As usual, Madelaine had been dancing with some young man. When she had returned, Colin had accidently let out a sonorous burp. She had indignantly suggested that he should have an early night if that was the best he could offer in the way of conversation. He had agreed that that was probably for the best.

As he sat in his office looking at the half-empty whisky bottle, he pictured the man from the cemetery buying a packet of cheroots at the hotel bar and joining Madelaine after he had gone to bed.

Milverton attempted to cry, but he found that he couldn't. He pulled out a handkerchief and blew his nose. As he pushed it back into his jacket pocket, he felt something that must have slipped down inside the lining. By wiggling his finger through a small tear in the pocket and pushing the object with his other hand, he was able eventually to extract a sixpenny bit, with a hole in its centre, which he had found on the pavement outside his house nearly two years earlier.

Chapter Four

I imagine Ingram and Pollock's progress along the railway line between Partick and Yorkhill Stations shortly after seven o'clock on 16
June 1954. The sun would have been shining on their backs. The
tops of the rails would have caught its reddish light. The gravel between the sleepers would have been covered with an uneven layer of
coal dust. Robert, with his jacket draped over one arm and one shirt-
sleeve rolled up, was holding his other arm out at an awkward angle
in order to see the injury to his elbow. They crunched in single file
along the narrow gap between the two sets of rails. Periodically, Ingram would stoop to rub at the grass stains on his trouser legs. Just
before they reached the bridge across the River Kelvin, they had to
step over the rails to avoid a goods train that was chugging away
from the town centre. There were two engines pulling a seemingly
endless succession of oil tanks.

When I was four, I had a friend who had a beautiful railway layout
that his father had built for him. There were green hills and trees.
There was a station with hand-painted figures on the platform, including a little Indian file of five children, positioned by my friend's
father to celebrate a family holiday. There was a policeman cycling
up a hill between two rows of houses. There was the comic detail of
a drunk man holding a tiny black bottle and dozing near the wall of
the goods depot. But what I liked most was the little steam engine,
puffing real steam, that trailed a line of goods trucks in a broad circle
round the layout. An oil tank, mounted on a grey plastic wagon, was
painted a matt black that just cried out to be touched. One day, I did
so, derailing the train and earning a punch in the eye which ended
the friendship.

As the pair approach Yorkhill Station, Pollock puts his jacket
back on and pushes his hair behind his ears. Two or three people are
waiting for a train on the platform across the rails on their right, but
the platform on the left is empty save for a porter who is sweeping

up some litter. Pollock goes first, running up the ramp on to the platform. Their shadows stretch out ahead of them.

The stationmaster appears in the entrance to the ticket office with a smoking pipe gripped between his teeth. When he sees the two hoodlums running on to his platform, he starts shouting. The pipe falls, cracking its stem. He runs towards them. The porter raises his broom and joins him, but, on catching sight of Ingram's knife, he drops the broom and runs towards the waiting room. He collides with a plump woman, heavily laden with shopping, as she steps on to the platform. She falls back, shedding fruit and vegetables, and he ends up sitting astride her.

The stationmaster grabs hold of Pollock's left arm, slowing him down. Ingram slashes out with his knife. Its point pierces the stationmaster's earlobe, ripping part of it off and scoring the skin of his neck. He releases Pollock, loses his balance as he tries to turn towards Ingram and cracks open his head on the platform. The porter struggles back on to his feet and runs towards Ingram without thinking, but the hoodlum comes to a halt in front of him, threatening him with the knife and beckoning him with the fingers of his other hand. Pollock looks back and shouts at Ingram. The porter holds up both hands with the fingers spread wide. Ingram merely lands a kick on his genitals and starts after Pollock. They run along the railway line for a short distance and then scramble over the wall at the foot of Kelvinhaugh Street.

In the winter of 1990, I went to that very spot. The railway line runs parallel to the river, crossing Sandyford Street on an iron bridge. To the right of the bridge a row of stone arches support the line. The wall down which they scrambled is on the left. Beyond the line, there is a square stone tower with a clock face and two arched windows on its north side. The water of Yorkhill Quay is visible under the bridge. Tower blocks, built long after these events, rise in the misty distance. I photographed this scene from Sandyford Street in front of Kelvinhaugh Primary School. Yorkhill rose behind me with the hospital on its summit and tenements encircling its southern and eastern slopes.

After taking the photograph, I walked to the wall and looked along Kelvinhaugh Street. This was the most southerly point of Ingram and Pollock's wanderings on that fateful day. The descent from the railway embankment had added coal and moss stains to Ingram's suit. His hat was awry. His face was streaked with sweat. When Pollock, his arms at full stretch, finally let go of the rim of the wall and landed awkwardly beside him, Ingram dragged the unfortunate man up by his lapels and held him close to his feverishly working face. 'It's aw your fault, ya bastard. If ye hudnae been late we'd uv caught McGuigan earlier.' Ingram drew his knife and pushed Pollock back against the wall.

Pollock felt his innards heave. Sweat began to slide down his back and gathered inside the waistband of his trousers. At that moment, in a hospital across town, my mother's confinement was moving inexorably towards its messy conclusion.

In my father's book collection, there was a richly illustrated history of medieval Europe which I liked to look through when he was out. In it was one reproduction that I would return to again and again, of St Catherine's martyrdom, dating from the late fourteenth century. The saint was pictured in an emerald gown embroidered about the bodice with a diamond lattice of gold thread. Her face and bared shoulders were rendered in a very pure white, her eyebrows were thin, dark semicircles and her hairline was well back from her forehead. In front of her was a curious wooden wheel with curved blades set at intervals around its rim. Behind her, a well-dressed man with unshaven, bestial features was pushing her towards the wheel. She reminded me of my favourite photograph of my mother.

The photograph stood on the mantelpiece in the sitting room of my father's house. My nineteen-year-old mother was patting her dog. Her hair was pulled tightly back from her forehead. Her eyebrows were pencilled in. Her skin was unnaturally pale because the film had been over-exposed. I still do not know exactly what happened to St Catherine on that wheel, but the picture aroused a morbid curiosity in me, which was mixed with a strange excitement that I was unwilling to admit even to myself.

Childbirth presented my young mind with a similar mystery and a similar violent conclusion. No one would explain what had happened to my mother. As the years passed, I went back again and again to that picture of St Catherine, thinking that the secret lay there. Other scenes of cruelty would evoke a certain guilty pleasure in me, but no other picture would make me feel as if I was on the brink of a revelation.

While my martyr mother lay in the Royal Maternity Hospital on Rottenrow, enduring agonies that her heart could not long sustain, Ingram was holding his knife at Pollock's throat by the embankment at the foot of Kelvinhaugh Street.

Pollock noticed that Ingram's eyes were raised so high in their sockets that his irises had all but disappeared. His lips were moving. His hands were trembling. He was holding back Pollock's head by the hair. Pollock could feel the blade pricking the taut skin under his jaw.

'Dinnae dae it, Ingram. Ye cannae operate without me,' he pleaded, trying to move his lips as little as possible. Ingram was holding his breath.

'Whit are they daein', Mammy?' said a voice behind them.

'Come away frae there, Maria,' a woman shouted. Ingram started breathing again. He pulled his arm away and retracted the blade. He let go of Pollock's hair. Pollock doubled over and started coughing. Ingram turned to see a little blond-haired girl looking at him and pushing her left forefinger into one of her nostrils. She was standing at the corner on the opposite side of the street. A woman was running down Sandyford Street towards her. The little girl turned to look at her and said, 'Mammy, those men were kissin' each other.'

Two men appeared at the gate of the brass foundry on the other side of Sandyford Road. They looked at Ingram and Pollock. Ingram straightened the brim of his hat and set it at its usual angle. He brushed down his jacket with both hands and buttoned it up. Pollock straightened up and attempted to smile at the little girl. The woman grabbed her arm so roughly that the girl's nail must have caught on the skin inside her nostril, for her nose started to bleed and she burst into tears.

'See when a get you home tae yer faither,' said the woman. She started to pull the girl up the street. One of the men shouted over to her and laughed while the other closed the foundry gate.

In 1990, the brass foundry was gone. Yorkhill Station was gone. My mother was gone. McCluskie was gone. Ingram and Pollock were gone. However, I still have the history book containing the painting of St Catherine, and the photograph of my mother now stands on my desk beside one of my father. On that winter afternoon, I stood for a moment with my gloved hand pressed against the embankment. I didn't know what I hoped to find there. I returned my camera to its case and looked back up the street. Fiona was standing by her car, waiting for me. Occasionally, the breeze would whip up the skirts of her coat. A gull, gliding overhead, let out two harsh screeches and then banked towards the river.

Now, that day too is gone and I sit here at my desk, looking at a spectacular sunset, while from the pavement down below I hear the angry sounds of Fiona's footsteps receding into the distance.

PART FOUR

Chapter One

I try to tell myself that nothing has changed. My room is the same as it was yesterday. I see the same view through my window. But I am wrong. The clouds form different patterns today. There are different people on the street. Fresh dust is falling in my room, some of it composed of Fiona's skin. My hopes of yesterday are gone.

I take solace in considering the fate of Colin Milverton; perhaps because it was so much worse than anything I can envisage happening to me. On the day following his police interview in August 1954, Inspector Greig paid a visit to his house while he was at work. The sky was overcast. Madelaine opened the door immediately after the inspector rang the bell. She hesitated in the doorway.

'I'm sorry to catch you at an inconvenient moment, Mrs Milverton.'

'I was on my way out, inspector.'

'I won't keep you very long.'

Some such exchange must have taken place. It is hot today. I am tired. I close my eyes and cover them with my hands. Dangerous vision of Fiona walking across my room in a skirt so short it barely covers the tops of her stockings. No. No. I imagine Madelaine turning and going back into the house. Her tight pencil skirt forces her to place one foot in front of the other when she walks. Once in the lounge, the inspector sits down, resting his arms on his legs and feeding the brim of his hat between his finger and thumb. He has trimmed his moustache. Madelaine notices the thin line of recently exposed skin above his upper lip.

He explains that he has come to see the letter that she received from Campbell McCluskie two years earlier. He points out that he hasn't got a warrant but that he could easily get one. She gets angry. He reflects upon her 'absurd affectations' (as he would later describe them). He feels weary of the case, which, he believes, has been responsible for his recent indigestion.

Madelaine goes upstairs. The telephone makes a noise, which leads him to suppose that she is using an extension. The daily help is using the vacuum cleaner in the dining room. Five minutes later, Madelaine returns. She appears agitated. He asks her where the letter is. She tries to evade the question, but finally admits that she can't find it. It is not in its hiding place. Madelaine puts her hand up to her mouth. The inspector notices the light from the windows catching on her nail varnish. She says, 'O my God, it wasn't dated. You don't believe my husband ...?'

'Your husband?' said the inspector.

'No, it's not possible. He's just not that kind of man.'

The atmosphere is close. Greig puts his hat down on the arm of the chair and wipes his neck with his handkerchief. Madelaine begins to cry. The inspector clears his throat. Madelaine blows her nose. Somewhat foolishly, he wonders if she realises the significance of her words.

'I think we're in for thunder,' he says.

Meanwhile, in his flat across town, Donald Usher, reflecting on Madelaine's phone call, writes in his diary, 'Everything going swimmingly.' In his office in G—— Street, Milverton finishes dictating a letter, sighs and rubs his eyes. In the back garden of her house in Balloch, my Aunt Wilma stands holding me. She is smiling and twisting round towards the camera. I am wearing a hat with a wavy brim. Flowers and bushes form a hazy background and dark clouds are gathering in the sky. On the back of the photograph the words 'Our nephew, Ian, 17th August 1954' are written in faded pencil. Even then, I was a fat, unlovable child.

Two days later, the inspector presented his findings about Milverton to the Procurator Fiscal. They drank coffee. Sunlight reflected off the polished surface of the desk. The Procurator looked through the papers in the pale yellow file lying open in front of him. Greig sat with his legs crossed, balancing his saucer on his knee. After a while, the Procurator said, 'Yes, inspector, I think we can proceed with the prosecution. There is one thing that still troubles me, however. You have found no evidence to prove that Milverton arranged to meet McCluskie in the Botanic Gardens.'

'Unfortunately not; but it seems clear that Milverton thought the playwright was having an affair with Madelaine. I believe that McCluskie brought the letter with him to prove that the affair had ended long before.'

'And the murder weapon, the knife, it did come from Laing's Restaurant?'

And so we find Milverton in a room in a police station, staring into a mug with his elbows on a table. The tea has a bitter flavour.

The rim of the mug is chipped on one side, exposing a semicircle of gritty beige china dotted with black. A uniformed policeman is sitting by the door with his arms crossed, looking at the opposite wall. Between the slats of the Venetian blind on the room's only window, Milverton can see the blackened wall of a tenement and part of its roof.

The policeman stands up when Inspector Greig and Cairncross enter. The inspector sits down directly opposite Milverton. The table is so narrow that their knees touch. Milverton feels uncomfortable, but does not move for fear of offending the inspector. Cairncross takes out his notebook, looks at his watch and writes the date and time at the top of a fresh page. Milverton has a sip of tea.

'Well, Mr Milverton, I trust you had a comfortable night?'

Milverton remains silent, scrutinising his fingernails and wondering why he can never keep them clean.

That night, in his cell, he wrote about the interrogation in his pocket diary. It had lasted two hours. The inspector had read him transcripts of the previous interviews and asked him to explain their numerous inconsistencies. Milverton had been tired and confused. He had told the inspector that at first he had considered his relationship with his wife to be a private matter, of no relevance to the police inquiry.

He had a very upset stomach, which made it nearly impossible for him to sleep. When he finally dozed off, he dreamed that he was walking through a maze of streets, trying to get rid of a knife. With a sudden shift typical of dreams, he found himself in his sitting room at home holding a mug of tea. Inspector Greig was standing by the settee with his trousers round his ankles. Madelaine was kneeling down, gripping the inspector's buttocks and sucking his penis. He smiled at Milverton and said, 'So you took the knife after all, Mr Milverton.' Milverton tried to explain that it was a mug of tea he was holding, but the inspector merely laughed and then, making a curious clucking noise, started tickling Madelaine under the chin.

Milverton was woken by someone clattering the door of his cell. His teeth ached. There was an unpleasant taste in his mouth. It took him a moment to recollect that he had been formally charged with the murder of the playwright Campbell McCluskie.

At a preliminary hearing, Milverton was refused bail and his trial was set to begin on 14 October, one hundred and twenty days after McCluskie's murder. After the hearing, he was transferred to Barlinnie Prison. It was raining when he arrived. His belongings were taken from him. He was given a shower and a prison uniform. Then he was put into a cell with a burglar named Dougal Dougalston.

During his first weeks in prison, Milverton endured a number of bewildering meetings. Donald Usher visited him shortly after his arrival. The solicitor was unable to act on Milverton's behalf, because he had been cited as a witness for the prosecution. Therefore he had taken the liberty of calling on a lawyer friend, Peter Quimby, who was already in the process of securing the services of an advocate called Duncan Harvey. Milverton said nothing. He sat looking at the surface of the table. He imagined that an irregularly shaped patch, where the varnish had worn through, represented the plan of a strange island to which he might escape if he could only understand the true import of what Usher was saying.

Quimby and Harvey duly arrived. Sunlight streamed through the semicircular window. The stone walls were painted cream. Through the door's barred opening, Milverton could see the back of a warder's head. Harvey (curling grey hair and sideburns; shaving rash) opened a leather portfolio on the table. As he perused its contents, he hummed a tune that Milverton recognised but could not name. Quimby (tall; eyes close together; unusually wide face) sat beside him, occasionally reading over his shoulder. After several minutes, Harvey turned to Quimby and said, 'Perhaps we should go for diminished responsibility.'

'I didn't kill McCluskie,' said Milverton suddenly.

Both men turned to look at him. Harvey sighed.

'I'm not guilty.'

'But, Mr Milverton, we can't find anyone to back up your statements,' said Harvey. Once again Milverton recounted his movements on the day of McCluskie's death. The advocate jotted down some notes. His lower jaw made occasional sideways movements as he wrote, which reminded Milverton of his son. With a sudden pang, he wondered if James was his son. He became distracted and forgot what he was saying. The two lawyers exchanged glances. Later, as they waited for the warder to unlock the door, Milverton heard Quimby say, 'Holst, wasn't it?'

'I beg your pardon,' replied Harvey. The door was closed behind them with a sharp clang. Milverton was escorted back to his cell.

Madelaine also visited him with the two children. The warder remained in the room, standing impassively by the door. Occasionally he would shift his weight from foot to foot, or change the positions of his arms, but never once did Milverton see him move.

Afterwards, Milverton could not recall what Madelaine was wearing. He had tried to avoid looking at her. Her daughter, Anne, in a flowery dress, had sat on a chair on the other side of the room and started swinging her feet, which didn't quite reach the floor. Her thick black hair almost reached her waist. She was wearing ankle socks and patent shoes. She had fallen asleep in the back garden the previous weekend and had burned her face and the fronts of her legs. The skin on the backs of her legs was still pale. The words 'milky white thighs' had passed through his mind, causing an unpleasant, acidic sensation in his stomach.

'She's too old to be wearing dresses that short,' he had said irritably.

After that, Madelaine had done most of the talking. Milverton had barely responded. He had gouged loose a varnished sliver from the table surface and started to push it round in circles with his forefinger. Madelaine's voice had sounded unnaturally bright. Her conversation had mainly concerned domestic matters. James had spent most of the visit standing just behind her. After their muted greetings, neither of the children had spoken. However, James had burst into tears when the time had come to leave. Milverton had found himself unable to look either of them in the eye.

That night, Milverton climbed into the lower bunk about an hour before lights out. He carefully placed his pocket diary under his pillow, said goodnight to Dougalston and turned to face the wall. The burglar continued playing patience and muttering to himself. Just before the lights were turned off, he urinated noisily into the bucket. Milverton squeezed his eyes shut and hoped that his cellmate had not dropped his cigarette stub into the bucket. He pictured the soggy paper shedding tobacco into the yellow liquid and felt his gorge rising.

Dougalston pulled himself on to the top bunk. Milverton's mind raced. He remembered the first time he had seen Madelaine at the dance; the play of light on her exposed back. He pictured her turning and smiling at him, like the beautiful lady in the 'Bella Donna' story. He thought of James crying in the visiting room. There was no longer any doubt in his mind that he was the boy's father. He felt ashamed that he had doubted it.

The image of the cell fades. Once again, I am alone in my room. Once again, I remember running my clumsy hand up Fiona's thigh; the small ladder where my soiled thumbnail caught on her stocking; the brief glimpse I had of the bare tops of her legs; the dark hairs curling round the elastic of her pants; Fiona pushing me away and striding across the room; the small smudge of blood on her heel where her shoes had rubbed; her angry face; her unattainable beauty.

Chapter Two

From a letter to his son that Milverton wrote shortly before his execution, we learn that he left his office on the evening of McCluskie's murder at about quarter to eight, after decanting the remains of his malt whisky into his hip flask. No one witnessed his departure, although Milverton saw the janitor making a cup of tea in the little room attached to his office by the building's entrance.

The streets were relatively quiet. The sun shone in his eyes as he made his way towards Central Station. There was no wind. His mouth felt dry. He hurried into the shade of the buildings on Hope Street and then turned north. When he reached the corner of Sauchiehall Street, he saw a young woman in a light blue striped dress looking in a shop window. She had thick black hair and resembled Vivien Leigh. A slim white belt emphasised her hips. He started to follow her. He noticed that her stocking was worn through on her right heel, revealing a smudge of blood every time she raised her foot.

As they made their way along Sauchiehall Street, he tried to imagine what it would be like to have her as his wife. She stopped to look in the window of a shoe shop. A small, dapperly dressed man was locking the door. He checked the lock twice, nodded at her and then walked away, whistling. She started walking again. Milverton paused in front of the shoe shop to allow her to get ahead.

When she reached the corner of Sauchiehall Street and Douglas Street, she stopped and looked at her watch. Then she headed towards Blytheswood Square, where she met a man in a pinstriped suit. Milverton watched them walking arm in arm down St Vincent Street.

McCluskie would have noticed the flock of starlings wheeling overhead; the sunlight striking the upper storeys of the buildings beside him; the heart-rending precision of the shadows cast on the cream stone by various architectural details; the sunlight spreading across the western sky, forming irrevocable combinations of shapes and colours.

It occurred to Milverton that he had never stayed in a hotel in

Glasgow. Several practical difficulties intruded on his thoughts. He panicked and started walking south. By the time he wrote the letter, he found it impossible to recall which streets he had taken and how he had come to be back in Blytheswood Square. He sat down on some steps leading up to an entrance on the north side of the square.

It was exactly eight thirty. He had a sudden clear image of the cottage in Bembridge, on the Isle of Wight, where he had intended to take his family that summer. The advertisement he had seen for it in a guidebook had been illustrated with an engraving: a slim man in a suit and fedora stooping to unlock the front door.

A woman walked by. She was wearing a silk scarf tied at the side of her neck, a tight-fitting top curving low at the back and a black skirt. She turned her head and smiled at Milverton as she passed close to a lamp post. When she reached the northwest corner of the square, he stood up, brushed down the seat of his trousers and started to follow her.

From Blytheswood Square she turned left on Sauchiehall Street and headed towards Charing Cross. Once or twice, she looked back and smiled at him, but he made no attempt to catch up with her. Instead he indulged in futile charades of looking in shop windows or fastening his shoelaces.

He felt a sense of boundless freedom as he walked after her. The evening sunlight brought out the beautiful tones of the red sandstone buildings around Charing Cross. She headed along Woodlands Road, her shadow stretching towards him. His own was thankfully tucked away behind him; out of sight out of mind, as his mother used to say when dressing him.

It occurred to him that she might be a prostitute. He conjured with that idea, imagining her in conventional settings – red lights, scarlet hangings. He had never plucked up the courage to go with a prostitute. The banknotes in his pocket suddenly took on a new significance. But the memory of Madelaine lying on the floor of his study with her legs apart temporarily unmanned him. He remembered the blackmailer in the cemetery. He remembered the letter. The woman entered a pub in the next block.

Milverton was thrown into a quandary. The green frosted glass on the lower part of the window prevented him from seeing into the pub. He didn't know what kind of clientele it would have. He didn't know whether he could bring himself to talk to the woman. He looked up the hill across the road, where the windows of the higher buildings still caught the sunlight. Had he been sober, it is almost certain that he would not have gone in. He might even have gone home.

Inside was a fug of cigarette smoke, noise and sweat. His eyes watered as he made his way to the bar. He ordered a double whisky and tried not to look at people too closely. The threat was all in his imagination; most people in the place were workers out for a drink and a chat. He took a swig of whisky and rubbed his eyes with the back of his hand. Then he checked that the two ten-pound notes were still in his pocket.

When he got to the end of the bar, he saw her sitting at a table in an alcove. A man was standing talking to her. He noticed that her hand was resting on the man's sleeve and that she was staring into his eyes. Milverton turned to go, but she caught sight of him and beckoned him over. The man swivelled round, raised the brim of his hat and looked Milverton up and down, before walking away. She said something to him as he left and then smiled at Colin.

'Huv ye no got a drink fer me,' she said. 'That's no very polite.' Milverton became flustered and apologised. He downed his whisky in one gulp, asked her what she was drinking and went to the bar. He was convinced that people were staring at him. When he returned to the table, she changed chairs and, patting the seat she had vacated, she said, 'Come on 'n' sit here. It's still warm.' Unbearably hot and red in the face, Milverton looked about him self-consciously. The woman grabbed his arm and leaned towards him. Perfume wafted up from between her partially exposed breasts. He felt her hand brush his thigh under the table.

'We're gonnae get on jist fine,' she said.

Milverton suddenly blurted out, 'How much is it for the whole night?' and pulled the two banknotes from his pocket.

She drew back, saying, 'Pit them awa; you'll huv the polis doon on us. Noo, we'll jist huv a few drinks here, an' then a'll take ye tae ma place. Ye've mair than enough. Dinnae bother yer heed aboot it.'

Milverton had three more double whiskies. The room was beginning to spin, when they were joined by a man with a deeply lined face.

'Nae worries, pal. Me 'n' Margarita'll see ye awright,' he said. 'She's goat a body on 'er some men wid kill fer.' So saying, he leaned over and squeezed one of her breasts.

'Fuck aff, ye big bastard,' she said, pushing his hand away.

Milverton's eyes were losing focus. The man and woman helped him to his feet and, supporting him on either side, took him out of the pub. After turning down one of the streets leading off Woodland

Road, the pair led him through a labyrinth of streets. When they eventually stopped, he had no idea where he was.

'Right, pal,' said the man, 'gie ten pounds tae the lady 'n' she'll go in an' make things ready fer ye.' Swaying slightly, Milverton pulled out his money. The man took both notes and handed one to the woman. She smiled, rolled it up and allowed Milverton to push it down her cleavage. Then she kissed him, pressing her tongue into his mouth, and crossed the street to the nearest close. 'A envy ye, pal. Yer in fer the night uv yer life. Just gie her a couple of minutes 'n' follow her up. It's the top flat on the right.'

Milverton was hardly aware that the man had pocketed the other ten-pound note. After those specified minutes had run their agonising course, he climbed unsteadily up the stairs of the close. On reaching the top landing, he knocked loudly four times on the right-hand door. The short interval that followed was filled with the sounds of distant revels. A dog barked. The door opened an inch and he glimpsed a narrow, pointed nose and the gleam of an eye beneath a tangled grey eyebrow.

'Who is it?' came a high, wavering voice from inside.

'I dinnae ken.'

'Who is it?' repeated the voice.

'I tell't you, I dinnae ken.' The door was slammed shut. Falling on his knees, Milverton began to pound it with both fists.

When Milverton had described this sorry episode to Inspector Greig, the inspector replied, 'Do you honestly expect us to believe this claptrap, Mr Milverton? A Mr Murdoch of Park Road has made a statement to the effect that, while walking his dog at quarter to nine on the evening of the murder, he saw a fat, balding man standing in a close near the Doublet.'

However, in his final letter to his son, Milverton concluded,

It is, above all, important that you believe me. I know that I have doubted and wronged you and that I haven't always been the best father, but if you believe me, then my life will not have been altogether wasted.

My world has now shrunk to this tiny cell. My metal bedstead is painted blue. My blankets are grey. My table is yellow. I play chess with my guards, who bring my food, take out my excrement and record my actions in a diary. My advocate has put through a final appeal for leniency, but, for all his bravado, I can sense that he is not optimistic.

When you read this, you will already be a young man. Don't make the mistakes I have made. Beauty is a dangerous lie. Do not trust it. Your mother may have told you things about me, but please believe me when I tell you that only on one occasion did she have cause to fault my behaviour.

Be careful in your dealings with women. Please learn from my experiences. I stood on that foul smelling landing, the drunken dupe of a cheap harlot, knocking on that door and crying out for sex, with no more dignity than a dog howling in the night.

I freely admitted to the police that I was drunk. I did not know where I was. It was chance that brought me to Park Road; chance. This playwright, this Campbell McCluskie might well have fornicated with your mother. God only knows how many others there were. But I did not seek him out. I didn't even know who he was. I am not a killer, James.

At a little after twenty-five past ten, Colin Milverton came to the corner of Park Road and South Woodside Road. He never knew what prompted him to turn down that side street. Perhaps he hoped to catch a tube train back into town. The sky was coloured a deep red above the warehouses and buildings on the far side of the Kelvin, but the sun was no longer visible.

At the point where the road swung north, he caught sight of a man lying against the wall at the back of the West Princes Street tenements. He stopped and called out to him, but the man didn't respond. When Milverton started walking again, his foot struck something which skittered along the road for a short distance. He bent to pick it up, nearly falling over as he did so.

A steak knife, he thought, after scrutinising it in the fading light. The blade felt sticky near its point, so he dropped it and rubbed his fingers on his trouser leg.

'Are you all right?' he said to the man, but again there was no reply.

Chapter Three

I imagine Campbell pausing at the entrance of the One-O-One Restaurant, shortly after taking his leave of Tommy Skelton. The playwright has only two-and-a-half hours left of life, but even at this hour I don't believe that his fate was inevitable. He is still young. He believes that he has started upon his finest piece of work to date. Perhaps he imagines himself going home. He would apologise to Helen. Through sheer effort of will, he would see her once again as a desirable and mysterious stranger. They would make love. The evening sunlight, the trees in the park, the university tower, the shadow of a passing bird – all would participate in their pleasure. They would have a baby – a little girl with a purple face and matted, black eyelashes, uttering her first cry. He would write his novel and find a new agent.

But no; he walks to a pub on Renfield Street and buys himself another half-bottle of whisky. Nothing will now avert the tragedy unfolding across town in a stark hospital room overlooking Rottenrow.

One afternoon, some eighteen months earlier, Campbell set himself the task of describing everyone who walked past him as he sat in a doorway in Sauchiehall Street. The resulting passage has the appearance of a poem:

> An old lady wearing a black hat and a black,
> fur collared coat, whose ankles seem
> unnaturally thin in relation to her shoes.
>
> Just behind her, complaining about her speed,
> another old lady hobbles along wearing a
> similar coat and carrying a leather hold-all,
> in the unzipped opening of which is visible
> a cabbage partially wrapped in newspaper.

A young woman with a Paisley scarf tied
about her head, dressed in a thick jacket
buttoned to the neck, a long skirt and
caramel coloured boots which emphasise
the thickness of her calves.

An old man with a weather beaten, bald head,
hair trailing over his ears in greasy,
yellow strands, his chin stubbled with
white hairs distinct against his skin,
who mutters in my direction, 'Whit're ye
fuckin' lookin' at ya cunt?'

A middle-aged woman in a turquoise turban
and an artificial fur coat, who keeps
adjusting her pace to maintain
her distance behind the man.

I wonder how many people he passed as he walked from the restaurant to the pub and from there to the tram stop on Sauchiehall Street. I wonder if anyone else was waiting for the tram. I picture a short queue. At the front, a businessman with his jacket draped over his arm scrutinises the timetable. A shop assistant stands beside him, rocking back and forth on her heels. An old man in a black suit mops his face with a handkerchief. Campbell focuses on the matrix of wrinkles on the old man's neck and notices the black-bordered card poking out of his jacket pocket. Then the playwright draws his fingers through his hair (apparently a characteristic gesture, but one only referred to by his lover and biographer Mary Ryder) and, shielding his eyes, looks along the street which rises in a gentle gradient towards the evening sun. But, of course, I borrowed the people in that queue from a bus stop I was waiting at on Sauchiehall Street three weeks ago. The bus windscreen caught the early evening sunlight. I stepped aboard, scattering loose change on the floor. The driver swore under his breath.

No record remains of Campbell's movements between buying the half-bottle of whisky and meeting Lillian Cawdor in the Doublet. Consequently, Inspector Greig was able to use this temporal hiatus as a clean sheet on which to project his own vision of events. He convinced the Procurator Fiscal (and ultimately the jury) that the playwright caught a tram on Sauchiehall Street at a little after 8.30

p.m. on 16 June 1954; that he sat on the upper deck on the right-hand side and was, therefore, unable to see Milverton dashing from a nearby doorway to catch the tram at the last possible moment.

I agree with the inspector up to a point. However, my research identifies Nicholas Skeres, rather than Milverton, as the man who made that dash from doorway to tram.

Using my own memories of a recent bus journey, I picture Campbell paying the conductor and then pulling out the novel *Bend Sinister* from his pocket. The shadow of the seat in front falls across the book. Floating dust is picked out by the sun's rays. The tram hums and rattles. Campbell remembers the spring morning in New York in 1951 when he bought the book. Outside, the white façade of the Royal Hotel passes; then a lamp post with a bell-shaped shade; then his father's shop. Campbell opens his book and slips the tram ticket he is using as a bookmark inside the back cover. Helen Miriam will put the book, complete with tram ticket, in the place reserved for it in Campbell's bookcase, when it is returned to her shortly before Christmas 1954.

Campbell tries to read, but his attention keeps wandering. Perhaps he looks at the tenement block that curves round the northeast corner of Charing Cross. Does he try to imagine the lives going on behind its windows? Does he notice the ornamentation around the clock?

The critic Swinbourne described Campbell's life as 'an obsessive acquisition of experiences', and then went on to argue that there was something inherently selfish in the playwright's attitude to the world. 'Just as Campbell found it difficult to look at a young woman without imagining her sexual compliance,' he reasoned, 'so he found it hard to accept that the world could be indifferent to his presence.' Campbell's notebooks from the last six months of his life would seem to support this argument. They are filled with detailed accounts of all his past love affairs, and descriptions of Glasgow which combine acute perception with an almost unbearable sense of loss.

As I sat on that bus and looked at the tenements on Woodlands Road, I recalled a scurrilous passage from McCluskie's last notebook, in which he imagined the simultaneous events taking place in a tenement block one winter's evening:

> In a storeroom, at the back of a grocer's shop on the ground floor, a man in an apron, with a notebook and a well licked pencil, makes an inventory of his rationed stock. On the top

floor, a naked woman on all fours is taken from behind by an exultant but slender man, who grips her hips and sobs with ecstasy, while her husband reaches out to open the bedroom door. At a dining table in a third floor flat, a man with Brylcreemed hair carefully unscrews the back of a wireless set and places the screws in an ashtray, already containing three buttons, two needles, a thimble and a ha'penny piece. In another flat on the same floor, a woman, holding a baby to her breast, repeatedly strikes a little boy on the shaven back of his head, while his older sister sits on the couch with her thumb in her mouth, staring in wonder at the tracery of veins on her mother's breast. A dog slinks away (eye whites showing, tail between its legs) from a pile of elaborately coiled excrement by the door in the hallway of a flat on the first floor.

Campbell got off the tram towards the western end of Woodlands Road and headed down Eldon Street. Shortly afterwards, as the tram slowed to turn on to Park Road, Nicholas Skeres, holding his hat, jumped to the pavement, stumbled, nearly fell, regained his balance and looked about him with murderous intent.

On Eldon Street, Campbell heard some ominous shouts coming from one of the flats on the left. He passed a curiously angled house on the right with a portico supported by square pillars, and a church with a large rose window but no steeple. He stopped by the gateway to Kelvingrove Park and looked up the broad path and wooded slope that he had descended that morning. He took a swig of whisky and wiped his mouth with the back of his hand. Then he turned round and saw Lillian Cawdor entering the Doublet. Beguiled by the sway of her shapely bottom, he turned away from the gate and followed her into the pub.

Tonight, I feel quite exhausted. I was going to conclude this chapter differently, but for the life of me I cannot remember how.

Earlier today, I had a meeting with Professor Williams. It was his phone call yesterday that interrupted my narrative. I told him that it was outrageous of him to intrude upon my sabbatical and that I should have been given much more notice of any meeting. He alluded to allegations of serious misconduct, spoke of a question mark hanging over my job and, not to put too fine a point on it, blackmailed me into agreeing to the meeting.

I marvel at how little the professor's office has changed during the years since I first entered it. Not so the professor. He has turned into an embittered old man. His wrinkles provide a graphic record of unhappiness and disappointment, which makes it all the more surprising that he should devote so much care to dying his remaining hair.

What Fiona told him of last week's events, I do not know. But it would appear that she withdrew her allegation of sexual harassment late yesterday afternoon, after the professor had telephoned me. As he sat with his elbows on the desk and his fountain pen bridging the gap between his pale hands, his frustration was almost palpable. For nearly a week, he had had me where he wanted me, but now his hopes were dashed.

Nevertheless, I felt rather foolish sitting there with my head lowered and the edge of the chair digging into my plump calves. Moreover, the professor still had something up his sleeve – evidence of Fiona's duplicity. It transpired that Fiona had shown him some of my drafts of the biography, at a time when I had been convinced of her support and enthusiasm, if not of her affections. Professor Williams pointed his fountain pen at me and said, 'From what little I have seen of your efforts, it is clear that you have made a fundamental error. You have identified too closely with your subject. In fact, I found quite risible your attempts to ape McCluskie's style. I mean, the man was a mediocrity after all. As for your dramatic reconstructions, the less said about them the better.'

My anger got the better of me. I told him that his hatred of McCluskie and his persistent attempts to thwart me both stemmed from the fact that his wife had had sex with the playwright. That got to him. He blanched, insisted that Campbell was an inveterate liar, that the playwright's sexual prowess was all in his head. Bluff and bluster, bluff and bluster; my job is secure. Once again the professor is discomfited. But why did Fiona betray me?

Outside, a smooth-haired mongrel is weaving about the pavement, nose to the ground, in pursuit of a scent. Moths are gathering round the lamp post, and a bat flits after them. A woman in a flat across the road stands up, presses both hands into the small of her back and looks out on the street for a moment before drawing the curtains. Further down the street, I can see a couple embracing. Both are wearing leather jackets. The girl has buried her face in the man's neck and is rubbing his hip with her raised thigh. I have a peculiar feeling that I have seen them somewhere before and that he is peering over her shoulder at my window: strange tired thoughts.

Chapter Four

The weather this morning is cloudy and dull. Perhaps, if I could muster more energy, I might be able to make sense of all that I have learned. Time and again I have felt close to the revelation I am seeking – to the secret link that binds my fate to McCluskie's. But those moments passed, leaving me with the impression that if I had only studied the events more closely, they would have disclosed their store of truth.

In just such a manner, Inspector Greig came close to discovering the truth about McCluskie's murder. Shortly after Milverton's arrest, he knocked on the door of Cairncross's office and entered without waiting for a reply. The detective was interviewing a young woman. She fell silent when the door opened. The inspector noticed that her eyes were wide with fear and that the exaggerated curves of her painted-on eyebrows were rendered ludicrous by her expression. When he caught a whiff of her unusual scent, he had a sudden recollection of her sitting at a table in a nightclub with another woman and two men.

'Excuse me, Cairncross,' he said. 'I wonder if you could give me the transcript of the Milverton interview.'

Cairncross did not hide his annoyance. 'This is Inspector Greig, Miss Torrance,' he said to the young woman as he reached across the desk for a yellow folder that was lying next to his upturned hat. When he picked the folder up, his hat tipped over and several type-written sheets followed it on to the floor. To reach them Cairncross had to work his way into the narrow gap between the desk and the wall. In the process the desk was jolted, a cup was upset and luke-warm tea poured over the edge on to the hat.

'It's a bit uv a squeeze in here,' said Miss Torrance, laughing. Cairncross mopped up the tea with his hankie, returned his, now stained, hat to the desk and started to rearrange the papers in the folder. Greig shook his head slowly from side to side. He thought that Miss Torrance looked a lot prettier now that she had regained her self-assurance. 'But why', he wondered, 'had she been so disturbed by the interruption?'

He then found himself gazing at the damp patch on Cairncross's hat, which stopped just short of its silk band and vaguely resembled a lion rampant. It struck him that he had seen Miss Torrance on another occasion. He pictured rain on a window, but at that moment Cairncross handed him the folder, breaking his train of thought.

'Funny, that detail about the dog, after what Chapman told us,' said Cairncross.

The inspector made a non-committal grunt, apologised to Miss Torrance for the intrusion and left.

Back in his office, he thought about the two men he had seen with Miss Torrance. After a moment, he managed to put names to their faces – Paul McGuigan and Ingram Farqueson – both notorious gangsters. He wondered what her relationship with them was. Shortly afterwards, he remembered that Ingram had different-coloured eyes and that he was on the run for McGuigan's murder. It would be Cairncross who would remind him, later that afternoon, that McGuigan had been killed on the same day as Campbell McCluskie.

Neither the inspector nor Cairncross had any suspicion that Ingram and Pollock made their way along Kelvinhaugh Street early in the evening of 16 June. What mind could embrace the multitude of events taking place at that same moment throughout Glasgow; the whole mass of movements on the spinning globe? And yet, there amidst everything, my own tiny form, poised near my mother's dilated cervix, was being manipulated in unimaginable ways by a doctor's practised hands.

Ingram and Pollock turned left up Yorkhill Street. Ingram walked in silence. Pollock had problems keeping up with his long stride. Every so often, he would run for a few yards and then slow down to a walk again, as he tried to maintain his position slightly behind Ingram. When they turned right on to Haugh Road, Pollock said, 'Whit're we gonnae dae, Ingram? Meikle'll be waitin' fer us at yoor place.'

'We've got tae go back. A've got ma money stashed there, ya stupit bastard.'

The shadows of the tenements on their left slanted across the road to reproduce their angled chimneys on the façade opposite. Pollock hesitantly tapped Ingram's shoulder and pointed at a small corner shop ahead of them, where a grey-haired, portly man was lifting a box of vegetables from the display in front of the window.

'Yon bastard can gie us the money,' said Pollock.

'Aye, mibbe he can,' replied Ingram. They slowed their pace, to allow the man to get inside with the box, and then they ran to the shop entrance. When they entered, the shopkeeper was standing in the gap at the end of the counter, unlocking the door to the store-room with the box of vegetables under one arm. At the sound of the bell, he said, 'A've closed up fer the day.' He placed the box on the counter and turned to look at them. Ingram had already drawn his knife and was running across the room towards him. 'A've paid fer protection,' the man added and, without thinking, pushed the box towards Ingram. Some carrots rolled on to the floor. Ingram slipped on one and fell back into Pollock, who was in turn thrown back on to a bag of potatoes. Ingram's knife slid across the bare floorboards until it struck the base of the counter. The shopkeeper noticed the white eagle inlaid in the handle when he picked it up and held it out in front of him.

Ingram struggled to his feet and then ran at him, screaming in fury. The terrified man tried to tighten his grip on the knife, but his arm was easily pushed aside and he was punched on the nose. Blood spurted. He fell back and banged his head on the edge of the counter. Ingram grabbed his shirt, pulling off two buttons, and noticed a silver St Christopher's medal among his glistening chest hairs.

'A might uv fuckin' known it,' he yelled and let go of him. The shopkeeper slumped back unconscious. Ingram kicked him hard in the side of the chest. Then he retrieved his knife and rifled through the man's pockets. In a drawer behind the counter, Ingram found one five-pound note and about ten shillings in loose change. He took the note and threw the drawer across the room.

'We be'er get oot o'here,' said Pollock.

At the end of Haugh Road, they would have seen the tennis courts and bowling green beside Kelvin Way, and Kelvingrove Park beyond; the stately façades of Park Terrace rising above the trees; the Museum and Art Gallery; the university straddling Gilmorehill across the river; bluish shade stretching out to the east of the trees; reddish orange pockets of light scattered over the grass; the violet hue of the sky overhead; evening traffic on Argyle Street.

At that same moment, McCluskie shed his collar and tie on the stairs of the One-O-One Restaurant. Milverton was following a young woman towards Blytheswood Square. And in a hospital corridor smelling of antiseptic, which resounded with the efficient footsteps of nurses, voices and distant muted screams, my father sat hunched on a chair, praying, no doubt, for the deliverance of my mother, whatever the cost.

Ingram, his suit stained here and there, loose hairs falling over his eyes, dragged Pollock across the road by his elbow. Pollock would later tell the police that by that stage of the evening his only desire was to get away from Ingram. His subsequent actions tend to contradict this assertion.

When 'Fingers' McGloag happened upon them about five minutes later, a short distance along Kelvin Way, Ingram was standing at the kerb with his legs apart, combing his hair and looking in the mirror of a car. Pollock was sitting on the bonnet, swinging his foot. McGloag was a slimly built man with unusually long fingers, whose careful attempts at parting his hair were always confounded by a cow's lick on the back of his head. He was carrying a bag of bowling balls, from which his bowling shoes were slung. He was a very talented housebreaker and pickpocket, whose services Johnny Meikle had made use of from time to time.

'A didnae think a'd meet yoo here, Ingram,' he said.

'Why, in God's name, is every fucker in this toon so surprised tae see me today?'

'Here, go easy, Ingram,' said Pollock.

'A thought you wir aff tae Inverness wi' Molly. A didnae mean ony harm, Ingram.'

'Whit dae ye mean, "Inverness"?'

'A saw her getting on the Inverness train this mornin' when a wis workin' the station. A thought yoo were awready on it.'

'You must'uv been dreamin', pal. Molly's at home noo, makin' ma fuckin' tea. D'ye hear. You've been fuckin' seein' things.'

McGloag wanders away. Ingram and Pollock continue along Kelvin Way. Pollock, stepping on and off the pavement, says, 'Fir fuck's sake, Ingram, we cannae go back to your place. Meikle'll kill us.' The regularly spaced cast iron lamp posts are mute witnesses to their passage, aligning their shadows with those of the railings and the trees. People stroll in the park. A couple lie on the grass kissing.

They turn right into the park, following their own shadows (tiny heads; long legs; Frankenstein boots) across the river. Today, the stone bridge is still there with its fat-bellied balusters. (I photographed it in 1990. Fiona was standing beside me. Two women were leaning on the coping. One had shining blond hair, which I wanted to stroke and keep stroking until all this madness might pass.) Ahead, the statue of a soldier sits on a monument, looking back over his shoulder. A path steadily rises to the right. The hillside is covered with trees, but above them it is just possible to see the chimneys and roof of McCluskie's house.

Ingram and Pollock turn left at the end of the bridge. The Gothic spire of the university now stands on their left. The path rises and then descends towards the Eldon Street exit. They can see one side of Park Road and the church on its corner. It is interesting to note that McCluskie walked down this same path just over twelve-and-a-half hours earlier. When they reach the gateway, two men approach. Ingram recognises them as Meikle's bodyguards, the ex-heavyweight Welsh and the fat, balding Grogan. Welsh is holding a British service revolver, with a newspaper draped over it in a not altogether plausible manner.

'Meikle is not a happy man, Ingram,' he says. 'He disnae like it when things get messy.' The group of men remain there for some ten minutes. Despite all the threats and insults, Ingram realises that he and Pollock are in no immediate danger. He concludes, quite correctly, that Meikle still needs him and he wonders if Meikle has troubles of his own. Welsh advises him that they will take him to Meikle the following morning. Pollock and Ingram are allowed to go. They turn right on to Eldon Street. Welsh directs Grogan to keep an eye on them. Grogan is about to argue, but thinks better of it. Welsh grins, slips the revolver inside his jacket and walks away along Gibson Street.

It is exactly eight thirty on the evening of 16 June 1954. Ingram, a slim man in a grey suit and fedora, stoops to unlock the door of his flat. For only the second time that day, he thinks about Molly. As soon as he opens the door, he senses that she is gone. Something clicks inside him. I think of the final scene of *The Life and Death of Doctor Frost*. Sitting alone in his mansion, Frost hears a distant baying sound, as of a hound in the night; the last of a series of events, subtly introduced into the play, of which Frost's sinister mentor warned him. At that moment, Frost perceives the pattern that has shaped his life and death.

Ingram tears through all the rooms of the flat like an overwound mechanism, shouting and smashing things up. Pollock stands quietly in a corner, fearful of drawing attention to himself. Outside, Grogan hears the rumpus and retreats into a nearby close-mouth. A couple of minutes later, a handsome young man in a green tweed suit sways past without seeing him.

*

The human heart has four chambers. The flow of blood through them is mainly controlled by the heart muscle. Its motions are coordinated by an ellipse-shaped clump of tissue operating through a branching network of nerve fibres. A member of the University Medical Faculty once told me (in answer to a question that did not reveal my personal tragedy) that in rare cases a chemical disturbance, possibly resulting from stress, can lead to ventricular fibrillation. In his innocence of my grief, he compared this condition to a bird panicking in a cage.

'That's a good metaphor for many emotional states,' I said. His eyebrows were still raised quizzically when I retreated into my own private Hell. Today, my torments are, if anything, worse. At nine o'clock on the evening of 16 June 1954, it seems that I was still entangled in the umbilical cord. I can barely imagine my mother's sufferings. I do not even know at what point in the proceedings the doctor grasped my head with the bloodied instrument that left (still visible) indentations on my temples.

In my mind's eye I see my mother screaming and straining up on her elbows to peer over the material that has been stretched between her knees. The doctor's masked face appears for a moment, beaded with sweat, which a nurse wipes off with a white towel.

Across town, in a pub called the Doublet, Ingram Farqueson has just finished his second double whisky. Pollock and several other customers peer nervously at him from time to time. Only Pollock realises the full extent of the danger. Ingram rarely drinks alcohol.

At one end of the bar, Campbell McCluskie is standing with an attractive young woman, his hand resting on the inward curve of her lower back. He, too, is drinking whisky. A man with a very broad posterior and a cloth cap is leaning further along the bar. At another table, half hidden by a wooden pillar, sits a man in a black pinstriped suit. A hat with a white band is hanging from a nail on the pillar. Groups of men sit chatting, smoking and drinking, but there are no other women. Blackened beams stretch across the room. The smoke-stained walls were once white.

I imagine Ingram turning to Pollock and saying, 'Here, is that no Lillian Cawdor?'

'Aye, it is. So what?'

Campbell had become a regular client of Lillian's during the months before his death. The playwright's drinking had got so bad that he proved to be a poor performer. Consequently, he was less onerous than her other clients. He also paid well for her company.

Lillian admitted to Cairncross that she had a certain affection for the playwright, because of the funny things he said. When she was first interviewed by the police, she was too frightened to tell them about the incident in the pub, which only emerged much later, after Ingram disappeared.

'A'll have her,' said Ingram. 'Any port in a storm.'

'Jesus, Ingram. We dinnae want any mair trouble.'

Campbell's voice was getting louder. Lillian tried to grasp his arm, but he pulled it away from her. He turned his back on the bar, spread his arms and said in a loud but slightly blurred voice,

And all should cry, Beware! Beware!
His flashing eyes, his floating hair!
Weave a circle round him thrice,
And close your eyes with holy dread,
For he on honey-dew hath fed
And drunk the milk of Paradise.

What little Ingram heard of this recital was jumbled by anger, drink, ignorance, prejudice and jealousy. He made a beeline for the playwright, jaw thrust forward, neck sinews knotted, fists clenched.

'Shu'up wi' aw that Papish nonsense, ya fuckin' bastard!'

Campbell's arms dropped to his sides. He coolly retrieved his whisky and, looking at the fuming hoodlum as steadily as his condition would permit, said, 'All Protestants are hypocritical arseholes.'

Then something peculiar happened. As Ingram reached into his pocket and said, 'A'm gonnae fuckin' kill you,' Campbell noticed the red face, shadowed by his cap and framed by woolly sideburns, of the man with the broad posterior leaning further along the bar. With his curved yellow claw, the latter scatched his bulbous nose, upon which there was an unpleasant tracery of purple veins. At the sight of him, Campbell seemed to lose countenance. Lillian took the playwright's arm and said, 'Let's go back to mine, Campbell.' Something glittered on the periphery of her vision.

'No here, Ingram. No here,' someone said.

'He's got a knife.' This from somewhere to her left.

'Jist pit the knife awa fir the time bein'.' This last statement was spoken with an air of conviction. Campbell and Lillian were permitted to leave. White, staring faces fell back on either side. When she looked back from the doorway, Lillian saw, standing near Ingram with his back to her, a man in a black pinstriped suit and a hat with a white band. His jacket was raised in such a way as to suggest a hidden revolver being pointed at Ingram.

As she and Campbell climbed the dimly lit stairs of her close, he kept muttering to himself and shaking his head. Suddenly, he said, 'Have you ever seen Rannoch Moor?'

'Naw, a've never been further than Dunoon.'

'It's the most desolate place on Earth.'

Once in the flat, she put the kettle on for tea. While the water heated, Campbell sat in the room's only chair. He noticed a copy of *Men Only* lying under the bed. Lillian stretched her back and unbuttoned her blouse. Then she pulled her blouse free of her skirt and unfastened her bra, but did not remove it.

'Fuckin' thing's killing me,' she said. She took a cigarette and offered Campbell one from the packet. He shook his head and flipped through the magazine. Then he laughed, looked at the cover ('January 1954; caricature of Terry Thomas; fingerprints of the playwright' – Cairncross's notebook) and threw it back on the floor.

After drinking her tea, Lillian took off her blouse, bra and skirt. She was about to take off her pants, when Campbell said, 'Let me.' She lay on the bed. I picture her raising her bottom to allow him to pull her pants free. I picture the red light shimmering on her stockings.

'Campbell started footerin' wi' his fly, but then stopped. He liked lookin',' she told Cairncross defiantly. 'A mean thir's worse things done by men. But he wis lookin' at ma pants. Ye see, they wir caught roond ma ankle. "Yir a fuckin' pervert, McCluskie," a tell't him, 'n' kicked them awa.'

Campbell fell asleep after finishing. Lillian cleaned herself up, got dressed and poured a drink. She switched on the radio and started to read. After about half an hour or so, she shook him.

'Come on, Campbell; it's time ye wir aff. A've got tae get ma beauty sleep.' He groaned once or twice and then she was fairly certain he said, 'I feel so cold.'

The opening sentence of Milverton's final letter to his son leaves us with the trembling ghost of a coincidence, for he wrote, 'I feel so old.'

Night and day, rotating shifts of prison guards kept an eye on Milverton. He played draughts and chess with them. The Reverend John McKinley also made frequent visits. McKinley, a man of nondescript appearance with a grumbling appendix, gave Milverton a Bible during his first visit. During subsequent visits, it was all he could do to keep Milverton from talking about his wife. Certain passages in the Old Testament seemed to stimulate the condemned man into making intriguing disclosures about her infidelities.

Seven days before his execution, Milverton asked if he could read one of Campbell's plays. Behind the scenes a panic-stricken rush went on in order to satisfy this request, which resulted in Coultts sending a copy of the de luxe edition of *The Life and Death of Doctor Frost* to the prison.

Milverton began to read it after receiving word that his final appeal had failed. The guards noticed that he displayed a marked excitement while he read and that he finished it in one sitting. It was also noted that when he stopped reading he said, 'It all makes sense now.' Then he placed it on his bedside table under the Bible.

On Wednesday 9 February, the guards checked his weight with particular care. He was then taken for a walk round the exercise yard. Afterwards, he described in his pocket diary the young tree, bare of leaves, and the rimed gravel path.

On the south-facing wall of the yard, he noticed a window that was set a little apart from the others and he tried to picture a different life going on behind it. He imagined a leisurely sentence during which he could watch the tree grow to maturity. Every autumn, it would cover the yard with dead leaves.

'Why, that's your cell,' his guard replied, smiling at the question.

'Of course, it is,' said Milverton, thinking about the cruelty of those high, curved windows that reveal nothing but slates, chimneys and sky.

After dinner, he played chess with one of the guards. He won, but could not rid himself of the suspicion that the guard had let him do so. The guards' conversation seemed unnaturally bright. Milverton thought of visits to the dentist when gas was administered. In his diary, he scribbled down a few random memories: a mouldy bathroom floor in a flat in Oxford; Madelaine dancing in a dress cut low at the back; a writing exercise of his son's about an aborted holiday.

At eight thirty on the following morning, the Reverend McKinley arrived, rubbing his side. He rifted and whispered to the guard, 'Mayonnaise; an unfortunate weakness.' Twenty-eight minutes later, one of the guards opened the cell's other door. Its outer side was painted red. I imagine Milverton taking in the sight of the noose; of the lever; of the trapdoor crossed by two planks – all within fourteen paces of his cell – and experiencing the same shock of recognition that we experience when we finally discern the old crone's profile in the picture of the young woman.

The guard pressed him lightly on the back to encourage him forward. His death certificate (a photocopy of which was shown to me by his son) laconically cites as the cause of death 'fractal dislocation of the second and third vertebrae'.

Two weeks after the hanging, Detective Cairncross handed in his resignation. Then he walked through the corridors to Inspector Greig's office, carrying a folder under his arm. He entered without knocking and slammed the folder down on the inspector's desk. Greig rubbed the skin under his eyes, stroked his moustache and yawned. Neither of them spoke. The inspector opened the folder with leisurely movements. In it was a coroner's report about a body that had been fished out of the Clyde three weeks earlier. It had been identified with some difficulty as that of one Charles Mainwaring. Cairncross had underlined a paragraph describing serious fractures that had been inflicted on two fingers of the right hand, possibly as much as a year before his death. The pathologist believed that the tendons of those fingers had also been severed at the same time.

'Madelaine's missing lover, don't you agree?' said Cairncross.

'That is not my concern,' replied the inspector, closing the folder and slowly pushing it to one side.

From the doorway, Cairncross added, 'Oh and I've heard rumours that an investor from the building trade has saved Donald Usher's firm from bankruptcy.'

Without looking up, Greig replied, 'Rumours and speculation have no place in a murder inquiry.' On the walls were four maps of Glasgow marked with pins linked by vari-coloured threads.

I, too, have a map of Glasgow on my wall. On it I have marked the positions of McCluskie's four residences in the city. I have also marked the movements of the playwright, Ingram and Milverton on the day of McCluskie's death.

A letter arrived from Fiona this morning. She has forgiven my indiscretion and suggests that we might meet up again in October, when my sabbatical is over. The letter also included a disturbing confession that has burdened my mind with the almost intolerable sense of a missed opportunity.

As if that were not bad enough, a prospective student, whom I had invited over to discuss his proposal, failed to show up this morning. As a consequence, I was not able to settle down to my writing until late this afternoon.

I little thought when I sat down four months ago to type out this biography, which has obsessed me for nearly twenty years, that I would finish it today, on the thirty-eighth anniversary of the play-wright's murder. It seems apt somehow. The weather, too, has lived up to the occasion. It has been a hot, still day. Far too hot, one would have thought, for the leather jacket worn by that young man who is currently arguing with a dapperly dressed pensioner on the corner.

The evening sun makes me feel melancholy. So much of McCluskie's life has eluded me. So much of my own life has been wasted in searching for its key. There is a red line, traced on my map, that begins and ends at the position of Ingram's flat on Eldon Street. When I looked at it a moment ago, I was suddenly reminded of a girl called Marion MacDonald, whom I once loved.

They have resolved their argument. The pensioner is now walking past my window, licking his unpleasant lips. A woman is shaking a little girl by the arm in a nearby close-mouth and I can hear the tinkling sound of an approaching ice cream van. Beyond the roofs opposite I can see a burnished crane. The sky in the west is a beautiful shade of violet.

At five past ten on the evening of his death, McCluskie insisted on writing out for Lillian, on a sheet of paper torn from her rent book, the poem from which he had recited earlier that evening. However, after putting down the first two lines, he lost interest, folded the paper up with a banknote, handed it to her and asked if he could have the bottle of stout that was standing on her windowsill. Then he made his unsteady way out into the close. At that very moment, my head began making its way into the birth canal, while the doctor, with unforeseen irony, asked my mother to make one last effort.

Twenty-five minutes later, he held up my bruised and bloodied form, but it is unlikely that my mother saw it. Valuable seconds were lost, while a nurse cut the umbilical cord, before anyone became aware of my mother's distress. Further seconds were lost before a stethoscope unveiled the sound of her fibrillating heart. As I was rushed from the room and the full extent of the danger was finally appreciated, the doctor who had delivered me took the desperate measure of cutting into her chest, in the forlorn hope of massaging her heart back into its normal rhythm.

Later, they believed that oxygen deprivation had led to her death at the moment of my birth, although more than one cruel person has suggested that this notion is merely the egotistical conceit of a lonely person.

                    *   *   *   *

Shortly afterwards, McCluskie emerged on to West Princes Street and stumbled in the direction of the Kelvin, periodically swigging stout from the bottle. It is probable that he threw the bottle into the goods depot before relieving himself by the wall at the back of the tenements.

It was at this vulnerable moment that Ingram and Pollock attacked him. Ingram kicked him in the back. Campbell fell forward on one knee. Pollock, drawing the steak knife from his pocket, made a wild lunge at him, but Campbell parried it, knocking the knife to the ground. While the playwright grappled with Pollock, Ingram picked up the knife and, after weaving three times about the struggling pair, managed to stab Campbell above his eye. The hoodlum was surprised at how quickly he lost consciousness. Pollock dusted himself off. Ingram wiped the knife handle thoroughly, dropped it and they headed off quickly in the direction of Great Western Road with Grogan in discreet pursuit.

Colin Milverton discovered Campbell perhaps two minutes before he died. Milverton was drunk. He sat down, cradled the playwright's head in his arms and started to weep. A dog appeared round the corner, panting, its sharp muzzle close to the ground. Light from a street lamp caught in its eyes as it gave Milverton a frightened sideways glance. He noticed the white diamond splash on its chest. To avoid putting weight on its front right paw, it held it off the ground in a heart-rending manner when it stopped to sniff the air.

Epilogue

I discovered Dr McDuffy's body on the morning of 16 June 1992. It was an unpleasant sight which I am loath to recreate for you now. Suffice it to say that he had hanged himself with a curtain cord. Judging by references he made at the end of the biography to my appointment with him, it is clear that, in his despair and mounting paranoia, he had confused the dates. As a consequence, he had carried out his final act a day earlier than he had intended.

I found the letter from 'Fiona' on his desk. I have taken the liberty of changing the names of both her and her father whenever they appear in the biography, because of the sensitive nature of her involvement with the biographer. When I spoke to her, she feared that her letter might have in some way contributed to Dr McDuffy's suicide. However, I have spoken to a psychologist, who assured me that, given the obsessive nature of Dr McDuffy's biography, it is probable that he had been planning his death for some time.

Her sensitive confession that she had desired the biographer sexually on only one occasion in her teens, and of the respect that she subsequently felt for his restraint, would have convinced any normal man that life was full of unforeseen possibilities.

Should any doubts remain about Dr McDuffy's state of mind, I should like to point out that, although he was a plump man, by no stretch of the imagination could he be described as fat.

A word about my editorial policy. All quotations from Campbell's plays are from a recent edition that restores the strong language lost in more timorous times. I have left the text of the typescript very much as it was. Its curious mirror-like structure – the division of the biography into two distinct books – is clearly deliberate. However, I have excised some erotic scenes that I felt owed more to Dr McDuffy's fantasies than to the life of the playwright.

In the second book, 'The Death of Campbell McCluskie', it is clear that Dr McDuffy is imaginatively recreating many of the events he describes. While it is true that the biographer had access to all the police interviews relating to McCluskie's murder, the other conversations he records seem rather stagey. Indeed, his Glaswegian argot more accurately reflects that used by Campbell in his plays than anything spoken on the streets of Glasgow at the time.

It is almost as if Dr McDuffy was using the events of that fateful day to construct a fiction in the style of Campbell McCluskie and thereby to make himself Campbell's creative equal. Or perhaps he was trying to produce the novel that Campbell himself never had the time to write. That said, all of Dr McDuffy's recreations are based closely on the facts he unearthed during many years of scrupulous research, and all contain details supplied by witnesses of the actual events.

The prologue did not form part of the original typescript, but was discovered amongst Dr McDuffy's papers. I have published it here, both to provide the biography with an appropriately thespian air, and to help clarify some of the mysteries of the text. One mystery that I could not clear up is that of the page from the last chapter which Dr McDuffy must have burned in an ashtray shortly before his suicide. I have indicated its position in the biography with asterisks.

To those readers who may still doubt that Campbell McCluskie ever existed, I need only draw your attention to a graveyard in Clydebank where a plain white cross commemorates the life of the museum curator Mr Alan Cairns, born 1 April 1922, died 2 September 1981; to a letter from Campbell's sister, Dorothy, authorising publication of the biography; to the yellow ticket in my possession, upon which is written:

'The Irresistible Rise of Tam McLean'
A Play in Five Acts
by
Campbell McCluskie
16th June, 1968
Admit One, Evening Perf. 7.30 p.m.
Citizens' Theatre

A.W.M.
Oxford
20 January 1995

www.awenpublications.co.uk

Also from Awen Publications:

The Long Woman
Kevan Manwaring

An antiquarian's widow discovers her husband's lost journals and sets out on a journey of remembrance across 1920s England and France, retracing his steps in search of healing and independence. Along alignments of place and memory she meets mystic Dion Fortune, ley-line pioneer Alfred Watkins, and a Sir Arthur Conan Doyle obsessed with the Cottingley Fairies. From Glastonbury to Carnac, she visits the ancient sites that obsessed her husband and, tested by both earthly and unearthly forces, she discovers a power within herself.

'A beautiful book, filled with the quiet of dawn, and the first cool breaths of new life, it reveals how the poignance of real humanity is ever sprinkled with magic.' *Emma Restall Orr*

Fiction ISBN 978-1-906900-44-1 £9.99
The Windsmith Elegy Volume 1

Exotic Excursions
Anthony Nanson

In these stories Anthony Nanson charts the territory between travel writing and magic realism to confront the exotic and the enigmatic. Here are epiphanies of solitude, twilight and initiation. A lover's true self unveiled by a mountain mist … a memory of the lost land in the western sea … a traveller's surrender to the allure of ancient gods … a quest for primeval beings on the edge of extinction. In transcending the line between the written and the spoken word, between the familiar and the unfamiliar, between the actual and the imagined, these tales send sparks across the gap of desire.

'He is a masterful storyteller, and his prose is delightful to read … His sheer technical ability makes my bones rattle with joy.' *Mimi Thebo*

Fiction/Travel ISBN 987-0-9546137-7-8 £7.99

Mysteries
Chrissy Derbyshire

This enchanting and exquisitely crafted collection by Chrissy Derbyshire will whet your appetite for more from this superbly talented wordsmith. Her short stories interlaced with poems depict chimeras, femmes fatales, mountebanks, absinthe addicts, changelings, derelict warlocks, and persons foolhardy enough to stray into the beguiling world of Faerie. Let the sirens' song seduce you into the Underworld …

'All of the pieces in *Mysteries* are entertaining. But they also speak twice. Each one has layers of meaning that touch on the ultimate that cannot be put into words and speak to our inner landscapes that are so full of desire for meaning. Chrissy's journey, elaborately retold in the arena of mythology, is our own journey.' *Kim Huggens*

Fiction/Poetry ISBN 978-1-906900-45-8 £8.99

By the Edge of the Sea: short stories
Nicolas Kurtovitch

Nicolas Kurtovitch is one of the leading literary figures in the French-speaking country of New Caledonia in the South Pacific. The twelve short stories in *By the Edge of the Sea* are written with a poet's sensitivity to style and the significance of what's left unsaid. They convey an enchantment of place in their evocation of physical settings; an enchantment too of the conscious moment; a big-hearted engagement with indigenous cultures and perspectives; and arising from all these a sense of possibility permeating beyond what the eye can see. This seminal first collection of Kurtovitch's stories appears here in English for the first time, together with an introduction to the author's work and New Caledonian background.

'This collection of stories retains its appeal and importance, its freshness, a quarter-century after it first appeared, and that can now be appreciated for the first time by an English-speaking public thanks to Anthony Nanson's careful and sensitive translation.' *Peter Brown*

Fiction ISBN 978-1-906900-53-3 £9.99

The Firekeeper's Daughter
Karola Renard

From the vastness of Stone Age Siberia to a minefield in today's Angola, from the black beaches of Iceland to the African savannah and a Jewish-German cemetery, Karola Renard tells thirteen mythic stories of initiation featuring twenty-first-century kelpies, sirens, and holy fools, a river of tears and a girl who dances on fire, a maiden shaman of ice, a witch in a secret garden, Queen Guinevere's mirror, and a woman who swallows the moon. The red thread running through them all is a deep faith in life and the need to find truth and meaning even in the greatest of ordeals.

'In her lively and vivid stories, Karola Renard points a finger towards the mythic threads that run through life's initiations.' *Martin Shaw*

Fiction ISBN 978-1-906900-46-5 £9.99

Green Man Dreaming: reflections on imagination, myth, and memory
Lindsay Clarke

The transformative power of imagination, the elusive dream world of the unconscious, our changing relationship to nature, and the enduring presence of myth – these subjects have preoccupied Lindsay Clarke throughout the thirty years since he emerged as the award-winning author of *The Chymical Wedding*. Assembled in this definitive collection are the major essays, talks, and personal reflections that he has written, with characteristic verve and insight, on these and other themes relating to the evolution of consciousness in these transitional times.

Speculative, exploratory, salty with wit, and interwoven with poems, this book brings the Green Man and the Daimon into conversation with alchemists, psychologists, gods, and Plains Indians, along with various poets and novelists the author has loved as good friends or as figures in the pantheon of his imagination. This lively adventure of the spiritual intellect will take you through shipwreck and spring-water into the fury of ancient warfare, before dropping you into the dark descent of the Hades journey and urging you on to the fabled land beyond the Peach Blossom Cave. Through a reverie of images and ideas, *Green Man Dreaming* puts us closely in touch with the myths and mysteries that embrace our lives.

Fiction ISBN 978-1-906900-56-4 £15.00

Lightning Source UK Ltd.
Milton Keynes UK
UKHW020645040219
336711UK00010B/322/P